영미시의 감상과 이해

영미시의 감상과 이해

황치복 지음

도서출판 동인

여러 장르의 영미문학에 있어서 소홀히 할 수 없는 분야는 단연 시문학일 것이다. 고대에서부터 현대에 이르기까지 시문학은 전반적으로 다른 분야에 상당한 영향을 끼쳤다고 볼 수 있다. 현대에 이르러 인문학이 위기를 겪고 있다 하더라도, 전 세대에 걸쳐 영시에 대한 독자들의 사랑은 여전히 지속되고 있다고 본다.

하지만 영문학 계열의 학부나 대학원의 시험, 특히 중등영어 임용고시와 같이 목전에 큰 시험을 앞두고 있는 독자들에게는 수험서와 같은 지침서가 필요하다는 것을 느꼈다. 그래서 그동안 대학에서 영미문학 강의를 해오면서 모아두었던 자료들을 정리하여 용기 있게 출판을 하게 되었다.

본 저자는 지난 19년 동안 시행되어 왔던 중등영어 임용고시의 문학 장르의 기출문제를 철저히 분석하여, 시험을 준비하는 학생들에게 무엇이 필요한지를 분석할 수 있었다. 따라서 본 저서는 일반 영문학과 시험은 물론 중등영어 임용고시 등과 같은 시험을 준비하는 독자들에게 하나의 지침서가 될 것으로 확신한다. 저서의 내용은 영시 읽기의 기초라고 할 수 있는 영시의 형식과 문학적 기법을 시작으로, 16세기부터 현대에 이르기까지 영국과 미국의 시대별 주요작가와 시를 다루었으며, 임용고시에서 출제되었던 영시는 물론 기출분석을 통해 출제가 예상되는 영시도 다루었다.

물론 영시의 출제 비중이 아주 작은 부분을 차지한다 하더라도, 기본적인 영시기법의 정확한 이해와 영어해석능력을 고양한다면, 교양을 위한 영시에 대한 감상과 이해는 물론 여러 시험을 준비하는 데 길잡이가 될 것으로 확신한다.

　　마지막으로 늦은 초고 제출에도 불구하고, 출판을 허락해주신 도서출판 동인 이성모 사장님과 직원 여러분께 감사드리고 싶다. 더불어 본 저서가 나오기까지 항상 옆에서 많은 조언을 해주신 정철성 교수님께도 감사를 표하는 바이다.

2015년 9월
황치복

| 차 례 |

II. 영국시

제6장 빅토리아 시대 영국시

제7장 20세기 영국시

III. 미국시

I

영미시 읽기의 기초

제1장
시의 형식

시는 언어로 이루어져 있고 언어의 기본단위인 단어는 소리와 의미로 구성된다. 하나의 시에서 단어들이 지닌 의미는 서로 연계되어 의미의 그물을 이루고 이것이 그 시의 주제를 이루게 된다면 단어들이 지닌 소리들 또한 소리의 그물을 이루게 되는데 이것이 그 시의 소리체계가 되며 달리 말해서 그것은 운율체계를 이루게 된다. 따라서 시는 문장들로 짜인 바구니의 안에서 나오는 생각이 아니다. 시의 내용은 형식과 분리되어 존재할 수 없다.

1. 음성적 가치 Sound Values

시의 요소 중에 가장 주목할 만한 요소는 음성적 가치이다. 그러한 요소들은 시에서 어느 하나 절대로 빼놓을 수 없고, 서로 서로 보완해간다.

(1) 압운 Rhyme

운문의 연이 같은 동일한 음성의 마지막 단어를 가졌을 때 압운 또는
압운을 가졌다 또는 압운의 운영체계를 가졌다고 불린다. 다시 말해 압운
은 두 개 이상의 단어가 마지막 강세가 있는 철자부터 끝까지 같을 때를
말한다.

Atalanta in Calydon

Algernon Charles Swinburne (1837-1909)

Come with bows bent and with emptying of qu<u>ivers</u>,
   Maiden most prefect, lady of l<u>ight</u>,
With a noise of winds and many r<u>ivers</u>,
   With a clamour of waters, and with m<u>ight</u>:
Bind on thy sandals, O thou most fl<u>eet</u>,
Over the splendour and speed of thy f<u>eet</u>:
For the faint east quickens, the wan west sh<u>ivers</u>,
   Round the feet of the day and the feet of the n<u>ight</u>.

위의 시에서 qu<u>ivers</u>, r<u>ivers</u>, sh<u>ivers</u>; l<u>ight</u>, m<u>ight</u>, n<u>ight</u>; and fl<u>eet</u>, f<u>eet</u>
들은 압운의 그룹들이다. 각 각운 그룹 단어들에 밑줄 친 철자들은 발음이
같고, 철자들이 같다. 그리고 철자는 같지는 않지만 소리 값이 같은 단어들
을 사용한 압운들도 있다.

Stanzas for Music

Lord Byron (1788-1824)

There be none of Beauty's d<u>aughters</u>
   With a magic like th<u>ee</u>;

And like music on the waters
　　Is thy sweet voice to me:
· · · · · · · · ·
With a full but soft emotion
Like the swell of Summer's ocean.

　압운을 이용한 효과는 무수히 많이 존재한다. 이러한 압운의 사용은 우리로 하여금 소리가 조화되어 울리는 듯한 경험을 하게끔 해준다. 부가적으로 압운의 패턴 사용은 기대심을 자극하여 다음에 올 연속적인 단어의 예측하고 다음에 올 단어를 맞추게 한다. 미적 즐거움의 한 종류는 예측을 만족시키는 데에 있다.

　강음절이 행의 마지막에 위치하여 끝날 때 그것을 '남성압운' (masculine)이라 하고, 이것은 강한 느낌을 주며 어조가 다른 것보다 좀 더 긍정적이다. 약음절이 행의 마지막에 위치하여 끝날 때 그것을 '여성압운' (feminine)이라 한다. 여성압운의 효과는 좀 더 우아하고, 남성압운으로 끝나는 행보다 좀 더 연속적인 느낌을 준다.

　특별한 종류의 압운은 '유사음'(inexact or slant rhyme)이다. 이 압운의 소리의 단어들은 같지 않고, 다만 좀 더 유사하다. 예를 들어, 에밀리 디킨즈(Emily Dickinson)의 한 시에서 유사음의 사용은 pain-tune, know-do, obey-bee, come-fame이다. 부정확한 압운은 규칙적인 같은 소리의 재현으로 만들어진 일반적인 암시를 계속 유지하지만, 그것을 강요하지는 않는다.

　우리는 늘 압운을 운문 행의 마지막에서 찾고자 기대한다. 통례적인 압운의 사용을 '각운'(end rhyme)이라 한다. 어떤 시인들은 그들의 음성 멜로디를 행의 중간에 위치시켜 시를 장식하기도 한다. 이를 '중간운'(internal rhyme)이라 한다. 이러한 중간운의 사용은 각운의 결합력을 더욱 향상시키기도 한다.

The Rime of the Ancient Mariner

Samel Taylor Coleridge (1772-1834)

The fair breeze bl<u>ew</u>, the white foam fl<u>ew</u>,
The furrow followed free;
We were the <u>first</u> that ever b<u>urst</u>
Into that silent sea.

Down dropped the breeze, the sails dropped down,
'Twas sad as sad could be;
And we did speak only to break
the silence of the sea!

이 시의 첫 연의 첫 번째와 세 번째 행에서 정확한 'internal rhymes'이 사용되었다. blew-flew; first-burst이 중간운의 사용이다. 두 번째 연 첫 행에서 독자들은 다시 breeze와 상응하는 압운을 찾으려 하지만 그것은 없다. 그리고 세 번째 행에서 speak-break는 압운처럼 보이지만 이것도 압운은 아니다. 때때로 이러한 사용을 '시각운'(eye rhyme)이라 한다. 이러한 교묘한 사용은 그 연의 주제와 관계를 가지고 있다.

(2) 두운법과 모음운 Alliteration and Assonance

여러 가지의 단어들의 첫 머리에 같은 소리의 반복이나 같은 자음의 반복을 말한다. 다음의 시는 사무엘 테일러 콜리지(Samel Taylor Coleridge)의 「노수부의 노래」("The Rime of the Ancient Mariner")의 한 구절이다. 이 시는 f, b, w, s의 연속된 두운법이 사용되었다.

The fair breeze blew, the white foam flew,
The furrow followed free,
We were the first that ever burst
Into that silent sea.

이 따분한 두운법의 사용은 시의 행에서 큰 효력을 부여하기 위해 중간운의 사용과 함께 일어난다. 작가가 모음의 소리는 반복하면서, 주위의 자음소리를 바꾸면 이것을 '모음운'(assonance)이라고 한다. 비록 모음운은 종종 두운법으로 쓰이지만 그것은 더욱 구별하기 어렵다. 그래서 독자들은 보는 즉시 작가가 부가적으로 부여한 의미나 감정의 톤을 찾기가 힘들다.

Dolores (Notre-Dame des Sept Douleurs)

Algernon Charles Swinburne (1837-1909)

Cold eyelids that hide like a jewel
　Hard eyes that grow soft for an hour; · · ·

동일한 두운법과 모음운의 패턴은 소리의 유사성과 관계되어있지만, 철자는 동일하지 않다.

(3) 의성어 Onomatopoeia

의성어는 자연의 소리를 모방한 단어의 소리이다. "hum" 또는 "clatter" 또는 "moo" 같은 많은 보통 단어들은 그것들의 이름과 비슷하다. 시에 있어 그러한 단어들은 오직 자연의 소리를 암시함을 의미한다. 단어의 소리가 직접적으로 의성어와 관계는 없지만, 두운법과 모음운은 의성어적 효과에 공헌한다.

2. 작시 Versification

모든 음성적 가치는 운율(rhythm)과 율격(meter), 음보(foot) 그리고 절 형식인 연(stanza)을 포함하는 작시로 집합적으로 알려진 구조적 실행과 관련되어있다.

(1) 운율과 율격 그리고 음보 Rhythm, Meter and Foot

모든 언어에서 가장 중요한 요소는 리듬이다. 우리는 아마 그것을 악센트(accent) 즉 강세(stress)의 규칙적인 재현이라고 정의 내렸을 것이다. 영어에서 어떤 다음절 단어라도 하나의 음절은 다른 것들보다 하나의 강한 강세를 갖는다. 그리고 단음절이 홀로 있을 때만 강세가 주어진다고 생각되어왔을 것이다. 하지만 문단에서 단음절이 다른 단어들과 연합된다면 문단에서의 의미에 따라 강세와 약세가 주어진다. 따라서 악센트가 있는 음절을 강음절이라 하며, 물리적으로 강하게 높게 길게 발음하는 것을 의미하나 현대영어에서는 특히 어떤 음절을 강조하는 것을 말하며, 이것을 스트레스라고 한다. 따라서 스트레스란 말은 보다 포괄적인 뜻을 가진 악센트란 말과 동의어로 쓰이는 일이 많다. 보통 약음절 하나 혹은 두 개를 사이에 두고 스트레스가 되풀이되는 것이 영시의 원칙이다.

Frost at Midnight

Samel Taylor Coleridge (1772-1834)

The Fróst perfórms its sécret mínistrý,
Unhélped by ány wînd. The ówlet's cry
Cáme lóud-and hárk, agâin! lóud as befóre.
The ïnmátes of my cóttage, áll at rést,

Have léft me tó that sólitúde, which súits
Abstrúser músings: sáve that át my síde
My crádled ínfant slúmbers péacefullý.
'Tis cálm indéed! so cálm, that ít distúrbs
And véxes méditátion with its stránge
And extréme sílentnéss.

열 개의 행 중 6개의 행이 같은 패턴이다. 약세와 강세가 정확하게 교대하고 있다. 나머지 중 세 개의 행도 한 점에서만 지켜지지 않고, 거의 정확하게 지켜진다. 이 이상적인 패턴을 운문의 율격(meter)이라고 한다. 영시에서 가장 중요한 율격은 약세+강세로 구성된 "the iamb or iambic foot"(약강격, ˘ ´)이다. 많은 양의 영시가 "the iamb or iambic foot"으로 쓰여졌다. 약강격의 행들은 안정적이고 분위기 있는 느낌을 시 안에서 준다. "the trochee or trochaic foot"(강약격, ´ ˘)이다. 이것은 강세+약세로 구성되어 있다. 이것은 다른 2음절의 율격이다. 강세가 음절에서 먼저 나오고, 뒤에 약세가 오는 것이다. 강약격 행들은 힘 있고, 박력 있는 느낌을 준다. 3음절의 율격으로 되어있는 영시도 종종 보인다. 그 중 보다 흔한 것을 "the anapest"(약약강격, ˘ ˘ ´)이라 한다. 이것은 "iambic foot"과 비슷해 보이는데, 이것은 강세가 율격의 마지막에 위치하여 "rising meter"라고 한다. 약약강격의 행은 가볍고, 신속한 느낌을 준다. 3음절로 되어 있는 율격 중 하락하는 운보를 "dactyl or dactylic foot"(강약약격, ´ ˘ ˘)이라고 한다. 이것은 속도가 느려지는 느낌을 주고, 약음절이 두 개이므로 차분한 느낌 역시 준다. 이러한 기본적 율격을 몇몇씩 바꾸어가며 사용해가며 시를 작성하는 것도 가능하다.

A Hymn to God the Father

John Donne (1572-1631)

Wilt thou forgive that sin where I begun,
 Which was my sin, though it were done before?
Wilt thou forgive that sin, through which I run,
 And do run still, though still I do deplore?
 When thou hast done, thou hast not done,
  For I have more.

Wilt thou forgive that sin which I have won
 Others to sin, and made my sin their door?
Wilt thou forgive that sin which I did shun
 A year or two, but wallow'd in, a score?
  When thou hast done, thou hast not done,
   For I have more.

I have a sin of fear, that when I have spun
 My last thread, I shall perish on the shore;
But swear by thyself, that at my death thy Son
 Shall shine as he shines now, and heretofore;
  And, having done that, thou hast done;
   I fear no more.

한 예로 존 던(John Donne)의 이 작품은 각 연이 약강5보격(iambic pentameter) 4행, 약강4보격(iambic tetrameter) 1행, 약강2보격(iambic dimeter) 1행으로 결합된 6행으로 된 시이며, 각운은 ababab로 되어 있다. 작가는 이렇게 치밀하게 논리적으로 전개함과 동시에 동음이의어(pun)를 사용하여 구원을 향한 개인적 열망을 표현하고 있다.

| 정리

* **운율**Rhythm: 영시의 운율은 강음의 주기적인 반복에 의해서 일어나는 것이다. 이처럼 시간적 과정에 있어서 음의 일정한 단위가 규칙적으로 반복됨으로써 일어나는 시의 운율에는 음의 수와 음의 강약에 의한 것 이외에 음의 장단에 의한 것이 있다.

* **음보**Foot: 영시의 운율의 기본요소는 시를 구성하고 있는 각 단어의 음절(syllable)이다. 이 음절에는 강세(stress)가 있는 것과 없는 것이 있어서, 시를 읽을 때 음의 강약이 생기게 되는 것이다. 이러한 음절이 둘 내지 셋이 모여서 운율의 기본 단위인 음보를 형성하게 된다. 음보의 종류는 이음보의 종류에는 기본적으로 다음과 같은 것이 있다.

  1. 약강(iambic)   2. 강약(Trochee)
  3. 약약강(Anapest)   4. 강약약(Dactyl)
  5. 강강(Spondee)   6. 약약(Pyrrhic)

* **율격**Meter: 운율의 2차적 단위인 시행(line or verse)을 이루고 또 이 시행이 몇 개 합해서 더 큰 운율 단위인 연(stanza)을 이루게 된다. 이렇게 해서 이루어지는 시의 여러 가지 운율형식을 율격이라고 부른다. 그리고 율격에 관한 연구를 운율학(prosody)이라 하고 율격에 의한 운문의 작법을 작시법(versification)이라고 한다. 한 시행에는 음보가 한 개 내지 여덟 개가 있다.

(2) 시의 행 Line of Verse

시의 리듬에서 다른 요소는 '휴지'(Pause)라고 알려진, 자연스러운 멈춤이다. 많은 시 행의 중간에서 그 시의 최고조에서 떨어지는 부분에 간결한 중단을 만든다. 능숙한 시인은 그 시의 외형의 끝에서 휴지부를 찾아낼 수 있다. 휴지부의 위치는 내부의 표시와 일치한다. 독자들은 행들의 의미 또는 다른 형식상의 요소들과 함께 휴지부의 위치를 준수함으로써 효과적인 낭독을 하기 위해 그 실마리들을 찾을 수 있다. 시의 행들은 더 나아가 'end stopped' 또는 'run on'으로 나뉠 수 있다. 'end stopped line'은 생각의 논리적 단위와 일치하여 그 행들은 늘 구두점과 함께 끝난다. 'run on line'은 생각의 부분을 유지하거나, 생각의 두 단위의 부분이다. 이것은 구두점과 함께 시가 끝나거나, 생각의 단위가 두 개 혹은 더 이상의 행들에 걸쳐 있어, 소수의 행들만이 끝이 난다. 다시 말해 시인들은 시의 이 특성을 효과의 다양성을 위해 교묘하게 다룰 수 있다.

(3) 시연 Stanza Forms

연(連), 절(節). 일정한 운율적 구성으로서 배열된 시의 단위를 말한다. 원래 정형시의 용어이며, 연에는 2행으로부터 14수 행의 것이 있고 행수에 따라서 특수한 명칭으로 불린다.

① 이행연(Two-line Stanza, Couplet)은 각운을 밟는 2행으로 이루어지는 연이다. 두 번째 행에서 그 연은 끝이 난다. 각운을 가진 이행연은 열려있다. 즉, 두 번째 연은 이어져있어 첫 이행연부터 다음 것까지 운문은 자유롭게 느껴지고, 계속되는 느낌을 준다.

② 삼행연(Three-line Stanza, Triplet, Tercet)은 3행으로 연이 이루어진다.

이것은 영웅 2행연구의 연속적인 변화로 나타난 것이고, 압운 형식은 일반적으로 aaa bbb처럼 세 개의 행들이 같은 압운을 가지며, 이외도 aba aab 등도 있다. '3운구법'(terza rima)은 3행으로 된 연으로 단테 (Dante)가 신곡(神曲)에서 썼으며 약강 5보격(iambic pentameter)의 각 연(aba)은 다음 연과 압운을 통해 연결된다. (bcb, cdc, etc.)

The Triumph of Life

Percy Bysshe Shelley (1792-1822)

As in that trance of wondrous thought I lay,	a
This was the tenor of my waking dream: —	b
Methought I sat beside a public way	a
Thick with summer dust, and a great stream	b
Of people there was hurrying to and fro,	c
Numerous as gnats upon the evening gleam, . . .	b

③ 사행연(Four-line Stanza, Quatrain)은 4행연은 행의 길이나 압운을 밟는 방법도 일정하지 않다. 행들이 약강 5보격(iambic pentameter)으로 되어 있으면, 이것을 'heroic or elegiac stanza'이라고 한다. 그리고 이 중에서 약강 4보격 또는 약강 3보격으로 되고 압운 형식이 'x a x a'로 된 것을 발라드연(Ballad Stanza)이라 부른다. 그러나 저 발라드가 모두 저 연의 형식으로 구성된 것은 아니다. 다른 변화의 것은 두 번째 rhyme을 첫 번째 rhyme이 둘러 싼(a b a b) 형식이다. 이 행을 'envelope quatrain' 또는 약강 4보격(iambic tetrameter)에서는 'Memoriam stanza'라고 한다. 또 하나의 재미있고 특별한 변화의 것은 '루바이야트 4행시'(Rubaiyat quatrain)라고 한다. 이것은 'iambic pentameter'이면서 a a x a의 압운을

가지고 있다.

④ 칠행연(Seven-line Stanza)은 4행연과 3행연이 결합된 형식도 있지만 이 연 중에서 주목할 것은 제왕운인데, 약강 5보격으로 되고 압운이 ababbcc로 되어있다. 스코틀랜드의 왕 제임스 1세가 이 시형을 사용했다고 해서 'royal'이라는 명칭이 붙었다고 한다. 그리고 이것은 초서 (Chaucer)와 그의 후계자들이게 효과적으로 사용되었다.

⑤ 팔행연(Eight-line Stanza, Ottava Rima)은 8행연에서 가장 유명한 형식은 팔행연구이다. 약강 5보격으로 된 6행 다음에 2행 연 하나가 첨부되고 압운 형식은 ababcc로 된 것을 8행연구라고 부른다. 이것은 각 연에서 연속된 3개의 각운의 두 세트를 찾아내는 정교한 솜씨가 필요하다. 이것은 긴 시에서 커다란 성공을 거두었다.

⑥ 구행연(Nine-line Stanza) 중에서 가장 중요한 것은 '스펜서식 시연' (Spenserian stanza)이다. 이것은 약강 5보격으로 된 8행 다음에 약강 6보격으로 된 1행을 첨부한 것이고 압운 형식은 ababbcbcc로 된다. 에드먼드 스펜서(Edmund Spenser)가 『선녀 여왕』(*The Faerie Queene*)을 위해 고안하였고 키츠(Keat)와 바이런(Byron)에 의해 성공적으로 사용되었다.

Childe Harold's Pilgrimage

Lord Byron (1788-1824)

Once more| upon| the wa|ters! yet| once more!	a
And the| waves bound| beneath| me as| a steed	b
That knows his rider. Welcome to their roar!	a
Swift to their guidance, wheresoe'er it lead!	b
Though the strained must should quiver as a reed,	b
And the rent canvas fluttering strew the gale,	c

still must I on; for I am as a weed,	b
Flung from the rock, on Ocean's foam to sail	c
Where'er| the surge| may sweep,| the tem|pest's breath| prevail.	c

처음의 8개 행은 약강 5보격(iambic pentameter)이고, 9번째 행은 약강 6보격(iambic hexameter or Alexandrine)이다.

(4) 소네트, 14행의 구성의 시 The Sonnet

소네트라는 용어는 서정적인 14행의 약강격 5음보의 운율을 가진 시를 나타내는 여러 가지 방식 중의 하나이다. 그것들의 압운에 의한 구별과 논리적 발달에 의한 두 가지 기본적인 형식들은 영어에 빈번히 존재한다. '페트라츠카식 또는 이탈리안 소네트'(The petrarchan or Italian sonnet)는 a b b a, a b b a, c d e, c d e의 압운을 가진다. 마지막 여섯 행의 압운은 가지각색으로 여러 가지가 가능하다.

On First Looking into Chapman's Homer

John Keats (1795-1821)

Much have I travell'd in the realms of gold,	a
And many goodly states and kingdoms seen;	b
Round many western islands have I been	b
Which bards in fealty to Apollo hold.	a
Oft of one wide expanse had I been told	a
That deep-brow'd Homer ruled as his demesne;	b
Yet did I never breathe its pure serene	b
Till I heard Chapman speak out loud and bold:	a
Then felt I like some watcher of the skies	c
When a new planet swims into his ken;	d

Or like stout Cortez when with eagle eyes   e

    He star'd at the Pacific — and all his men   c

Look'd at each other with a wild surmise —   d

    Silent, upon a peak in Darien.   e

이 시는 전형적인 이탈리안 소네트(페트라츠카식 소네트)로 전대절의 운율구조는 abba, abba이고, 후소절의 운율구조는 cde, cde이다. 키츠는 이 소네트에서 호머(Homer)를 통해서 말로만 들었던 그리스문학을 접한 뒤, 그 기쁨을 새로운 행성을 발견한 천체 관측가나 탐험 끝에 신세계를 발견한 탐험가의 기쁨으로 병치시키고 있다.

(5) 자유시 Free Verse

비록 다른 단어, 구, 구조 등의 반복 양식을 사용하나 행에서 정형화된 율격이나 정기적으로 되풀이되는 리듬을 피한 시이다. 그렇다고 산문을 임의대로 쪼개어 행으로 나눈 것은 아니다. 어법에 있어서 수사법과 상징을 사용하며 생각의 흐름과 시행의 흐름이 평행 구조를 이룬다. 월트 휘트먼(Walt Whitman)이 선구자이다.

(6) 무운시 Blank Verse

각운(脚韻)이 없는 약강(弱强) 5보격(步格) 시행으로, 영어로 된 극시와 산문시의 대표적 운문 형식이며, 이탈리아어와 독일어 극시의 표준형식이기도 하다. 무운시의 풍부함과 자유로움을 제대로 살리려면, 각 행의 강세와 휴지(pause)의 위치를 변화있게 구사하고 언어의 변화하는 음감과 감정적 뉘앙스를 잘 반영하며, 각 행들을 내용에 따라 단락으로 묶는 시인의 기교가 필요하다. 그리스 · 로마의 각운 없는 영웅시를 변형 · 발전시킨 무운시는 다른 고전 운율과 함께 16세기경 이탈리아에 도입되었다.

제2장

문학적 기법

시의 문학적 기법은 시의 형식을 통하여 강화될 수 있다. 시 전체는 물론이고 시의 부분들에 있어서도 묘사하고 있는 다양한 여러 가지의 시형들이 있게 마련이다. 그래서 형식과 내용은 서로 보완적으로 공존하게 된다. 또한 시에 있어서 최소한의 내용은 물론 시어들이다. 시어들이 지니고 있는 각별하고 독특한 함축적인 의미나 의미의 뉘앙스 및 비유적인 언어(figurative language) 때문에 특수한 이유에서 시어들이 세심하게 선별되고 있다. 따라서 시의 의미는 시가 전달하고자 하는 중심적인 사상이나 메시지이기에 이러한 개념은 시의 주제로 부각되며, 시의 화자나 배경과 밀접한 관계를 이룬다고 할 수 있다. 그러므로 시 읽기에 있어서 시어에 담겨진 문학적인 기법뿐만 아니라 시가 담고 있는 비유적 언어를 이해하는 것은 시를 감상하는 첫 걸음일 것이다.

1. 시의 언어 The Language of Poem

시는 일종의 응집력 있는 언어적 표현이기에 언어의 쓰임새는 중요하다. 따라서 사용되는 언어의 용도는 인간의 경험이 강도를 높이고 경험의 폭을 확장시키는 경험적 측면의 문학적 용도와 언어의 실용적 목적으로서의 정보전달의 용도로 구분할 수 있다. 따라서 시의 언어는 그 의미가 고도로 함축된 언어가 되며 언어의 정확한 의미의 구분이 중요한 기능을 발휘할 수 있다.

(1) 외연 Denotation

외연이란 어떤 개념이 적용되는 대상 범위로서, 예컨대 동물이라는 개념의 외연은 소·말·개·고양이·호랑이 따위다. 인간이라는 개념의 외연은 과거에 존재했던 개개의 인간, 현재 생존하고 있는 개개의 인간, 장차 태어나게 될 개개의 인간들 전체가 된다. 이것을 확장하여 '아무개는……' 이라는 형식의 조건문을 충족시키는 전체를 이 조건문의 외연이라고 한다. 외연의 개념을 새롭게 정리하여 얻은 개념이 바로 '집합'이다. 따라서 고도로 함축적인 문서정보를 해독하기 위해서 거쳐야 할 단계는 이와 같은 언어의 의미 습득단계이며, 그때 접하게 되는 의미가 바로 외연적 의미라고 할 수 있으며, 문학 이해의 가장 기본적인 부분이다.

(2) 내연 내포, Connotation

의미작용의 1단계인 외연이 기표와 기의가 합쳐져 의미를 만드는 것이라면, 의미작용의 2단계인 내연은 외연에서 만들어진 의미가 다시 기표가 된다. 즉, 외연은 언어에서 '말해지고 있는 것'을 의미하고, 내포는 말해지는 것 이외의 '다른 무엇'을 의미하는 것이다. 내포는 그 기호를 사용하는 사용자의 느낌이나 감정, 문화적 가치와 관계해서 만들어진다. 다시 말해 기호에 인간의 감정이나 평가가 더해져서 만들어진다는 뜻이다. 따라서 사전적 의미의 외연보다는 상징적이고 암시적인 의미인 내연이 시의 의미를 결정한다. 일반적으로 내연은 시의 의미의 요지를 강화시켜주고 태도와 가치를 제시함으로써 시의 의미를 풍부하게 만들게 한다.

2. 심상 Imagery

심상이란 우리의 상상력에 떠오르는 어떤 것, 즉 우리의 정신 속에 맺힌 영상을 말하는데, 시적 이미지를 통해서 시인이 말하는 어떤 감정이나 생각을 우리는 체험하게 된다. 이러한 이미지를 떠올리게 하는 언어를 심상 또는 이미저리라고 말한다. 이 심상에는 시각적, 청각적, 후각적, 미각적, 촉각적 심상 등이 있다. 이렇게 추상적 의미보다는 감각적 인식을 통하여 얻게 되는 심상을 통하여 시인의 이미지 창출을 통한 함축적인 시어 및 비유적인 시적 기교를 얻게 된다.

In a Station of the Metro

Ezra Pound (1885-1972)

The apparition of these faces in the crowd
Petals on a wet, black bough.

에즈라 파운드(Ezra Pound)는 파리 지하철역에서 기차를 기다리는 창백한 얼굴을 한 유령과도 같은 사람들의 모습을 꽃나무에 달려 있는 꽃잎에 비유하고 있다. 이 두 이미지의 상반된 모습으로 죽음과 초자연적인 느낌을 주고 반면에 삶과 재생의 느낌을 준다.

Ulysses

Alfred Lord Tennyson (1809-1892)

There lies the port; the vessel puffs her sail:
There gloom the dark, broad seas. My mariners,
Souls that have toil'd, and wrought, and thought with me —
That ever with a frolic welcome took
The thunder and the sunshine, and opposed
Free hearts, free foreheads — you and I are old;
Old age hath yet his honour and his toil;
Death closes all: but something ere the end,
Some work of noble note, may yet be done,
Not unbecoming men that strove with Gods.
The lights begin to twinkle from the rocks:
The long day wanes: the slow moon climbs: the deep
Moans round with many voices. Come, my friends,
'Tis not too late to seek a newer world.

테니슨(Tennyson)의 이 시에는 dark, thunder, sunshine, twinkle, moan 등과 같은 시어로 우리에게 시각적이고 청각적인 요소를 많이 제공한다. 독자에게 전달되는 이미지 즉, 개개의 상을 통틀어 심상이라고 말한다.

Those Winter Sundays

Robert Hayden (1913-1980)

Sundays too my father got up early
And put his clothes on in the blueblack cold,
Then with cracked hands that ached
From labor in the weekday weather made
Banked fires blaze. No one ever thanked him.

I'd wake and hear the cold splintering, breaking.
When the rooms were warm, he'd call,
And slowly I would rise and dress,
Fearing the chronic angers of that house,

Speaking indifferently to him,
Who had driven out the cold
And polished my good shoes as well.
What did I know, what did I know
Of love's austere and lonely offices?

　　헤이든(Hayden)은 20세기 초에 인종적 편견으로 고통받는 흑인들의 어두운 과거를 자신의 시에 되살리며, 이러한 경험을 예술적 보편성으로 형상화시켰다. 특히 아버지에 대한 시인의 회상은 감각적인 다양한 심상을 통하여 흑인 가정의 고단한 삶과 애환을 생생하게 전한다.

3. 직유 Simile

직유는 비유법 중 가장 간단하고 명쾌한 형식으로, 2개의 사물을 직접적으로 비교하여 표현하는 방법이다. 내포된 비유를 사용하는 은유법과 달리 겉으로 드러나는 비유이므로 묘사가 정확하고 논리적 · 설명적인 것이 특징이다. 즉 하나의 사물을 나타내기 위해 다른 사물의 비슷한 속성을 직접 끌어내어 비교하므로, 공식적인 비교표현 매체를 사용하여 유사성을 명백히 지적한다. 이 때 비유되는 사물과 비유하는 사물은 '마치 ~같다', '~인 양', '~같은', '~처럼' '~듯이'의 형식으로 연결한다.

VIII. Wedded Love
The Wedding-Day

Edmund Spenser (1552?-1599)

From "Epithalamion"

Tell me, ye merchants' daughters, did ye see
So fayre a creature in your towne before?
So sweet, so lovely, and so mild as she,
Adorned with beauty's grace and vertue's store?
Her goodly eyes lyke saphyres shining bright;
Her forehead ivory white;
Her cheekes lyke apples which the sun hath rudded;
Her lips lyke cherries charming men to byte;
Her brest lyke to a bowl of cream uncrudded;

에드먼드 스펜서(Edmund Spenser)는 자신의 연인을 사파이어라는 보석이나 빨간 사과와 체리에 비유하였으며, 워드워즈(William Wordsworth)는 자신의 고독한 처지를 골자기 위에 떠다니는 구름에 비유하였다.

Ode: Intimations of Immortality from Recollections of Early Childhood

William Wordsworth (1770-1850)

Thus blindly with thy blessedness at strife?
Full soon thy soul shall have her earthly freight,
And custom lie upon thee with a weight,
Heavy as frost, and deep almost as life!

4. 은유 Metaphor

직유처럼 연결어를 사용하지 않고서도 두 대상을 비유할 수 있는데, 이러한 비유를 은유라고 한다. 원관념은 숨기고 보조관념만 드러내어 표현하려는 대상을 설명하거나 그 특징을 묘사하는 표현법이다. 원관념과 비유되는 보조관념을 같은 것으로 봄으로 'A(원관념)는 B(보조관념)다'의 형태로 나타난다. 대표적으로 로버트 프란시스(Robert Francis)의 시 「사냥개」("The Hound") 에서 원관념으로 life가 나오며, 보조관념으로 the hound가 사용되는 같은 은유가 나타난다.

The Hound

Robert Francis (1901-1987)

Life the hound
Equivocal
Comes at a bound
Either to rend me
Or to befriend me.
I cannot tell
The hound's intent
Till he has sprung
At my bare hand
With teeth or tongue.
Meanwhile I stand
And wait the event. (2006년 중등영어 임용고시 기출문제)

또한 에밀리 디킨슨(Emily Dickenson)의 시에서 시인은 자연에 심취한 화자를 술에 취한 것으로 비유하고 있다. 각 연의 세부적인 묘사가 모두 술과 관련된 은유로 이어지고 있다. 여기서 술에 취한다는 것은 자연에 취한다는 것을 의미하며 더 나아가 신성에 취한다는 의미로 볼 수 있다.

I taste a liquor never brewed

Emily Dickinson (1830-1886)

I taste a liquor never brewed —
From Tankards scooped in Pearl —
Not all the Frankfort Berries
Yield such an Alcohol!

Inebriate of air — am I —
And Debauchee of Dew —
Reeling — thro' endless summer days —
From inns of molten Blue —

When "Landlords" turn the drunken Bee
Out of the Foxglove's door —
When Butterflies — renounce their "drams" —
I shall but drink the more!

Till Seraphs swing their snowy Hats —
And Saints — to windows run —
To see the little Tippler
Leaning against the — Sun!

5. 의인법 Personification

의인법은 동물이나 다른 대상물 또는 관념에 인간성을 부여하는 수사법을 말한다. 의인법에서는 무생물이나 추상적 개념에 생명을 주는 것이기에 일종의 특별한 은유로도 볼 수 있다. 이러한 의인법은 윌리엄 블레이크 (William Blake)나 셸리(P. B. Shelley) 그리고 존 던(John Donne)의 시에서 볼 수 있다.

The Tiger

William Blake (1757-1827)

TIGER, Tiger, burning bright
In the forests of the night,
What immortal hand or eye
Could frame thy fearful symmetry?

To Night

Percy Bysshe Shelley (1792-1822)

Wrap thy form in a mantle gray,
　　　　Star-inwrought!
Blind with thine hair the eyes of Day;
Kiss her until she be wearied out,
Then wander o'er city, and sea, and land,
Touching all with thine opiate wand—
　　　　Come, long-sought!

When I arose and saw the dawn,
　　　　I sighed for thee;

When light rode high, and the dew was gone,
And noon lay heavy on flower and tree,
And the weary Day turned to his rest,
Lingering like an unloved guest.
    I sighed for thee.

Death be not proud, though some have called thee

John Donne (1572-1631)

Death be not proud, though some have called thee
Mighty and dreadfull, for, thou art not so,
For, those, whom thou think'st, thou dost overthrow,
Die not, poore death, nor yet canst thou kill me.
From rest and sleepe, which but thy pictures bee,
Much pleasure, then from thee, much more must flow,
And soonest our best men with thee doe goe,
Rest of their bones, and soules deliverie.

6. 풍유 Allegory

풍유는 추상적인 것을 구체화시키는 효율적인 비유법의 일종으로 원관념
을 뒤에 숨기고 보조관념만으로 숨겨진 본래의 의미를 암시하는 방법이다.
일명 우화법이라고도 하는데, 이면에 숨겨진 의미가 풍자적·암시적인 내
용이 많다. 특히 풍자시에서 풍자하고자 하는 뜻을 뒤에서 암시하고 비근
한 다른 사물이나 관념으로 비유 표현한다. 즉 시인은 표면적 이야기나 의
미에도 관심을 부여하지만, 주된 관심사는 바로 이면에 있는 궁극적인 의
미에 있으며, 주로 교훈적인 의도를 지닌다.

Because I could not stop for Death

Emily Dickinson (1830-1886)

Because I could not stop for Death —
He kindly stopped for me —
The Carriage held but just Ourselves —
And Immortality.

We slowly drove — He knew no haste
And I had put away
My labor and my leisure too,
For His Civility —

We passed the School, where Children strove
At Recess — in the Ring —
We passed the Fields of Gazing Grain —
We passed the Setting Sun —

Or rather — He passed us —
The Dews drew quivering and chill —
For only Gossamer, my Gown —
My Tippet — only Tulle —

We paused before a House that seemed
A Swelling of the Ground —
The Roof was scarcely visible —
The Cornice — in the Ground —

Since then — 'tis Centuries — and yet
Feels shorter than the Day
I first surmised the Horses' Heads
Were toward Eternity —

디킨슨(Dickinson)은 이 시에서 내세와 불멸성에 대한 명상을 표현하고 있다. 죽음이 영인인 화자에게 마차로 드라이브를 시켜주는 신사로 의인화되었으며, 여행과정 전체는 사람의 일생에 대한 풍유로 볼 수 있다.

7. 상징 Symbol

상징은 어떤 대상이나 사람, 상황이나 행동 등이 실제보다 더 강한 뜻을 지니게 하는 수사법을 의미하며, 가장 고도의 시적 이미지 중의 하나이다. 따라서 어떤 단어나 구절이 문자 그대로 지시하는 바를 넘어 그 이상의 어떤 것을 의미하는 것을 말한다. 대표적으로 윌리엄 블레이크(William Blake)의 「병든 장미」("The Sick Rose")와 로버트 프로스트(Robert Frost)의 「가지 않는 길」("The Road Not Taken") 그리고 T. S. 엘리엇(Eliot)의 「황무지」("The Waste Land")에서 찾아볼 수 있다.

The Sick Rose

William Blake (1757-1827)

O Rose thou art sick.
The invisible worm,
That flies in the night,
In the howling storm:

Has found out thy bed
Of crimson joy:
And his dark secret love
Does thy life destroy.

The Road Not Taken

Robert Frost (1874-1963)

Two roads diverged in a yellow wood,
And sorry I could not travel both
And be one traveler, long I stood
And looked down one as far as I could
To where it bent in the undergrowth;

Then took the other, as just as fair,
And having perhaps the better claim,
Because it was grassy and wanted wear;
Though as for that the passing there
Had worn them really about the same,

And both that morning equally lay
In leaves no step had trodden black.
Oh, I kept the first for another day!
Yet knowing how way leads on to way,
I doubted if I should ever come back.

I shall be telling this with a sigh
Somewhere ages and ages hence:
Two roads diverged in a wood, and I—
I took the one less traveled by,
And that has made all the difference.

The Waste Land

T. S. Eliot (1888-1965)

I. The Burial of the Dead

April is the cruellest month, breeding
Lilacs out of the dead land, mixing
Memory and desire, stirring
Dull roots with spring rain.

. . . . . .

8. 환유 Metonymy

환유는 한 낱말 대신 그것과 가까운 다른 낱말을 사용하는 것이다. 즉 한 사물의 용어가 그 사물과 경험상 밀접한 연관 관계를 지니게 된 다른 사물에 적용되는 것으로, 원인과 결과, 소유자와 소유물, 발명자와 발명물, 포함하는 것과 포함되는 것을 서로 교환하는 비유이다. 예를 들어 wealth를 rich person으로, age를 old man을 표현하여 추상적 명사를 갖고 구체적 대상을 표현하고, head and heart를 갖고 intellect and affection을 표시하여 구체적 명사를 갖고 추상적 대상을 표현하고, Grey hair를 old age를, the sun을 heat of the sun을 나타내어 결과로 원인을, 원인으로 결과를 표현한다. 대표적으로 셸리(Shelly)의 시에서 그 예를 찾아볼 수 있다.

To Night

Percy Bysshe Shelley (1792-1822)

When I arose and saw the dawn,
    I sighed for thee;
When light rode high, and the dew was gone,
And noon lay heavy on flower and tree,
And the weary Day turned to his rest,
Lingering like an unloved guest.
    I sighed for thee.

9. 제유 Synecdoche

제유 전체와 부분, 일반과 특수가 서로 다른 것을 제시하는 비유이며, 사물의 한 부분이 전체의 표현에 이바지하는 표현법이다. 예를 들어, 빵이 식량을, 감투가 벼슬을 나타내는 것에서 그 예를 볼 수 있다. 은유와 직유가 원관념과 보조관념의 유사성에 기대어 의미의 전이가 일어난다면 환유와 제유 같은 대유법은 원관념과 보조관념의 인접성에 기대어 의미의 전이가 일어난다고 할 수 있다. 제유의 한 예를 셰익스피어(Shakespeare)의 소네트와 알프리드 테니슨(Alfred, Lord Tennyson)의 시에서 볼 수 있다.

Sonnet LXXI

William Shakespeare (1564-1616)

Nay, if you read this line, remember not
The hand that writ it, for I love you so,
That I in your sweet thoughts would be forgot,
If thinking on me then should make you woe.

Break, Break, Break

Alfred, Lord Tennyson (1809-1892)

Break, break, break,
On thy cold gray stones, O Sea!
And I would that my tongue could utter
The thoughts that arise in me.

10. 반어법 Irony

반어법은 기본적으로 균열이나 불일치에서 시작하는 표현으로 표현의 효과를 높이기 위해 실제와 반대되는 의미로 하는 말이다. 따라서 항상 말이나 진술의 실제적 의미와 다른 암시적 의미 사이의 대조에서 생기며, 익살이나 비꼬는 효과를 갖는다. 그리고 반어법은 뜻하는 바와 상반되게 표현하는 이 법인 언어상의 반어법(verbal irony), 화자의 말과 뜻하는 내용 사이의 불일치가 아니라 저자가 의도하는 뜻과 화자가 하는 말 사이의 불일치를 의미하는 극적인 반어법(dramatic irony), 실제 상황과 적절하게 보이는 의도된 상황 사이의 불일치, 또는 기대하는 것과 실제적으로 일어나는 상황과의 불일치가 일어날 경우를 나타내는 상황적 반어법(situational irony)이 있다. 그 예로 기대했던 것과 실제로 일어나는 상황과의 불일치의 묘사를 통해서 인간의 행위를 반어적으로 표현한 토머스 하디(Thomas Hardy)의 시와 윌리엄 블레이크(William Blake)의 시에서 다양한 반어적 표현이 나온다.

Channel Firing

Thomas Hardy (1840-1928)

That night your great guns, unawares,
Shook all our coffins as we lay,
And broke the chancel window-squares,
We thought it was the Judgment-day

And sat upright. While drearisome
Arose the howl of wakened hounds:
The mouse let fall the altar-crumb,
The worms drew back into the mounds,

The glebe cow drooled. Till God called, "No;
It's gunnery practice out at sea
Just as before you went below;
The world is as it used to be:

The Chimney Sweeper

William Blake (1757-1827)

When my mother died I was very young,
And my father sold me while yet my tongue
Could scarcely cry "'weep! 'weep! 'weep! 'weep!"
So your chimneys I sweep & in soot I sleep.

There's little Tom Dacre, who cried when his head
That curled like a lamb's back, was shaved, so I said,
"Hush, Tom! never mind it, for when your head's bare,
You know that the soot cannot spoil your white hair."

And so he was quiet, & that very night,
As Tom was a-sleeping he had such a sight!
That thousands of sweepers, Dick, Joe, Ned, & Jack,
Were all of them lock'd up in coffins of black;

And by came an Angel who had a bright key,
And he opened the coffins & set them all free;
Then down a green plain, leaping, laughing they run,
And wash in a river and shine in the Sun.

Then naked & white, all their bags left behind,
They rise upon clouds, and sport in the wind.

And the Angel told Tom, if he'd be a good boy,
He'd have God for his father & never want joy.

And so Tom awoke; and we rose in the dark
And got with our bags & our brushes to work.
Though the morning was cold, Tom was happy & warm;
So if all do their duty, they need not fear harm.

11. 역설 Paradox

역설은 겉으로 보기에는 명백히 모순되지만 어쨌거나 진실을 담고 있는
진술이나 상황을 말한다. 그래서 시에서 가끔 강조적인 표현으로 주의를
환기시키기 위해서 사용하는 상반되는 한 쌍의 사상이나 말, 이미지, 태도
등을 제시하는 방법이다. 역설의 가치는 충격을 준다는 점에서 일반적으로
숨겨진 사실을 폭로한다는 점에서 자가당착적인 성격을 띠고, 평범한 서술
에서 벗어난 뒤틀린 표현을 의미하기도 한다. 윌리엄 워즈워스(William
Wordsworth)와 존 던(John Donne) 그리고 엘리엇(T. S. Eliot)의 시에서 그
예를 볼 수 있다.

My Heart Leaps Up

William Wordsworth (1770-1850)

My heart leaps up when I behold
   A rainbow in the sky:
So was it when my life began;
So is it now I am a man;
So be it when I shall grow old,
   Or let me die!

The Child is father of the Man;
And I could wish my days to be
Bound each to each by natural piety.

Batter My Heart

John Donne (1572-1631)

Batter my heart, three-personed God, for you
As yet but knock, breathe, shine, and seek to mend;
That I may rise and stand, o'erthrow me, and bend
Your force to break, blow, burn, and make me new.
I, like an usurped town to another due,
Labor to admit you, but oh, to no end;
Reason, your viceroy in me, me should defend,
But is captived, and proves weak or untrue.
Yet dearly I love you, and would be loved fain,
But am betrothed unto your enemy;
Divorce me, untie or break that knot again,
Take me to you, imprison me, for I,
Except you enthrall me, never shall be free,
Nor ever chaste, except you ravish me.

The Waste Land

T. S. Eliot (1888-1965)

April is the cruellest month, breeding
Lilacs out of the dead land, mixing
Memory and desire, stirring
Dull roots with spring rain.

12. 인유 Allusion

인유는 역사나 신화 등에 나오는 것이나 기존 문학작품에 나오는 것을 인용하거나 암시하여 쓰는 것을 말한다. 따라서 과거의 역사나 문학을 언급하여 풍부한 함축적인 의미와 상징적인 의미를 나타내는 방법으로 다른 작품이나 사건이 지니는 사상이나 정서를 이용하여 자신의 작품의 정서나 사상을 강화시키는 효과를 나타낸다. 엘리엇(T. S. Eliot)의 "The Waste Land"와 로버트 프로스트(Robert Frost)의 "Out, Out—"에서 특히 많은 인유를 볼 수 있으며, 오스틴 클락(Austin Clark)과 예이츠(W. B. Yeats)의 시 그리고 알렉산더 포프(Alexander Pope)의 시에서도 다양한 예를 볼 수 있다.

Penal Law

Austin Clark (1896-1983)

Burn Ovid with the rest. Lovers will find
A hedge-school for themselves and learn by heart
All that the clergy banish from the mind,
When hands are joined and head bows in the dark.

Leda and the Swan

William Butler Yeats (1865-1948)

A sudden blow: the great wings beating still
Above the staggering girl, her thighs caressed
By the dark webs, her nape caught in his bill,
He holds her helpless breast upon his breast.

How can those terrified vague fingers push
The feathered glory from her loosening thighs?
And how can body, laid in that white rush,
But feel the strange heart beating where it lies?

A shudder in the loins engenders there
The broken wall, the burning roof and tower
And Agamemnon dead.
                Being so caught up,
So mastered by the brute blood of the air,
Did she put on his knowledge with his power
Before the indifferent beak could let her drop?

Sound and Sense

Alexander Pope (1688-1744)

True ease in writing comes from art, not chance,
As those move easiest who have learned to dance.
'Tis not enough no harshness gives offense,
The sound must seem an echo to the sense:
Soft is the strain when Zephyr gently blows,
And the smooth stream in smoother numbers flows;
But when loud surges lash the sounding shore,
The hoarse, rough verse should like the torrent roar;
When Ajax strives some rock's vast weight to throw,
The line too labors, and the words move slow;
Not so, when swift Camilla scours the plain,
Flies o'er the unbending corn, and skims along the main.
Hear how Timotheus' varied lays surprise,
And bid alternate passions fall and rise!

13. 과장법 Overstatement

과장법은 대상의 중요성을 부각시키기 위하여 그 대상에 대한 사실이나 정서를 확대할 목적으로 과장해서 표현하는 일종의 수사법이다. 로버트 번즈(Robert Burns)의 시와 셰익스피어(Shakespeare)의 「오셀로」(*Othello*)에서 간단한 과장법을 찾아 볼 수 있다.

A Red, Red Rose

Robert Burns (1759-1796)

O my Luve is like a red, red rose
    That's newly sprung in June;
O my Luve is like the melody
    That's sweetly played in tune.

So fair art thou, my bonnie lass,
    So deep in luve am I;
And I will luve thee still, my dear,
    Till a' the seas gang dry.

Till a' the seas gang dry, my dear,
    And the rocks melt wi' the sun;
I will love thee still, my dear,
    While the sands o' life shall run.

And fare thee weel, my only luve!
    And fare thee weel awhile!
And I will come again, my luve,
    Though it were ten thousand mile.

Othello (Act III, Scene 3)

William Shakespeare (1564-1616)

I did say so.
Look, where he comes. Not poppy nor mandragora,
Nor all the drowsy syrups of the world,
Shall ever medicine thee to that sweet sleep
Which thou owedst yesterday.

14. 과소법 Understatement

과소법은 실제보다 과소하게 표현하거나 극히 언어를 절제해서 쓰는 방법
으로 이것 역시 언급하고 있는 대상이나 문제를 확대하는 효과를 가져 올
수 있다. 현대 흑인 시인인 샘 커니쉬(Sam Cornish)가 재즈 음악가 레이 찰
스(Ray Charles)를 묘사하는 시에서, 시인은 절제된 언어와 아이러니가 빚
어내는 황량하고 우울한 분위기를 만들어낸다.

Ray Charles

Sam Cornish (1943-)

do you
dig ray
charles

when the
blues are
silent

in his throat
& he rolls
up his
sleeves

15. 모순어법 Oxymoron

모순어법은 양립할 수 없는 말을 서로 짜 맞추는 표현으로, '쾌락의 고통'
이나 '사랑의 증오'와 같은 엘리자베스 시대의 연애시에 나오는 기발하고
독단적인 수사법이다. 이것은 또한 인간의 지각과 논리를 초월하는 기독교
적 신비를 드러내는 종교시에서 많이 사용된다.

Tears, Idle Tears

Lord Alfred Tennyson (1809-1892)

Tears, idle tears, I know not what they mean,
Tears from the depth of some divine despair
Rise in the heart, and gather to the eyes,
In looking on the happy autumn-fields,
And thinking of the days that are no more.

Fresh as the first beam glittering on a sail,
That brings our friends up from the underworld,
Sad as the last which reddens over one
That sinks with all we love below the verge;
So sad, so fresh, the days that are no more.

Ah, sad and strange as in dark summer dawns
The earliest pipe of half-awakened birds

To dying ears, when unto dying eyes
The casement slowly grows a glimmering square;
So sad, so strange, the days that are no more.

Dear as remembered kisses after death,
And sweet as those by hopeless fancy feigned
On lips that are for others; deep as love,
Deep as first love, and wild with all regret;
O Death in Life, the days that are no more!

16. 돈호법 Apostrophe

돈호법은 사람이나 사물의 이름을 불러 독자의 주의를 강하게 환기시키는
수사법으로, 실제로 존재하지 않는 인물이나 추상적 존재, 인격화된 무생
물에게 말을 거는 방법이다. 존 키츠(John Keats)의 시에서 간단한 예를 볼
수 있다.

Ode on a Grecian Urn

John Keats (1795-1821)

Thou still unravish'd bride of quietness,
Thou foster-child of silence and slow time,
Sylvan historian, who canst thus express
A flowery tale more sweetly than our rhyme:
What leaf-fring'd legend haunts about thy shape
Of deities or mortals, or of both,
In Tempe or the dales of Arcady?
What men or gods are these? What maidens loth?

What mad pursuit? What struggle to escape?
What pipes and timbrels? What wild ecstasy?

17. 기상 Conceit

기상은 상식적으로는 결부시킬 수 없는 두개 이상의 관계로부터 공통성을
발견하여 억지로 결부시키는 수사법으로 규모가 큰 비유 형식을 취하는
경우가 많다. 16-17세기의 영국문학, 특히 형이상시에서 흔히 찾아볼 수 있
다. 존 던의 시 "Flea"에서 말하는 사람과 그의 연인의 피를 빨아먹은 벼룩
이 두 사람이 하나가 된 혼인의 잠자리에 비유된 것은 그 일례이다.

The Flea

John Donne (1572-1631)

Mark but this flea, and mark in this,
How little that which thou deniest me is;
It sucked me first, and now sucks thee,
And in this flea our two bloods mingled be;
Thou know'st that this cannot be said
A sin, nor shame, nor loss of maidenhead,
    Yet this enjoys before it woo,
    And pampered swells with one blood made of two,
    And this, alas, is more than we would do.

Oh stay, three lives in one flea spare,
Where we almost, nay more than married are.
This flea is you and I, and this
Our mariage bed, and marriage temple is;
Though parents grudge, and you, w'are met,

And cloistered in these living walls of jet.
      Though use make you apt to kill me,
      Let not to that, self-murder added be,
      And sacrilege, three sins in killing three.

Cruel and sudden, hast thou since
Purpled thy nail, in blood of innocence?
Wherein could this ·flea guilty be,
Except in that drop which it sucked from thee?
Yet thou triumph'st, and say'st that thou
Find'st not thy self, nor me the weaker now;
      'Tis true; then learn how false, fears be:
      Just so much honor, when thou yield'st to me,
      Will waste, as this flea's death took life from thee.

18. 풍자 Satire

풍자는 새로운 사회의 등장에 적응하지 못하는 구세대나 불합리한 권력의 가치관이나 체제를 공격하기 위한 문학적 기법이다. 대상에 대해 부정적비판적 태도를 취하므로 아이러니(Irony)와 비슷하지만 아이러니보다는 날카롭고 노골적인 공격 의도를 지닌다. 대상의 약점을 폭로하고 비판하는 데 있어 직접적인 공격을 피하고 모욕, 경멸, 조소를 통해 간접적으로 빈정거리거나 유머의 수단을 이용한다. 그런 점에서 풍자는 코믹(comic)의 하위 개념이지만 코믹은 공격의 과정에서 부수적으로 파생될 뿐이지 그 자체가 목적은 아니다. 풍자시에 관해서 가장 특출한 풍자시인은 포프(Pope)와 스위프트였다. 스위프트와 포프의 풍자시는 도덕적 긴박성으로 활기차게 되고 운명의 비극적 느낌에 의해 고양되었기 때문에 위대하다.

Verses on the Death of Dr. Swift, D. S. P. D.

Jonathan Swift (1667-1745)

> Yet, should some neighbour feel a pain
> Just in the parts where I complain,
> How many a message would he send?
> What hearty prayers that I should mend?
> Inquire what regimen I kept,
> What gave me ease, and how I slept?
> And more lament when I was dead,
> Than all the sniv'llers round my bed.
>
> My good companions, never fear;
> For though you may mistake a year,
> Though your prognostics run too fast,
> They must be verify'd at last.

19. 현현 Epiphany

현현은 평범하고 일상적인 대상 속에서 갑자기 경험하는 영원한 것에 대한 감각이나 통찰을 뜻하는 말로, 원래 'epiphany'는 그리스어로 '귀한 것이 나타난다'는 뜻이며, 기독교에서는 신의 존재가 현세에 드러난다는 의미로 사용되어 왔다. 평범한 대상이나 풍경이 주는 돌연한 계시의 체험은 영국의 낭만파 시인들에 의해 일찌감치 주목된 바 있다. 윌리엄 워즈워스(W. Wordsworth)의 『서곡』(*Prelude*)에는 현현의 순간들이 인상적으로 묘사되어 있으며, 셸리(Shelley)는 이러한 경험이 시를 영원하게 만드는 계시의 "순간들"(moments)이라 말했다.

20. 대구 Antithesis

대구 도는 대조는 동일구법에 따라, 사물의 종류·성질 등이 비슷하거나 상반된 것을 나란히 두는 구의 형태로, 서술을 장중하게 하거나 풍염하게 하는 문장상의 효과가 있는 시적 표현의 기초 기법이다. 이와 같이 대구는 일반적으로 종교적인 시에 사용되며 E. 블레이크, E. 휘트먼, T. S. 엘리엇, 알렉산더 포프 등이 효과적으로 구사하였다.

An Essay on Man: Epistle II

Alexander Pope (1688-1744)

Know then thyself, presume not God to scan;
The proper study of mankind is man.
Plac'd on this isthmus of a middle state,
A being darkly wise, and rudely great:
With too much knowledge for the sceptic side,
With too much weakness for the stoic's pride,
He hangs between; in doubt to act, or rest;
In doubt to deem himself a god, or beast;
In doubt his mind or body to prefer;
Born but to die, and reas'ning but to err;
Alike in ignorance, his reason such,
Whether he thinks too little, or too much:
Chaos of thought and passion, all confus'd;
Still by himself abus'd, or disabus'd;
Created half to rise, and half to fall;
Great lord of all things, yet a prey to all;
Sole judge of truth, in endless error hurl'd:
The glory, jest, and riddle of the world!

II

영국시 읽기

고대, 중세의 영국시 (−1485)

ca. 450 :	Anglo-Saxon Conquest	
597 :	St. Augustine arrives in Kent; beginning of Anglo-Saxon conversion to Christianity.	
0871-0899 :	Reign of King Alfred	
ca. 1200 :	Beginnings of Middle English literature.	
1360-1400 :	The summit of Middle English literature: Geoffrey Chaucer; *Piers Plowman*; *Sir Gawain and the Green Knight*.	
1485 :	William Caxton's printing of Sir Thomas Malory's *Morte Darthur*, one of the first books printed in England.	

初기의 영국역사가 가경자 비드(Bede)가 쓴 『영국인 교회사』(*Historia ecclesiastica gentis Anglorum*)에 의하면, 영어로 된 최초의 시는 7세기 후반에 나온 것으로 되어 있다. 그것을 쓴 캐드먼(Caedmon)은 일자무식의 목동이 었으나, 꿈에서 영감을 얻어 천지창조를 찬송하는 짧은 시 「찬미가」 ("Hymn")를 지었다. 그 뒤에는 성서를 바탕으로 시를 지었는데, 이것이 영 국의 토착적 시형식을 정착시킨 효시라고 한다. 고대영어로 쓰인 시는 사실 상 전부 두운시인 것이 특색이다. 한 행에 4개의 강세가 있고, 2번째와 3번 째 강세 사이에 휴지부가 있으며, 앞부분과 뒷부분이 두운으로 연결되는 것

이 이 형식이다. 형식 위주에다 상투적 표현들이 주류를 이루지만, 뛰어난 시의 경우에는 이러한 정형성이 지루하게 느껴지지 않고 오히려 시의 배경을 이루는 문화적 토양의 풍요로움으로 강한 인상을 남긴다. 그 밖의 표현 방식으로는 케닝(kenning)이 있는데, 사물을 비유적인 복합명사, 예컨대 '바다'를 '백조길', '고래길' 등으로 표현하는 방법이다. 그 밖에도 한 가지 뜻을 다른 말로 반복 표현하는 방식이 있으며, 반복 때마다 새로운 의미가 중첩된다. 이러한 시의 기교가 400년 동안 거의 변함없이 이어져온 사실은 앵글로색슨 문화의 극단적인 보수성을 드러내준다. 고대영시의 대부분은 10세기 후반과 11세기 초반에 씌어진 4편의 필사본에 보존되어 있다. 『베어울프』(Beowulf) 사본, 『엑서터서』(Exeter Book), 『주니어스』(Junius) 필사본, 『베르첼리』(Vercelli Book) 사본 등이 그것이다. 연대를 확정지을 수는 없으나, 『베어울프』 사본에 실린 『방랑자』(The Wanderer)를 비롯해, 초기 시로 간주되었던 그 밖의 작품들을 9-10세기의 작품으로 보는 것이 학계의 통설이다. 작가를 확실하게 밝힐 수 있는 시는 더욱 드물다. 그 중 많은 작품이 현재까지 남아 있는 가장 중요한 시인은 키너울프(Kynewulf)이다. 고대영시 가운데 세속적 재물이나 영광 또는 우애의 상실을 한탄하는 시를 통틀어 애가(elegy)라고 한다. 이 부류의 전형적 예로서 유명한 『베어울프』가 있다. 이 작품은 용사 베어울프가 괴물인 그렌델 일당과 싸워서 이기는 무용담을 그린 것이지만, 승리는 언제나 잠시뿐이고 싸움은 다시 일어나기 마련이라는 작가의 역사의식 때문에 작품 전체에 애가의 분위기가 깔려 있다.

12세기말까지 영국 시는 프랑스 시로부터 크게 영향을 받았다. 이 시기의 가장 뛰어난 시는 『부엉이와 나이팅게일』(The Owl and the Nightingale)로서, 당시 유행하던 논쟁 형식을 취하고 있다. 제목에 나오는 두 마리 새가 위생습관, 용모, 결혼노래, 예견, 신앙양태 등 다양한 화제를 놓고 논쟁을 벌이는데, 나이팅게일은 삶의 즐거움을, 부엉이는 삶의 어두운 측면을 대변한다. 13세기에 이르러 성서이야기, 성자의 생애, 라틴어나 프랑스어를 모르는 사람을 위한 도덕교훈 등을 담은 교훈시가 대두하게 되었다. 중세 시대 내내 유행한 로맨스 시가 처음 나타난 것도 13세기이며, 짐승을 등장시킨 해학풍 장시가 출현한 것도 이 시기이다. 중세 영어로 쓰인 세속 서정시에 가장 자주 나타나는 주제는 봄철과 낭만적 사랑이며, 대개가 노래로 불리기 위해 쓰인 듯하다. 종교적 서정시를 지배한 것은 열정적 분위기이며, 사랑의 시에서 표현을 빌린 경우가 많다.

후기 중세 및 초기 르네상스 시대인 1350-1550년에 영문학의 본질과 발전을 규정한 가장 주요한 요인 중 하나는 이 시대 초기에 영국이 처해 있던 특수한 언어적 상황이었다. 전체 인구 가운데 문자를 해독하는 소수의 사람들은 보통 2개 국어 심지어 3개 국어를 사용했다. 문학적 언어매체의 측면에서 영어는 라틴어나 당시 영국에서 널리 사용된 프랑스어의 앵글로 노르만(Anglo-Norman) 방언과의 경쟁에서 불리한 입장에 있었다. 뿐만 아니라 영어 내에서도 방언마다 차이가 심한 것이 토착어 문학의 유통을 가로막는 요인으로 작용했다. 그럼에도 불구하고 문자문화는 흑사병의 창궐(1347-51), 백년전쟁 및 장미전쟁과 같은 국내외의 고질적인 군사적 충돌, 사회적·정치적·종교적 불안정 등의 강력한 저해요인에 직면하면서 끈질기게 살아남았고, 또 번창하기에 이르렀다.

중세 후기 영시에 있어서 운을 밟지 않는 두운시가 14세기 중엽에 다시 나타났다. 14세기 말엽의 두운시는 고대영어 시대의 전통을 극히 표면적으로만 이어받았거나 자체의 형식을 발전시킨 것이다. 이와 같은 두운시 운동은 지금 볼 때 다소 기이해 보일 뿐 별로 주목할 만한 작품을 남기지 못한 사소한 문학적 현상으로 생각될지 모르나, 이름이 밝혀지지 않은 어느 단일 저자의 작품으로 여겨지는 4편의 시만은 예외이다. 기사도 로맨스인『가웨인 경과 녹색기사』(*Sir Gawayne and the Grene Knight*), 2편의 설교시

『인내』(*Patience*), 『순결』(*Purity*), 그리고 『진주』(*Pearl*)라는 제목으로 알려진 애가체 꿈 우화가 그것이며, 모두 1400년경의 단일 필사본 안에 들어 있다. 그 밖의 유명한 작품으로 윌리엄 랭런드(William Langland)의 길고 난해하며 아름다운 두운시 『농부 피어스』(*Piers Plowman*)가 있다. 이 두운시 운동은 대체로 15세기 초에 끝났지만 궁정시가는 더 오래 그 맥이 이어졌다. 14세기 후반에 이르러서는 궁정과 귀족사회에서 영어가 앵글로 노르만 프랑스어를 대체하게 되는데, 이러한 언어의 자국어화 과정은 제프리 초서(Geoffrey Chaucer)와 같은 기질이나 관심을 지닌 작가들이 많이 나올 수 있는 여건을 조성해 주었다. 또한 영어를 문어로서 확립한 초서의 천재성이 이 과정을 촉진시키고 그 발전 방향을 제시했다는 것도 의심할 여지가 없다. 초서는 부르조아 출신의 런던 사람으로서 궁정인·외교관·공무원 등 여러 경력을 거쳤다. 그의 초기 시는 '궁정풍'이라는 용어와 관련된 견해나 가치관을 담고 있으며, 아주 초기의 시는 당시의 프랑스 연애시에서 형식과 내용을 빌려온 것이었다. 그러나 그가 새로운 문학적 시도로서 결국 10음절, 즉 약강 5보격의 시행을 터득한 것은 영시에 있어 극히 중요한 계기가 되었다. 이렇게 닦은 기량은 처음에 7행시 등 연시가(聯詩歌) 형식으로, 뒤에 가서는 『캔터베리 이야기』(*The Canterbury Tales*)의 대부분을 이루는 10음절 2행연구체(聯句體)로 나타나게 되었다. 초서의 주요업적은 이야기체 시 분야에서 이루어졌다. 그는 초기에 보인 프랑스 궁정연애시 특히, 그가 번역한 『장미 이야기』(*Roman de la Rose*)의 영향에서 차츰 이탈리아 문학, 특히 단테·페트라르카·보카치오 등에 대한 관심으로 옮아갔다. 초서는 이야기체 시의 기교를 『캔터베리 이야기』에서 최고로 발휘했는데, 이 장시는 런던을 출발해 성 토머스 베킷의 사원을 참배하고 돌아오는 순례자 일행이 들려주는 이야기들을 담은 미완성 작품이다. 시인 자신이 아니라 순례자 개개인이 각자의 이야기를 들려준다는 가상의 구조는 작가의 입장을 매우 자유롭게 만들었고, 그렇게 함으로써 초서는 여러 장르를 섭렵할 수 있었다. 예컨대 경건한 전설, 파블리오*(fabliaux), 기사 로맨스, 통속 로맨스, 동물우화 등이 그것이다.

Middle English Lyrics

Sumer is icumen in*

Sumer is icumen in,
Lhude sing cuccu!
Groweþ sed and bloweþ med
And springþ þe wde nu,
Sing cuccu!

Awe bleteþ after lomb,
Lhouþ after calue cu.
Bulluc sterteþ, bucke uerteþ,
Murie sing cuccu!

- 익살조의 우화시
* 이 시에는 경쾌한 리듬과 아름다운 여운이 감도는 [u:] 음이 각운을 이루면서 봄의 즐거운 정경과 조화를 이룬다. 시각으로 파악할 수 있는 꽃동산과 푸른 숲을 배경으로 온갖 동물들의 우렁찬 합창이 청각적으로 어우러져 새로운 계절의 생동감을 더해 준다.

※ "Sumer Is Icumen In" (also called the Summer Canon and the Cuckoo Song) is a medieval English rota of the mid-13th century. The title translates approximately to "Summer Has Come In" or "Summer Has Arrived" (Roscow 1999). The song is composed in the Wessex dialect of Middle English. Although the composer's identity is unknown today, it may have been W. de Wycombe. The manuscript in which it is preserved was copied between 1261 and 1264 (Wulstan 2000, 8). This rota is the oldest known musical composition featuring six-part polyphony (Albright 1994), and is possibly the oldest surviving example of independent melodic counterpoint.[citation needed] It is sometimes called the Reading Rota because the earliest known copy of the composition, a manuscript written in mensural notation, was found at Reading Abbey; it was probably not drafted there, however (Millett 2004). The British Library now retains this manuscript (Millett 2003a).

Cuccu, cuccu, wel singes þu cuccu;

Ne swik þu nauer nu.

Pes:

Sing cuccu nu. Sing cuccu.

Sing cuccu. Sing cuccu nu!

The Prologue to the Canterbury Tales*

Geoffrey Chaucer (1340(?)-1400)

Whan that Aprille with his shoures soote

The droghte of Marche hath perced to the roote,

And bathed every veyne in swich licour,

Of which vertu engendred is the flour;

Whan Zephirus eek with his swete breeth

Inspired hath in every holt and heeth

The tendre croppes, and the yonge sonne

Hath in the Ram his halfe cours y-ronne,

And smale fowles maken melodye,

That slepen al the night with open ye,

(So priketh hem nature in hir corages);

Than longen folk to goon on pilgrimages,

---

* 켄터베리 이야기의 시작이 되는 부분이 바로 이 "General Prologue" 부분인데, 이 부분에서
는 켄터베리 이야기의 중심틀이 되는 부분을 담당하고 있다고 할 수 있다. 우선 상황을 설명
하는 내용이 들어가고, 사람들이 여관에 하나둘씩 모이는 그러한 장면을 그려낸다. 그리고
동시에 여관에서 함께 순례에 동참하게 되는 사람들의 인물을 묘사하는 장면도 상당히 많이
등장한다. "기사는 어떻고.. 수녀는 어떻고.." 이러한 부분이 여기에 모두 등장하고 있는 모
습이다. 이러한 인물 묘사가 끝나면, 여관주인의 제안이 시작되고, 프롤로그 마지막 부분에
는 누가 가장 먼저 이야기를 시작하게 될 것인지를 결정하는 부분이 등장한다.

When he nyhtegale singes*

Harley MS. (c. 1310.)

When the nyhtegale singes,
    The wodes waxen grene,
Lef ant gras ant blosme springes
    In Averyl, Y wene;
Ant love is to myn herte gon
    With one spere so kene,
Nyht ant day my blod hit drynkes ·
    Myn herte deth me tene.

Ich have loved al this yer
    That Y may love na more;
Ich have siked moni syk,
    Lemmon, for thin ore,
Me nis love neuer the ner,
    Ant that me reweth sore;
Suete lemmon, thench on me,
    Ich have loved the yore.
Suete lemmon, Y preye thee,
    Of love one speche;
Whil Y lyve in world so wyde
    Other nulle Y seche.
With thy love, my suete leof,
    My blis thou mihtes eche;
A suete cos of thy mouth
    Mihte be my leche.

---

* Springtime이라는 시에서는 봄철에 느낄 수 있는 자연의 아름다움과 시인 자신의 비참한 현
실을 대조시키고 있다. 이루어지지 않은 사랑의 아픔은 자연의 신선함과 즐거움 때문에 더
심화 되지 않을 수 없다. 이런 심정은 16세기 서정시에서 더욱 짙게 부각된다.

Suete lemmon, Y preye thee
    Of a love-bene:
Yef thou me lovest, ase men says,
    Lemmon, as I wene,
Ant yef hit thi wille be,
    Thou loke that hit be sene;
So muchel Y thenke vpon the
    That al y waxe grene.

Bituene Lyncolne ant Lyndeseye,
    Norhamptoun ant Lounde,
Ne wot I non so fayr a may,
    As y go fore ybounde.
Suete lemmon, Y preye the
    Thou lovie me a stounde;
Y wole mone my song
    On wham that hit ys on ylong.

Blow, Northern Wind*

Anonymous. (c. 1300)

ICHOT a burde in boure bryht,
That fully semly is on syht . . .

---

* 1. Ichot: "Ich wot", I know (of). 1b burde: maiden. 1c boure bryht: bright bower. 2. fully semly... syht: very pleasing to sight. 3. menskful: worshipful. 4. feir: fair. 5. fonde: deal with. 6. wurhliche: worthy. 7. won: multitude. 8. y nuste: I knew not. 9. lussomore in londe: lovelier n earth. 10. suetyng: sweetling, sweetheart. 11. lefliche: lovely. 12. fonge: finger, take between ands. 13. murthes: mirths, joys. 14. mote heo monge: may she mingle. 15. brid: bird. 16. breme: glorious. 16b lossom: lovesome, lovely. 17. rode: the rood, the cross. 18. lure: face. 19. lumes: beams. 20. bleo: colour. 21. suetly swyre: darling neck. 22. hue, heo: she. 23. clannesse: cleanness, purity. 24. parvenke: periwinkle. 25. solsecle: sunflower. 25b lealté: loyalty. 26. carke: care, worry. 26b dare: am in dismay. 27. won: wan. 28. slake: lessen.

With lokkes lefliche ant longe,

With frount ant face feir to fonge,

With murthes monie mote heo monge,

    That brid so breme in boure.

With lossom eye grete ant gode,

With browen blysfol under hode . . .

Hire lure lumes liht,

Ase a launterne a nyht,

Hire bleo blykyeth so bryht.

    So feyr heo is ant fyn.

A suetly swyre heo hath to holde,

With armes shuldre ase mon wolde.

Spring*

About 1310. MS Harl. 2253, f71v.

Lenten ys come with love to toune,

With blosmen & with briddes roune,

That al this blisse bryngeth;

Dayes eyes in this dales,

Notes suete of nyhtegales;

    Uch foul song singeth.

The threstelcoc him threteth oo;

Away is huere wynter wo,

    When woderove springeth.

---

* This poem takes up a common theme of medieval love-poetry, the contrast between the coming of spring, when all creatures choose their mates, and the lover's own frustrations. The movement of thought can be paralleled more concisely in the lover's complaint in John Gower's late-C14 *Confessio Amantis* ('The Lover's Confession')

This foules singeth ferly fele,
Ant wlyteth on huere wynter wele,
    That al the wode ryngeth.

The rose rayleth hire rode;
The leves on the lyhte wode
    Waxen al with wille.
The mone mandeth hire bleo;
The lilie is lossom to seo,
    The fenyl & the fille.
Wowes this wilde drakes;
Miles murgeth huere makes,
    Ase strem that striketh stille.
Mody meneth, so doth mo;

Ichot ycham on of tho,
    For love that likes ille.

The mone mandeth hire lyht,
So doth the semly sonne bryht,
    When briddes singeth breme;
Deawes donketh the dounes,
Deores with huere derne rounes

Domes forte deme;
Wormes woweth under cloude,
Wymmen waxeth wounder proude,
    So wel hit wol hem seme,
Yef me shal wonte wille of on,
This wunne weole y wole forgon
    Ant wyht in wode be fleme.

Now shrinketh rose and lily-flower*

Nou skrinketh rose ant lylie-flour,
  That whilen ber that suete sauour
  In somer, that suete tyde;
  Ne is no quene so stark ne stour,
  Ne no leuedy so bryht in bour
  That ded ne shal by glyde.
  Who-se wol fleysch lust forgon
  Ant heuene blis abyde,
  On Iesu be is thoht anon,
  That therled was ys side.

From Petresbourh in o morewenyng,
  As y me wende o my pleyghyng,
  On mi folie y thohte;
  Menen y gon my mournyng
  To hire that ber the heuene kyng,
  Of merci hire bysohte:
  'Ledy, preye thi sone for ous

---

* For the Feast of the Immaculate Conception, here's a medieval poem in praise of the Virgin Mary. The opening lines set the poem in autumn or winter, but the poem turns from depicting the transience of earthly life (a familiar theme in medieval poetry, on which see also this poem and this one; and also this and this —I said it was familiar!) to an appeal for salvation which is full of hope. This makes it appropriate for Advent. The shift from the winter setting, when "the rose and lily wither", to the poem's main subject may seem a little abrupt, but we should probably remember that flower imagery is extremely common in Middle English lyrics to describe both Christ and the Virgin Mary; there's an implicit contrast between the earthly rose and lily, which fade and die, and the heavenly "rose of Sharon, lily of the valley". Mary is the "Lady, flower of alle thing, rosa sine spina", as this carol has it; and in this superb fifteenth-century poem, Christ is the flower which bloomed in Bethlehem, and Mary the branch on which he grew.

That ous duere bohte,
Ant shild vs from the lothe hous
That to the fend is wrohte.

제2장

16세기 영국시 (1485-1603)

1485 : Accession of Henry VII inaugurates age of the Tudor sovereigns.

1509 : Accession of Henry VIII.

1517 : Martin Luther's Wittenberg Theses; beginning of the Reformation.

1534 : Henry VIII acknowledged "Supreme Head on Earth" of the English church.

1557 : Publication of *Tottel's Miscellany*, containing poems by Sir Thomas Wyatt, Henry Howard Earl of Surrey, and others.

1558 : Accession of Queen Elizabeth I.

1576 : The Theatre, the first permanent structure in England for the presentation of plays, is built.

1588 : Defeat of the Spanish Armada.

1603 : Death of Elizabeth I; accession of James I, first of the Stuart line.

1. 시대적 배경

화려한 업적을 남긴 문학사 가운데서도 엘리자베스 시대와 스튜어트 왕조 초기는 가장 화려한 시대를 대변한다. 동시에 이 시기는 모든 면에서 영국 사회를 변모시킨 광범위한 분열로 인해 엄청난 충격을 던져준 때이기도 하다. 이러한 사회변동에 지적 혁명이 수반되어, 새로운 과학, 새 종교, 새로운 인본주의 앞에 중세적 통합은 붕괴되기에 이른다. 새로운 세기를 대변한 철학자는 실험의 꾸준한 축적을 통한 과학의 점진적 발전을 옹호한 프랜시스 베이컨(Francis Bacon)이었고, 지식의 일반원칙을 체계화시키는 것은 불가능하다고 본 회의주의자 미셸 드 몽테뉴(Michel de Montaigne)였다. 인본주의와 청교도주의는 무지몽매와 민간전통에 대해 반대했으나, 다행히 그 어느 쪽도 건강한 대중의 취향을 오래 외면하지 못했다. 이 시기에는 장르의 교배작용이 계속 이루어져 많은 성과를 낳았다. 귀족풍 목가에 대중적 설화가 끼어들고, 서정시에는 발라드, 희극에는 로맨스, 비극에는 풍자, 시에는 산문이 섞이게 되었다. 언어 역시 급격한 팽창을 계속하여, 고급문학작품이 거리낌 없이 구어표현을 빌려왔다. 여러 층의 청중을 대상으로 동시에 말을 걸 줄 알고, 상충하는 경험과 세계관을 한 곳에 연결 지을 줄 알았던 엘리자베스 시대 사람들은 문학작품에도 복합성과 힘을 부여했다.

(1) 엘리자베스 시대의 시

영국의 시는 1570년대 후반에 갑작스럽게 꽃피기 시작했다. 우아함과 세련미를 과시하는 유려한 예술성 쪽으로 취향이 바뀌게 된 결정적 계기는 에드먼드 스펜서와 필립 시드니의 작품에서 비롯되었다. 에드먼드 스펜서(Edmund Spenser)의 『요정여왕』(The Faerie Queene)은 엘리자베스 시대의 대표적인 시로, 형식은 중세의 우화시에다 이탈리아풍의 낭만적 서사시를 융합시킨 것이다. 스펜서는 원래 엘리자베스 여왕을 상징하는 요정의 여왕 글로리아나의 궁정에서 온 12명의 기사가 12개의 미덕을 찾아다니는 것을 12편으로 나누어 그리려고 구상했으나 실제로는 6편밖에 완성하지 못했다. 글로리아나의 사랑을 추구하는 아서(Arthur)는 매 편마다 나오며, 완벽한 인간인 '장엄'(magnificence)의 모범으로 나타난다. 여유롭게

서서히 진행되는 9행시연과 고아한 언어는 자주 뛰어나게 감각적인 효과를 자아낸다. 1591년 발표된 필립 시드니(Philip Sidney)의 『아스트로펠과 스텔라』(*Astrophel and Stella*) 역시 소네트(14행시) 연작형식을 크게 유행시킨 계기가 되었다. 이 시가 교만한 미녀와 실연당한 애인의 이야기를 재기발랄한 솜씨로 다룬 페트라르카(Petrarca)풍의 재현인 데 비해, 1609년에 출판된 셰익스피어(W. Shakespeare)의 소네트집은 그 전통을 뒤엎어놓은 듯 전혀 다른 세계를 제시하고 있다. 그러나 소네트와 서정시는 엘리자베스 시대 운문의 일부 전통을 나타낼 뿐이다. 이와는 달리 엘리자베스 시대 특유의 우아함을 외면한 형식으로 풍자시(satire)가 있다. 풍자시는 원래 한탄과 연관된 것이지만, 당대인들은 그 용어가 그리스의 사티로스(Satyros), 즉 반인반수의 신에서 유래한 것으로 잘못 해석해 형식과 내용을 합치시킨 나머지 욕설과 매도에 치중하는 시를 썼다. 풍자시 작가들은 '불평객'이라는 새로운 유형의 인물을 유행시켰다.

(2) 스튜어트 왕조 초기의 시

1640년대의 정치적 붕괴와 그 직전부터 점차 증가된 사회적·문화적 일탈현상으로 스튜어트 왕조 초기에는 어떤 합일점도 찾아보기 어렵다. 고급문학과 저급문학 간의 괴리가 점차 심해짐에 따라 엘리자베스 시대의 작품들이 지녔던 강렬함은 거의 사라졌다. 이런 분위기에서, 시를 미덕을 권장하는 설득자로 보았던 옛 생각은 낡은 것으로 치부되었고, 특히 합리적으로 균형 잡힌 2행연구의 시와 자서전 및 소설 등이 새로운 문학 형식으로 대두된 것이 이 시대의 전반적인 특징이다. 시에서는 존 던(John Donne)이 형이상학파라고 알려진 전통을 대변한다. 그는 16세기의 핵심 전통인 평이한 시 전통의 정점에 있었다. 그의 언어는 항상 극적이며, 운문은 '강렬한 시행'·불협화음·일상회화체를 사용하고 있다. 존 던은 최초의 런던 출신 시인이라고 할 만하다. 초기 풍자시와 애가들은 바쁜 대도시의 분위기를 가득 담고 있으며, 최고 걸작이라 여겨지는 연가나 소네트는 상호 모순되는 태도·역설·우발성 등을 끊임없이 드러내고 있어 도시생활의 근대적인 모습을 실감나게 한다. 그는 전통적인 육체와 영혼의 이분법을 거부하여, 정신적·종교적 맥락으로만 사용되던 언어로 애인을 열렬히 찬양하는 경우도 빈번했다. 존 던은 마지못해 교회 직분을 가짐으로써 사회적 명망을 얻었겠지만, 그의 종교시조차 세속시와 마찬가지로 자기 확신과 자기비하 사이의 갈등을 드러내고 있다. 존 던의 영향력은 매우 컸다. 그의 추종자 중 가장 흥미있는 사람들은 조지 허버트(George Herbert), 리처드 크래쇼(Richard Crashaw), 헨리 본(Henry Vaughan) 등의 종교 시인들이다. 실제로 경건한 신앙심을 지녔으며 부유한 집안 출신인 조지 허버트는 존 던의 고통스런 자아를 대신해서 자비롭고 명상에 잠긴 확고한 신념을 표현했다. 로마 가톨릭교도인 리처드 크래쇼는 찬양시를 통해 대륙의 바로크 문학이 지닌 감각적 환희와 풍요로움을 소개했다. 헨리 본의 시는 심원한 자연주의와 신비스런 황홀경을 표현하고 있다. 그러나 던의 가장 뛰어난 후계자는 앤드루 마블(Andrew Marvell)이다. 마블의 뛰어난 작품은 군더더기가 없고 긴장감이 있으며 표현이 정확할 뿐만 아니라 궁정시풍의 서정적인 우아함과 청교도적인 언어의 절제가 독특하게 결합되어 있다. 이와는 대조적으로, 넓은 의미에서 벤 존슨의 전통을 따른 것은 사회적 성격의 시였다. 이 부류의 시는 고전의 명증성과 무게를 지닌 동시에 교양 있는 분별력, 격식에 대한 존중, 내면적인 자족감이라는 이상을 진지하게 받아들였다. 즉 그것은 일반대중이 공유한 가치관과 규범을 표현한 시였다. 존슨에게 있어서 평이한 문체란 노력과 절제 및 통제의 산물이었다. 그러나 그를 계승한 로버트 헤릭(Robert Herrick), 토머스 커루(Thomas Carew),

존 서클링(Sir John Suckling) 경, 리처드 러블레이스(Richard Lovelace) 등의 궁정시인들은 세련됨과 환락이라는 요소를 더욱 부각시키는 경향을 보였다.

2. 주요 작가와 작품

(1) 윌리엄 셰익스피어 William Shakespeare, 1564-1616

셰익스피어는 1564년 잉글랜드 중부의 스트랫퍼드 어폰 에이번(Stratford-upon-Avon)에서 출생하였다. 정확한 출생일은 알려지지 않고 있으며, 4월 26일은 그가 유아세례를 받은 날로 최초의 기록이다. 그가 태어난 마을은 아름다운 자연에 둘러싸인 영국의 전형적인 소읍이었고, 아버지 존 셰익스피어는 비교적 부유한 상인으로 피혁 가공업과 중농을 겸하고 있었다. 아버지가 읍장까지 지낸 유지였으므로, 당시의 사회적 신분으로서는 중산계급에 속해 있었기 때문에 셰익스피어는 풍족한 소년시절을 보낸 것으로 짐작된다.

당시 스트랫퍼드 어폰에 훌륭한 초·중급학교가 있어서 라틴어를 중심으로 한 기본적인 고전교육을 받았으며, 뒤에 그에게 필요했던 고전 소양도 이때 얻은 것으로 볼 수 있다. 그러나 1577년경부터 가세가 기울어져 학업을 중단했고 집안일을 도울 수밖에 없었다. 학업을 중단하고 런던으로 나온 시기는 확실치가 않다. 다만 1580년대 후반일 것으로 생각되며, 상경의 동기가 극단과 어떤 관계였는지의 여부도 알 수 없으나, 1592년에는 이미 그가 유수한 극작가의 한 사람이었다는 사실을 선배 극작가인 R. 그린의 질투어린 비판을 통하여 알 수 있다.

    1590년을 전후한 시대는 엘리자베스 1세 여왕 치하에서 국운이 융성한 때였으므로 문화면에서도 고도의 창조적 잠재력이 요구되었던 시기였다. 이러한 배경을 얻어 그의 천분은 더욱 빛날 수 있었다. 당시의 연극은 중세 이래의 민중적·토착적 전통이 고도로 세련되었으며, 특히 그리스·로마의 고전을 소생시킨 르네상스 문화의 유입을 맞아 새로운 민족적 형식과 내용의 드라마를 창출해내려는 때이기도 하였다.

    그러나 1592-1594년 2년간에 걸친 페스트 창궐로 인하여 극장 등이 폐쇄되었고, 때를 같이하여 런던 극단도 전면적으로 개편되었다. 이때부터 신진극작가인 셰익스피어에게 본격적인 활동의 기회가 주어졌다. 그는 당시의 극계를 양분하는 세력의 하나였던 궁내부장관 극단의 간부 단원이 되었고, 그 극단을 위해 작품을 쓰는 전속 극작가가 되었다. 그는 이 극단에서 조연급 배우로서도 활동했으나 극작에 더 주력하였다. 그리고 이 기간을 전후해서 시인으로서의 재능도 과시하여 「비너스와 아도니스」("Venus and Adonis", 1593)와 「루크리스」("Lucrece", 1594) 등 두 편의 장시를 발표하기도 하였다.

    1599년 템스강 남쪽에 글로브 극장(The Globe)을 신축하고 엘리자베스 1세 여왕의 뒤를 이은 제임스 1세의 허락을 받아 극단명을 '임금님 극단'(King's Men)이라 개칭하는 행운도 얻었다. 그러나 이런 명칭은 당시의 관례였을 뿐 상업적인 성격을 띤 일반 극단과 차이가 없었다. 1613년 그의 마지막 작품인 『헨리 8세』를 상연하는 도중 글로브 극장이 화재로 소실되었다. 1616년 4월 23일 52세의 나이로 고향에서 사망하였다.

Hamlet*

To be, or not to be (Act III, Scene 1)

To be, or not to be: that is the question:
Whether 'tis nobler in the mind to suffer
The slings and arrows of outrageous fortune,
Or to take arms against a sea of troubles,
And by opposing end them? To die: to sleep;
No more; and by a sleep to say we end
The heart-ache and the thousand natural shocks
That flesh is heir to, 'tis a consummation
Devoutly to be wish'd. To die, to sleep;
To sleep: perchance to dream: ay, there's the rub;
For in that sleep of death what dreams may come
When we have shuffled off this mortal coil,
Must give us pause: there's the respect
That makes calamity of so long life;
For who would bear the whips and scorns of time,
The oppressor's wrong, the proud man's contumely,
The pangs of despised love, the law's delay,
The insolence of office and the spurns
That patient merit of the unworthy takes,

---

* 'To be or not to be, that is the question'. Read Hamlet's famous soliloquy by Shakespeare below, along with a modern translation and explanation of what 'To be or not to be' is about. We've also pulled together a bunch of facts about the famous soliloquy, and have the 5 most famous film performances of 'to be or not to be'.

'To be or not to be' is the most famous soliloquy in the works of Shakespeare—probably, even, the most famous soliloquy anywhere. That is partly because the opening words are so interesting, memorable and intriguing but also because Shakespeare ranges around several cultures and practices to borrow the language for his images, and because he's dealing here with profound concepts, putting complex philosophical ideas into the mouth of a character on a stage, communicating with an audience with a wide range of educational levels.

When he himself might his quietus make
With a bare bodkin? who would fardels bear,
To grunt and sweat under a weary life,
But that the dread of something after death,
The undiscover'd country from whose bourn
No traveller returns, puzzles the will
And makes us rather bear those ills we have
Than fly to others that we know not of?
Thus conscience does make cowards of us all;
And thus the native hue of resolution
Is sicklied o'er with the pale cast of thought,
And enterprises of great pith and moment
With this regard their currents turn awry,
And lose the name of action. —Soft you now!
The fair Ophelia! Nymph, in thy orisons
Be all my sins remember'd.

Sonnet 18: Shall I compare thee to a summer's day?*

Shall I compare thee to a summer's day?
Thou art more lovely and more temperate.

---

* The speaker opens the poem with a question addressed to the beloved: "Shall I compare thee to a summer's day?" The next eleven lines are devoted to such a comparison. In line 2, the speaker stipulates what mainly differentiates the young man from the summer's day: he is "more lovely and more temperate." Summer's days tend toward extremes: they are shaken by "rough winds"; in them, the sun ("the eye of heaven") often shines "too hot," or too dim. And summer is fleeting: its date is too short, and it leads to the withering of autumn, as "every fair from fair sometime declines." The final quatrain of the sonnet tells how the beloved differs from the summer in that respect: his beauty will last forever ("Thy eternal summer shall not fade...") and never die. In the couplet, the speaker explains how the beloved's beauty will accomplish this feat, and not perish because it is preserved in the poem, which will last forever; it will live "as long as men can breathe or eyes can see."

Rough winds do shake the darling buds of May,
And summer's lease hath all too short a date.
Sometime too hot the eye of heaven shines,
And often is his gold complexion dimmed;
And every fair from fair sometime declines,
By chance, or nature's changing course, untrimmed;
But thy eternal summer shall not fade,
Nor lose possession of that fair thou ow'st,
Nor shall death brag thou wand'rest in his shade,
When in eternal lines to Time thou grow'st.
      So long as men can breathe, or eyes can see,
      So long lives this, and this gives life to thee.

(2008년 교육과정 평가원 기출문제)

Sonnet 29: When, in disgrace with fortune and men's eyes*

When, in disgrace with fortune and men's eyes,
I all alone beweep my outcast state,
And trouble deaf heaven with my bootless cries,
And look upon myself and curse my fate,
Wishing me like to one more rich in hope,
Featured like him, like him with friends possessed,

---

* One of Shakespeare's often quoted lines from "Sonnet 29" was dedicated along with many other sonnets to a young man that is greatly loved. Not much is known about Shakespeare's personal life; therefore, it is impossible to make assumptions about the romantic aspect of these poems. The Shakespearean sonnet follows a set pattern. It has fourteen lines with three quatrains [4 line verses] and a couplet at the end. The rhyme scheme is abab, cdcd, efef, gg. The first eight lines of Shakespeare's sonnet always present an argument which shows his unhappiness with what he does. Beginning with the ninth line, "yet," —, present a splendid image of a morning lark that "sings hymns at heaven's gate." This image epitomizes the poet's delightful memory of his friendship with the youth and compensates for the misfortunes he has lamented.

Desiring this man's art and that man's scope,
With what I most enjoy contented least;
Yet in these thoughts myself almost despising,
Haply I think on thee, and then my state,
(Like to the lark at break of day arising
From sullen earth) sings hymns at heaven's gate;
        For thy sweet love remembered such wealth brings
        That then I scorn to change my state with kings.

Sonnet 55: Not marble, nor the gilded monuments*

Not marble, nor the gilded monuments
Of princes, shall outlive this powerful rhyme;
But you shall shine more bright in these contents
Than unswept stone, besmear'd with sluttish time.
When wasteful war shall statues overturn,

---

* Sonnet 55 is one of Shakespeare's most famous works and a noticeable deviation from other sonnets in which he appears insecure about his relationships and his own self-worth. Here we find an impassioned burst of confidence as the poet claims to have the power to keep his friend's memory alive evermore. Some critics argue that Shakespeare's sudden swell of pride in his poetry was strictly artificial—a blatant attempt to mimic the style of the classical poets. "It is difficult on any other hypothesis to reconcile the inflated egotism of such a one as 55 with the unassuming dedications to the Venus and Lucrece, 1593 and 1594, or with the expressions of humility found in the sonnets themselves, e.g. 32 and 38" (Halliwell-Phillipps, 304). However, many believe that such an analysis ignores Shakespeare's paramount desire to immortalize his friend in verse, and not himself (as was the motive of most classical poets). "The Romans say: Because of my poem I will never die. Shakespeare says: Because of my poem you will never die....What distinguishes Shakespeare is that he values the identity of the beloved; he recognizes that the beloved has his own personal immortality, in no way dependent on poetry" (Martin, 158). By focusing on the word live, Shakespeare uses the language itself to emphasize his authorial intentions. Notice the word choices of outlive (2), living (8), oblivious (9), and live (14).

And broils root out the work of masonry,
Nor Mars his sword nor war's quick fire shall burn
The living record of your memory.
'Gainst death and all-oblivious enmity
Shall you pace forth; your praise shall still find room
Even in the eyes of all posterity
That wear this world out to the ending doom.
So, till the judgment that yourself arise,
You live in this, and dwell in lovers' eyes.

Sonnet 116: Let me not to the marriage of true minds*

Let me not to the marriage of true minds
Admit impediments. Love is not love
Which alters when it alteration finds,
Or bends with the remover to remove:
O no; it is an ever-fixed mark,
That looks on tempests, and is never shaken;
It is the star to every wandering bark,
Whose worth's unknown, although his height be taken.
Love's not Time's fool, though rosy lips and cheeks
Within his bending sickle's compass come;

---

* Sonnet 116 is about love in its most ideal form. The poet praises the glories of lovers who
have come to each other freely, and enter into a relationship based on trust and
understanding. The first four lines reveal the poet's pleasure in love that is constant and
strong, and will not "alter when it alteration finds." The following lines proclaim that true
love is indeed an "ever-fix'd mark" which will survive any crisis. In lines 7-8, the poet claims
that we may be able to measure love to some degree, but this does not mean we fully
understand it. Love's actual worth cannot be known; it remains a mystery. The remaining
lines of the third quatrain (9-12), reaffirm the perfect nature of love that is unshakeable
throughout time and remains so "ev'n to the edge of doom", or death.

Love alters not with his brief hours and weeks,

But bears it out even to the edge of doom.

　　If this be error and upon me proved,

　　I never writ, nor no man ever loved.

Sonnet 129: Th'expense of spirit in a waste of shame*

Th' expense of spirit in a waste of shame

Is lust in action; and till action, lust

Is perjured, murd'rous, bloody, full of blame,

Savage, extreme, rude, cruel, not to trust,

Enjoyed no sooner but despisèd straight,

Past reason hunted; and, no sooner had

Past reason hated as a swallowed bait

On purpose laid to make the taker mad;

Mad in pursuit and in possession so,

Had, having, and in quest to have, extreme;

A bliss in proof and proved, a very woe;

Before, a joy proposed; behind, a dream.

　　All this the world well knows; yet none knows well

　　To shun the heaven that leads men to this hell.

---

* This, one of the most famous sonnets, explores the reaction of the human psyche to the promptings of sexual urges. The folk wisdom of omne animal post coitum triste est, which is often quoted in connection with this sonnet, is banal in comparison to the ideas developed here. One has to look back to the ancient Greek world, and to the plays of Euripides, especially The Bacchae and Hippolytus, to find an equivalent. Particularly striking is the torrent of adjectives describing the build up of desire, and the imagery of the hooked fish which portrays the victim of lust as a frenzied animal expending its last vital energies in paroxysms of rage and futile struggle, even though it is inevitably doomed.

Sonnet 130: My mistress' eyes are nothing like the sun;*

My mistress' eyes are nothing like the sun;
  Coral is far more red than her lips' red;
  If snow be white, why then her breasts are dun;
  If hairs be wires, black wires grow on her head.
  I have seen roses damask'd, red and white,
  But no such roses see I in her cheeks;
  And in some perfumes is there more delight
  Than in the breath that from my mistress reeks.
  I love to hear her speak, yet well I know
  That music hath a far more pleasing sound;
  I grant I never saw a goddess go;
  My mistress, when she walks, treads on the ground:
    And yet, by heaven, I think my love as rare
    As any she belied with false compare.

(2009년 중등영어 임용고시 기출문제)

(2) 에드먼드 스펜서 Edmund Spenser, 1552–1599

에드먼드 스펜서는 런던 출신으로 미완성의 대작인 장편 서사시 『페어리 퀸』(*The Faerie Queene*)으로 불후의 명성을 남겼다. 후세 시인들에게 큰 영향을 끼쳤기 때문에 시인 중의 시인이라 불린다. 케임브리지 대학 재학 중 당시 유럽의 문학적 추세에 물들어 F. 페트라르카(Francesco Petrarca)와

---

* Sonnet 130 is the poet's pragmatic tribute to his uncomely mistress, commonly referred to as the dark lady because of her dun complexion. The dark lady, who ultimately betrays the poet, appears in sonnets 127 to 154. Sonnet 130 is clearly a parody of the conventional love sonnet, made popular by Petrarch and, in particular, made popular in England by Sidney's use of the Petrarchan form in his epic poem Astrophel and Stella.

J. 뒤벨레(Joachim Du Bellay)의 작품을 번역하고, 『사랑의 찬가』(*Hymnes in honour of love and beautie*) 등을 쓴 것도 이 무렵이었으며, 이 두 편은 후에 『4편의 찬가』(*Four Hymnes*, 1596)에 수록되었다. 대학 졸업 후 그는 학우를 통하여 레스터 백작이나 시드니 등, 당시 유력인사들의 지우를 얻어 궁정인으로서 출세하려고 하였으며, 동시에 시작에도 주력하여 1579년에는 목가적인 처녀시집 『목양자의 달력』(*Shepherd's Calender*)을 출판하여 유명해졌다.

그러나 레스터 백작의 실각으로 말미암아 1580년 본의 아니게 아일랜드 총독의 비서로 부임하여, 그 후 생애의 태반을 이 변경에서 지내게 되었다. 시드니의 전사를 애도한 시 「아스트로펠」("Astrophel")은 그곳에서 쓴 것이다. 1589년 『페어리 퀸』의 제1-3권 원고를 챙겨 런던에 상경, 이듬해 출간된 이 작품은 열광적인 반응을 불러일으켰으며, 작품 속에서 비유로 칭송되었던 엘리자베스 여왕은 그에게 연금을 하사하기까지 하였다. 그러나 전직의 소원은 이루어지지 않아 1591년에 유형지처럼 느껴지는 임지로 돌아가 『콜린 클라우트 다시 돌아오다』(*Colin Clout's ComeHome Again*, 1595)를 쓰면서 울분을 달랬다.

1594년 엘리자베스 보일과 결혼하여 『결혼 축가』(*Epithalamion*)에서 그의 기쁨을 노래하였으며, 그녀에 대한 구애에서 태어난 것이 연애시의 걸작이라 불리는 『연애 소곡집』(*Amoretti*)이다. 1596년에 재차 상경하여 옛 작품 둘을 포함한 『4편의 찬가』와 『페어리 퀸』 제4-6권 및 산문 『아일랜드의 현상에 대한 견해』(*A short View of the Present State of Ireland*)를 공표하였다. 1598년 그의 공관은 아일랜드 민중의 반란으로 불타버렸으며, 『페어리 퀸』의 나머지 원고도 이때 함께 불타버린 것 같다. 이듬해 런던에서 실의 속에 죽자 그의 유해는 웨스트민스터 대성당의 '시인의 한 모퉁이'에 매장되었다. 『페어리 퀸』에서 그가 보여준 약동하는 이미지의 아름다움은 예로부터 많은 시인을 사로잡았으며, 그의 '스펜서 시체'라는 형식의 아름다운 음악성은 절찬을 받아왔다. 그러나 최근 이 작품 속에는 엘리자베스 왕조의 정신적 풍토가 지닌 모든 문제점이 시인의 깊은 관찰로 묘사되었다 하여, 새로운 각도에서 재평가되고 있다.

Amoretti LXVIII: Most Glorious Lord of Life*

Most glorious Lord of life, that on this day,
Didst make thy triumph over death and sin:
And having harrow'd hell, didst bring away
Captivity thence captive, us to win:
This joyous day, dear Lord, with joy begin,
And grant that we for whom thou diddest die,
Being with thy dear blood clean wash'd from sin,
May live for ever in felicity.
And that thy love we weighing worthily,
May likewise love thee for the same again:
And for thy sake, that all like dear didst buy,
With love may one another entertain.
So let us love, dear love, like as we ought,
Love is the lesson which the Lord us taught.

---

* Spenser's sonnets in his Amoretti sonnet cycle reveal a complexity that foretells that of the then upcoming Epithelamion. Spenser accomplished (at least) two ends with his Amoretti: (1) he chronicled his difficult courtship of Elizabeth Boyle and (2) he gave a sonneteer's representation of the Anglican daily liturgy as laid out in the Book of Common Prayer. Any analysis of Amoretti 68 has to include consideration of both aspects.

Amoretti LIV: Of this worlds Theatre in which we stay*

Of this worlds Theatre in which we stay,
My love lyke the Spectator ydly sits
Beholding me that all the pageants play,
Disguysing diversly my troubled wits.
Sometimes I joy when glad occasion fits,
And mask in myrth lyke to a Comedy:
Soone after when my joy to sorrow flits,
I waile and make my woes a Tragedy.
Yet she beholding me with constant eye,
Delights not in my merth nor rues my smart:
But when I laugh she mocks, and when I cry
She laughes, and hardens evermore her hart.
What then can move her? if not merth nor mone,
She is no woman, but a sencelesse stone.

(3) 토마스 와이엇 Thomas Wyatt, 1503-1542

16세기 영국의 서정 시인으로 이탈리아 소네트 형식을 영국에 도입한 인물로 서리 백작과 함께 엘리자베스 왕조 시의 황금기 기반을 닦은 사람으로 유명하다. 케임브리지 대학에서 배우고 외교관으로서 헨리 8세를 섬기는 한편 유럽 각국의 대사를 역임하여 그 수완을 높이 평가받았는데, 정

---

* This is a poem that bemoans a woman being completely unmoved by a man's actions. The theatre and the different type of plays the wannabe lover claims to be adept in, are really different aspects or spheres of life. He is left feeling confused and frustrated by her lack of interest in him. Unrequited love is probably the most obvious. The poetic voice (Spenser) explores his frustration that he cannot get this woman (Boyle) to notice him, despite all his best efforts.

쟁으로 말미암아 두 차례나 투옥 당하였다. 시인으로서는 일찍이 대륙의
문학을 가까이 하여 여러 모로 실험을 시도한 서정 시인으로 알려져 있는
데, 특히 이탈리아의 소네트 형식을 영국에 도입해서 서리 백작과 함께 엘
리자베스 왕조 시의 황금기 기반을 닦은 사람으로 유명하다.

My Lute Awake*

My lute awake! perform the last
Labour that thou and I shall waste,
And end that I have now begun;
For when this song is sung and past,
My lute be still, for I have done.

As to be heard where ear is none,
As lead to grave in marble stone,
My song may pierce her heart as soon;
Should we then sigh or sing or moan?
No, no, my lute, for I have done.

---

* This poem begins with the speaker addressing his lute, calling for it to awaken and join him
in performing one last labor before they are done. That labor is to sing of his failed
attempts to capture the heart of a woman he loves. He goes on to speak of how cruelly his
beloved has repelled his advances. The speaker repeats his claims that he has given up, and
both he and his lute are done with this. This heartbreak turns to accusation in the fourth
stanza, where he begins to address his love directly, rather than his lute. He accuses the
unnamed woman of being 'proud of the spoil' of hearts that she was won. 'Spoil,' in this
case, meaning captured treasure or profits.

The Long Love that in my Thought doth Harbour*

The longë love that in my thought doth harbour
And in mine hert doth keep his residence,
Into my face presseth with bold pretence
And therein campeth, spreading his banner.
She that me learneth to love and suffer
And will that my trust and lustës negligence
Be rayned by reason, shame, and reverence,
With his hardiness taketh displeasure.
Wherewithall unto the hert's forest he fleeth,
Leaving his enterprise with pain and cry,
And there him hideth and not appeareth.
What may I do when my master feareth
But in the field with him to live and die?
For good is the life ending faithfully.

---

* Sir Thomas Wyatt the Elder has written his poem loosely based on the work by Petrarch entitled Rima 140. At first glance, both poems seem to be dealing with love. Upon closer reading one can tell that the author means much more. Coming from a courtly status in the court of King Henry VIII Wyatt could mean love as a metaphor for service and pledge of honor to ones king. After examining lines one and two, the honor one has pledged to his king is inescapable and always present not only in ones mind but his heart as well. Lines three and four imply that regardless of how one truly feels the king or lord a courtier owes service to will embed his thoughts and cause into the servants mind. This poem has a clear reflection of the influences of Petrarch. Focusing on unattainable love was a clear influence to Petrarch so it makes sense for Wyatt's poem to mimic that. Despite the suffering caused by things unattainable, a courtier must still perform his duties to those in court in order to be considered honorable or virtuous. These poems both seem to complain about the every day pressures found in such a society built upon honor and servitude.

(4) 필립 시드니 Philip Sidney, 1554-1586

영국 군인이자 정치가이며 시인 겸 평론가인 시드니는 스텔라에게 부치는 소네트를 쓰기 시작하고 그녀를 위해 목가적인 로맨스 『아케이디아』(*Arcadia*)를 쓰기 시작했다. 그는 E. 스펜서 등 문인과 사귀면서 그들의 후원자 역할만 하고 있었지만 사후에 유고가 발표되자 일약 시인·평론가로서 존경을 받았다. 시드니는 켄트펜스허스트 출생으로 헨리 시드니(Sir Henry Sidney)의 장남이다. 엘리자베스 여왕의 총신으로 명문 출신이었으나, 1583년 나이트(knight)의 작위를 받을 때까지는 작위가 없어서 막대한 유산을 물려받을 처지였으나 가난한 생활을 하였다. 옥스퍼드에서 유학하면서 F. 그레빌(F. Grevil), W. 캠덴(William Camden)과 친교를 맺고, 유럽 대륙 각지를 여행하였다. 귀국한 이듬해 에섹스 백작인 월터 데베르의 지기를 얻고, 그의 딸 피네로페를 알게 되었다.

1578년 레스터 하우스에 모인 문학자 그룹인 아레오파거스(Areopagus)에 가입하여 E. 스펜서와 사귀게 되었다. 이 무렵부터 스텔라에게 부치는 소네트를 쓰기 시작하고, 1581년경에는 누이동생인 펨브로크 백작부인의 윌튼 하우스에서 그녀를 위해 목가적인 로맨스 『아케이디아』를 쓰기 시작하였다. 1583년 F. 월싱검의 딸 프랜시스와 결혼하고, 1585년 프리신겐 총독이 되었으며, 이듬해 주트펜 구원군에 지원 참가하여 치명상을 입었다. 그 때 빈사상태에 있던 병사에게 자기의 물을 준 이야기는 유명한데, 당시 신사의 이상적인 상(像), 기사도 정신의 전형이라 하여 추앙받았다. 그의 죽음을 온 국민이 애석히 여겼고, E. 스펜서의 『아스트로펠』을 비롯하여 200편에 이르는 애가가 바쳐졌다. 생전의 그는 E. 스펜서 등 문인과 사귀면서 그들의 후원자 역할만 하고 있었지만 사후에 유고가 발표되자 일약 시인·평론가로서 존경을 받았다. 그의 저서는 2편의 시를 제외하고는 모두 사후에 출판되었다. 주요 저서는 『아케이디아』, 『아스트로펠과 스텔라』 (*Astrophel and Stella*) 그리고 『시의 변호』 등이 있다.

Astrophel and Stella 1: Loving in truth, and fain in verse my love to show*

Loving in truth, and fain in verse my love to show,
That she, dear she, might take some pleasure of my pain,
Pleasure might cause her read, reading might make her know,
Knowledge might pity win, and pity grace obtain, —
I sought fit words to paint the blackest face of woe;
Studying inventions fine, her wits to entertain,
Oft turning others' leaves to see if thence would flow
Some fresh and fruitful showers upon my sun-burned brain.
But words came halting forth, wanting invention's stay;
Invention, nature's child, fled step-dame Study's blows,
And others' feet still seemed but strangers in my way.
Thus, great with child to speak, and helpless in my throes,
Biting my truant pen, beating myself for spite,
Fool, said my muse to me, look in thy heart and write.

---

* Sidney's actions of writing about how to compose a love sonnet allow him to do just that: compose a love sonnet. With this in mind, he warns the reader that the emotions expressed in the entire sonnet sequence stem directly from the heart-thus, he cannot be held rationally responsible. The statements in this first sonnet make clear that Sidney (who already can be identified with the author of the love sonnets) is conflicted in his role as a zealous lover and a self-critical poet. This sonnet demonstrates the first of many clashes between reason and passion that appear in the sonnet sequence. He already seems to know that he will never truly win Stella, but he cannot help but desire her. This conflict between contradicting forces is a crucial element of the sequence.

Astrophil and Stella 2: Not at first sight, nor with a dribbèd shot*

Not at first sight, nor with a dribbèd shot,
    Love gave the wound which while I breathe will bleed:
    But known worth did in mine of time proceed,
Till by degrees it had full conquest got.
I saw, and liked; I liked, but lovèd not;
    I loved, but straight did not what love decreed:
    At length to love's decrees I, forced, agreed,
Yet with repining at so partial lot.
    Now even that footstep of lost liberty
Is gone, and now like slave-born Muscovite
I call it praise to suffer tyranny;
    And now employ the remnant of my wit
        To make myself believe that all is well,
        While with a feeling skill I paint my hell.

Astrophil and Stella 5: It is most true, that eyes are formed to serve**

It is most true, that eyes are formed to serve
The inward light; and that the heavenly part

---

* Sidney presents himself as a passive participant in the progression of love. He has no control over his emotions. Moreover, because of the slow and steady progression of his emotions, he was unable to guard himself in any way. He is a slave to love and has no power to escape it. By presenting himself as a slave to a sort of happy tyranny, Sidney both justifies and excuses his actions. According to his inflexible Protestant background, Sidney's desire for Stella is inappropriate and must be restrained at all times. But if he is not under his own control, existing as nothing more than a slave to love, he cannot be judged as completely responsible for his behavior.

** This poem is essentially a series of moral axioms upended in the end with a final strange conclusion. Sidney uses the term "true" frequently in the sonnet in order to play with the

Ought to be king, from whose rules who do swerve,
Rebels to Nature, strive for their own smart.

It is most true, what we call Cupid's dart,
An image is, which for ourselves we carve;
And, fools, adore in temple of our heart,
Till that good god make Church and churchman starve.

True, that true beauty virtue is indeed,
Whereof this beauty can be but a shade,
Which elements with mortal mixture breed;
True, that on earth we are but pilgrims made,
And should in soul up to our country move;
True; and yet true, that I must Stella love.

Astrophel and Stella 15: You that do search for every purling spring*

You that do search for every purling spring
    Which from the ribs of old Parnassus flows,
    And every flower, not sweet perhaps, which grows
    Near thereabouts into your poesy wring;
You that do dictionary's method bring

---

reader's mind and toy with the meaning of the term. All of the force he establishes with the idea of truth in the first thirteen lines is used in the last line to prove his final truth: that he must love Stella. The closing phrase is the first deeply personal note of the poem, and it gains its power from the contrast with the previous thirteen lines. Astrophel agrees to become a "rebel to Nature" and a "foole" to Cupid's power. Yet, he emphasizes that he does not have a choice in the decision; he "must" love Stella with an urgency that is beyond his control.

* Sidney also critiques plagiarism and imitation in sonnets 1, 3, and 6. As in the other sonnets, Sidney maintains that inspiration is only lacking in poetry if it does not stem directly from the heart. His muse is Stella, and he does not need to use the methods of other poets (the dictionary, mythological images, and so on) in order to express his true feelings. This sonnet is simultaneously tongue-in-cheek because, although he may not plagiarize, Sidney does utilize classical mythology and florid language in other sonnets in this sequence.

Into your rhymes, running in rattling rows;
You that poor Petrarch's long-deceasèd woes
With new-born sighs and denizened wit do sing;
You take wrong ways, those far-fet helps be such
As do bewray a want of inward touch,
And sure at length stol'n goods do come to light.
But if, both for your love and skill, your name
You seek to nurse at fullest breasts of Fame,
Stella behold, and then begin to endite.

Astrophel and Stella 74: I never drank of Aganippe well*

I never drank of Aganippe well,
Nor ever did in shade of Tempe sit,
And Muses scorn with vulgar brains to dwell:
Poor layman I, for sacred rites unfit.
    Some do I hear of poets' Fury tell,
But (God wot) wot not what they mean by it;
And this I swear, by blackest brook of hell,
I am no pick-purse of another's wit.
    How falls it then, that with so smooth an ease
My thoughts I speak, and what I speak doth flow
In verse, and that my verse best wits doth please?
Guess we the cause: 'What, is it thus?' Fie, no;
    'Or so?' Much less. 'How then?' Sure, thus it is:
    My lips are sweet, inspired with Stella's kiss.

---

* In this sonnet, Astrophel steps out of character to construct a witty reference to the stolen kiss. This sonnet is widely considered to be the comic masterpiece of the sonnet sequence because of Astrophel's tongue-in-cheek response and lack of remorse for the kiss. (Compare Alexander Pope's later "The Rape of the Lock.")

(5) 월터 롤리 Walter Raleigh, 1552-1618

1569년 의용병으로 위그노 전쟁에 참가하고, 1578년 이복형 길버트의 북아프리카 탐험에 수행하였다. 또 1580년 아일랜드 반란을 진압한 공으로 엘리자베스 1세의 총애를 받아 기사 작위를 서임 받았다. 진흙길 위에 값진 망토를 펼쳐 여왕을 지나가게 하였다는 전설은 유명하다. 1587년 근위대장으로 임명되어 광대한 영지와 상업상의 특권을 부여받아 궁정에서 세력을 떨쳤다. 북아메리카를 탐험, 플로리다 북부를 '버지니아'로 명명하고 식민을 행하였으나 실패하였다. 감자와 담배를 영국으로 도입한 사실로도 유명하다.

그 후 여왕의 총애를 잃어 한때 투옥되기도 하였다. 제임스 1세 때에는 반역사건에 연루되어 투옥, 옥중에서 『세계사』(*The History of the World*)를 저술하였다. 1616년 출옥하고 다음해 오리노코 강 탐험을 시도했으나 실패, 1618년 귀국하자 그는 부하들이 에스파냐령에서 난폭한 행위를 하였다는 혐의로 처형되었다. E. 스펜서의 친구로서 서정시인으로도 유명했는데, 작품은 30편 정도가 남아 있을 뿐이다.

The Nymph's Reply to the Shepherd*

If all the world and love were young,
And truth in every Shepherd's tongue,
These pretty pleasures might me move,
To live with thee, and be thy love.

---

* Sir Walter Raleigh's "The Nymph's Reply to the Shepherd" is a satiric reply to Christopher Marlowe's "The Passionate Shepherd to His Love." The irony of this satire is that a mythological spirit depicted as a maiden is more realistic than the shepherd. The flaw in the shepherd's pastoral lyric of invitation ironically pointed out by this maiden is that the idyllic life that he and the nymph will share is limited by its temporality.

Time drives the flocks from field to fold,
When Rivers rage and Rocks grow cold,
And Philomel becometh dumb,
The rest complains of cares to come.

The flowers do fade, and wanton fields,
To wayward winter reckoning yields,
A honey tongue, a heart of gall,
Is fancy's spring, but sorrow's fall.

Thy gowns, thy shoes, thy beds of Roses,
Thy cap, thy kirtle, and thy posies
Soon break, soon wither, soon forgotten:
In folly ripe, in reason rotten.

Thy belt of straw and Ivy buds,
The Coral clasps and amber studs,
All these in me no means can move
To come to thee and be thy love.

But could youth last, and love still breed,
Had joys no date, nor age no need,
Then these delights my mind might move
To live with thee, and be thy love.

(6) 크리스토퍼 말로 Christopher Marlowe, 1564-1593

엘리자베스 왕조 연극의 선두에 섰던 '대학재사'의 대표적인 인물인
영국 극작가 겸 시인이다. 특징으로는 물욕·지식욕·정복욕 등 한결 같이

인간으로서의 규범을 벗어난 욕망에 휘말려 거의 좌절해 가는 주인공을 삼았다는 것이다. 주요 작품에는 『포스터스 박사』(Dr. Faustus), 『탬벌린 대왕』(Tamburlaine the Great) 등이 있다.

그는 캔터베리 출생으로 셰익스피어로 그 절정에 이른 엘리자베스 왕조 연극의 선두에 섰던 대표적인 인물이다. 제화공의 아들로 태어나 장학금으로 케임브리지 대학을 졸업하였다. 재학 중에는 영국의 첩보기관에도 관계한 듯하다. 그래서인지 그의 최후도 1593년 5월 30일, 딥트퍼드의 주점에서 술값으로 사소한 다툼 끝에 동료 밀정에게 찔려 죽었다. 생전에 워터 롤리경 등의 진보적인 지식인들과 친교를 맺었고, 신을 부정하는 논문을 썼다고 하여 그가 죽은 뒤 체포령이 내리는 등, 29년의 짧은 생애에 파문이 그칠 날이 없었다. 그가 만들었던 극의 공통적인 특징으로는 물욕 · 지식욕 · 정복욕 등 한결같이 인간으로서의 규범을 벗어난 욕망에 휘말려 거의 좌절해 가는 주인공을, 그것도 구성의 졸렬함 따위에는 아랑곳하지도 않고 당대 연극의 기조를 이루었던 무운시로 낭랑하게 읊은 점이다. 시작에는 정열적인 미완의 서사시 『히어로와 리앤더』(Hero and Leander) 등이 있다.

The Passionate Shepherd to His Love*

Come live with me and be my love,
And we will all the pleasures prove,
That Valleys, groves, hills, and fields,
Woods, or steepy mountain yields.

---

* "The Passionate Shepherd to His Love" is a pastoral poem, meaning it is set in an idealized version of the countryside, where life is good and the air is sweet. Plot-wise, the poem basically comes down one lover saying to another lover: "move to the country with me and once you're there we can play by the river, listen to the birds sing, and I'll even make you

And we will sit upon the Rocks,
Seeing the Shepherds feed their flocks,
By shallow Rivers to whose falls
Melodious birds sing Madrigals.

And I will make thee beds of Roses
And a thousand fragrant posies,
A cap of flowers, and a kirtle
Embroidered all with leaves of Myrtle;

A gown made of the finest wool
Which from our pretty Lambs we pull;
Fair lined slippers for the cold,
With buckles of the purest gold;

A belt of straw and Ivy buds,
With Coral clasps and Amber studs:
And if these pleasures may thee move,
Come live with me, and be my love.

The Shepherds' Swains shall dance and sing
For thy delight each May-morning:
If these delights thy mind may move,
Then live with me, and be my love.

---

some bohemian chic clothing to boot." The poem was first published—or at least part of it
was—in 1599 in a hodgepodge poetry collection called The Passionate Pilgrim, but people
who have spent decades in libraries studying Marlowe think that it was likely written in the
mid—to late 1580s, a few years before his death. This places the composition of the poem
somewhere near the beginning of Marlowe's career, and definitely before he became a
bigshot in the Renaissance theater world.

17세기 영국시 (1603-1660)

(1588 : The Spanish Armada.)

1603 : Death of Elizabeth Tudor, accession of James Stuart.

1605 : The Gunpower Plot; last effort of English Catholic extremists.

1620 : First emigration of Pilgrims of the New World.

1625 : Death of James I, accession of Charles I.

1641 : Outbreak of Civil War: theaters closed, 1642.

1649 : Execution of Charles I, beginning of Common wealth and Protectorate, known inclusively as the Interregnum (1649–60)

1660 : End of the Protectorate, Restoration of Charles II.

(1688 : Abdication of James II, last Stuart king of England.)

1. 시대적 배경

영문학사에서 17세기는 1603년 스튜어트(Stuart)가의 첫 왕인 제임스 1세 (James I)가 즉위할 때부터 1660년 찰스 2세(Charles II)가 복위할 때까지를 말한다. 이 시기는 격동의 시기로서 향후 영국의 정치, 사회, 종교의 향방을 가늠하는 사건들이 발생하게 된다. 영국의 정치적 문제들은 종교적 갈등과 맞물려있는 복합적 요소로서 엘리자베스 튜더 왕조 시기의 잠복기를 거쳐 튜더 왕조에 이르러 내란과 혁명으로 분출된다. 과세권을 둘러싸고

국왕과 의회 사이에 갈등이 야기되자, 찰스 1세는 오랜 기간 동안 의회를 소집하지 않음으로써 국민의 반감을 사게 된다. 정치적 불만은 또한 종교적 갈등에 의해 악화되었으며, 종교적 갈등은 신교와 구교, 국교와 비국교, 온건한 종파들과 과격한 종파들의 대립으로 복잡한 양상으로 치닫게 되었다. 내란의 직접적인 동기는 찰스가 청교도가 대다수를 이루는 스코틀랜드에 영국교회의 체제와 『공동 기도서』를 강요하면서 비롯되었다.

1642년 보수세력의 귀족과 국교도의 지지를 받는 왕당파와 비국교도 및 청교도, 중산층의 지지를 받은 의회파 사이에 전쟁이 시작된다. 이 전쟁은 왕당파의의 패배와 찰스 왕의 체포로 이어지면서 결국은 왕의 처형이라는 극단적인 사건으로 종결되었고, 그 결과 영국은 1649년에 공화정을 선포한다. 이 내란은 결국 왕과 의회 사이의 권력투쟁이었으며, 동시에 국교와 비국교간의 종교분쟁이기도 했다. 올리버 크롬웰(Oliver Cromwell)에 의해 시작된 공화정은 성공을 거두지 못한다. 공화정의 통치는 영국민이 바라던 안정과 자유를 보장해 주지 못했다. 1653년 크롬웰은 의회를 해산하고 독재정치를 감행한다. 1658년 크롬웰이 갑자기 사망하자, 영국은 공화정을 포기하고 다시 왕정을 복고하게 된다.

(1) 청교도 혁명 Puritan Revolution

청교도 혁명은 영국인들의 의식세계에 커다란 영향을 끼치게 된다. 청교도 혁명과 내란으로부터 나타난 한 가지 보편적인 진리는 어떠한 방법으로도 오직 한 가지 보편적인 진리를 얻는 것이 불가능하다는 것이었다. 종교 의식 및 교리를 비롯한 제반 사회적 가치문제에 있어서도 오직 한 가지 믿음 내지 진리는 불필요한 것처럼 보였다. 피를 수반한 긴 전쟁을 치르고 나니 결국 어떤 사람도 꼭 옳을 수가 없고 어떤 사람도 그릇될

수가 없다는 것이 영국인들의 의식 속에 깊게 자리 잡게 되었다. 이제 영국사회는 계급과 획일과 개인적인 관계의 개념에 입각한 사회에서 다수와 관용의 개념에 입각한 사회로 바뀌게 된다. 즉, 전제국가에서 활기 있고 실리주의적인 다원주의 국가로 옮겨가게 된 것이다.

문학의 발달 면에서 1660년 찰스 2세가 복위함에 따라 많은 사람들은 20년간의 내전과 공화정 아래서 갖게 된 정치적 희망과 지복천년의 기대를 고통스럽게 재평가해야 했다. 효율적인 검열제도의 도입으로 대담한 공화정 시대의 이단적 사상은 출판금지 당했다. 1660년 이전의 가장 뛰어난 논객이었던 존 밀턴(John Milton)은 더 이상 그런 분위기의 글을 쓰지 않았으며, 공적 활동으로부터 은퇴를 강요당한 채 종교적 투쟁과 신념을 다룬 시인 『실락원』(*Paradise Lost*), 『복락원』(*Paradise Regained*), 『투사 삼손』(*Samson Agonistes*)을 쓰는 데 전념했다. 이 작품들은 인간 역사 속에 신의 뜻이 드러나는 미묘한 방식을 탐구한 것으로, 밀턴 자신이 커다란 믿음과 희망을 걸었던 혁명이 실패한 사실에 대한 그의 단호한 반응으로 보아야 한다. 『넘치는 은혜』(*Grace Abounding*), 『천로역정』(*The Pilgrim's Progress*, 1부 1678 · 2부 1684)을 쓴 존 버니언이나 자서전 『백스터 유고집』(*Reliquiae Baxterianae*)을 쓴 리처드 백스터 같은 비국교도들은 17세기의 청교도 정신을 개인적인 글로 기록한 사람들이다. 반면 청교도적 반응이 매우 날카로운 작품을 쓴 새뮤얼 버틀러의 의사영웅시체 풍자문학으로 『휴디브라스』(*Hudibras*)가 있는데, 당시 큰 인기를 얻었으며 18세기까지 영향을 미쳤다. 왕당파 역시 그들 나름대로 패배와 복권의 경험을 기록한 전기나 자서전을 남겼고, 그 밖에도 뛰어난 연대기 작가들, 걸출한 일기작가 존 이블린(John Evelyn)과 새뮤얼 피프스(Samuel Pepys), 궁정재사로 알려진 수많은 시인들이 배출되었다. 궁정재사들의 시보다 훨씬 뛰어난 수준의 시를 남긴 사람은 존 드라이든(John Dryden)이다. 그는 당시의 사회문제를 진지하게 다루었고, 말년

에는 유베날리스·펠시우스·베르길리우스 등의 고전작품을 번역하거나
보카치오와 초서의 작품을 훌륭하게 번안하기도 했다.

(2) 형이상학파의 시와 시인들 Metaphysical Poets

17세기에 연애 서정시와 종교적 서정시를 썼던 일군의 시인들인 존
던(John Donne), 조지 허버트(George Herbert), 에이브라함 쿨리(Abraham
Cowley)들을 형이상학파 시인들이라고 지칭한다. 이들의 시는 재치 있는
기상(conceit)과 기발한 이미지의 사용으로 엘리자베스 시대에 유행했던 낭
만적 분위기를 자아냈던 전통적 연애시와 대조를 이룬다.

* **Definition of Metaphysical Poetry**
  : The poetry is intellectual, analytical, psychological, bold, absorbed in
    thoughts of death, physical love, religious devotion.
  − philosophical poetry dealing with metaphysics
  − emotional apprehension of thought
  − psychological analysis of the emotions of love and religion
  − logical elements
  − the sense of the complexities and contradictions of life
  − passion is interwoven with reasoning

2. 주요 작가와 작품

(1) 존 던 John Donne, 1572-1631

존 던은 런던 출신으로 가톨릭교도인 부모 사이에서 태어나 가톨릭의
영향을 받으며 자랐다. 1584년 옥스퍼드 대학에 들어갔으나 중퇴하고,

1591년 법률학을 연구하기 시작하여 케임브리지 대학에서 공부한 후 1592년 링컨스 인(Limcoln's Inn) 법학원에 들어가 정계나 법조계에서 입신할 뜻을 굳혔다. 그리하여 1596년과 1597년 2회에 걸쳐 에식스 백작을 따라 에스파냐 원정에 종군하였고, 귀국한 후에 국새상서 T. 에저튼 경의 비서가 되었다. 그러나 그의 조카 A. 모어와의 비밀결혼이 발각되어 직위도 잃고, 1602년까지 감옥에 갇혀 있었다. 이 무렵에 에스파냐 문학을 비롯한 각국의 문학사상에 흥미를 느껴 풍자시와 서정시를 썼고, 가톨릭 신앙에 대해서는 회의적이었다. 출옥 후 비록 자유의 몸이 되기는 하였으나, 정신적으로나 물질적으로 괴로운 생활이 15년간이나 계속되었다.

1608년 중병에 걸렸을 때에는 끊임없이 자살을 생각하여 『자살론』(Biathanatos)을 쓸 정도였다. 이때 가톨릭으로부터 영국국교로 개종하게 된다. 불우한 가운데서도 1609년에는 뛰어난 종교시 「신성 소네트」("The Holy Sonnets")를 썼고, 이어서 애가 「세계의 해부」("An Anatomy of the World")와 그 속편 「영혼의 걸음」("Of the Progress of the Soul")을 썼다. 1611년 대륙을 여행하고 돌아와서는 국왕의 조언을 받아들여 1615년에 성직자에 임명되어 국왕 앞에서 설교한 일도 있다. 1617년 아내를 여의고 마지막 대륙의 여행에서 돌아와 성 바오로 대성당의 주임사제가 되어 죽을 때까지 그 직에 있었다. 르네상스의 변동기에 산 그의 생애에 어울리게 던의 시도 젊은 시절의 연애시와 만년의 종교시로 대별할 수 있다.

『노래와 소네트』(Songs and Sonnets)로 대표되는 연애시는 상냥함·야유·자조·절망·저주 등 사랑의 온갖 심리를 대담하고 정치한 이미지를 구사하여 표현한 뛰어난 작품이다. F. 페트라르카 류의 상투적인 연애시를 배격하고, 불굴의 정열과 냉철한 논리와 해박한 지식의 통일을 이룩한 이들 작품으로, 17세기 영국의 형이상적 시인의 제1인자로서 위치를 굳혔을 뿐만 아니라 T. S. 엘리엇, W. B. 예이츠 등 20세기의 현대 시인에게도 깊은

영향을 끼쳤다. 기지의 제왕이라는 말을 듣던 그의 면모는 만년의 설교에도
여실히 나타나 명설교로도 이름이 알려졌다. 「유물」("The Relic"), 「매장」
("The Funeral") 「성자의 반열에 오름」("The Canonization") 등이 유명하다.

An Anatomy of the World*

'Tis all in pieces, all coherence gone,
All just supply, and all relation;
Prince, subject, father, son, are things forgot,
For every man alone thinks he hath got
To be a phoenix, and that then can be
None of that kind, of which he is, but he.

Satire III**

To adore, or scorn an image, or protest,
May all be bad; doubt wisely; in strange way

---

* 존 던은 이 시를 그의 친구이자 패트론인 로버트 두루어리 경의 14세 된 어린 딸의 죽음을
추념하기 위해 지었다. 던의 시의 기본적인 주제는 이 세상을 함께 묶어 주고 있던 가냘프
지만 귀중한 상호 공감의 끈들이 끊어져 나가 버려서 이 세상이 부패되고 붕괴되었다는 것
이다. 이 시에 나타나는 다른 상징들로는 에덴동산 및 인류타락의 이야기, 황금시대의 신화,
인간과 인간의 도덕생활이 우주적 관심의 중심이 되었던 오랜 지구 중심적 우주관의 붕괴
등을 들 수 있다. 제시하는 일반적인 관점으로 예전에는 이 세상이 이상적이었고 질서정연
했으나 지금은 급속히 악화되어가고 있으며 실상 그 역사가 오래되었고, 많은 형식으로 표
현이 되어오고 있었다. 통일성의 상실을 애도하고 있는 이 시는, 가능한 한 여러 무리의 교
묘한 상응관계를 끌어냄으로써 통일성을 시험해본, 단의 기지에 넘치고 외견상 괴팍해 보
이는 시들의 대응물에 지나지 않는다. 비록 「세계의 해부」가 그 대담하고 기운찬 시들보다
덜 압축된 시이기는 하지만, 가장 위대한 만가들이 바로 그렇듯이 그 주제를 탈개인화시키
고 보편화시키는 구실을 하는 웅장한 애가로 서서히 발전한다.

** During Donne's era, Christianity was divided between Roman Catholicism (on the one

To stand inquiring right, is not to stray;

To sleep, or run wrong, is. On a huge hill,

Cragged and steep, Truth stands, and he that will

Reach her, about must and about must go, . . .

The Indifferent*

I can love both fair and brown,

Her whom abundance melts, and her whom want betrays,

Her who loves loneness best, and her who masks and plays,

Her whom the country formed, and whom the town,

Her who believes, and her who tries,

Her who still weeps with spongy eyes,

And her who is dry cork, and never cries;

I can love her, and her, and you, and you,

I can love any, so she be not true.

---

hand) and various Protestant sects (on the other). Protestantism, which had begun with the revolt of Martin Luther against the Roman Catholic Church, had generated, by Donne's time, a variety of different denominations and theologies, including those of Luther, John Calvin, and the Anglican church in England. Thus people living in Donne's time had crucial decisions to make about which church, if any, to embrace. Even though Roman Catholicism was technically illegal in Donne's day in England, many English people used the freedom of their own consciences to continue to believe in Catholic doctrines, even if they could not legally be practicing members of an established Catholic church.

* "The Indifferent" has three nine-line stanzas following a rhyme scheme of abbacccdd with varied meter. Each stanza has two parts, with the last two lines consisting of a rhyming couplet. Donne employs his famous sardonic wit; here is a man whose "love" is non-exclusive and can be directed at multiple women at the same time. The title reflects the attitude of the speaker in the first stanza.

A Valediction: Forbidding Mourning*

As virtuous men pass mildly away,
 And whisper to their souls to go,
Whilst some of their sad friends do say,
 "The breath goes now," and some say, "No,"

So let us melt, and make no noise,
 No tear-floods, nor sigh-tempests move;
 'Twere profanation of our joys
 To tell the laity our love.

Moving of the earth brings harms and fears,
 Men reckon what it did and meant;
 But trepidation of the spheres,
 Though greater far, is innocent.

Dull sublunary lovers' love
 (Whose soul is sense) cannot admit
 Absence, because it doth remove
 Those things which elemented it.

But we, by a love so much refined
 That our selves know not what it is,

---

* The speaker explains that he is forced to spend time apart from his lover, but before he leaves, he tells her that their farewell should not be the occasion for mourning and sorrow. In the same way that virtuous men die mildly and without complaint, he says, so they should leave without "tear-floods" and "sigh-tempests," for to publicly announce their feelings in such a way would profane their love. The speaker says that when the earth moves, it brings "harms and fears," but when the spheres experience "trepidation," though the impact is greater, it is also innocent.

Inter-assured of the mind,

Care less, eyes, lips, and hands to miss.

Our two souls therefore, which are one,

Though I must go, endure not yet

A breach, but an expansion,

Like gold to airy thinness beat.

If they be two, they are two so

As stiff twin compasses are two:

Thy soul, the fixed foot, makes no show

To move, but doth, if the other do;

And though it in the center sit,

Yet when the other far doth roam,

It leans, and hearkens after it,

And grows erect, as that comes home.

Such wilt thou be to me, who must,

Like the other foot, obliquely run;

Thy firmness makes my circle just,

And makes me end where I begun.

Good-Friday, 1613, Riding Westward*

Let man's soul be a sphere, and then, in this,

Th' intelligence that moves, devotion is;

And as the other spheres, by being grown

---

* John Donne wrote this poem during a westward ride from Warwickshire to Montgomery,

Subject to foreign motion, lose their own,
And being by others hurried every day,
Scarce in a year their natural form obey;
Pleasure or business, so, our souls admit
For their first mover, and are whirl'd by it.
Hence is't, that I am carried towards the west,
This day, when my soul's form bends to the East.
There I should see a Sun by rising set,
And by that setting endless day beget.
But that Christ on His cross did rise and fall,
Sin had eternally benighted all.
Yet dare I almost be glad, I do not see
That spectacle of too much weight for me.
Who sees Gods face, that is self-life, must die;
What a death were it then to see God die ?
It made His own lieutenant, Nature, shrink,
It made His footstool crack, and the sun wink.
Could I behold those hands, which span the poles
And tune all spheres at once, pierced with those holes ?
Could I behold that endless height, which is
Zenith to us and our antipodes,
Humbled below us ? or that blood, which is
The seat of all our soul's, if not of His,
Made dirt of dust, or that flesh which was worn
By God for His apparel, ragg'd and torn ?
If on these things I durst not look, durst I

Wales. It is a sincere meditation on one of the most important days in the Christian calendar, the day on which Christians commemorate the Crucifixion of Jesus. There appears to be no satire or sarcasm in this poem, and for Donne this poem is relatively restrained with regard to poetic conceits. The imagery tends to clarify rather than confuse the poet's points, and his prostration before Christ appears heartfelt and moving.

On His distressed Mother cast mine eye,

Who was God's partner here, and furnish'd thus

Half of that sacrifice which ransom'd us ?

Though these things as I ride be from mine eye,

They're present yet unto my memory,

For that looks towards them; and Thou look'st towards me,

O Saviour, as Thou hang'st upon the tree.

I turn my back to thee but to receive

Corrections till Thy mercies bid Thee leave.

O think me worth Thine anger, punish me,

Burn off my rust, and my deformity;

Restore Thine image, so much, by Thy grace,

That Thou mayst know me, and I'll turn my face.

Holy Sonnets: Death, be not proud*

Death, be not proud, though some have called thee

Mighty and dreadful, for thou art not so;

For those whom thou think'st thou dost overthrow

Die not, poor Death, nor yet canst thou kill me.

From rest and sleep, which but thy pictures be,

Much pleasure; then from thee much more must flow,

And soonest our best men with thee do go,

Rest of their bones, and soul's delivery.

---

* This is essentially the main point of the entire poem. Donne tells Death to not be proud. Some people have called Death powerful, but Donne claims Death is not. Death may believe he has defeated those who die, but Donne states those people do not truly die because their souls live on in the afterlife. According to Donne and the poem, people who die are only dead momentarily, then they live along with all other spirits in Heaven. This is why Donne claims Death cannot kill him.

Thou art slave to fate, chance, kings, and desperate men,

And dost with poison, war, and sickness dwell,

And poppy or charms can make us sleep as well

And better than thy stroke; why swell'st thou then?

One short sleep past, we wake eternally

And death shall be no more; Death, thou shalt die.

Break of Day*

'Tis true, 'tis day, what though it be?

O wilt thou therefore rise from me?

Why should we rise because 'tis light?

Did we lie down because 'twas night?

Love, which in spite of darkness brought us hither,

Should in despite of light keep us together.

Light hath no tongue, but is all eye;

If it could speak as well as spy,

This were the worst that it could say,

That being well I fain would stay,

And that I loved my heart and honour so,

That I would not from him, that had them, go.

---

* Today, a love poem in rhymed couplets from John Donne, who lived in the late 16th and early 17th century. About two hundred years after his birth, Dr. Samuel Johnson dubbed him a "Metaphysical Poet", part of (and in truth, founder of) a loosely associated group of poets who used art, history and religion as extended metaphor (known as a conceit, a word which here has absolutely nothing to do with being stuck-up. The Metaphysical Poets delighted in using what was considered unusual imagery and syntax in their poems. Expediency caused him to convert from Catholicism to the Anglican church; Donne was eventually forced by King James I to become an Anglican clergyman (by royal decree preventing him from occupying any other job, no less).

Must business thee from hence remove?
Oh, that's the worst disease of love,
The poor, the foul, the false, love can
Admit, but not the busied man.
He which hath business, and makes love, doth do
Such wrong, as when a married man doth woo.

(2) 앤드루 마블 Andrew Marvell, 1621-1678

마블은 요크셔 주의 목사 아들로 출생하여 케임브리지 대학을 졸업하고 4년에 걸친 대륙여행 후, 의회파에 속하는 귀족의 딸 가정교사가 되었다. 이 때 서정시 『정원』(*The Garden*) 등 많은 시를 썼다. 1657년 라틴어 비서관으로서 밀턴(Milton)을 도왔으며, 이듬해부터 죽을 때까지 20년간, 고향인 헐에서 국회의원으로 활약하였다. 왕정복고 후, 익명으로 정치적 풍자문서를 발표하여 궁정과 의회의 지도자를 통렬히 비판하였다. 전원의 우아하고 고요한 생활, 그 곳에서의 명상을 묘사한 것이 많고, 강인한 지성과 부드러운 감성의 뛰어난 결합은 그의 시의 매력으로 평가된다. 그의 시는 고전 고대의 전통을 따르면서도 영국적이고, 또 르네상스에서 18세기에 이르는 전환기 시이기도 하다.

Bermudas*

Where the remote Bermudas ride
In th' ocean's bosom unespy'd,
From a small boat, that row'd along,

---

* In "Bermudas," Marvell consciously imitates the poetry of praise that appears in the Book

The list'ning winds receiv'd this song.

What should we do but sing his praise
That led us through the wat'ry maze
Unto an isle so long unknown,
And yet far kinder than our own?
Where he the huge sea-monsters wracks,
That lift the deep upon their backs,
He lands us on a grassy stage,
Safe from the storm's and prelates' rage.

An Horatian Ode upon Cromwell's Return from Ireland*

That thence the royal actor borne
The tragic scaffold might adorn,
While round the armed bands
Did clap their bloody hands.
He nothing common did or mean

---

of Psalms, which is part of the Old Testament. Marvell was writing during the early modern period, and the Book of Psalms was a favorite source of inspiration for poets wanting to praise their patrons or members of the court, especially Kings and Queens. However, Marvell's poem departs from this tradition by placing the song of praise in the mouths of English Puritan settlers, who are leaving their homeland in order to found a new, Eden-like community of believers in the Bermudas. Marvell wrote the poem in couplets of rhyming iambic tetrameter.

* Marvell wrote this poem to commemorate Oliver Cromwell's return to England after a military expedition to Ireland. Cromwell defeated the Irish Catholic and English Royalist Alliance in a series of battles, thereby eliminating a major threat to the newly formed English Republican government. Marvell models his poem on the odes of the Roman poet, Horace, who fought on the side of Roman Republicans but eventually accepted Augustus Caesar's rule and the ensuing peace. The poem is ambivalent about the rule and execution of King Charles I, even though Marvell clearly praises Oliver Cromwell's leadership.

Upon that memorable scene,

> But with his keener eye
> The axe's edge did try;

Nor call'd the gods with vulgar spite
To vindicate his helpless right,

> But bowed his comely head
> Down as upon a bed.

The Definition of Love*

My love is of a birth as rare
As 'tis for object strange and high;
It was begotten by Despair
Upon Impossibility.

Magnanimous Despair alone
Could show me so divine a thing
Where feeble Hope could ne'er have flown,
But vainly flapp'd its tinsel wing.

And yet I quickly might arrive
Where my extended soul is fixt,

---

* Scholars often connect Marvell's "The Definition of Love" to John Donne's metaphysical lyrics, due to the elaborate imagery and the neo-platonic implications of love between souls or minds that is distinct from the physical body. The poem constitutes an exploration of love by depicting two perfect yet irreconcilable loves—the love of the speaker, and the love of his lover. These two loves are perfect in themselves and they face each other in an opposition of perfection, but, according to the speaker's formulation, that same condition prevents them from meeting in the physical sphere. The poem is composed of eight stanzas, each of which features four lines of iambic tetrameter that rhyme alternately, in a pattern of ABAB, CDCD, and so forth.

But Fate does iron wedges drive,
And always crowds itself betwixt.

For Fate with jealous eye does see
Two perfect loves, nor lets them close;
Their union would her ruin be,
And her tyrannic pow'r depose.

And therefore her decrees of steel
Us as the distant poles have plac'd,
(Though love's whole world on us doth wheel)
Not by themselves to be embrac'd;

Unless the giddy heaven fall,
And earth some new convulsion tear;
And, us to join, the world should all
Be cramp'd into a planisphere.

As lines, so loves oblique may well
Themselves in every angle greet;
But ours so truly parallel,
Though infinite, can never meet.

Therefore the love which us doth bind,
But Fate so enviously debars,
Is the conjunction of the mind,
And opposition of the stars.

(3) 조지 허버트 George Herbert, 1593-1633

조지 허버트는 영국의 목사이자 형이상파의 시인인 허버트는 귀족의 혈통을 받아 학자의 길을 걸었으나, 도중에 성직자의 꿈을 갖고 37세의 나이에 가난한 마을의 목사가 되었다. 그 후 죽을 때까지 3년 동안 종교 시집 『성당』(*The Temple*)을 펴냈다. 약 160편의 단시로 이루어진 작품은 그의 친구이며 시인인 존 던의 영향을 받은 것으로 보이며, 영혼의 갈등과 신의 사랑을 던의 시처럼 정묘하게 분석, 묘사하였다. 구어적 표현, 비근한 이미지, 유연한 시형이 특색이다.

The British Church*

I joy, dear mother, when I view
Thy perfect lineaments, and hue
    Both sweet and bright.
Beauty in thee takes up her place,
And dates her letters from thy face,
    When she doth write.

  A fine aspect in fit array,
Neither too mean nor yet too gay,
    Shows who is best.
Outlandish looks may not compare,

---

* (5) Possibly refers to the ecclesiastical practice of dating by the Church Year.
(13-18) Refers to the Roman Catholic Church, to which the allegory in Revelation, xvii.3-6, was frequently applied by Protestants.
(20-25) Refers to the Nonconformist Churches.
(29) double-moat: protect against a twofold danger.

For all they either painted are,
    Or else undress'd.

    She on the hills which wantonly
Allureth all, in hope to be
        By her preferr'd,
Hath kiss'd so long her painted shrines,
That ev'n her face by kissing shines,
        For her reward.

    She in the valley is so shy
Of dressing, that her hair doth lie
        About her ears;
While she avoids her neighbour's pride,
She wholly goes on th' other side,
        And nothing wears.

    But, dearest mother, what those miss,
The mean, thy praise and glory is
        And long may be.
Blessed be God, whose love it was
To double-moat thee with his grace,
        And none but thee.

The Pilgrimage*

I travell'd on, seeing the hill, where lay
My expectation.

---

* George Herbert did not have a comfortable relationship with God. The images in his poetry

A long it was and weary way.
The gloomy cave of Desperation
 I left on th' one, and on the other side
The rock of Pride.

 And so I came to fancy's meadow strow'd
With many a flower:
Fain would I here have made abode,
But I was quicken'd by my hour.
 So to care's copse I came, and there got through
With much ado.

 That led me to the wild of Passion, which
Some call the wold;
A wasted place, but sometimes rich.
Here I was robb'd of all my gold,
 Save one good Angell, which a friend had ti'd
Close to my side.

 At length I got unto the gladsome hill,
Where lay my hope,
Where lay my heart; and climbing still,
When I had gain'd the brow and top,
 A lake of brackish waters on the ground
Was all I found.

---

often remind us of the First World War poets in their bleak view of life. But whereas in the
verse of Owen and Sassoon the landscape has been blasted by enemy artillery, in Herbert's
the fire is friendly: the perpetual Passchendaele through which he trudges has been made by
God.

Jordan (I)*

Who says that fictions only and false hair
Become a verse? Is there in truth no beauty?
Is all good structure in a winding stair?
May no lines pass, except they do their duty
       Not to a true, but painted chair?

Is it no verse, except enchanted groves
And sudden arbours shadow coarse-spun lines?
Must purling streams refresh a lover's loves?
Must all be veil'd, while he that reads, divines,
       Catching the sense at two removes?

Shepherds are honest people; let them sing;
Riddle who list, for me, and pull for prime;
I envy no man's nightingale or spring;
Nor let them punish me with loss of rhyme,
       Who plainly say, my God, my King.

Jordan (II)**

WHen first my lines of heav'nly joyes made mention,
Such was their lustre, they did so excell,

---

* Herbert's "Jordan (I)" is very difficult to understand because understanding the poem depends completely upon understanding the allusions that pepper the poem, the allusions that are scattered throughout. Remembering that Herbert was a devout Christian Anglican and minister, after resigning his parliamentary career, it is easier to understand the first and central allusion in the title: Jordan. There are two "Jordan" poems and both discuss writing poetry.

** In "Jordan (II)," Herbert explains the difficult task he faces in writing poetry that speaks to

That I sought out quaint words and trim invention;
My thoughts began to burnish, sprout, and swell,
Curling with metaphors a plain intention,
Decking the sense, as if it were to sell.

Thousands of notions in my brain did runne,
Off'ring their service, if I were not sped:
I often blotted what I had begunne;
This was not quick enough, and that was dead.
Nothing could seem too rich to clothe the sunne,
Much lesse those joyes which trample on his head.

As flames do work and winde, when they ascend,
So did I weave my self into the sense.
But while I bustled, I might heare a friend
Whisper, How wide is all this long pretence!
There is in love a sweetnesse readie penn'd;
Copie out onely that, and save expense.

Redemption*

Having been tenant long to a rich lord,
   Not thriving, I resolvèd to be bold,
   And make a suit unto him, to afford
A new small-rented lease, and cancel th' old.

---

the profound significance of his religious devotion. As a poet, he is inclined to use
dramatic, expressive, and flowery language. But his religious outlook implores modesty and
therefore, rich, overzealous language is just not in that spirit of modesty and piety.
* George Herbert's poem, Redemption, is a sonnet dealing with the mankind's search for
God. It is a parable and a sermon on the Biblical lines, using the landlord/tenant analogy,

In heaven at his manor I him sought;
   They told me there that he was lately gone
   About some land, which he had dearly bought
Long since on earth, to take possessiòn.

I straight returned, and knowing his great birth,
   Sought him accordingly in great resorts;
   In cities, theaters, gardens, parks, and courts;
At length I heard a ragged noise and mirth

   Of thieves and murderers; there I him espied,
   Who straight, Your suit is granted, said, and died.

Virtue*

Sweet day, so cool, so calm, so bright,
The bridal of the earth and sky;
The dew shall weep thy fall to-night,
   For thou must die.

Sweet rose, whose hue angry and brave
Bids the rash gazer wipe his eye;

---

the landlord being God and the tenant being every man. The poem relates to man's fallen state and the myth of crucifixion. As in a number of parables in the Bible in which God is presented as the landowner and humankind as the tenat, here also the speaker, a 'tenant long to a rich lord' resolved to meet the landowner for a more affordable deal: 'A new small-rented lease' in cancellation of the old contract. The first quatrain thus deals with the mankind's problematic since the Fall.

* George Herbert's poem entitled, "Virtue," uses images of things that are "sweet" and full of life, and couples them with the dark side of life: inevitable death.

Thy root is ever in its grave,
　　　And thou must die.

Sweet spring, full of sweet days and roses,
A box where sweets compacted lie;
My music shows ye have your closes,
　　　And all must die.

Only a sweet and virtuous soul,
Like season'd timber, never gives;
But though the whole world turn to coal,
　　　Then chiefly lives.

The Pulley*

　When God at first made man,
Having a glass of blessings standing by,
"Let us," said he, "pour on him all we can.
Let the world's riches, which dispersèd lie,
　　　Contract into a span."

---

* "The Pulley" is both a myth of origins and a moral and spiritual fable; these two genres overlap because, for Herbert, one's devotional responsibilities are perfectly consistent with and flow inevitably from who one is. Despite the brevity and simplicity of the poem, several key facts are affirmed. For example, this version of the Creation myth emphasizes the dignity of humankind, bestowed by a God who is thoughtful, generous, and kind. The story of Creation in the Book of Genesis is astonishing: A spiritual breath raises dusty clay to life in the form of Adam. In Herbert's poem, the Creation seems even more splendid, as humankind is described as the sum and epitome of all the world's riches, and God is a being who communicates easily and cordially with His creation.

So strength first made a way;
Then beauty flowed, then wisdom, honour, pleasure.
When almost all was out, God made a stay,
Perceiving that, alone of all his treasure,
    Rest in the bottom lay.

"For if I should," said he,
"Bestow this jewel also on my creature,
He would adore my gifts instead of me,
And rest in Nature, not the God of Nature;
    So both should losers be.

"Yet let him keep the rest,
But keep them with repining restlessness;
Let him be rich and weary, that at least,
If goodness lead him not, yet weariness
    May toss him to my breast."

(4) 헨리 본 Henry Vaughan, 1622-1695

헨리 본은 웨일스 브레컨셔 란산트프레드 출신으로 '형이상학파 시인'의 한 사람이다. 옛날 실루리아 인이 살았다고 하는 웨일스의 고향 마을을 사랑하여 스스로 실루리스트(Silurist)라고 불렀다. 또 옥스퍼드 대학 출신의 의사로서 내란 때에는 왕당파의 군의관으로도 출정하였다. 문필 활동은 라틴어 시문의 번역으로부터 시작하여 시집 『어스크 강의 백조』(*Olor Iscanus*) 등의 세속적인 시를 쓴 뒤, 병상에서의 종교적 체험을 전환점으로 하여 신비주의적 색채를 띠게 되었다. "어느 날 밤 나는 영원을 보았도다"로 시작되는 「세상」("The World")와 워즈워스에 영향을 주었다는 「퇴행」("The

Retreat") 등의 시를 포함하는 종교시집 『불꽃 튀는 부싯돌』(*Silex Scintillans*)
은 대표적 작품이다. 그의 시는 당대에는 인정을 받지 못하였으나, 100년
이 지난 뒤부터 재평가 받았다.

Regeneration*

A WARD, and still in bonds, one day
    I stole abroad . . .
My walke a monstrous, mountain'd thing . . .
    And as a Pilgrims Eye
      Far from reliefe,
Measures the melancholy skye
    Then drops, and rains for griefe.

The Retreat**

Happy those early days! when I
Shined in my angel infancy . . .
When yet I had not walked above

---

* The poem takes us on a journey. Various natural features act as symbols or emblems, including the seasons and the scenery. For the first time, some words are given to the poet. In a Herbert-like move, God speaks right at the end to resolve the puzzle. The words 'Where I please' echo the Bible passage from the Gospel of John. The poet's response forms the concluding couplet. It is a prayer for God to breath on him, which could refer to Christ breathing on his disciples so that they might receive the Holy Spirit (John 20:22), or to the Song of Solomon, the great love poem of the Bible (Song of Songs 4:16). The poet asks that he may die to his old sinful self, while there is still time, before he has to face physical death. This is the moment of regeneration.

** Vaughan expresses his nostalgic thought to go back to heaven from where he has come to

A mile or two from my first love,
And looking back, at that short space,
Could see a glimpse of His bright face . . .
Some men a forward motion love;
But I by backward steps would move,
And when this dust falls to the urn,
In that state I came, return.

(5) 에드먼드 월러 Edmund Waller, 1606-1687

월러는 이튼 학교와 케임브리지 대학교에서 공부한 뒤 일찍이 젊은
나이에 정계에 진출하여 하원의원이 되었다. 원래 부유한 가정에서 태어난
그는 부유한 런던 상인의 상속녀와 결혼했지만 그녀는 3년 만에 죽었다.
그 뒤 도로시 시드니 부인에게 구혼했으나 실패하고 1644년 메리 브레이
시와 결혼했다. 월러는 매끄럽고 규칙적인 시형을 채택함으로써, 17세기
말에 영웅시체 2행 연구가 시적 표현의 지배적인 양식으로 사용될 수 있는
토대를 마련했다. 그는 생전에 탁월함을 충분히 인정받아, 존 드라이든은
'월러가 우리 시의 운율을 바꾸어놓았다'라고 하면서 알렉산더 포프와 함
께 그를 본떠 영웅시체 2행 연구를 가장 농축된 형태로 발전시켰다. 영문
학사에서 매우 유명한 서정시이자 그의 초기 시인 『가자, 사랑스런 장미
여!』(*Go, lovely Rose!*) 등을 비롯한 시 몇 편은 1645년 그의 시집이 나오기 20
여 년 전부터 널리 알려졌다. 그러나 공인된 초판은 1664년에 나왔다. 1655

---

the earth. He desires a backward movement of life so that he gets back his childhood
innocence and insight of his infancy. But his soul halts and staggers on the way of his
retreat as it is intoxicated with the worldly pursuits, and the pleasures of the world. He
realizes that it is not possible to go back to the pure innocence and insight of infancy.
Death can alone enable him to go back to his childhood days of innocence and perfection.

년『호국경(크롬웰)에게 바치는 찬사』(*Panegyrick to my Lord Protector*)를 발표했으나, 1660년에는 유명한 시 「폐하에게 행복이 돌아오기를」("To the King, upon his Majesties happy return")을 선보였다. 말년에도 「신시」("Divine Poems")를 비롯한 시를 썼으며, 1690년에 『월러 시집 제2부』(*The Second Part of Mr. Waller's Poems*)가 출간되었다.

Go, lovely Rose*

Go, lovely Rose —
　　　Tell her that wastes her time and me,
　　　That now she knows,
When I resemble her to thee,
How sweet and fair she seems to be.

　　　Tell her that's young,
And shuns to have her graces spied,
　　　That hadst thou sprung
In deserts where no men abide,
Thou must have uncommended died.

　　　Small is the worth
Of beauty from the light retired:
　　　Bid her come forth,

---

* "Go, Lovely Rose" has preserved Waller's reputation as a poet, in part, because of its simplicity of language. The poem marks a movement away from the seriousness of metaphysical poetry to a form reflecting less weighty subjects. The rose, personified as a creature able to deliver speeches and die on command, must urge the woman — beautiful but fragile, tangible but tenuous — to "Suffer herself to be desired/ And not blush so to be admired." Waller employs ambiguity in the word "suffer."

Suffer herself to be desired,
And not blush so to be admired.

Then die—that she
The common fate of all things rare
May read in thee;
How small a part of time they share
That are so wondrous sweet and fair!

(6) 리처드 크래쇼 Richard Crashaw, 1612-1649

크래쇼는 열성적이고 박식한 목사의 아들로 태어나 케임브리지에서
공부하면서 라틴어 · 그리스어 · 히브리어 · 에스파냐어 · 이탈리아어를 배
웠다. 졸업하던 1634년에 성서의 주제를 다룬 라틴어 시집 『성구집』
(*Epigrammatum Sacrorum Liber*)을 출판했다. 그는 초기에는 세속시를 썼고,
후기에는 활기차고 장식적인 문체와 번뜩이는 재치가 담긴 종교시를 쓴
것으로 유명하다. 대체로 전기의 세속시는 그가 이상으로 생각하는 아름다
운 여인의 미덕을 다루었고, 후기의 종교시는 관능적인 사랑이 아닌 신앙
과 성모 마리아에 관한 주제를 다루었다. 특히 그는 과장된 비유와 기발한
심상을 적용하여 세속과 신앙, 눈물과 황홀, 감각적인 것과 정신적인 것 등
을 역설적인 기법으로 표현하였다. 초기 세속시로 대표적인 것은 "Wishes,
to his(supposed) Mistress"로, 126행으로 이루어진 3행절 시로서 독특한 리
듬을 갖고 있다.

제1차 청교도혁명(1642-1651) 중에 크래쇼는 로마 가톨릭 쪽으로 기
울어져 피터 하우스에서 목사직을 유지할 수 없게 되자, 청교도들이 자신
을 쫓아내기 전에 스스로 물러났다. 그는 1646년에 라틴어와 영어로 된 종

교시와 세속시가 들어 있는 시집 『성당으로의 발걸음: 성시, 기타 뮤즈의 기쁨』(*Steps to the Temple: Sacred Poems, with other Delights of the Muses*)을 냈다. 그는 1644년 프랑스로 가서 로마 가톨릭교도가 되었다. 죽기 몇 개월 전에는 로레토에 있는 산타카사 성당의 참사회원 자리를 얻기도 했다. 1652년 파리에서 종교시집 『우리 주께 찬양』(*Carmen Deo Nostro*)을 재출판했는데, 여기에는 그가 그린 12장의 삽화가 들어 있다. 새로 첨가된 시 가운데 아빌라의 성녀 테레사에게 바친 「불타는 가슴으로」("From the Flaming Heart")에 덧붙여진 시행은 그의 최고 걸작으로 꼽힌다.

On the Wounds of Our Crucified Lord*

O these wakeful wounds of thine!
Are they mouths? or are they eyes?
Be they mouths, or be they eyne,
Each bleeding part some one supplies.

Lo! a mouth, whose full-bloomed lips
At too dear a rate are roses.
Lo! a bloodshot eye! that weeps
And many a cruel tear discloses.

---

* The poem reveals two miracles simultaneously: that of eternal life and that of the transformation of the profane into the sacred. For ordinary people to understand what God offers through the sacrifice of His son, they must work with what they know, which are things of this world. The poem shows how even the most minute of earthly details reveal God's plan. It focuses more narrowly as it progresses, from the statue or painting to the wounds to the fluids emanating from the wounds. Such a complete immersion into earthly details emphasizes Crashaw's view of the glory of creation and redemption. Similarly, the humor and bathos of the poem are balanced by the miracle of salvation.

O thou that on this foot hast laid
Many a kiss and many a tear,
Now thou shalt have all repaid,
Whatsoe'er thy charges were.

This foot hath got a mouth and lips
To pay the sweet sum of thy kisses;
To pay thy tears, an eye that weeps
Instead of tears such gems as this is.

The difference only this appears
(Nor can the change offend),
The debt is paid in ruby-tears
Which thou in pearls didst lend.

(7) 벤 존슨 Ben Jonson, 1573-1637

벤 존슨은 런던 출신으로 웨스트민스터 학교를 졸업한 후, 벽돌 쌓는 일과 군대 생활 등을 거친 후 연극계에 들어섰다. 동료 배우를 결투로 죽이고 투옥되어, 한 때 가톨릭으로 개종한 일도 있었다. 최초의 기질희극『십인 십색』(*Every Man in His Humour*)은 낭만적인 셰익스피어 희극에 대한 반항으로서 고전적·풍자적·사실적인 작품을 지녀, 당시 사회적 위선에 시달린 민중의 환영을 받았고, '기질희극'의 유행을 유도하였다. 뒤이은 작품『모두 기분 언짢아』(*Every Man Out of His Humour*)는 당시의 극작가들을 통렬히 풍자하였다 하여 2년간에 걸친 '무대싸움'으로 번져 투옥당하기도 하였다.

존슨의 작품은 모든 면에서 셰익스피어(Shakespeare)의 작품과 강력한 대조를 이루고 있다. 그는 당시의 낭만적 조류를 배격하고 고전적 기준을 되찾으려 하였다. 셰익스피어는 『햄릿』(*Hamlet*) 속에서 보여준 바와 같이 아리스토텔레스의 '3일치의 법칙'이나 그 밖의 규칙들과 같은 고전적 극작 이론에 정통해 있었으나, 자신의 극작에서는 그러한 규칙에 얽매이지 않고 어디까지나 자유로운 상상을 원칙으로 삼았다. 그러나 존슨에게는 고전적 규칙들이란 필요에 따라 쓸 수도 있는 개념이 아니라, 모든 작가가 반드시 지켜야 할 절대명령과도 같은 것이었다.

On my First Son*

Farewell, thou child of my right hand, and joy;
My sin was too much hope of thee, lov'd boy.
Seven years tho' wert lent to me, and I thee pay,
Exacted by thy fate, on the just day.
O, could I lose all father now! For why
Will man lament the state he should envy?
To have so soon 'scap'd world's and flesh's rage,
And if no other misery, yet age?
Rest in soft peace, and, ask'd, say, "Here doth lie
Ben Jonson his best piece of poetry."
For whose sake henceforth all his vows be such,
As what he loves may never like too much.

---

* Written around 1603, Ben Jonson's deceptively plain elegy, "On My First Son," consists of one twelve-line stanza of iambic pentameter rhyming couplets. Taking the form of a "classical" consolatio expressing the Christian-Platonic-Stoic reasons to celebrate the child's release from the pains of human life, the poem poignantly stages the tension between the "poet's" wish for this intellectual consolation and his emotional expressions of paternal grief. By seeking reasons for the death of his "loved boy," the father reveals his own religious doubts, which test and contradict both the Christian teachings of acceptance and the literary decorum of the elegiac form.

Inviting a Friend to Supper*

Nor shall our cups make any guilty men;
But, at our parting we will be as when
We innocently met. No simple word
That shall be uttered at our mirthful board,
Shall make us sad next morning or affright
The liberty that we'll enjoy tonight.

To Celia**

Drink to me only with thine eyes,
    And I will pledge with mine;
  Or leave a kiss but in the cup
    And I'll not ask for wine.
The thirst that from the soul doth rise
    Doth ask a drink divine;
But might I of Jove's[2] nectar[3] sup,
    I would not change for thine.
I sent thee late a rosy wreath,

---

* Ben Jonson's Inviting a Friend to Supper, serves as a reassuring end-of-holiday reminder that it's not impossible "to eat, drink and be merry" and still get up for work the next day. Ben Jonson's poem, number 101 (CI) of his Epigrams balances the luxury and liberty of happy home-dining with the classical ideal of restraint. The whole collection is dedicated to the author's most steadfast patron, William Herbert, the Earl of Pembroke, and he is the guest to whom Jonson is making his graceful and witty invitation. Others will be present, but the guest who will bring grace to the otherwise worthless supper is William Herbert.

** "To Celia" by Ben Jonson has been related with the love felt this modern period although it is from the Renaissance many years ago. The poem To Celia also has symbolisms in it. These symbolisms contribute to the poem being powerful to its readers. These symbolisms are greatly influenced by the renaissance culture—cup, Jove's nectar, and wreath.

Not so much honouring thee

As giving it a hope that there

It could not withered be;

But thou thereon didst only breathe,

And sent'st it back to me,

Since when it grows and smells, I swear,

Not of itself but thee!

(8) 로버트 헤릭 Robert Herrick, 1591-1674

헤릭은 런던 출신으로 1620년 케임브리지 대학교 졸업한 뒤, 1623년 성공회 목사가 되었고, 1629년 데본셔의 딘프라이어의 목사로 부임하였다. 내란 때인 1647년 청교도에 의해 성직에서 쫓겨나 런던에 돌아왔다가, 1662년 다시 그곳 목사로 부임하여 생애를 마쳤다. 왕당파 서정시인인 그의 시작품은 『헤스페리데스』(*Hesperides, or the Works both Human and Divine of Robert Herrick Esq.*)에 수록되어 있다. 존슨의 시풍을 계승하여 격조를 갖춘 목가적 서정시를 발표, 신변의 가련한 것들의 아름다움을 정묘하게 읊었다.

To the Virgins, to make much of Time*

GATHER ye rosebuds while ye may,

Old Time is still a-flying:

And this same flower that smiles to-day

To-morrow will be dying.

---

* From the title, we can tell that the speaker is addressing this poem to a group of virgins.

The glorious lamp of heaven, the sun,

    The higher he's a-getting,

The sooner will his race be run,

    And nearer he's to setting.

That age is best which is the first,

    When youth and blood are warmer;

But being spent, the worse, and worst

    Times still succeed the former.

Then be not coy, but use your time,

    And while ye may, go marry:

For having lost but once your prime,

    You may for ever tarry.

Delight in Disorder*

A sweet disorder in the dress

Kindles in clothes a wantonness;

A lawn about the shoulders thrown

He's telling them that they should gather their "rosebuds" while they can, because time is quickly passing. He drives home this point with some images from nature, including flowers dying and the sun setting. He thinks that one's youth is the best time in life, and the years after that aren't so great. The speaker finishes off the poem by encouraging these young virgins to make good use of their time by getting married, before they're past their prime and lose the chance.

* Much poetry of the late sixteenth and early seventeenth centuries incorporates the idea of a "slight disorder in the dress" as well as in the hair of its female subjects. Ben Jonson notes that there is something suspicious about a woman who is always neatly dressed: What is she hiding? He calls for the "sweet neglect" of "robes loosely flowing, hair as free" in the woman who would capture his heart. Similarly, Richard Lovelace bids Amarantha to "dishevel Her Hair," letting it fly "as unconfined/ As its calm ravisher, the wind," that she might "shake [her] head and scatter day." Probably the best known of all poems with this bent is Robert Herrick's "Delight in Disorder."

Into a fine distraction;

An erring lace, which here and there

Enthrals the crimson stomacher;

A cuff neglectful, and thereby

Ribands to flow confusedly;

A winning wave, deserving note,

In the tempestuous petticoat;

A careless shoe-string, in whose tie

I see a wild civility:

Do more bewitch me, than when art

Is too precise in every part.

Corinna's going a Maying*

Get up, get up for shame, the Blooming Morne

Upon her wings presents the god unshorne.

        See how Aurora throwes her faire

        Fresh-quilted colours through the aire:

        Get up, sweet-Slug-a-bed, and see

        The Dew-bespangling Herbe and Tree.

Each Flower has wept, and bow'd toward the East,

Above an houre since; yet you not drest,

        Nay! not so much as out of bed?

        When all the Birds have Mattens seyd,

---

* The title of this poem is particularly interesting in that it asserts unequivocally that Corinna will take part in the activities of May morning, although there is no certainty in the text that she will do so. The poem is a dramatic monologue, with the lover-speaker seeking to persuade his sweetheart to get out of bed and join the other youths "to fetch in May." Her reactions to his entreaties are unrecorded. She remains no more than a name, as the interest of the poem resides in the speaker's rhetorical strategies to work his will upon her.

And sung their thankful Hymnes: 'tis sin,
Nay, profanation to keep in,
When as a thousand Virgins on this day,
Spring, sooner than the Lark, to fetch in May.

Rise; and put on your Foliage, and be seene
To come forth, like the Spring-time, fresh and greene;
And sweet as Flora. Take no care
For Jewels for your Gowne, or Haire:
Feare not; the leaves will strew
Gemms in abundance upon you:
Besides, the childhood of the Day has kept,
Against you come, some Orient Pearls unwept:
Come, and receive them while the light
Hangs on the Dew-locks of the night:
And Titan on the Eastern hill
Retires himselfe, or else stands still
Till you come forth. Wash, dresse, be briefe in praying:
Few Beads are best, when once we goe a Maying.

Come, my Corinna, come; and comming, marke
How each field turns a street; each street a Parke
Made green, and trimm'd with trees: see how
Devotion gives each House a Bough,
Or Branch: Each Porch, each doore, ere this,
An Arke a Tabernacle is
Made up of white-thorn neatly enterwove;
As if here were those cooler shades of love.
Can such delights be in the street,
And open fields, and we not see't?

Come, we'll abroad; and let's obay
The Proclamation made for May:
And sin no more, as we have done, by staying;
But my Corinna, come, let's goe a Maying.

There's not a budding Boy, or Girle, this day,
But is got up, and gone to bring in May.
A deale of Youth, ere this, is come
Back, and with White-thorn laden home.
Some have dispatcht their Cakes and Creame,
Before that we have left to dreame:
And some have wept, and woo'd, and plighted Troth,
And chose their Priest, ere we can cast off sloth:
Many a green-gown has been given;
Many a kisse, both odde and even:
Many a glance too has been sent
From out the eye, Loves Firmament:
Many a jest told of the Keyes betraying
This night, and Locks pickt, yet w'are not a Maying.

Come, let us goe, while we are in our prime;
And take the harmlesse follie of the time.
We shall grow old apace, and die
Before we know our liberty.
Our life is short; and our dayes run
As fast away as do's the Sunne:
And as a vapour, or a drop of raine
Once lost, can ne'r be found againe:
So when or you or I are made
A fable, song, or fleeting shade;

> All love, all liking, all delight
>> Lies drown'd with us in endlesse night.
> Then while time serves, and we are but decaying;
> Come, my Corinna, come, let's goe a Maying.

(9) 존 밀턴 John Milton, 1608-1674

밀턴은 런던 출신으로 대서사시 『실낙원』(*Paradise Lost*)의 저자로서 셰익스피어에 버금가는 대시인으로 평가된다. 신흥 중산계급인 공증인 · 금융업자의 집안에서 태어났다. 그의 조부는 로마 가톨릭교도로 자영 농민이었는데, 아버지가 신교로 개종하였기 때문에 두 사람 사이는 절연되었다고 한다. 그래서 밀턴은 작곡에 재능이 있던 아버지로부터 청교도적인 강렬한 기질과 음악 애호의 소질을 이어받고 문예부흥적인 교양을 몸에 익혔다. 7세에 성 바울 학원에 입학하여 라틴어 · 그리스어 · 헤브라이어를 배웠고, 청교도 신학자 T. 영으로부터 신학 지도를 받았다.

이러한 환경에서 인문주의와 청교도주의가 밀턴의 생애와 사상의 틀이 되었던 것이다. 1625년 케임브리지 대학 크라이스트 칼리지에 입학하였는데, 그의 단정하고 수려한 용모와 청순한 생활태도 때문에 '크라이스트 대학의 숙녀'라는 별명을 얻었다. 이미 이때의 밀턴의 라틴어 시는 다른 어떤 영국인에게도 추종을 불허하는 높은 수준에 도달하여 있었다. 1626년에 쓴 짧은 반가톨릭적인 서사시 『11월 5일』에서 생생하게 악마와 지옥을 묘사하였다. 최초로 영어로 쓴 시 「그리스도 강탄의 아침에」("Hymn On The Morning Of Christ's Nativity")는 종교적 주제에 있어서나 기교적 원숙에 있어서 성년에 도달하였고, 또 그의 장래의 방향을 선언한 작품이었다. 1631년에 발표한 「쾌활한 사람」("L'Allegro")과 「침사의 사람」("Il

Penseroso")은 엄격한 청교도적 정신과는 아주 대조적인 문예부흥적인 향기가 높이 풍기는 우미한 심정을 토로한 작품이다. 이때부터 아버지가 희망하였던 성직자가 되는 길을 버리고, 시작에 전념하였다.

대학을 졸업하고, 1632-1638년의 약 6년간 런던 서쪽 교외의 호튼에서 전원생활을 하면서, 그의 위대한 테마인 선악 갈등의 최초의 연극적 표현이며, 후기의 3대작의 시풍을 암시한 가면극 『코머스』(Comus)와, 신의 섭리를 소원하면서 새로운 희망으로 사는 결의를 피력한 목가적 작품이며 불의의 해난사고로 죽은 친구를 추도한 시 『리시다스』(Lycidas)를 발표하였다. 1638년 대륙으로 건너가, 파리에서는 그로티우스와, 이탈리아 피렌체에서는 갈릴레이와 알게 되었으나, 고국의 정치적 동란이 위급함을 듣자 그리스 여행계획을 취소하고 1639년 귀국하였다.

그의 저작의 5분의 4를 차지하는 산문 작품(1641-1660)은 3종류로 대별된다. 제1은 새로운 예루살렘의 도래를 믿고, 감독제도하에 있던 영국 국교회를 비판하여 성서중심주의를 전개한 여러 논문이다. 그리고 제2는 M. 파우엘과의 불행한 결혼을 경험하고, 자연과 이성을 근거로 하여 성서의 권위에 도전한 4편의 『이혼론』(Doctrine and Discipline of Divorce)이다. 마지막으로 제3은 교육론과 검열 없는 출판의 자유를 주장한 『아레오파지티카』(Areopagitica) 외에 찰스 1세의 처형을 지지하고 크롬웰의 라틴어 비서관이 되어 공화제를 옹호한 일련의 논쟁문서, 즉 『왕과 위정자의 재임』(The Tenure of Kings and Magistrates)과 『우상파괴자』(Eikonoklastes), 『영국 국민을 위해 변호하는 서』(Defensio pro Populo Anglicano) 등이다.

인간의 원죄와 그 죄로 인한 낙원상실의 비극적 사건을 다룬 대서사시 『실낙원』은 1667년에 출간되었는데, 그 모럴은 바로 밀턴 자신이 말한 것처럼 "영원의 섭리를 설파하고, 인간에 대한 신의 길의 정당함을 역설하는" 것이며, 그 목적은, 작중에서 활약하는 악마 사탄의 강렬한 성격 때문에 때로 반대의 인상을 주기도 하나, 대체로 달성되었다고 할 수 있다. 이어서 내놓은 『복낙원』(Paradise Regained)과 『투사 삼손』(Samson Agonistes)은 1671년에 1권으로 출판되었다. 『복낙원』은 광야에서 그리스도가 사탄의 유혹을 물리침으로써 그가 최후의 시련에도 이겨낼 수 있음을 보여 준 대서 사시로, 더욱 그리스도의 인간적인 역할로서 인간이 견고한 성실과 신의 의지에 대한 겸손한 순종을 가지고 행하면 어떤 일을 할 수 있는가를 가르친 것이고, 『투사 삼손』은 구약성서에 나오는 영웅 삼손이 자신의 비참함과 치욕에만 마음을 빼앗기고 있던 상태에서, 마음을 돌이켜 사심 없는 겸손과 억제를 배워 정신적으로 힘을 회복한 결과, 자신을 재차 신에게서 선택받은 전사(戰士)라고 느끼게 된 과정이 묘사되어 있다.

이 외에 이단의 신학을 포함한 『그리스도교 교의론』(De Doctrina Christiana), 미완성의 『영국사』(History of Britain), 『간이 라틴어 문법』, 『논리학』, 『사신집』(Epistolae Familiares)과 『연설집』(Prolusiones Oratoriae) 『모스크바 소사』(A Brief History of Moscovia) 등이 있다.

Paradise Lost: The First Book*

Of man's first disobedience, and the fruit
Of that forbidden tree whose mortal taste
Brought death into the World, and all our woe,

---

* The poem opens with an invocation; that's when the speaker asks the muses —ancient deities thought to inspire poetry and art—to inspire him, give him the ability to perform, etc. We see speakers talk to their muses in the beginning of a lot of epic poems; check out the first lines of the Iliad. He asks the muses to sing about "man's first disobedience" (1), the Forbidden Fruit, his exile from Eden, his eventual redemption through Jesus Christ, etc. Soon, the scene shifts to a burning inferno; we're in Hell with Satan, only Hell isn't below the earth but somewhere way out in the middle of nowhere, a place Milton calls Chaos.

With loss of Eden, till one greater Man

Restore us, and regain the blissful Seat,

Sing, Heavenly Muse . . .

Paradise Lost: The third Book*

HAIL, holy Light, offspring of Heaven first-born!

Or of the Eternal coeternal beam

May I express thee unblamed? since God is light,

And never but in unapproached light

Dwelt from eternity-dwelt then in thee,

Bright effluence of bright essence increate!

Or hear'st thou rather pure Ethereal Stream,

Whose fountain who shall tell? Before the Sun,

Before the Heavens, thou wert, and at the voice

Of God, as with a mantle, didst invest

The rising World of waters dark and deep,

Won from the void and formless Infinite!

Thee I revisit now with bolder wing,

Escaped the Stygian Pool, though long detained

In that obscure sojourn, while in my flight,

Through utter and through middle Darkness borne,

With other notes than to the Orphean lyre

I sung of Chaos and eternal Night,

---

* Milton addresses the light emanating from Heaven, saying it is God's first "offspring." This is the second invocation of the poem. The poet is now revisiting Heaven, after having spent the first two books in Hell. He still feels the heavenly light, but he can't see it because he's blind. This doesn't prevent him from writing poetry, however. He's too tough for that. The poet hasn't forgotten about other famous blind poets and prophets, such as Homer and Tiresias; he's "equal" to them in blindness and hopes to be "equal" to them in fame.

Taught by the Heavenly Muse to venture down

The dark descent, and up to re-ascend,

Though hard and rare. Thee I revisit safe,

And feel thy sovran vital lamp; but thou

Revisit'st not these eyes, that rowl in vain

To find thy piercing ray, and find no dawn;

Sonnet 19: When I consider how my light is spent*

When I consider how my light is spent,

    Ere half my days, in this dark world and wide,

    And that one Talent which is death to hide

    Lodged with me useless, though my Soul more bent

To serve therewith my Maker, and present

    My true account, lest he returning chide;

    "Doth God exact day-labour, light denied?"

    I fondly ask. But patience, to prevent

That murmur, soon replies, "God doth not need

    Either man's work or his own gifts; who best

    Bear his mild yoke, they serve him best. His state

Is Kingly. Thousands at his bidding speed

    And post o'er Land and Ocean without rest:

    They also serve who only stand and wait."

---

* John Milton's Sonnet XIX, sometimes known as "When I Consider How My Light Is Spent," opens with the narrator reflecting on the fact that he has become blind before half his life has been lived. He is profoundly distressed at the prospect of no longer being able to use his greatest talent, writing, and fears that God might be displeased and punish him for not using it—just as, in a biblical parable, God punished the servant who had not used the money entrusted to him but had hidden it instead. He asks himself whether God could possibly expect the same service from him, being impaired, that God expects from those without an overwhelming handicap.

18세기와 왕정복고 시대 영국시 (1660-1798)

1660 :	Charles II restored to the English throne.
1688-89 :	The Glorious Revolution : deposition of James II and accession of William of Orange.
1700 :	Death of John Dryden.
1707 :	Act of Union unites Scotland and England, which thus become "Great Britain."
1714 :	Rule by house of Hanover begins with accession of George I.
1744-45 :	Death of Pope and Swift.
1784 :	Death of Samuel Johnson.
1789 :	The French Revolution begins.

1. 시대적 배경

포프 이후 18세기의 시단에 토머스 그레이나 크리스토퍼 스마트 같은 주
목할 만한 시인이 몇 명 등장했다. 1780년대에 로버트 번스의 『스코틀랜드
방언으로 쓴 시집』(*Poems, Chiefly in the Scottish Dialect*)이 출판되어 성공을 거
둠으로써, 스코틀랜드 어휘와 발라드 양식도 시어에 새로운 활력을 불어넣
을 수 있음이 효과적으로 입증되었다. 그 밖의 중요한 시인들로 올리버 골
드스미스와 새뮤얼 존슨이 있다. 존슨은 뛰어난 시인이긴 하나 주로 산문

에 정력을 쏟아 부었으며, 일찍부터 런던에서 문필을 생업으로 삼았다. 1주일에 2번씩 『램블러』(*The Rambler*, 1750-52)지에 기고한 논설은 문학이나 도덕의 문제들을 인상적인 방식으로 다룬 글로서, 절정에 이른 그의 능력을 보여주고 있다. 그의 분석력은 2가지 업적, 즉 혁신적인 『영어사전』(*Dictionary of the English Language*)과 셰익스피어 희곡집(1765)에서 입증되고 있다. 제임스 보즈웰의 권위 있는 『존슨 전기』(*Life of Samuel Johnson*)는 그 주인공의 윤리적 성실성이나 풍부한 지성에 대한 깊은 존경심과 더불어, 그의 사사로운 습관과 태도를 세세히 전달하면서 항상 찬사만 늘어놓지 않는 객관적인 관점을 독특한 방식으로 결합시킨 작품이다.

2. 주요 작가와 작품

(1) 알렉산더 포프 Alexander Pope, 1688-1744

포프는 런던 출신으로 아버지는 직물도매상으로, 12세 때 앓은 병으로 평생 불구의 몸이 되었다. 아버지가 가톨릭 신자였기 때문에 정규교육을 받지 못하였으나 독학으로 고전을 익혔고, 타고난 재능으로 21세에 이미 시집 『목가집』(*Pastorals*)을 발표하였다. 이후 『비평론』(*Essay on Criticism*)을 발표하여 영국 시단에서 확고한 지위를 얻었다. 익살스러운 주제를 격조 있는 시형으로 노래한 풍자 영웅시 『머리카락을 훔친 자』(*The Rape of the Lock*), 자연묘사에 뛰어난 『윈저의 숲』(*Windsor Forest*)을 발표한 후, 호메로스의 역시 『일리아스』(*Ilias*)와 『오디세이』(*Odyssey*)에 의해서 경제적인 성공도 거두었다.

「엘로이스로부터 아벨라르에게로」("Eloisa To Abelard")와 「불행한 부

인을 애도하는 노래」("Elegy To The Memory Of An Unfortunate Lady")에
서는 그의 작품으로는 드물게 풍부한 정서가 있지만, 대표작은 역시 풍자
시인 「우인열전」("The Dunciad")이다. 이것은 자기가 싫어하는 출판업
자·시인·학자 들을 철저하게 조롱한 작품이다. 보편적인 진리는 이미 그
리스나 로마의 고전을 통해 알 수 있으므로 근대시인은 그에 대한 완벽한
표현을 가하는 일이 과제이며, 이것이 그의 시론의 핵심이었다. 당시의 이
신론(deism)에 바탕을 둔 철학시인 『인간론』(An Essay on Man)은 사상의 깊
이가 있는 것은 아니나 표현의 묘에서 뛰어난 역작이다.

An Essay on Criticism
Part I*

Be sure yourself and your own reach to know,
How far your Genius, Taste, and Learning go,
Launch not beyond your depth, but be discreet,
And mark that point where Sense and Dulness meet.
Nature to all things fix'd the limits fit,
And wisely curb'd proud man's pretending wit.

---

* "An Essay on Criticism" is written in heroic couplets, which consist of two rhyming lines
that are written in iambic pentameter. Lines written in iambic pentameter consist of five
iambs, which are metrical feet that have two syllables, one unstressed syllable followed by
one stressed syllable, as in 'belong' or 'along.' Heroic couplets are typically used when writing
traditional and idealistic poetry, a quality that reiterates the serious tone of Pope's poem.
Pope saw the poem less as an original composition and more as a collection of the insights
of other writers. His goal was to combine the wisdom of others to help produce a sort of
definitive guideline from which critics could learn.

The Rape of the Lock
Canto III*

. . . oft the fall foredoom
Of foreign tyrants and of nymphs at home;
Here thou, great Anna! whom three realms obey,
Dost sometimes counsel take — and sometimes tea.
. . .

In various talk th' instructive hours they pass'd,
Who gave the ball, or paid the visit last;
One speaks the glory of the British queen,
And one describes a charming Indian screen;
. . .

Snuff, or the fan, supply each pause of chat,
With singing, laughing, ogling, and all that.
. . .

The hungry judges soon the sentence sign,
And wretches hang that jury-men may dine;
. . .

The skilful nymph reviews her force with care:
"Let Spades be trumps!" she said, and trumps they were.
. . .

---

* The Rape of the Lock is a humorous indictment of the vanities and idleness of 18th-century high society. Basing his poem on a real incident among families of his acquaintance, Pope intended his verses to cool hot tempers and to encourage his friends to laugh at their own folly. The poem is perhaps the most outstanding example in the English language of the genre of mock-epic. The epic had long been considered one of the most serious of literary forms; it had been applied, in the classical period, to the lofty subject matter of love and war, and, more recently, by Milton, to the intricacies of the Christian faith.

An Essay on Man, Epistle I*

'Tis ours to trace him only in our own.
  He, who thro' vast immensity can pierce,
  See worlds on worlds compose one universe,
  Observe how system into system runs,
  What other planets circle other suns,
  What vary'd Being peoples ev'ry star,
  May tell why Heav'n has made us as we are.
  But of this frame the bearings, and the ties,
  The strong connexions, nice dependencies,
  Gradations just, has thy pervading soul
  Look'd thro'? or can a part contain the whole?

Is the great chain, that draws all to agree,
  And drawn supports, upheld by God, or thee?

(2) 존 드라이든 John Dryden, 1631-1700

드라이든은 왕정복고기의 대표적인 문인으로 다방면에 걸쳐서 많은 저술을 남겼다. 노샘프턴셔의 청교도 집안에서 태어나, 그 환경에 어울리는 교육을 케임브리지 대학에서 받았으나 찰스 2세에 의한 왕정복고가 이루어지자, 일변하여 국교회를 신봉해서 궁정과의 관계를 맺었다. 또한 제

---

* Pope's first epistle seems to endorse a sort of fatalism, in which all things are fated. Everything happens for the best, and man should not presume to question God's greater design, which he necessarily cannot understand because he is a part of it. He further does not possess the intellectual capability to comprehend God's order outside of his own experience. These arguments certainly support a fatalistic world view. According to Pope's thesis, everything that exists plays a role in the divine plan. God thus has a specific intention for every element of His creation, which suggests that all things are fated.

임스 2세가 즉위하자 왕과 같은 종파인 로마 가톨릭으로 개종하였다. 이같이 그때그때의 지배자가 바뀜에 따라 청교주의·국교회파·가톨릭교 등으로 옮겨 지조를 지키지 못한 것은 사실이나, 몇 가지 신앙을 주제로 한 장시에서 볼 수 있는 것처럼, 참된 영혼의 근거를 찾으려고 하는 진지한 태도라고도 볼 수 있다. 1688년의 명예혁명 때 충성을 서약하지 않았던 탓으로 그 이후에는 '계관시인' 및 그 밖의 직함이나 궁정의 보호도 상실하고, 고전 번역 등으로 불우하게 만년을 보냈다. 시에 있어서는 초기의 작품으로 『경이의 해』(*Annus Mirabilis*)도 좋기는 하나, 비교적 후기의 영웅시형이라고 부르고 있는 대구시형을 사용한 수편의 정치적 풍자시의 세계가 그의 본래의 특색이다.

가장 유명한 『압살롬과 아히도벨』(*Absalom and Achitophel*)은 구약성서에 나오는 인물을 빗대어서 왕에게 적대하는 사람들을 사정없이 공격하였으며, 뚜렷한 인물묘사가 풍자를 더욱 통렬히 표현하였다. 똑같은 형태의 풍자시에는 『훈장』(*The Medal*), 『플렉크노 2세』(*Mac Flecknoe*)가 있다. 신앙을 취급한 시에는 국교회를 옹호한 『세속인의 종교』(*Religio Laici*)와 가톨릭교로 개종한 후에 쓴 우화시 『암사슴과 표범』(*The Hind and the Panther*)이 있다.

비평가로서는 격조를 존중하는 고전파의 테두리 안에 머물러 있으면서도 대담한 구상과 명석하면서도 설득력이 있는 문장으로, 고전과 당대문학, 외국과 자기 나라와의 문학비교를 시도하여 종래에는 반드시 중시하였다고 볼 수 없었던 셰익스피어, 초서, 밀턴 등이 얼마나 뛰어났는지를 말하고 있는 점은 그만큼 비평안의 탁월함을 말해 주는 것으로서, '영국 비평의 아버지'라고 불린다.

Year of Wonders*

Yet, London, Empress of the Northern Clime,
By an high fate thou greatly didst expire;
Great as the worlds, which at the death if time
Must fall, and rise a nobler frame by fire.

As when some dire Usurper Heav'n provides,
To scourge his Country with a lawless sway,
His birth, perhaps, some petty Village hides,
And sets his Cradle out of Fortunes way:

Till fully ripe his swelling fate breaks out,
And hurried him to mighty mischief on:
His Prince surpriz'd at first, no ill could doubt,
And wants the pow'r to meet it when know.

Such was the rise of this prodigious fire,
Which in mean buildings first obscurely bred,
From thence did soon to open streets aspire,
And straight to Palaces and Temples spread.

---

* It is autumn, 1666, and in the lead-mining village of Eyam in Derbyshire, England, Anna
  Firth is reflecting on the past year, in which two-thirds of the village's population had died
  from the effects of the bubonic plague. Anna is keeping house for Michael Mompellion, the
  village rector, who has been sitting in his room and refusing food and company since his
  wife, Elinor, had died. Elizabeth Bradford, the daughter of a wealthy family who had fled the
  village and the plague, returns and demands assistance from the rector, who rouses from his
  room only long enough to angrily turn her away.

Absalom and Achitophel*

In pious times, ere priest-craft did begin,
Before polygamy was made a sin;
When man, on many, multipli'd his kind,
Ere one to one was cursedly confin'd:
When Nature prompted, and no Law deni'd
Promiscuous use of concubine and bride;
Then, Israel's monarch, after Heaven's own heart,
His vigorous warmth did variously impart
To wives and slaves . . .

What prudent men a settled throne would shake?
For whatsoe'er their sufferings were before,
That change they covet makes them suffer more.
All other errors but disturb a state;
But innovation is the blow of fate.
If ancient fabrics nod, and threat to fall,
To patch the flaws, and buttress up the wall,
Thus far 'tis duty; but here fix the mark:
For all beyond it is to touch our Ark.
To change foundations, cast the frame anew,
Is work for rebels who base ends pursue:

---

* The political situation in Israel (England) had much to do with David's (Charles II's) virility,
which, though wasted on a barren queen, produced a host of illegitimate progeny, of which
by far the fairest and noblest is Absalom (duke of Monmouth). David's kingly virtues are
equally strong but unappreciated by a great number of Jews (Whigs), who, because of a
perverse native temperament, want to rebel. Although David provides no cause for rebellion,
as the wiser Jews (Tories) point out, a cause is found in the alleged Jebusite (Catholic) plot
to convert the nation to the Egyptian (French) religion. The plot miscarries, but it does
create factions whose leaders are jealous of David and oppose his reign.

At once divine and human laws control;

And mend the parts by ruin of the whole.

The tamp'ring world is subject to this curse,

To physic their disease into a worse.

To the Memory of Mr. Oldham*

Farewell, too little and too lately known,

Whom I began to think and call my own;

For sure our souls were near ally'd; and thine

Cast in the same poetic mould with mine.

One common note on either lyre did strike,

And knaves and fools we both abhorr'd alike:

To the same goal did both our studies drive,

The last set out the soonest did arrive.

Thus Nisus fell upon the slippery place,

While his young friend perform'd and won the race.

O early ripe! to thy abundant store

What could advancing age have added more?

It might (what nature never gives the young)

Have taught the numbers of thy native tongue.

But satire needs not those, and wit will shine

Through the harsh cadence of a rugged line.

A noble error, and but seldom made,

---

* John Dryden's elegy "To the Memory of Mr. Oldham" presents a tribute in verse to the
poetic achievement of John Oldham (1653-1683), whom Dryden knew as a younger
contemporary. Although he produced a variety of poems and translations, Oldham gained
fame through his highly topical Satyrs upon the Jesuits (1681). In twenty-five lines of heroic
couplets, an unusual verse form for an elegy, Dryden laments Oldham's premature death and
assesses his literary merit.

When poets are by too much force betray'd.
Thy generous fruits, though gather'd ere their prime
Still show'd a quickness; and maturing time
But mellows what we write to the dull sweets of rhyme.
Once more, hail and farewell; farewell thou young,
But ah too short, Marcellus of our tongue;
Thy brows with ivy, and with laurels bound;
But fate and gloomy night encompass thee around.

(3) 새뮤얼 버틀러 Samuel Butler, 1612-1680

잉글랜드 우스터셔 출신으로 성장하여 몇몇 귀족의 서기를 지냈는데, 청교도의 치안관 새뮤얼 루크 경을 섬길 때 비국교파와 공화주의에 대한 반감을 8음절 대구로 영웅시 비슷하게 썼다. 이것이 『휴디브래스』(Hudibras)로서 결혼 뒤 런던에 가서 그 제1부와 제2부를 1662년과 1663년에 냈다. 1660년의 왕정복고 직후에 낸 셈이어서 시대에의 편승으로도 여겨진다. 청교주의를 독선적인 이상주의로 간주하고 있던 왕당파는 이것을 환영했고, 찰스 2세는 연금을 보냈다고 한다. 1678년 제3부가 출판되었다.

이 작품은 당시 유행했던 대륙문학의 영향도 받아서, 주인공 휴디브래스는 세르반테스의 돈키호테를, 부하인 랠포는 산초를 각각 본뜬 것이며, 또 곱사등이 주인은 완고한 장로파, 부하는 독립교회파이다. 그들은 세속적인 악의 시정을 목표로 길을 떠나는데, 그 위선과 이기주의는 민중의 조소와 바늘 끝 같은 작자의 독설로 희롱 당한다. 전체적으로 성격이 유형적이라는 점과 악의 있는 풍자가 과격한 점 등 결점도 많으나 광신적인 청교도를 두들기는 인상 깊은 운문에는 독창성과 근대성이 들어 있다. 19세기의 동성동명의 소설가 S. 버틀러와 구별하기 위하여 '휴디브래스의 작자'라고 한다.

Hudibras Part I*

When civil fury first grew high,
And men fell out, they knew not why;
When hard words, jealousies, and fears,
Set folks together by the ears,
And made them fight, like mad or drunk,
For Dame Religion, as for punk

Hudibras' Religion
From "Hudibras"

FOR his religion, it was fit
To match his learning and his wit;
'Twas Presbyterian, true blue;
For he was of that stubborn crew
Of errant saints, whom all men grant
To be the true Church Militant;
Such as do build their faith upon
The holy text of pike and gun;
Decide all controversies by
Infallible artillery;

---

* Sir Hudibras, a Presbyterian knight, is among those who rode out against the monarchy during England's civil war. He is a proud man, one who bends his knee to nothing but chivalry and suffers no blow but that which was given when he was dubbed a knight. Although he has some wit, he is shy about displaying it. He knows Latin, Greek, and Hebrew; indeed, his talk is a piebald dialect, so heavily is it larded with Greek and Latin words and tags. He is learned in rhetoric, logic, and mathematics, and he frequently speaks in a manner demonstrating his learning. His notions fit things so well that he is often puzzled to decide what his notions are and what reality is.

And prove their doctrine orthodox
By apostolic blows, and knocks;
Call fire, and sword, and desolation,
A godly, thorough Reformation.
. . .

A sect, whose chief devotion lies
In odd perverse antipathies;
In falling out with that or this,
And finding somewhat still amiss;
More peevish, cross, and splenetic,
Than dog distract or monkey sick.

(4) 앤 핀치 Anne Finch, Countess of Winchilsea, 1661-1720

오래된 시골 가문에서 태어난 앤 킹스밀(Anne Kingsmill)은 찰스 2세의 궁정에서 공주의 시녀가 되었다. 그곳에서 그녀는 콜로넬 핀치(Colonel Heneage Finch)를 만나 1684년에 그들은 결혼했다. 제임스 2세의 짧은 통치기간 동안에 그들은 궁정에서 번영을 누렸지만 1688년의 왕의 실각으로 그들은 강제로 퇴역하여 마침내 영국의 남부 해안가 근처 켄트지역의 이스트웰의 아름다운 가문의 영지에 정착하게 되었다. 여기서 콜로넬 핀치는 1712년에 윈칠시 백작이 되고 여기서 앤 핀치는 대부분이 시를 썼는데 그녀의 말로는 "고독과 시골의 안정감"에 영향을 받은 시이고 "자연적으로 부드럽고 시적 상상력에 영감 받은 주제"로 이루어진 시라고 했다. 그녀의 *Miscellany Poems on Several Occasions, Written by a Lady*는 1713년에 발간되었다. "The Spleen"이란 시는 그녀와 다른 많은 세련된 사람들이 고통 받고 명성을 얻어 신비한 우울증적인 병의 묘사인데 포프(Pope)는 작품 *The Rape of the Lock*에서 여신 Spleen을 자극할 적에 그 시를 언급한 듯 했다.

하지만 핀치의 더 큰 명성은 1세기가 더 지나 시인 워즈워스(Wordsworth)가 그녀가 시선을 외부 자연에 고정하고 "종종 경탄할만하고 정숙하고 부드럽고 열정적인" 문제라며 칭송했을 때 얻게 된다.

핀치의 시에는 세 가지가 밑으로 연결되어 있다. 그녀는 귀족이며 그녀의 자연은 쇠퇴하고 있고 그녀는 여성이란 점이다. 이런 것 중 어떤 것도 그녀가 그 세기의 전환점에서 여전히 "시나 긁적이는 여편네"라는 조롱을 받게 되는 것에 자신을 노출시키지 않으려 한 것이다. 예를 들어 그녀의 뛰어난 시중 많은 편수가 들어 있는 "The Petition for an Absolute Retreat"는 고독의 기쁨을 노래하고 있다. 그럼에도 현격하게 그녀는 시를 발간하는 것을 선택했다. 핀치가 발간하려는 이유는 그녀의 여성은 단지 사소한 추구에만 적합하다는 상념에 대한 경멸 때문이었을 것이다. 「시의 서시」("The Introduction")에서 그녀는 여성은 "자연적인 바보라기보다 교육에 열외된 바보들"이라고 주장하고 종종 인류의 반을 공적생활에서 제외시키는 폐해에 대한 언급을 하고 있다. 하지만 핀치는 여성의 본보기라 할 수 있는 예리한 시각과 자족적인 시인이었다.

Adam Posed*

Could our first father, at his toilsome plow,
Thorns in his path, and labor on his brow,
Clothed only in a rude, unpolished skin,
Could he a vain fantastic nymph have seen,
In all her airs, in all her antic graces,

---

* In her poem "Adam Posed," Anne Finch employs allegory. She imagines "a vain, fantastic nymph" who intrudes in the biblical creation narrative to confront humanity's "first father." Adam, busy at his "toilsome plow," seems to have already fallen from Paradise as he is

Her various fashions, and more various faces;

How had it posed that skill, which late assigned

Just appellations to each several kind!

A right idea of the sight to frame;

T'have guessed from what new element she came;

T'have hit the wav'ring form, or giv'n this thing a name.

To Death*

O King of terrors, whose unbounded sway

All that have life must certainly obey;

The King, the Priest, the Prophet, all are thine,

Nor would ev'n God (in flesh) thy stroke decline.

My name is on thy roll, and sure I must

Increase thy gloomy kingdom in the dust.

My soul at this no apprehension feels,

But trembles at thy swords, thy racks, thy wheels;

Thy scorching fevers, which distract the sense,

And snatch us raving, unprepared, from hence;

At thy contagious darts, that wound the heads

Of weeping friends, who wait at dying beds.

---

already experiencing "thorns in his path" and the grueling reality of performing hard labor to insure human survival.

Adam has been "assigned" the task of giving "appellations," or names, to each creation emerging from "the elements" of Eden, thus giving them a place in the terrestrial hierarchy over which he, even in his fallen state, presides.

* The author of "To Death" writes a piece of poetic literature that brings light to a tone of respect and resignation to death and its complete, unbridled power over human beings. Anne Finch uses rhetorical devices on showing the reader her views on death and how it's not the worst concept in a person's life. "To Death" has them of understanding. truth and fate as Finch shows the reader of her understanding on death and how it should be accepted in an overall.

Spare these, and let thy time be when it will;

My bus'ness is to die, and thine to kill.

Gently thy fatal scepter on me lay,

And take to thy cold arms, insensibly, thy prey.

The Spleen*

O'er me, alas! thou dost too much prevail:

   I feel thy Force, whilst I against thee rail;

I feel my Verse decay, and my crampt Numbers fail.

Thro' thy black Jaundice I all Objects see,

   As Dark, and Terrible as Thee,

My Lines decry'd, and my Employment thought

An useless Folly, or presumptuous Fault:

A Nocturnal Reverie**

When the loosed horse now, as his pasture leads,

Comes slowly grazing through th' adjoining meads,

Whose stealing pace, and lengthened shade we fear,

Till torn-up forage in his teeth we hear:

When nibbling sheep at large pursue their food,

And unmolested kine rechew the cud;

---

* "The Spleen" examines both a generalized public understanding of the condition and treatment of melancholy and her private suffering.

** "A Nocturnal Reverie" is a poem describing the beauty of nighttime and the speakers disappointment when it comes to an end. The majority of this poem contains detailed descriptions of a nighttime scene. Anne Finch uses night and day to create a metaphor comparing the busy world and peaceful solitude.

When curlews cry beneath the village walls,
And to her straggling brood the partridge calls;
Their shortlived jubilee the creatures keep,
Which but endures, whilst tyrant man does sleep.

(5) 토머스 그레이 Thomas Gray, 1716–1771

그레이는 런던 출신으로 이튼 칼리지를 거쳐 케임브리지 대학에서 공부하였다. 1739년부터 2년 남짓 H. 월폴과 함께 유럽을 여행하고 다녔으며, 귀국 후에는 케임브리지의 기숙사 안에서 은자와 같은 생활을 하였다. 정신활동의 폭은 넓었으며, 시 이외에 역사·식물·곤충·건축·음악 등에 조예가 깊었다. 그러나 선천적인 우울한 기질로 인하여 세상과의 접촉을 피하였으며, 1757년에 계관시인으로 천거되었으나 사퇴하고 1758년에 케임브리지의 근대사 교수로 임명되었는데도 강의는 하지 않았다. 작품은 적지만, 친구인 R. 웨스트가 죽은 무렵에 쓴 「봄의 노래」("Ode On The Spring"), 「멀리 이튼교를 바라보는 노래」("Ode on a Distant Prospect of Eton College") 등에서는 자연과 사회에 적응할 수 없는 고독감과 무상감이 흐르고 있다.

몇 년 동안 다듬은 끝에 완성한 「시골 묘지에서 읊은 만가」("Elegy Written in a Country Churchyard")는 명성도 재산도 얻지 못한 채 땅에 묻히는 서민들에 대한 동정을 애절한 음조로 노래한 걸작이며, 이 작품으로 18세기 중엽을 대표하는 시인이 되었다. 핀다로스풍의 송가 「시가의 진보」("The Progress of Poesy")와 「시선」("The Bard")에서는 풍부한 역사적 감각을 나타내었고, 또 북유럽의 고시를 번역하여, 시대를 앞선 낭만적 경향을 나타내었다. 선례를 가진 표현을 존중하는 그의 고전주의적 시풍은 난해한 편에 속한다. 사후에 출판된 일기와 편지는 우수한 산문으로 평가되고 있으며 당시의 전형적인 학자시인의 문체와 생활을 전하고 있다.

Ode on a Distant Prospect of Eton College*

Ye distant spires, ye antique towers
  That crown the watery glade,
Where grateful Science still adores
  Her Henry's holy shade;
And ye, that from the stately brow
Of Windsor's heights th' expanse below
Of grove, of lawn, of mead survey,
Whose turf, whose shade, whose flowers among
Wanders the hoary Thames along
  His silver-winding way:

Ah, happy hills! ah, pleasing shade!
  Ah, fields belov'd in vain!
Where once my careless childhood stray'd,
  A stranger yet to pain!
I feel the gales that from ye blow
A momentary bliss bestow,
As waving fresh their gladsome wing
My weary soul they seem to soothe,
And, redolent of joy and youth,
  To breathe a second spring.

---

* Two themes play through Gray's "Ode on a Distant Prospect of Eton College." The major theme is the inevitability of suffering, death, and unhappiness for humankind. Sad though the theme is, Gray tempers it with his own fatherlike concern in keeping this knowledge from the children. Because he knows that the "paradise" of their youth is brief, he tenderly allows them to enjoy it.

The Epitaph*

Here rests his head upon the lap of Earth
    A youth to Fortune and to Fame unknown.
Fair Science frown'd not on his humble birth,
    And Melancholy mark'd him for her own.

Large was his bounty, and his soul sincere,
    Heav'n did a recompense as largely send:
He gave to Mis'ry all he had, a tear,
    He gain'd from Heav'n ('twas all he wish'd) a friend.

No farther seek his merits to disclose,
    Or draw his frailties from their dread abode,
(There they alike in trembling hope repose)
    The bosom of his Father and his God.

(6) 윌리엄 콜린스 William Collins, 1721–1759

콜린스는 18세기 후반의 고전주의 시단에 낭만적인 시풍을 도입한 선구자의 한 사람이다. 옥스퍼드 대학교를 중퇴하고 런던으로 가서 문필생활

---

* Thomas Gray shows his discontent toward the way that life and death are categorized on this planet. He speaks of earth as a place which holds people for the time being that they are going through this grand cycle of what is called life.
When somebody only "rests his head upon the lap of Earth" it is not a way of approving the way that people are laid down for their final resting. The Epitaph shows , properly titled, the lot about how people are being brought up and brought down in a dark sort of way. Someone's personal epitaph is just a place where their head rests and Even "Fair Science frowned" on the aspects of the person's life and now the incapacity that they have toward this world. Their one and only sole purpose in this world is to waste space in the earth and rot away for eternity.

을 시작하였다. 1746년에 발표한 『송가집』(*Odes*)에는 유명한 「석양부」
("Ode to Evening")를 비롯한 「1746년 연두부」("Ode Written in the Year
1746"), 「간소부」("Ode to Simplicity") 등 그의 서정적 천품을 발휘한 작품
이 포함되어 있었으나, 낭만적인 시가 그 시대에는 일반에게 널리 받아들
여지지 못하였다.

Ode Written In The Beginning Of The Year 1746*

How sleep the brave, who sink to rest
By all their country's wishes blest!
When Spring, with dewy fingers cold,
Returns to deck their hallow'd mould,
She there shall dress a sweeter sod
Than Fancy's feet have ever trod.
By fairy hands their knell is rung;
By forms unseen their dirge is sung;
There Honour comes, a pilgrim grey,
To bless the turf that wraps their clay;
And Freedom shall awhile repair
To dwell, a weeping hermit, there!

---

* The whole theme of the poem is a praise to the courageous soldiers. Whho sacrificed their
lives in the name of their country. Poet created a beautiful image of their funeral, done by
nature. Poem consist lots of personifications spring, freedom, honour are the subjects.
Rhyme sheme is regular AABBCC. All the use of visual images are for displaying the praise
the pride of brave soldiers.

Ode To Evening*

If aught of oaten stop or pastoral song
May hope, chaste Eve, to soothe thy modest ear,
Like thy own solemn springs,
Thy springs, and dying gales,
O nymph reserved, while now the bright-haired sun
Sits in yon western tent, whose cloudy skirts,
With brede ethereal wove,
O'erhang his wavy bed:

Now air is hushed, save where the weak-eyed bat
With short shrill shriek flits by on leathern wing,
Or where the beetle winds
His small but sullen horn,
As oft he rises 'midst the twilight path,
Against the pilgrim borne in heedless hum:
Now teach me, maid composed,
To breathe some softened strain,
Whose numbers stealing through thy dark'ning vale
May not unseemly with its stillness suit,
As, musing slow, I hail
Thy genial loved return!

---

* "Ode to Evening," a single stanza of fifty-two lines, is addressed to a goddess figure
representing the time of day in the title. This "nymph," or "maid," who personifies dusk, is
"chaste," "reserv'd," and meek, in contrast to the "bright-hair'd sun," a male figure who
withdraws into his tent, making way for night. Thus "Eve," or evening, is presented as the
transition between light and darkness.

(7) 새뮤얼 존슨 Samuel Johnson, 1709-1784

새뮤얼 존슨은 1709년 스태퍼드셔 리치필드에서 서점 주인의 아들로 태어나 학비 부족으로 옥스퍼드 대학교를 중퇴하였으나, 후에 문학상 업적에 의하여 박사학위가 추증되어 '존슨 박사'라 불렸다. 26세 때 자신보다 20세나 연상인 미망인과 결혼하여 고향에서 사학을 열었다. 1737년에 런던으로 나온 그는 가난과 싸우면서 의회기사를 써주고 받는 원고료로 생계를 이어가면서, 잡지 『램블러』(*Rambler*)를 냈다. 풍자시 「런던」("London"), 「욕망의 공허」("The Vanity of Human Wishes") 등을 발표하면서 이름이 알려졌다. 1747년에 시작한 『영어사전』(*A Dictionary of the English Language*)을 자력으로 7년 만에 완성시킴으로써 사람들을 놀라게 하였다. 1762년에는 정부로부터 30파운드의 연금이 수여되었으며, 1763년에는 그를 중심으로 제자들이 문학 그룹 '더 클럽'을 조직하였다. 『존슨 전』의 저자 J. 보즈웰을 만난 것도 이때였다. J. 보즈웰은 『존슨 전』에서 그의 주위에 모여든 문인·평론가들의 인생론·문학론에 대한 논쟁과 활발한 대화·토론의 모습 및 그의 품격 있는 인품 등에 대해서 묘사하였다. 그는 1765년에 셰익스피어 전집을 출판하고, 그 서두에 훌륭한 셰익스피어론을 실었다. 그리고 17세기 이후의 영국 시인 52명의 전기와 작품론을 정리한 10권의 『영국시인전』(*Lives of the English Poets*)은 만년의 대사업으로 특히 유명하다. 존슨은 학자·문학자·시인이었을 뿐만 아니라, 'Talker Johnson'이라고도 불릴 만큼 담화의 명인이기도 하였다. "런던에 싫증난 자는 인생에 싫증난 자다"라고 말한 그는 진정으로 런던을 사랑한 사람이었다고 할 수 있다.

The Vanity of Human Wishes*

In full-blown dignity, see Wolsey stand,

Law in his voice, and fortune in his hand: 100

To him the church, the realm, their powers consign,

Thro' him the rays of regal bounty shine,

Turned by his nod the stream of honour flows,

His smile alone security bestows:

Still to new heights his restless wishes tower,

Claim leads to claim, and power advances power;

Till conquest unresisted ceased to please,

And rights submitted, left him none to seize.

At length his sov'reign frowns   the train of state

Mark the keen glance, and watch the sign to hate.

Wherever he turns he meets a stranger's eye,

His suppliants scorn him, and his followers lly;

At once is lost the pride of aweful state,

The golden canopy, the glittering plate,

The regal palace, the luxurious board,

The liveried army, and the menial lord.

With age, with cares, with maladies oppressed,

He seeks the refuge of monastic rest.

Grief aids disease, remembered folly stings,

And his last sighs reproach the faith of kings.

---

* Samuel Johnson's The Vanity of Human Wishes imitates, as its subtitle states, Juvenal's tenth
satire. The 368 lines of iambic pentameter in rhymed couplets do not claim to provide an
exact translation but rather to apply the poem to eighteenth century England. While Johnson
therefore feels free to modernize the allusions, he follows his model closely.

(8) 올리버 골드스미스 Oliver Goldsmith, 1728-1774

골드스미스는 롱포드 출신으로 더블린의 대학을 졸업한 다음, 에든버러와 라이든 대학에서 의학을 공부하였다. 그 후 유럽 각국을 떠돌아다녔는데, 1756년 런던에 돌아왔을 때는 빈털터리였다. 이 무전여행에서 얻은 것은 세계인으로서의 인생관이었으며, 이는 후일 『세계의 시민』(*The Citizen of the World*)이란 책으로 출판되었다. 작가로서 성공하기까지는 여러 잡지에 잡문을 기고하다가, 1761년에 문단의 원로인 S. 존슨의 호의로 그의 문학 그룹인 '더 클럽'의 회원이 되었다.

선량한 시골 목사 집안의 파란을 유머와 경쾌한 풍자를 곁들여 묘사한 소설 『웨이크필드의 목사』(*The Vicar of Wakefield*)가 존슨의 노력으로 60파운드에 팔림으로써 빚 때문에 투옥될 위기를 모면하게 되었다는 일화도 있다. 시로서는 「나그네」("The Traveller")와 「버림받은 마을」("Deserted village")이 대표작이다.

The Deserted Village*

Sweet Auburn, loveliest village of the plain,
Where health and plenty cheared the labouring swain,
Where smiling spring its earliest visit paid,
And parting summer's lingering blooms delayed,
Dear lovely bowers of innocence and ease,
Seats of my youth, when every sport could please,

---

* The Deserted Village is a long poem, its 430 lines distributed among twenty-five verse paragraphs of varying length. All the lines are given in heroic couplets. It is clear that Oliver Goldsmith as poet is the persona of the poem. The first-person narration is used to express a lamentation, as it were, for the passing of a way of life.

How often have I loitered o'er thy green,
Where humble happiness endeared each scene!
How often have I paused on every charm,
The sheltered cot, the cultivated farm,
The never-failing brook, the busy mill,
The decent church that topt the neighbouring hill,
The hawthorn bush, with seats beneath the shade,
For talking age and whispering lovers made!

낭만주의 시대 영국시 (1798-1832)

1789-1815 : Revolutionary and Napoleonic period in France.

1789 : The Revolution begins with the assembly of the States-General in May and the storming of the Bastille on July 14.

1793 : King Louis XVI executed; England joins the alliance against France.

1793-94 : The Reign of Terror under Robespierre. 1804: Napoleon crowned emperor.

1807 : British slave trade outlawed (slavery abolished throughout the empire, including the West Indies, twenty-six years later)

1811-20 : The Regency-George, Prince of Wales, acts as regent for George III, who has been declared incurably insane.

1815 : Napoleon defeated at Waterloo.

1820 : Accession of George IV.

1. 시대적 배경

낭만주의 시의 뚜렷한 특징은 개인의 감정과 사고가 새롭게 중요한 역할을 맡고 있다는 점이다. 18세기 시학의 주된 경향이 일반적인 것을 찬양하고 시인을 사회의 대변자로 보았던 반면, 낭만주의자들은 특수하고 독특한 경험에서 시의 근원을 찾았다. 시인은 자기 자신의 정신활동을 시의 기본 소재로 받아들일 수 있을 만큼 지각이 뛰어나기 때문에 다른 사람들과는 구별되는 개인이라고 여겨졌다. 시는 자체의 진리를 전달하는 것이며 성실성이야말로 그것을 판단할 수 있는 척도였다. 감정에 대한 이러한 강조는 곧 가장 강렬한 감정을 표현한 것이 최고의 시임을 뜻했고, 따라서 서정시가 새로운 중요성을 띠게 되었다. 낭만주의 이론은 신고전주의와는 달리 상상력에 상대적 중요성을 부여했다. 새뮤얼 존슨(Samuel Johnson)은 시의 구성요소를 '고안·상상·판단'이라고 보았지만, 판단이나 의식적 통제는 이차적인 것으로 여겨졌다. 따라서 당대 시인들은 무의식적 정신작용, 꿈과 환상, 초자연적 세계, 순수하고 원시적인 세계관을 크게 강조했다. 더나아가, 자연발생적이고 진지하고 강렬한 시는 기본적으로 창조적 상상력의 지시에 따라 만들어져야 한다는 입장이었다.

(1) 시

최초의 낭만주의자들인 윌리엄 블레이크(William Blake), 새뮤얼 테일러 콜리지(Samuel Taylor Coleridge), 윌리엄 워즈워스(William Wordsworth)는 당시의 지적 풍토에 불만을 갖고 있었다. 블레이크는 『순수의 노래』(*Songs of Innocence*, 1789)에서 그의 예언자적 생각을 처음 드러냈다. 『천국과 지옥의 결혼』(*The Marriage of Heaven and Hell*, 1790-93), 『경험의 노래』(*Songs of Experience*, 1794) 같은 작품에서는 그 시대의 위선과 분석적 이성이 당대의 사고를 지배함으로써 야기된 비정한 잔혹성을 공격했다. 그 뒤 블레이크는 시의 목표를 한 번 더 바꾸었다. 그는 『실락원』을 본떠 이야기체 서사시를 쓰려고 했던 계획을 바꾸어, 그보다 구성이 느슨한 상상의 이야기 시인 『밀턴』(*Milton*, 1804-08), 『예루살렘』(*Jerusalem*, 1804-20)을 썼다. 여기서도 그는 여전히 신화적 인물들을 등장시켜 상상력이 풍부한 시인을 사회의 영웅으로, 또 용서를 가장 위대한 미덕으로 그려내고 있다.

반면 워즈워스와 콜리지는 혁명의 의미를 좀 더 복잡하게 탐색하고 있었다. 워즈워스는 일생 동안 프랑스 혁명이라는 사건이 지닌 의미를 심사숙고했으며, 인간 개개인의 서글픈 운명과 전체 인류의 실현되지 못한 잠재성이라는 그의 이중적 관점에 부응할 만한 인간관을 전개하려고 애썼다. 자연과 인간정신 사이의 관계에 대한 그의 탐색은 자전적인 장시 「서곡」("The Prelude")에 뚜렷이 나타나 있다. 이 시기 동안 콜리지의 시도 워즈워스와 비슷한 발전단계를 거쳤다. 당대 정치에 곧 환멸을 느낀 콜리지 역시 자연과 인간정신의 관계를 탐구했다. 몽상 중에 떠올랐다고 하는 시 「쿠빌라이 칸」("Kubla khan")은 이국적인 작품의 새로운 지평을 열었고, 콜리지는 더 나아가 「노수부의 노래」("The Ancient Mariner")와 미완성작인 「크리스타벨」("Christabel")의 초자연주의에서도 이 분위기를 이용했다.

선배의 자유에 대한 열망을 공유했던 다음 세대의 시인들은 선배들의 경험으로부터 배워야 할 입장에 놓여 있었다. 퍼시 비셰 셸리(Percy Bysshe Shelley)는 인간해방의 열의와 시적 정열을 소유한 열렬한 혁명주의자였다. 초기 시 「매브 여왕」("Queen Mab"), 장시 「레온과 시스나」("Laon and Cythna"), 서정적 분위기의 극 『사슬에서 풀려난 프로메테우스』(*Prometheus Unbound*)에는 이러한 열기가 불타고 있다. 「서풍에 부치는 송시」("Ode to the West Wind")에서 뚜렷이 알 수 있듯이, 셸리는 자신을 시인이자 예언자라고 생각했다.

그와 대조적으로 존 키츠(John Keats)는 감각이 매우 예민한 시인이어서 「엔디미온」("Endymion") 같은 초기 시는 지나치게 화려하다는 느낌이 들 정도이다. 그러나 「성 아그네스 전야」("The Eve of St. Agnes"), 「나이팅게일에게」("To a Nightingale"), 「그리스 항아리에 부쳐」("On a Grecian Urn"), 「가을에」("To Autumn") 등의 송시 및 「히페리온」("Hyperion") 같은 후기 작품들은 절정에 달한 키츠의 기량을 보여주며, 복잡한 주제를 구체적으로 치밀하게 다룰 수 있는 능력을 드러낸다.

바이런(Byron)은 주제와 양식 면에서 볼 때 셸리나 키츠와는 구별된다. 『차일드 해럴드의 여행』(*Childe Harold's Pilgrimage*, 1812-18)와 걸작 『돈 주안』(*Don Juan*, 1819-24)은 바이런에게 대리자아를 제공했던 시들로, 그의 작품 중 가장 길다. 『차일드 해럴드의 여행』에서는 유럽의 사적지를 돌아다니는 냉혹하고 우수에 찬 유배자가, 『돈 주안』에서는 연애사건을 잇따라 일으키는 탕아가 등장한다. 바이런은 『맨프레드』(*Manfred*), 『카인』(*Cain*) 등의 극적인 시들을 발표해 유럽 전역에서 명성을 얻었으나, 오늘날에는 재치있고 역설적이며 덜 과장된 작품을 쓴 작가로 주로 기억된다.

2. 주요 작가와 작품

(1) 윌리엄 블레이크 William Blake, 1757-1827

윌리엄 블레이크는 런던 출신으로 정규교육은 제대로 받지 못하였고, 15세 때부터 판각가 밑에서 일을 배웠으며, 왕립미술원에서 공부한 적도 있다. 1783년 친구의 도움으로 『습작 시집』(*Poetical Sketches*)을 출판하였으며, 1784년 아버지가 죽은 후 판화 가게를 열어 채색인쇄법을 고안하였다. 어릴 때부터 비상한 환상력을 지녀 창가에서 천사와 이야기하고 언덕 위에 올라 하늘을 만진 체험이 있다고 하며, 그러한 신비로운 체험을 최초로 표현한 것이 『순수의 노래』(*Songs of Innocence*)이다. 이 시집은 자연과 인간의 세계에는 순수한 사랑과 아름다움으로 가득 차 있다는 사상이 기조를 이루며 『셸의 서』(*The Book of Thel*)는 그 속편이라고 할 수 있다. 『천국과 지옥의 결혼』(*The Marriage of Heaven and Hell*, 1790)에서는 스웨덴의 과학자 스베덴보리의 영향을 받으면서도 그것을 비판하여 인간의 근원에 있는 2개의 대립된 상태, 즉 이성과 활력의 조화가 새로운 도덕이 되어야 한다고 주장하였다. 그리하여 『순수의 노래』에 나오는 목가적인 동심의 세계는 『경험의 노래』(Songs of Experience)에서 일단 부정되어 분열되고 투쟁하는 현실세계의 어두운 면이 강조된다. 전자에서는 양의 순진함을 노래하였으나, 후자에서는 밤의 숲속에서 빛을 내는 호랑이의 존재에 시선을 돌리고 있다. 이러한 인간관과 이에 입각한 사회비판은 몇 권의 예언서를 낳았다.

미국의 독립을 노래한 『아메리카』(America a Prophecy) 이외에 『유럽』(Europe a Prophecy) 『유리젠 서』(The Book of Urizen) 등에 서사적 신화가 식각되었고, 나아가서 죄의 용서를 중심사상으로 하는 『밀턴』(John Milton, Paradise Lost)과 『예루살렘』(Jerusalem The Emanation of the Giant Albion)이 있다. 인간정신에는 언어를 매개로 하지 않고, 상징에 의하여 생각하는 영역이 있는데, 블레이크의 신화적 상징은 바로 그러한 원초적 체험을 표현하려고 한 것이었다. 시 『순수의 노래』, 『경험의 노래』, 『예루살렘』 등을 자신이 판화로 인쇄했을 뿐만 아니라 영, 그레이, 단테 등의 시와 구약성서의 『욥기』 등을 위한 삽화를 남김으로써 화가로서의 천재성도 보여주었다. 대부분은 동판화로, 손으로 채색한 독특한 색판을 겹쳐 나간 것들이지만, 섬세하고 우아한 선과 함께 독자적인 환상성과 장식성으로 가득 차 있다. 양식으로 볼 때 중세 및 매너리즘의 회화와 유사성이 있다고 지적되기도 하지만, 정신적 내용의 표현형식으로 블레이크가 스스로 창조해낸 양식으로 본다.

The Lamb*

Little Lamb who made thee
       Dost thou know who made thee
Gave thee life & bid thee feed.
By the stream & o'er the mead;
Gave thee clothing of delight,
Softest clothing wooly bright;
Gave thee such a tender voice,
Making all the vales rejoice!
       Little Lamb who made thee
       Dost thou know who made thee

       Little Lamb I'll tell thee,
       Little Lamb I'll tell thee!
He is called by thy name,
For he calls himself a Lamb:
He is meek & he is mild,
He became a little child:
I a child & thou a lamb,
We are called by his name.
       Little Lamb God bless thee.
       Little Lamb God bless thee.

---

* The poem begins with the question, "Little Lamb, who made thee?" The speaker, a child, asks the lamb about its origins: how it came into being, how it acquired its particular manner of feeding, its "clothing" of wool, its "tender voice." In the next stanza, the speaker attempts a riddling answer to his own question: the lamb was made by one who "calls himself a Lamb," one who resembles in his gentleness both the child and the lamb. The poem ends with the child bestowing a blessing on the lamb.

Holy Thursday*

Is this a holy thing to see,
In a rich and fruitful land,
Babes reducd to misery,
Fed with cold and usurous hand?

Is that trembling cry a song?
Can it be a song of joy?
And so many children poor?
It is a land of poverty!

And their sun does never shine.
And their fields are bleak & bare.
And their ways are fill'd with thorns.
It is eternal winter there.

For where-e'er the sun does shine,
And where-e'er the rain does fall:
Babe can never hunger there,
Nor poverty the mind appall.

---

* The poem begins with a series of questions: how holy is the sight of children living in misery in a prosperous country? Might the children's "cry," as they sit assembled in St. Paul's Cathedral on Holy Thursday, really be a song? "Can it be a song of joy?" The speaker's own answer is that the destitute existence of so many children impoverishes the country no matter how prosperous it may be in other ways: for these children the sun does not shine, the fields do not bear, all paths are thorny, and it is always winter.

Ah! Sun-flower*

Ah Sun-flower! weary of time,
Who countest the steps of the Sun:
Seeking after that sweet golden clime
Where the travellers journey is done.

Where the Youth pined away with desire,
And the pale Virgin shrouded in snow:
Arise from their graves and aspire,
Where my Sun-flower wishes to go.

London**

I wander thro' each charter'd street,
Near where the charter'd Thames does flow.
And mark in every face I meet
Marks of weakness, marks of woe.

---

* The Sunflower more closely represents human aspirations, with its face always looking toward the sun. That it follows the sun's progress from morning to evening shows that human aspirations must eventually end in death, symbolized by night in many of Blake's poems. The youth and virgin both have unfulfilled desires to which they seek satiation in the sunset, suggesting that their longings may be fulfilled in the next life.

** The poet expresses his disdain for the urban sprawl of post-Industrial Revolution London in terms as harsh as his praise for nature and innocence are pleasant. A society of people so tightly packed into artificial structures breeds evil upon evil, culminating with the "Harlot's curse" that harms both the young and the married. It is as if a system has been created specifically to destroy all that is good in humankind, a theme Blake takes up in his later works. The reader is warned off visiting or dwelling in London, and by implication urged to seek refuge from the world's ills in a more rural setting.

In every cry of every Man,
In every Infants cry of fear,
In every voice: in every ban,
The mind-forg'd manacles I hear

How the Chimney-sweepers cry
Every blackning Church appalls,
And the hapless Soldiers sigh
Runs in blood down Palace walls

But most thro' midnight streets I hear
How the youthful Harlots curse
Blasts the new-born Infants tear
And blights with plagues the Marriage hearse

The Chimney Sweeper*

When my mother died I was very young,
And my father sold me while yet my tongue
Could scarcely cry " 'weep! 'weep! 'weep! 'weep!"
So your chimneys I sweep & in soot I sleep.

---

* The entire system, God included, colludes to build its own vision of paradise upon the
labors of children who are unlikely to live to see adulthood. Blake castigates the government
(the "King") and religious leaders (God's "Priest") in similar fashion to his two "Holy
Thursday" poems, decrying the use of otherwise innocent children to prop up the moral
consciences of adults both rich and poor. The use of the phrase "make up a Heaven" carries
the double meaning of creating a Heaven and lying about the existence of Heaven, casting
even more disparagement in the direction of the Priest and King.

Introduction to the Songs of Innocence*

Piping down the valleys wild
Piping songs of pleasant glee
On a cloud I saw a child.
And he laughing said to me.

Pipe a song about a Lamb;
So I piped with merry chear,
Piper pipe that song again—
So I piped, he wept to hear.

Drop thy pipe thy happy pipe
Sing thy songs of happy chear,
So I sung the same again
While he wept with joy to hear

Piper sit thee down and write
In a book that all may read—
So he vanish'd from my sight.
And I pluck'd a hollow reed.

And I made a rural pen,
And I stain'd the water clear,

---

* The speaker urges his audience to listen to "the voice of the Bard!" who can see past, present, and future. In contrast to the "Introduction" for Songs of Innocence, this poem introduces a more mature and polished poetic voice in the bard. No rural shepherd converting his heart's songs to words using merely the tools at hand, this poet has heard "the Holy Word/ that walk'd among the ancient trees." This speaker's poetry is characterized by direct revelation rather than by the shepherds' inner melodies, and therefore holds the authority of both divinity and experience.

And I wrote my happy songs
Every child may joy to hear

The Garden of Love*

I went to the Garden of Love,
And saw what I never had seen:
A Chapel was built in the midst,
Where I used to play on the green.

And the gates of this Chapel were shut,
And Thou shalt not. writ over the door;
So I turn'd to the Garden of Love,
That so many sweet flowers bore.

And I saw it was filled with graves,
And tomb-stones where flowers should be:
And Priests in black gowns, were walking their rounds,
And binding with briars, my joys & desires.

The Ecchoing Green**

Old John, with white hair
Does laugh away care,
Sitting under the oak,

---

* The speaker visits a garden that he had frequented in his youth, only to find it overrun
  with briars, symbols of death in the form of tombstones, and close-minded clergy.
** The sun rises on a green field where birds sing and children play. As they play, "Old John

Among the old folk,
They laugh at our play,
And soon they all say.
'Such, such were the joys.
When we all girls & boys,
In our youth-time were seen,
On the Ecchoing Green.'

The Sick Rose*

O Rose thou art sick.
The invisible worm,
That flies in the night
In the howling storm:

Has found out thy bed
Of crimson joy:
And his dark secret love
Does thy life destroy.

---

with white hair" and other elderly observers laugh at their antics and remember a time when they were young, energetic, and playful. Eventually the little ones grow tired and the sun begins to set. The children gather back to their mothers and prepare for a night's rest.
* The speaker addresses a rose, which he claims is sick because an "invisible worm" has "found out thy bed/Of crimson joy." The rose symbolizes earthly, as opposed to spiritual, love, which becomes ill when infected with the materialism of the world. The rose's bed of "crimson joy" may also be a sexual image, with the admittedly phallic worm representing either lust or jealousy. The worm has a "dark secret love" that destroys the rose's life, suggesting something sinful or unmentionable.

(2) 새뮤얼 테일러 콜리지 Samuel Taylor Coleridge, 1772-1834

콜리지는 데본셔의 킹즈 스쿨 출신으로 그의 소년 시절 신동의 모습은 친구인 C. 램의 『엘리아 수필집』(*Essays of Elia*)에 쓰여 있다. 케임브리지 대학 졸업 후 친교를 맺은 W. 워즈워스와 1798년 『서정 가요집』(*Lyrical Ballads*)을 공저·출판하였는데, 이것은 영국 낭만주의에 기념할 만한 사건이 되었다. 서사시 「노수부의 노래」("The Rime of the Ancient Mariner"), 그리고 아편을 피우고 그 환상 속에서 창작하였으며, 영어로 쓰인 최초의 초현실주의 시라고 일컬어지는 「쿠빌라이 칸」("Kubla Khan"), 미완성의 서사시 「크리스타벨」("Christabel") 등 이상 3편의 대표작은, 환상적·상징적인 설정 속에서 인간 의식의 심연(深淵)을 탐구한 걸작이다. 이 밖에 「심야의 서리」 등의 '회화시'라고 불리는 몇 편의 독특한 작품도 1797-1798년이라는 짧은 시일에 쓰였다. 그러나 동시에 그의 시적 창작력은 급속히 감퇴되어, 그 괴로움을 노래한 「실의의 노래」(1802)가 최후의 수작이 되었다.

그러나 그는 이와 더불어 평론가·사상가로서 대성하였으며, 대표적 평론 『문학평전』(*Biographia Literaria*, 1817)과 강연·담화·수첩 등의 형식으로 셰익스피어론을 비롯한 많은 평론으로 평론사상의 거장의 위치를 확립하였다. 콜리지는 18세기 합리주의를 다음과 같이 비판하였다. 인간 최고의 능력으로서의 상상력의 우위를 강조한 이론적·철학적 방법론은 시적 직관에 뒷받침되었으며, 20세기의 '신비평' 등 후대에 큰 영향을 끼쳤다. 그의 사색은 종교와 정치영역까지 미쳤으며, 19세기 중엽의 그리스도교 사상에도 영향을 주었다. 오늘날에야 비로소 발간되는 그의 방대한 '수첩'은 프로이트를 예언하는, 심리적 통찰에 가득 찬 귀중한 인간기록이기도 하다. 가장 낭만주의적인 작품을 쓴 시인·사회비평가·문학평론가·신학자·심리학자로서 그는 인간 존재와 전우주의 본질적인 창조적 원칙을 해명하고자 노력하였다.

This Lime-tree Bower my Prison*

Wander in gladness, and wind down, perchance,
To that still roaring dell, of which I told;
The roaring dell, o'erwooded, narrow, deep,
And only speckled by the mid-day sun;
Where its slim trunk the ash from rock to rock
Flings arching like a bridge;—that branchless ash,
Unsunn'd and damp, whose few poor yellow leaves
Ne'er tremble in the gale, yet tremble still,
Fann'd by the water-fall!

. . .

So my friend
  Struck with deep joy may stand, as I have stood,
  Silent with swimming sense; yea, gazing round
  On the wide landscape, gaze till all doth seem
  Less gross than bodily; and of such hues
  As veil the Almighty Spirit, when yet he makes
  Spirits perceive his presence.

Kubla Khan**

A damsel with a dulcimer
  In a vision once I saw:

---

* "This Lime-Tree Bower My Prison" is a poem written by Samuel Taylor Coleridge during 1797. The poem discusses a time in which Coleridge was forced to stay beneath a lime tree while his friends were able to enjoy the countryside. Within the poem, Coleridge is able to connect to his friend's experience and enjoy nature through him, which keeps the lime tree from being a mental prison in addition to a physical one.

** The legendary story behind the poem is that Coleridge wrote the poem following an

It was an Abyssinian maid

And on her dulcimer she played,

Singing of Mount Abora.

. . .

Beware! Beware!

His flashing eyes, his floating hair!

Weave a circle round him thrice,

And close your eyes with holy dread

For he on honey-dew hath fed,

And drunk the milk of Paradise.

Frost at Midnight*

My babe so beautiful! it thrills my heart

With tender gladness, thus to look at thee,

And think that thou shalt learn far other lore

And in far other scenes!

. . .

But thou, my babe! shalt wander like a breeze

By lakes and sandy shores, beneath the crags

Of ancient mountain, and beneath the clouds,

Which image in their bulk both lakes and shores

---

opium-influenced dream. In this particular poem, Coleridge seems to explore the depths of dreams and creates landscapes that could not exist in reality. The "sunny pleasure-dome with caves of ice" exemplifies the extreme fantasy of the world in which Kubla Khan lives.

* In "Frost at Midnight," Coleridge explores the relationship between environment and happiness and also reflects on the idyllic innocence of childhood. The construction of this poem, in which Coleridge's infant son is the silent listener, is significant for Coleridge's musings on the above themes. In "Coleridge the Revisionary: Surrogacy and Structure in the Conversation Poems," Peter Barry highlights the "surrogacy" element that is present in many of Coleridge's conversation poems.

And mountain crags: so shalt thou see and hear
The lovely shapes and sounds intelligible
Of that eternal language, which thy God
Utters, who fro eternity doth teach
Himself in all, and all things in himself.
Great universal Teacher! he shall mould
They spirit, and by giving make it ask.

    Therefore all seasons shall be sweet to thee,
Whether the summer clothe the general earth
With greenness, or the redbreast sit and sing
Betwixt the tufts of snow on the bare branch
Of mossy apple-tree, while the nigh thatch
Smokes in the sunthaw; whether the eve-drops fall
Heard only in the trances of the blast,
Or if the secret ministry of frost
Shall hang them up in silent icicles,
Quietly shining to the quiet Moon.

(3) 윌리엄 워즈워스 William Wordsworth, 1770–1850

워즈워스는 잉글랜드 북부 컴벌랜드의 코커머스 출생이다. 변호사의 아들로 태어나 소년시절을 이 호수지방에서 보냈다. 8세 때 어머니를, 13세 때 아버지를 잃고 백부의 보호로 1787년 케임브리지 대학에 입학하였고, 재학 중에는 프랑스와 알프스 지방을 도보로 여행한 일도 있다. 1791년 학교를 마치자 다시 프랑스로 건너가 때마침 절정기에 이른 프랑스혁명의 이상에서 깊은 감명을 받았다. 오를레앙에 머무는 동안 A. 발롱이라는 여성과 사랑에 깊이 빠져 딸을 낳기까지 하였으나, 이 일은 오랫동안 비밀로 숨겨져 왔다.

1793년에 『저녁의 산책』과 『소묘풍경』을 출판하였는데, 시형은 상투적인 영웅대운이지만, 곳곳에 생생한 자연묘사가 돋보였다. 프랑스 혁명으로 영국과 프랑스 사이의 국교가 악화되자 그는 공화주의적인 정열과 조국애와의 갈등 때문에 깊은 고뇌에 빠졌다. 그 때 쓴 비극 『변경 사람들』에는 혁명과 고드윈적인 합리적 급진주의에 대한 반성이 엿보인다.

1795년, 친구의 도움으로 누이 도러시와 레이스다운으로 옮겨 조용한 자연과 누이의 자상한 애정으로 마음의 안정을 되찾아 갔다. 1797년 여름에는 다시 올폭스덴으로 전거하여 가까운 곳에 살고 있던 S. T. 콜리지와 친교를 맺으면서 그에게서 영향을 받았다. 1798년 이 두 시인은 공동으로 『서정가요집』(Lyrical Ballads)을 출판하였다. 이 책에서 콜리지는 초자연의 세계를, 워즈워스는 일상의 비근한 사건을 각각 다룸으로써 새로운 시경을 개척, 영문학사상 낭만주의 부활의 한 시기를 결정짓는 시집이 되었다. 여기에는 그의 초기 대표시 「틴턴 수도원」("Lines Composed A Few Miles above Tintern Abbey")이 포함되어 있다. 1800년 개정판을 냈으며, 영국 최초의 낭만주의 문학 선언이라고 볼 수 있는 그 서문에서 '시골 가난한 사람들의 스스로의 감정의 발로만이 진실된 것이며, 그들이 사용하는 소박하고 친근한 언어야말로 시에 알맞은 언어'라고 하여 18세기식 기교적 시어를 배척하고 있다.

초판이 발간된 지 얼마 안 되어 이들 세 사람은 독일로 여행을 떠나 고슬라에서 겨울을 보냈다. 향수 탓이었는지 그는 그 곳에서 한 영국 소녀를 주제로 한 『루시의 노래』를 썼고, 또한 자신의 시심이 성장해온 발자취를 내면적으로 더듬은 『서곡』(Prelude)을 집필하기 시작하였다. 1799년 독일에서 귀국한 뒤 누이와 함께 그래스미어 호반의 더브코티지에서 살았다. 1802년 누이의 친구 M. 허친슨과 결혼하였는데, 이 무렵 동생 존이 사고로 죽고, 콜리지가 병석에 눕게 되는 등 심로가 겹쳤고, 또 한편으로는 국외 정세의 변화로 해서 열렬한 애국자가 되었다.

그러나『서정가요집』이후의 10년간이 시작 면에서는 가장 왕성한 시기였으며, 그는 이 시기에 늙은 양치기와 그의 아들의 운명을 그린『마이켈』을 썼고, 대표작『서곡』(*The Prelude*)을 완성하였으며, 이 밖에 2권의 시집을 내 놓았다. 이 시집에는 「나는 홀로 구름처럼 헤매었다」("I Wandered Lonely as a Cloud"), 「홀로 추수하는 아가씨」("The Solitary Reaper") 등의 주옥같은 명시가 수록되었다.

시인으로서의 명성은 1820년경부터 점차 높아져 1843년에는 R. 사우디의 뒤를 이어 계관시인이 되었다. J. 톰슨, W. 쿠퍼 등에서 싹트기 시작한 자연에 대한 감수성이 워즈워스에 이르러 가장 심오해졌으며, 그리고 자연에의 미적 관심이 동양에 비하여 희박하였던 유럽에 있어 그와 같은 범신론적 자연관이 나타났다는 사실은 영문학에만 그치지 않고 유럽 문화의 역사상 커다란 뜻을 지녔다고 할 수 있다.

The Daffodils*

I wandered lonely as a cloud
That floats on high o'er vales and hills,
When all at once I saw a crowd,
A host, of golden daffodils;

---

* This poem, obviously inspired by Wordsworth's stomping grounds, is well-loved because of its simple yet beautiful rhythms and rhymes, and its rather sentimental topic. The poem consists of four six-line stanzas, each of which follow an ababcc rhyme scheme and are written in iambic tetrameter, giving the poem a subtle back-and-forth motion that recalls swaying daffodils.

Beside the lake, beneath the trees,
Fluttering and dancing in the breeze.

Continuous as the stars that shine
And twinkle on the milky way,
They stretched in never-ending line
Along the margin of a bay:
Ten thousand saw I at a glance,
Tossing their heads in sprightly dance.

The waves beside them danced; but they
Out-did the sparkling waves in glee:
A poet could not but be gay,
In such a jocund company:
I gazed—and gazed—but little thought
What wealth the show to me had brought:

For oft, when on my couch I lie
In vacant or in pensive mood,
They flash upon that inward eye
Which is the bliss of solitude;
And then my heart with pleasure fills,
And dances with the daffodils. (1998년 중등영어 임용고시 기출문제)

She Dwelt among the Untrodden Ways*

She dwelt among the untrodden ways
            Beside the springs of Dove,

---

* The poem celebrates an admired girl or young woman (a "Maid") by associating her with the
  beauties of nature. Both in its topic and its method, the poem is a prototypical representative

A Maid whom there were none to praise
　　And very few to love:

A violet by a mossy stone
　　Half hidden from the eye!
—Fair as a star, when only one
　　Is shining in the sky.

She lived unknown, and few could know
　　When Lucy ceased to be;
But she is in her grave, and, oh,
　　The difference to me! (2008년 중등영어 임용고시 기출문제)

The Solitary Reaper*

Behold her, single in the field,
Yon solitary Highland Lass!
Reaping and singing by herself;
Stop here, or gently pass!
Alone she cuts and binds the grain,
And sings a melancholy strain;

---

piece of Romantic writing. Other common Romantic traits of this work include its relatively simple, straightforward language; its emphasis on the personal, emotional expression of a particular speaker; its concern with rural life; its freedom from references to classical mythology (such as were often used in earlier poetry); and its short, lyric form.

* "The Solitary Reaper" is a short lyrical ballad, composed of thirty-two lines and divided into four stanzas. As the title suggests, the poem is dominated by one main figure, a Highland girl standing alone in a field harvesting grain. The poem is written in the first person and can be classified as a pastoral, or a literary work describing a scene from country life. The eyewitness narration conveys the immediacy of personal experience, giving the reader the impression that the poet did not merely imagine the scene but actually lived it.

O listen! for the Vale profound
Is overflowing with the sound.

No Nightingale did ever chaunt
More welcome notes to weary bands
Of travellers in some shady haunt,
Among Arabian sands:
A voice so thrilling ne'er was heard
In spring-time from the Cuckoo-bird,
Breaking the silence of the seas
Among the farthest Hebrides.

Will no one tell me what she sings? —
Perhaps the plaintive numbers flow
For old, unhappy, far-off things,
And battles long ago:
Or is it some more humble lay,
Familiar matter of to-day?
Some natural sorrow, loss, or pain,
That has been, and may be again?

Whate'er the theme, the Maiden sang
As if her song could have no ending;
I saw her singing at her work,
And o'er the sickle bending; —
I listened, motionless and still;
And, as I mounted up the hill,
The music in my heart I bore,
Long after it was heard no more.

My heart leaps up when I behold*

My heart leaps up when I behold
A rainbow in the sky:
So was it when my life began,
  So is it now I am a man,
So be it when I shall grow old
    Or let me die!
The child is father of the man:
And I could wish my days to be
Bound each to each by natural piety.

The Prelude**
Imagination and Taste, How impaired and Restored

In trivial occupations, and the round
        Of ordinary intercourse — our minds
        Are nourished and invisibly repaired;
        A virtue, by which pleasure is enhanced,
        That penetrates, enables us to mount,
        When high, more high, and lifts us up when fallen.

---

* Written on March 26, 1802 and published in 1807 as an epigraph to "Ode: Intimations of Immortality," this poem addresses the same themes found in "Tintern Abbey" and "Ode; Intimations of Immortality," albeit in a much more concise way. The speaker explains his connection to nature, stating that it has been strong throughout his life. He even goes so far as to say that if he ever loses his connection he would prefer to die.

** Wordsworth's blank-verse narrative, often achieving Miltonic sublimity, is punctuated by hauntingly recalled "spots of time" which Wordsworth links to intimations of his future poetic calling. These "spots" include the earliest moments of moral and spiritual awareness and are usually associated with an intensely felt response to nature.

This efficacious spirit chiefly lurks
Among those passages of life that give
Profoundest knowledge to what point, and how,
The mind is lord and master—outward sense
The obedient servant of her will.

The prelude
Introduction-Childhood and School Time

'twas my joy
With store of springes o'er my shoulder hung
To range the open heights . . .
Scudding away from snare to snare.

. . .

I heard among the solitary hills
Low breathings coming after me

. . .

I stood and watched
Till all was tranquil as a dreamless sleep.

. . .

for I would walk alone,
Under the quiet stars, and at that time
Have felt whate'er there is of power in sound
To breathe an elevated mood, by form
Or image unprofaned.

Ode

Intimations of Immortality from Recollections of Early Childhood*

Our birth is but a sleep and a forgetting.

. . .

Not in entire forgetfulness,
      And not in utter nakedness,
But trailing clouds of glory do we come
      From God, who is our home

. . .

The rainbow comes and goes,
      And lovely is the rose.

. . .

The cataracts blow their trumpets from the steep;
No more shall grief of mine the season wrong;
I hear the echoes through the mountains throng.

. . .

Whither is fled the visionary gleam?
Where is it now, the glory and the dream?

. . .

Mighty prophet! Seer blest!
      On whom those truths do rest,
Which we are toiling all our lives to find.

. . .

But for those obstinate questionings
      Of sense and outward things.

---

* "Ode; Intimations of Immortality" is a long and rather complicated poem about
Wordsworth's connection to nature and his struggle to understand humanity's failure to
recognize the value of the natural world. The poem is elegiac in that it is about the regret
of loss. Wordsworth is saddened by the fact that time has stripped away much of nature's
glory, depriving him of the wild spontaneity he exhibited as a child.

. . .

Hence in a season of calm weather
    Though inland far we be,
Our souls have sight of that immortal sea
    Which brought us hither,
    Can in a moment travel thither,
And see the children sport upon the shore,
And hear the mighty waters rolling evermore.

. . .

To me the meanest flower that blows can give
Thoughts that do often lie too deep for tears.

Composed upon Westminster Bridge, September 3, 1802*

Open unto the fields, and to the sky;
All bright and glittering in the smokeless air.
Never did sun more beautifully steep
In his first splendour, valley, rock, or hill.

(2013년 중등영어 임용고시 기출문제)

---

* "Composed upon Westminster Bridge, September 3, 1802" is an Italian sonnet, written in iambic pentameter with ten syllables per line. The rhyme scheme of the poem is abbaabbacdcdcd. The poem was actually written about an experience that took place on July 31, 1802 during a trip to France with Wordsworth's sister, Dorothy Wordsworth. The poem begins with a rather shocking statement, especially for a Romantic poet: "Earth has not anything to show more fair." This statement is surprising because Wordsworth is not speaking of nature, but of the city. He goes on to list the beautiful man-made entities therein, such as "Ships, towers, domes, theatres and temples." In fact, nature's influence isn't described until the 7th line, when the speaker relates that the city is "open to the fields, and to the sky." While the city itself may not be a part of nature, it is certainly not in conflict with nature. This becomes even more clear in the next line, when the reader learns that the air is "smokeless".

(4) 조지 고든 바이런 George Gordon Byron, Lord Byron, 1788-1824

　영국 런던에서 태어났으며 아버지는 미남이었으나, '미치광이 존'이라는 별명을 들을 정도로 방종한 가난뱅이 사관으로, 전처의 자식이 있었다. 후처로 들어온 바이런의 어머니 캐서린 고든은 스코틀랜드의 어느 부호의 재산 상속인이었으며, 바이런은 이 두 사람 사이에서 독자로 태어났다. 1791년 아내의 재산마저 탕진해 버린 아버지가 프랑스에서 방랑하다가 죽자, 그는 어머니의 고향인 스코틀랜드 북동부의 항구도시 애버딘에서 자랐다. 어머니는 변덕스러운 성격으로 오른 다리가 기형인 아들에게 냉담하기도 하였다. 독실한 청교도인 유모 메이 그레이의 칼뱅주의의 종교교육을 받아 후일 이 시인의 악마주의는 심각한 내부적 반항으로 승화되었다.

　1798년 제5대 바이런 남작이 죽음으로써 제6대를 상속하여, 조상 대대로 내려오는 노팅엄셔의 낡은 뉴스테드 애비의 영주가 되었다. 이듬해 런던에 올라와 다리지의 예비 칼리지를 거쳐 해로 스쿨에 다녔다. 다리는 부자유하였으나 수영과 크리켓도 잘 하였다. 1805년, 케임브리지 대학의 트리니티 칼리지에 들어가, 시집 『게으른 나날』(*Hours of Idleness*)을 출판하였다. 이 시집에 대한 『에든버러 평론』지의 악평에 분개하여 그는 당시의 문단을 비평한 풍자시 『잉글랜드의 시인들과 스코틀랜드의 비평가들』(*English Bards and Scotch Reviewers*)로 울분을 풀었다.

　그 후 생활태도에 대한 반성과 새로운 모험의 꿈을 안고 소작인의 아들과 종복, 친구 홉하우스를 데리고 배로 고국을 떠났다. 그는 이 때 이미 성년으로 상원에 의석을 두고 있었다. 리스본에서 육로로 에스파냐를 돌아보고, 몰타섬과 알바니아를 거쳐 아테네와 마라톤에 들렀으며, 스미르나에 머물면서 장편서사시 『차일드 해럴드의 편력』(*Childe Harold's Pilgrimage, Cantos I & II*)을 썼다. 그 후 2년 남짓한 긴 여행을 끝마치고 1811년에 귀국하였다. 1812년 상원에서 산업혁명기 방직공의 소요탄압에 항의하는 열변을 토해 이름을 떨쳤으며, 또『차일드 해럴드의 편력』의 출판으로도 생의 권태와 동경을 실은 분방한 시풍과 이국정서가 큰 호응을 얻어 일약 유명해졌다.

그 후 스콧의 뒤를 이어 담시『아바이도스의 신부』(*The Bride of Abydos*),『해적』(*The Corsair*),『라라』(*Lara, A Tale*) 등을 잇달아 출판하였으며, 반속적인 천재시인, 미남인 젊은 독신귀족이라 하여 런던 사교계의 총아로 등장하였고, 캐롤라인 램 남작부인, 이복누이 오거스터 리 부인, 옥스퍼드 백작부인 등과 관계를 가졌다. 1815년 양가의 딸인 애너벨러 밀뱅크와 결혼하였으며,『헤브라이 영창』(*Hebrew Melodies*),『파리지나』(*Parisina*)를 출판하였다. 그러나 딸 출생 후 아내의 별거 요구로 1816년 고국을 떠났다. 그해 여름을 셀리 부부와 스위스에서 지내면서,『차일드 해럴드의 편력』,『실롱의 죄수』(*The Prisoner of Chillon*) 등을 썼다.

셀리가 영국에서 온 이듬해인 1819년에는 테레사 귀치올리 백작부인과 동거생활을 하였는데, 그 동안에도『돈 주안』(*Don Juan*)을 계속하여 썼으며,『단테의 예언』(*The Prophecy of Dante*)과 4편의 시극『마리노 팔리에로』(*Marino Faliero*) 등을 썼다. 1822년에 셀리와 리헌트를 불러『리버럴』지를 발간하여, 풍자시『심판의 꿈』(*The Vision of Judgment*) 등을 발표하였으나, 셀리의 익사로 4호밖에 내지 못하고 폐간하였다. 1823년 그리스 독립군을 도우러 갔다가, 고난 끝에 1824년 4월 미솔롱기온에서 말라리아에 걸려 사망하였다. 그러나 바이런의 비통한 서정, 습속에 대한 반골, 날카로운 풍자, 근대적인 내적 고뇌, 다채로운 서간 등은 전 유럽을 풍미하였고, 한국에서도 일찍부터 그의 작품이 널리 애송되었다.

When we Two parted*

When we two parted
  In silence and tears,
Half broken-hearted
  To sever for years,
Pale grew thy cheek and cold,
  Colder thy kiss;
Truly that hour foretold
  Sorrow to this.

She Walks in Beauty**

She walks in beauty, like the night
  Of cloudless climes and starry skies;
And all that's best of dark and bright
  Meet in her aspect and her eyes;
Thus mellowed to that tender light
  Which heaven to gaudy day denies.
 . . .
And on that cheek, and o'er that brow,
  So soft, so calm, yet eloquent,

---

* The poem is highly autobiographical in that it recounts Byron's emotional state following the end of his secret affair with Lady Frances and his frustration at her unfaithfulness to him with the Duke.

** Byron wrote this poem about Mrs. Wilmot, his cousin Robert Wilmot's wife. It echoes Wordsworth's earlier "The Solitary Reaper" (1807) in its conceit: the speaker's awe upon seeing a woman walking in her own aura of beauty. While ostensibly about a specific woman, the poem extends to encompass the unobtainable and ideal. The lady is not beautiful in herself, but she walks in an aura of Beauty (Flesch 1).

The smiles that win, the tints that glow,

    But tell of days in goodness spent,

A mind at peace with all below,

    A heart whose love is innocent!

(5) 퍼시 비시 셸리 Percy Bysshe Shelley, 1792-1822

잉글랜드 필드플레이스 출신으로 섬세한 정감을 노래한 전형적인 서정시인으로, 영국 낭만파 중에서 가장 이상주의적인 비전을 그렸다. 작품이나 생애가 압제와 인습에 대한 반항, 이상주의적인 사랑과 자유의 동경으로 일관하여 바이런과 함께 낭만주의 시대의 가장 인기 있는 작가였다. 영국 남부 시골 귀족의 아들로, 이튼칼리지에서 옥스퍼드 대학으로 진학하였으나, 1811년 『무신론의 필연성』(*The Necessity of Atheism*)이라는 소책자를 출판·배포한 이유로 퇴학처분을 받았다. 1811년 여름 해리엇 웨스트브룩이라는 16세의 소녀와 결혼하였다. 무정부주의자이며 자유사상가인 W. 고드윈의 강력한 영향을 받아, 정치적 이상을 노래한 『매브 여왕』(*Queen Mab*)을 발표할 무렵, 고드윈의 딸 메리와 친해졌고, 애정 생활의 파탄을 비관한 해리엇은 1816년 투신자살했다. 그 해 메리와 정식 결혼한 그는 스위스를 여행, 시인 바이런과 알게 되어 교우관계가 시작되었다.

이 무렵의 작품은 '고독한 영혼'이란 부제가 붙은 서사시 『고독한 영혼』(*Alastor*), 정치시 『이슬람의 반란』(*The Revolt of Islam*), 플라톤의 『향연』의 번역 등이다. 영국정부를 비판한 『무질서한 가면극』(*The Masque of Anarchy*)과 워즈워스를 풍자한 『피터 벨 3세』(*Peter Bell the Third*)에 이어서, 16세기 로마에서 일어난 근친상간과 살인사건을 소재로 한 시극 대작 『첸치 일가』(*The Cenci*)와 대표작 『사슬에서 풀린 프로메테우스』(*Prometheus*

Unbound)를 발표하였다. 이 대표작이 발표되던 해에 셸리 부처는 이탈리아의 피사에 정착하였고, 『서풍의 노래』(*Ode to the West Wind*), 『종달새에 부쳐』(*To a Skylark*) 등 탁월한 서정시를 발표하였다. 1821년에는 이상적인 사랑을 노래한 시 『에피사이키디온』(*Epipsychidion*), 그리스 독립전쟁에 촉발된 『헬라스』(*Hellas*), 키츠의 죽음을 슬퍼하는 애가 『애도네이스』(*Adonais*), 시인의 예언자적 사명을 선언한 시론으로 유명한 『시의 옹호』(*A Defence of Poetry*) 등을 썼다. 장시 『생의 승리』(*The Triumph of Life*)를 미완성으로 남겨둔 채, 1822년 7월 스페치아 만을 요트로 항해 중 익사하였다.

Adonais: An Elegy on the Death of John Keats*

I weep for Adonais—he is dead!
    Oh, weep for Adonais! though our tears
    Thaw not the frost which binds so dear a head!

Ozymandias**

I MET a Traveler from an antique land,
Who said: "Two vast and trunkless legs of stone
Stand in the desert. Near them, on the sand,
Half sunk, a shattered visage lies, whose frown,

---

* Shelley wrote this long poem as an elegy for Shelley's close friend and fellow poet John Keats, who died in Rome of tuberculosis at the age of 26. The mood of the poem begins in dejection, but ends in optimism—hoping Keats' spark of brilliance reverberates through the generations of future poets and inspires revolutionary change throughout Europe. Adonis is the stand-in for Keats, for he too died at a young age after being mauled by a boar.
** The first-person poetic persona states that he met a traveler who had been to "an antique

And wrinkled lip, and sneer of cold command,
Tell that its sculptor well those passions read,
Which yet survive, stamped on these lifeless things,
The hand that mocked them and the heart that fed:
And on the pedestal these words appear:
"My name is OZYMANDIAS, King of Kings."
Look on my works ye Mighty, and despair!
No thing beside remains. Round the decay
Of that Colossal Wreck, boundless and bare,
The lone and level sands stretch far away."

(1999년 중등영어 임용고시 기출문제)

To a Skylark*

Hail to thee, blithe Spirit!
    Bird thou never wert,
That from Heaven, or near it,
    Pourest thy full heart
In profuse strains of unpremeditated art.

    Higher still and higher
    From the earth thou springest
Like a cloud of fire;

---

land." The traveler told him that he had seen a vast but ruined statue, where only the legs remained standing. The face was sunk in the sand, frowning and sneering. The sculptor interpreted his subject well. There also was a pedestal at the statue, where the traveler read that the statue was of "Ozymandias, King of Kings."

* The persona extols the virtues of the skylark, a bird that soars and sings high in the air. It flies too high to see, but it can be heard, making it like a spirit, or a maiden in a tower, or a glow-worm hidden in the grass, or the scent of a rose. The skylark's song is better than the sound of rain and better than human poetry.

                    The blue deep thou wingest,
And singing still dost soar, and soaring ever singest.
. . .

     Teach me half the gladness
               That thy brain must know,
          Such harmonious madness
               From my lips would flow
The world should listen then, as I am listening now.

To Wordsworth*

Poet of Nature, thou hast wept to know
That things depart which never may return:
Childhood and youth, friendship and love's first glow,
Have fled like sweet dreams, leaving thee to mourn.
These common woes I feel. One loss is mine
Which thou too feel'st, yet I alone deplore.
Thou wert as a lone star, whose light did shine
On some frail bark in winter's midnight roar:
Thou hast like to a rock-built refuge stood
Above the blind and battling multitude:
In honoured poverty thy voice did weave
Songs consecrate to truth and liberty,—
Deserting these, thou leavest me to grieve,
Thus having been, that thou shouldst cease to be.

---

* "To Wordsworth", this poem makes it seem as if Wordsworth died and Shelley is grieving him. However, he isn't! Wordsworth was alive long after Shelley had already passed. Instead, this poem is either speaking about someone else to Wordsworth or speaking about Wordsworth literally leaving and not his death. "To Wordsworth" is a poem of only one stanza. It contains fourteen lines and is written in iambic-pentameter. It has the rhyme scheme ABABCDCD-EEFGFG. It is an Italian Sonnet.

Mutability*

We are as clouds that veil the midnight moon;
  How restlessly they speed, and gleam, and quiver,
Streaking the darkness radiantly!—yet soon
  Night closes round, and they are lost forever:

Or like forgotten lyres, whose dissonant strings
  Give various response to each varying blast,
To whose frail frame no second motion brings
  One mood or modulation like the last.

We rest.—A dream has power to poison sleep;
  We rise.—One wandering thought pollutes the day;
We feel, conceive or reason, laugh or weep;
  Embrace fond woe, or cast our cares away:

It is the same!—For, be it joy or sorrow,
  The path of its departure still is free:
Man's yesterday may ne'er be like his morrow;
  Nought may endure but Mutability.

---

* In typical Romantic fashion, Shelley immediately places humans in the same physical realm as nature, opening with "We are as clouds." Immediately following, however, Shelley focuses on human agency and compares humans to things invented, this time using the simile "like forgotten lyres." (A lyre is a musical instrument, a Greek wind harp.) The purpose of the two comparisons is to emphasize the eternal human condition of change, in other words, to be mutable.

Mont Blanc*

Lines Written in the Vale of Chamouni

THE EVERLASTING universe of things
Flows through the mind, and rolls its rapid waves,
Now dark, now glittering, now reflecting gloom,
Now lending splendor, where from secret springs
The source of human thought its tribute brings
Of waters,—with a sound but half its own,
Such as a feeble brook will oft assume
In the wild woods, among the mountains lone,
Where waterfalls around it leap forever,
Where woods and winds contend, and a vast river
Over its rocks ceaselessly bursts and raves.

(6) 토머스 모어 Thomas Moore, 1779-1852

토머스 모어는 더블린 출신으로 주로 런던에서 지냈다. 어렸을 때부터 시에 몰두, 1809년 아나크레온의 번역 작품을 냈고, 이듬해 토머스 리틀 (Thomas Little)이라는 필명으로 시집을 내어 인정을 받았다. 1803년 버뮤다 제도 해군등기관이 되었으나 대역에게 일을 맡기고 캐나다와 미국을 여행, 후에 공금을 쓴 책임을 지고 이를 변상하느라 고생하였다. 1807-1834년에 서정 단시집 『아일랜드 가요』(*A Selection of Irish Melodies*)를 존 스티븐

---

* Mont Blanc is the highest peak in the Swiss Alps near the French/Italy border. Picture the young Shelley standing on a bridge over the Arvre River in the Valley of Chamonix, in what is now southeastern France. The poem resembles works of the earlier Romantics, specifically Wordsworth's "Tintern Abbey," which was a major influence on Shelley during his writing of this piece. Both poems "question the significance of the interchange between nature and the human mind" (Abrams 1740).

슨 경의 작곡으로 내어 그 민족적 감정으로 좋은 평을 얻었다. 그러나 그를 유명하게 만든 것은 이국적 정서가 넘치는 페르시아의 설화시 『랄라루크』(*Lalla Rookh*)였다.

그 동안 G. G. 바이런과 알게 되어 친교를 맺는 한편, 당시의 섭정 정부에 대한 통렬한 정치적 풍자시를 써서 커다란 반향을 일으켰다. 그 밖에 애국적인 시집이나 『파리의 파지 일가』(*The Fudge Family in Paris*) 등 영국인에 대한 유머러스한 풍자시로도 성공하였다.

Believe Me, If All Those Endearing Young Charms *

BELIEVE me, if all those endearing young charms,
    Which I gaze on so fondly to-day,
Were to change by to-morrow, and fleet in my arms,
    Like fairy-gifts fading away,
Thou wouldst still be ador'd, as this moment thou art,
    Let thy loveliness fade as it will,
And around the dear ruin each wish of my heart
    Would entwine itself verdantly still.

---

* The tune to which Moore set his words is a traditional Irish air, first printed in a London songbook in 1775. It is occasionally wrongly credited to Sir William Davenant, whose older collection of tunes may have been the source for later publishers, including a collection titled General Collection of Ancient Irish Music, compiled by Edward Bunting in 1796. Sir John Andrew Stevenson has been credited as responsible for the music for Moore's setting. It is thought that after Thomas Moore's wife, Elizabeth, was badly scarred by smallpox, she refused to leave her room, believing herself ugly and unlovable. To convince her his love was unwavering, Moore composed the 'Endearing' poem which he set to an old Irish melody and sang outside her bedroom door. He later wrote that this restored her confidence and re-kindled their love

It is not while beauty and youth are thine own,
   And thy cheeks unprofan'd by a tear,
That the fervour and faith of a soul can be known,
   To which time will but make thee more dear;
No, the heart that has truly lov'd never forgets,
   But as truly loves on to the close,
As the sun-flower turns on her god, when he sets,
   The same look which she turn'd when he rose.

'Tis The Last Rose of Summer *

   'TIS the last rose of summer,
      Left blooming alone;
   All her lovely companions
      Are faded and gone;
   No flower of her kindred,
      No rose-bud is nigh,
   To reflect back her blushes,
      Or give sigh for sigh.

   I'll not leave thee, thou lone one !
      To pine on the stem;
   Since the lovely are sleeping,
      Go sleep thou with them.
   Thus kindly I scatter

---

* The poem is set to a traditional tune called "Aislean an Oigfear" or "The Young Man's
Dream", which had been transcribed by Edward Bunting in 1792 based on a performance by
harper Donnchadh Ó hÁmsaigh (Denis Hempson) at the Belfast Harp Festival. The Poem
and the tune together were published in December 1813 in volume 5 of Moore's Irish
Melodies (full title: A Selection of Irish Melodies).

Thy leaves o'er the bed,
    Where thy mates of the garden
        Lie scentless and dead.

So soon may I follow,
    When friendships decay,
And from Love's shining circle
    The gems drop away.
When true hearts lie wither'd,
    And fond ones are flown,
Oh ! who would inhabit
    This bleak world alone ?

(7) 존 키츠 John Keats, 1795–1821

존 키츠는 런던 출신으로 마차 대여업자의 아들로 태어나 소년시절에
부모를 여의었다. 클라크 사숙 재학 중에 학교 도서를 모조리 탐독하였고,
특히 영국의 시인과 그리스·로마의 신화에 열중하였다. 졸업 후에는 생계
를 위하여 남의 집 서생이 되기도 하고, 병원에도 근무하면서 대시인이 될
희망을 품고 독서와 시작에 몰두하였다. 의학을 배운 5년 만에 의사 시험에
합격하여 개업면허증을 받았는데 그 성공은 키츠가 의학보다는 문학 공부
에 몰두하였다는 사정을 알고 있는 친구들의 시기심을 살 만큼 그의 특출
한 자질을 증명하는 하나의 사건이었다. 그러나 이듬해 그는 화가 세반과
비평가 J. H. L. 헌트 등 친구들의 격려로 병원 근무를 사직하고 시작에 전
념하게 되었다. 1817년 22세 때 처녀시집 『시집』을 출판하였고, 이듬해에
야심적인 장시 『엔디미온』(Endymion)을 발표하여 큰 발전을 보였다. 그러나
당시에는 그리스 신화에서 취재하여 이상미를 추구한 이 시가 혹평을 받았

을 뿐이었다. 이듬해에 패니 브라운과 사랑에 빠져 바로 약혼으로 진전되었는데, 그와 더불어 그의 생활도 폭과 깊이를 더하여 시에서도 비약적인 진보를 보여 잇달아 「그리스 항아리에 부치는 노래」("Ode on a Grecian Urn"), 「나이팅게일에게」("To a Nightingale"), 「가을에」("To Autumn") 등의 걸작을 써냈다. 이어 걸작 「하이피리언의 몰락」("The Fall of Hyperion")을 썼는데, 24세가 되던 1819년은 놀라울 만큼 그의 시가 많이 쏟아져 나오던 해였다. 병고에 시달리면서, 또 연애의 기쁨과 괴로움을 경험하면서 많은 명저를 냈으나, 이듬해에는 건강의 악화로 요양을 위하여 이탈리아로 건너갔다. 그러나 몇 달에 걸친 병상생활도 보람 없이 로마에서 25년 4개월이라는 짧은 생애를 끝마쳤다.

초기의 키츠는 감각미에 예민하여 짙은 색채를 즐겨 썼다. 특히 담시가 이 방면의 그 특징을 잘 나타내고 있다. 그러나 원숙기에 도달한 1819년의 키츠는 이미 단순한 감각미의 시인이 아니었다. 담담한 낙조의 경지에 들어가, 「그리스 항아리에 부치는 노래」의 마지막 구절 "아름다움이야말로 참이요, 참이야말로 아름다움"이라는 2행의 문장이 단적으로 나타내듯이 그는 영원한 모습에서 진선미의 조화, 또는 시인의 사명을 문제로 삼고 인생의 어두운 면을 괴로워하는 휴머니스트가 되어 있었다. 애인에게 보낸 연애서간도 그것을 읽는 사람으로 하여금 감동하게 하며, 또 그 서간에서 느끼는 인생경험과 시인으로서의 사명감은 25세도 채우지 못한 청년의 문장이라고는 생각하지 못할 만큼 깊은 것이다.

Bright Star! would I were steadfast as thou art*

Bright Star! would I were steadfast as thou art —
Not in lone splendour hung aloft the night,
And watching, with eternal lids apart,
Like Nature's patient sleepless Eremite,

The moving waters at their priestlike task
Of pure ablution round earth's human shores,
Or gazing on the new soft fallen mask
Of snow upon the mountains and the moors: —

No —yet still steadfast, still unchangeable,
Pillow'd upon my fair Love's ripening breast
To feel for ever its soft fall and swell,
Awake for ever in a sweet unrest;

Still, still to hear her tender-taken breath,
And so live ever, —or else swoon to death.

---

* "Bright Star!" considers a similar moment, and the sonnet is considered one of Keats's loveliest and most paradoxical. The speaker of the poem wishes he were as eternal as a star that keeps watch like a sleepless, solitary, and religious hermit over the "moving waters" and the "soft-fallen mask / Of snow." But while he longs for this unchanging state, he does not wish to exist by himself, in "lone splendor." Rather, he longs to be "Awake for ever" and "Pillowed upon my fair love's ripening breast." Unfortunately, these two desires —to experience love and to be eternal —do not go together. To love, he must be human, and therefore not an unchanging thing like the star.

On First Looking into Chapman's Homer*

Much have I travelled in the realms of gold,
   And many goodly states and kingdoms seen;
   Round many western islands have I been,
   Which bards in fealty to Apollo hold.
Oft of one wide expanse had I been told
   That deep-browed Homer ruled as his demesne;
   Yet did I never breathe its pure serene
   Till I heard Chapman speak out loud and bold:
Then felt I like some watcher of the skies,
   When a new planet swims into his ken;
   Or like stout Cortes when with eagle eyes
He stared 1 at the Pacific — and all his men
   Looked at each other with a wild surmise —
   Silent, upon a peak in Darien.

Ode to a Nightingale**

My heart aches, and a drowsy numbness pains
        My sense, as though of hemlock I had drunk,
Or emptied some dull opiate to the drains
        One minute past, and Lethe-wards had sunk:

---

* Keats has wide experience in the reading of poetry and is familiar with Homer's Iliad and Odyssey, but not until now has he had the special aesthetic enjoyment to be gained from reading Homer in the translation of George Chapman.

** Keats is in a state of uncomfortable drowsiness. Envy of the imagined happiness of the nightingale is not responsible for his condition; rather, it is a reaction to the happiness he has experienced through sharing in the happiness of the nightingale. The bird's happiness is conveyed in its singing.

'Tis not through envy of thy happy lot,
　　But being too happy in thine happiness, —
　　　　That thou, light-winged Dryad of the trees
　　　　　In some melodious plot
　　Of beechen green, and shadows numberless,
　　　　Singest of summer in full-throated ease.

La Belle Dame Sans Merci Ballad*

I.

O WHAT can ail thee, knight-at-arms,
　Alone and palely loitering?
The sedge has wither'd from the lake,
　And no birds sing.

II.

O what can ail thee, knight-at-arms!
　So haggard and so woe-begone?
The squirrel's granary is full,
　And the harvest's done.

III.

I see a lily on thy brow
　With anguish moist and fever dew,
And on thy cheeks a fading rose
　Fast withereth too.

---

* "La Belle Dame sans Merci" is a ballad, a medieval genre revived by the romantic poets. Keats uses the so-called ballad stanza, a quatrain in alternating iambic tetrameter and trimeter lines. The shortening of the fourth line in each stanza of Keats' poem makes the stanza seem a self-contained unit, gives the ballad a deliberate and slow movement, and is pleasing to the ear.

IV.

I met a lady in the meads,
   Full beautiful—a faery's child,
Her hair was long, her foot was light,
   And her eyes were wild.

Ode on Melancholy*

No, no, go not to Lethe, neither twist
     Wolf's-bane, . . .
. . . glut thy sorrow on a morning rose.
. . .

Or if thy mistress some rich anger shows,
    Emprison her soft hand, and let her rave,
       And feed deep, deep upon her peerless eyes.

. . .

Ay, in the very temple of Delight
    Veil'd Melancholy has her sovran shrine.
      Though seen of none save him whose strenuous tongue
    Can burst Joy's grape against his palate fine;
His soul shalt taste the sadness of her might,
      And be among her cloudy trophies hung.

---

* The "Ode to Melancholy" belongs to a class of eighteenth-century poems that have some form of melancholy as their theme. Such poetry came to be called the "Graveyard School of Poetry" and the best-known example of it is Thomas Gray's "Elegy in a Country Churchyard." The romantic poets inherited this tradition. One of the effects of this somber poetry about death, graveyards, the brevity of pleasure and of life was a pleasing feeling of melancholy.

Ode on a Grecian Urn*

O Attic shape! Fair attitude! with brede
       Of marble men and maidens overwrought.
. . .

Heard melodies are sweet, but those unheard
       Are sweeter.
. . .

therefore, ye soft pipes, play on;
Not to the sensual ear, but, more endear'd,
       Pipe to the spirit ditties of no tone.
. . .

Bold Lover, never, never canst thou kiss,
Though winning near the goal.
. . .

streets for evermore
       Will silent be; and not a soul to tell
       Why thou art desolate.

To Autumn**

1.

SEASON of mists and mellow fruitfulness,
       Close bosom-friend of the maturing sun;

---

* Keats has created a Greek urn in his mind and has decorated it with three scenes. The first
is full of frenzied action and the actors are men, or gods, and maidens. Other figures, or
possibly the male figures, are playing musical instruments. The maidens are probably the
nymphs of classical mythology. The men or gods are smitten with love and are pursuing
them. Keats, who loved classical mythology, had probably read stories of such love games
** "To Autumn" is one of the last poems written by Keats. His method of developing the

Conspiring with him how to load and bless
    With fruit the vines that round the thatch-eves run;
To bend with apples the moss'd cottage-trees,
    And fill all fruit with ripeness to the core;
        To swell the gourd, and plump the hazel shells
With a sweet kernel; to set budding more,
    And still more, later flowers for the bees,
    Until they think warm days will never cease,
        For Summer has o'er-brimm'd their clammy cells.

(8) 로버트 번스 Robert Burns, 1759–1796

스코틀랜드 에리셔 출신으로 각지의 농장을 돌아다니며 농사를 짓는 틈틈이 옛 시와 가요를 익혔으며, 스코틀랜드의 방언을 써서 자신의 사랑과 마을의 생활을 솔직하게 노래하였다. 최초의 시집 『주로 스코틀랜드 방언에 의한 시집』(*Poems, Chiefly in the Scottish Dialect*)으로 명성을 얻었으며, 한때는 에든버러에서 문단생활도 하였다. 그 후 고향에 돌아가 농장을 경영하였으나 실패하였고, 세금징수원으로 일하면서 옛 민요를 개작하기도 하고 시를 짓기도 하였다. 프랑스혁명에 공감하여 민족의 자유독립을 노래하여 당국의 주목을 받기도 하였다. 그의 시는 18세기 잉글랜드의 고전취미의 영향에서 벗어나, 스코틀랜드 서민의 소박하고 순수한 감정을 표현한 점에 특징이 있다. 『샌터의 탬』(*Tam o'Shanter*)을 비롯한 이야기시의 명작과, 『생쥐에게』(*To a Mouse*)와 『두 마리의 개』처럼 동물을 통하여 인도주의적 사상을 표현한 작품도 있으나, 역시 그의 진면목은 「둔 강둑」("The Banks

---

poem is to heap up imagery typical of autumn. His autumn is early autumn, when all the products of nature have reached a state of perfect maturity. Autumn is personified and is perceived in a state of activity.

of Doon")이나 「빨갛고 빨간 장미」("A Red, Red Rose")와 같이 자연과 여자를 노래한 서정시, 「올드 랭 사인」("Auld LangSyne")과 같은 가요에 있다. 지금도 그는 스코틀랜드의 국민시인으로 사랑과 존경을 받고 있다.

Auld Lang Syne*

Should auld acquaintance be forgot,
And never brought to mind?
Should auld acquaintance be forgot,
And days o' lang syne!

Chorus:
For auld lang syne, my dear
For auld lang syne,
We'll tak a cup o' kindness yet
For auld lang syne!

We twa hae run about the braes,
And pu'd the gowans fine,
But we've wander'd mony a weary foot
Sin' auld lang syne.

---

* Following his death, at the age of 37, Burns' poems traveled with the Scots diaspora and achieved international recognition as the influence of Scots increasingly took hold in all four corners of the globe. Today people from all parts of the world are familiar with his work, while his song 'Auld Lang Syne' is now widely sung to bring in the New Year, with the Scottish tradition of Hogmanay being, of course, internationally recognised.

A Red, Red Rose*

O my Luve is like a red, red rose
    That's newly sprung in June;
O my Luve is like the melody
    That's sweetly played in tune.

So fair art thou, my bonnie lass,
    So deep in luve am I;
And I will luve thee still, my dear,
    Till a' the seas gang dry.

Till a' the seas gang dry, my dear,
    And the rocks melt wi' the sun;
I will love thee still, my dear,
    While the sands o' life shall run.

And fare thee weel, my only luve!
    And fare thee weel awhile!
And I will come again, my luve,
    Though it were ten thousand mile.

---

* The poem opens with the speaker comparing his love to a "A Red, Red Rose" and to a
"melodie / That's sweetly play'd in tune!" In the second and third stanzas, the speaker
describes how deep his love is. And it's deep. He will love his "bonnie lass" as long as he
is alive, and until the world ends. At the end, he says adios, and notes that he will return,
even if he has to walk ten thousand miles.

빅토리아 시대 영국시 (1832-1901)

```
1832 : The First Reform Bill
1837 : Victoria becomes queen.
1846 : The Corn Laws repealed.
1850 : Tennyson succeeds Wordsworth as Poet Laureate.
1851 : The Great Exhibition in London.
1859 : Charles Darwin's Origin of Species published.
1870-71 : Franco-Prussian War.
1901 : Death of Victoria.
```

1. 시대적 배경

꼼꼼한 성찰은 후기 낭만주의 시대 문학에 반드시 등장하는 것으로, 시대 자체가 개개인의 작가와 마찬가지로 자기 분석적인 경향을 띠었다. 영국은 프랑스와의 오랜 전쟁(1793-1815)을 겪은 후 강대국이자 세계의 경제대국으로 부상했다. 세계 최초로 도시화·산업화된 사회라는 이 새로운 지위 때문에 이 시기에는 남다른 풍요·활력·자신감이 넘쳤다. 이 힘은 해외로 뻗어나가 대영제국의 발전으로 표현되었다. 국내에서는 급격한 사회변화와 격렬한 지적 논쟁이 일어났다. 산업이 가져다준 새로운 풍요와 전에 없던 새로운 종류의 도시빈민이 병존한다는 것은 이 길고 다양한 시기의 특징이랄 수 있는 많은 모순들 중 하나일 뿐이다. 종교에서는 신앙에 대한 유례없는 날카로운 공격과 때를 같이해 부흥운동이 절정에 달했다. 정치면에서는 경제적·개인적 자유에 대한 공약이 널리 퍼져 있었음에도 불구하고 정부의 권력이 점차 증대되었다. 빅토리아 시대의 치부인 거짓된 고상함은 사실 그만큼 심한 부도덕과 병행하고 있었다. 가장 근본적인 것은, 많은 작가들이 진보라고 받아들인 급격한 발전이 다른 사람들에게는 강한 향수를 불러일으키게 했다는 사실이다.

존 스튜어트 밀(John Stuart Mill)은 제러미 벤담(Jeremy Bentham, 1838)과 새뮤얼 테일러 콜리지(Samuel Taylor Coleridge, 1840)에 관한 평론에서 이러한 모순된 특성을 특유의 날카로움으로 간파했다. 그는 당시의 모든 사상가가 이 두 핵심 정신으로부터 많은 영향을 받았다고 주장했다. 그러나 끝까지 계몽주의를 주창한 벤담과 계몽주의에 대한 반동인 낭만주의를 대표하는 콜리지는 완전히 상반된 견해를 지녔다. 토머스 칼라일의 『의상철학』(*Sartor Resartus*, 1833-34)에서도 이와 비슷한 날카로운 논조를 느낄 수 있다. 스위프트와 스턴의 전통을 따르는 독특한 철학소설인 이 책에서 칼라일은 스스로 기계만능시대라고 보았던 당대에 새로운 정신적 각성을 부르짖었다.

(1) 초기 빅토리아 시대의 시

앨프레드 테니슨(Alfred Tennyson)은 『서정시집』(*Poems, Chiefly Lyrical*), 『시집』(*Poems*)으로 일찍 명성을 얻었다. 초기 작품에서 그는 후기 낭만주의 소재를 서정적으로 다루는 절묘한 재능을 발휘했다. 그의 작품들은 모두 키츠의 영향을 받아 1880년대의 프랑스 상징주의자들을 예견하게 한다. 그의 후기 작품이 지닌 가장 중요한 특징 중 하나는 빅토리아 시대 시가 형식면에서 이룬 최대의 혁신이라 할 수 있는 극적 독백의 사용이었다. 셸리에게서 깊은 영향을 받았던 로버트 브라우닝은 1842년 『극적 서정시집』(*Dramatic Lyrics*)을 발표하면서 독창적이면서도 현대적인 분위기를 찾아냈다. 제목이 시사하듯, 이 책은 극적 독백체의 시모음집이었다. 이 독백체는 브라우닝의 새로운 양식이 지닌 급진적인 독창성을 확실히 보여주었다. 즉 독자들이 범죄자나 인습에 얽매이지 않는 사람들의 정신상태와 공감하도록 만드는 효과를 지녔다. 시인 매슈 아널드의 처녀시집은 당시의 어두운 철학적 분위기에 대한 날카로운 인식과 서정적 우아함을 결합시킨 작품이다. 그러나 그의 가장 뛰어난 작품인 『스위스』(*Switzerland*), 『도버 해변』(*Dover Beach*), 『학자 집시』(*The Scholar-Gipsy*) 등은 항상 우울한 분위기이다. 1860년대 시에서 산문으로 돌아선 그는 『비평론』(*Essays in Criticism*), 『교양과 무질서』(*Culture and Anarchy*), 『문학과 독단』(*Literature and Dogma*)을 통해 생생하고 예리한 문학·사회·종교 비평을 선보였다.

(2) 후기 빅토리아 시대의 문학

후기 빅토리아 시대의 소설은 찰스 다윈(Charles Darwin) 시대의 많은 의문과 불확실성을 드러내지만, 미학적인 면에서는 새로운 세련미와 자신감을 보여주었다. 확신의 분위기를 만들어낸 대표적 인물 중 한 사람은 조지 엘리엇(George Eliot)이다. 그녀의 진보된 지적 흥미는 소설에 대한 한층 세련된 감각과 더불어 뛰어난 소설을 만들어내는 데 기여했다. 초기 소설 『애덤 비드』(*Adam Bede*), 『플로스 강변의 물방앗간』(*The Mill on the Floss*), 『사일러스 마너』(*Silas Marner*) 등은 영국의 전원생활을 주의 깊게 관찰한 연구서이다. 걸작 『미들마치』(*Middlemarch*)는 지방도시의 생활을 전례

없이 꼼꼼히 그려낸 작품으로, 2명의 주요 등장인물의 좌절된 이상주의에 초점을 맞추고 있다. 엘리엇과 같은 사실주의자인 앤소니 트롤럽(Anthony Trollope)은 바셋셔라는 가공의 마을을 배경으로 1867년에 완간된 6권의 장편소설 연작 중 첫 권인 『워든』(*The Warden*)으로 독자적인 소설양식을 확립했다.

　사실주의 소설이 융성함에 따라 그것과 정반대되는 로맨스가 부활한 것은 필연적이었다. 1860년대에는 새로운 하위 장르로 윌키 콜린스 등의 감각소설과 로버트 루이스 스티븐슨, 윌리엄 모리스, 오스카 와일드의 고딕 소설, 로맨스 및 모리스와 새뮤얼 버틀러의 유토피아 소설, H. G. 웰스의 초기 과학소설 등이 발표되어 전면적인 로맨스 부흥을 가져왔다. 토머스 하디는 이 세대의 가장 뛰어난 소설가라고 할 만하다. 그의 대표작은 전원생활을 다룬 비극적 소설인 『캐스터브리지의 시장』(*The Mayor of Casterbridge*), 『테스』(*Tess of the D'Urbervilles*), 『사생아 주드』(*Jude the Obscure*) 등이다. 이러한 소설에서는 가공의 웨식스 사람들과 풍경에 대한 뛰어난 묘사가 '모더니즘의 아픔'에 대한 복잡미묘한 느낌과 결합되어 나타난다. 라파엘 전파는 1848년에 형성되어 10년 후 비공식적으로 보강되었는데, 원래는 화가들의 모임으로 출발했으나 키츠로 대표되는 심미주의를 세기말의 데카당 운동과 연결시킨 문인들의 유파 역할도 했다. 단테 가브리엘 로제티의 시는 당대 생활을 미묘하게 다루면서 새로운 유형의 중세주의를 드러냈다. 모리스의 처녀시집이 보여준 놀라운 소재와 생생한 영상은 앨저넌 찰스 스윈번에 의해 더욱 발전되어, 『칼리돈의 아탈란타』(*Atalanta in Calydon*), 『시와 발라드』(*Poems and Ballads*)에서는 매혹적인 음악적 효과를 발휘하고 있다. 크리스티나 로제티의 섬세한 종교시는 라파엘 전파의 원래 목적인 경건성에 좀 더 충실한 것이라고 할 수 있다. 흥미를 끄는 이 시대의 또 다른 종교시인은 제러드 맨리 홉킨스(Gerard Manley Hopkins)로, 예수회 신부인 그의 작품은 그가 죽은 지 거의 30년 후인 1918년에『시집』
(*Poems*)으로 처음 엮어져 나왔다.

2. 주요 작가와 작품

(1) 크리스티나 로세티 Christina Rossetti, 1830-1894

런던 출신으로 D. G. 로세티의 누이동생으로, 어린 시절부터 시를 몹
시 좋아하였다. 1848년부터 오빠들의 결사인 '라파엘 전파'의 기관지에「꿈
의 나라」등 7편의 우수한 서정시를 익명으로 실었으며, 1862년에 최초의
시집『요귀의 시장, 기타』(*Goblin Market and other Poems*)를 발표하여 '라파엘
전파'의 시풍을 보였다. 그 후『왕자의 순력』(*Prince's Progress*)과 때 묻지 않
은 순결한 어린이의 마음을 노래한 동요시집『창가』(*Sing-Song*)『신작 시집』
(*New Poems*) 등을 차례로 발표하였다. 그녀의 작품은 세련된 시어, 확실한
운율법, 온아한 정감이 만들어내는 시경 등으로 신비적·종교적 분위기를
자아냈다. 또 큰오빠 D. G. 로세티와 공통된 색채감과 중세적 요소가 뚜렷
하여, 영국 여류시인의 대표적인 한 사람이다. 그녀는 신앙상의 이유에 의
한 두 차례의 실연으로 결혼을 단념하였으며, 그녀의 작품 중의 연애시의
대부분은 좌절된 사랑의 기록이다.

When I am dead, my dearest*

When I am dead, my dearest,
    Sing no sad songs for me;

---

* The first stanza of the poem describes the world of the living people. The poet addresses

Plant thou no roses at my head,
　　　　Nor shady cypress tree:
Be the green grass above me
　　　　With showers and dewdrops wet;
And if thou wilt, remember,
　　　　And if thou wilt, forget.

I shall not see the shadows,
　　　　I shall not feel the rain;
I shall not hear the nightingale
　　　　Sing on, as if in pain:
And dreaming through the twilight
　　　　That doth not rise nor set,
Haply I may remember,
　　　　And haply may forget.

Remember *

Remember me when I am gone away,
　　　　Gone far away into the silent land;
　　　　When you can no more hold me by the hand,
Nor I half turn to go yet turning stay.

---

her dearest one and asks him not to sing sad songs for her when she is dead. She does not want others to plant roses or shady cypress tree at her tomb. She likes her tomb with green grass associated with showers and dewdrops.

* "Remember" almost reads like an instruction manual. The speaker spends the first 8 lines telling her lover to remember her because, well, she'll be dead and they won't be able to chit chat anymore about their future or who hold hands. By the end of the poem, however, she changes her mind. At first she says it's okay if he forgets for a bit but then remembers her, but finally she realizes that it's probably better if he forgets her because remembering might just be too painful.

Remember me when no more day by day
        You tell me of our future that you plann'd:
        Only remember me; you understand
It will be late to counsel then or pray.
Yet if you should forget me for a while
        And afterwards remember, do not grieve:
        For if the darkness and corruption leave
        A vestige of the thoughts that once I had,
Better by far you should forget and smile
        Than that you should remember and be sad.

Up-Hill *

Does the road wind up-hill all the way?
    Yes, to the very end.
Will the day's journey take the whole long day?
    From morn to night, my friend.

But is there for the night a resting-place?
    A roof for when the slow dark hours begin.
May not the darkness hide it from my face?
    You cannot miss that inn.

Shall I meet other wayfarers at night?
    Those who have gone before.
Then must I knock, or call when just in sight?

---

* Over the course of a journey, the narrator asks her guide eight questions about the road ahead. The narrator asks if the roads are all up-hill and if the journey will take all day. The guide replies in the affirmative. Next, the narrator asks if there is a place to rest for the night and if the darkness will obscure said resting-place from their view.

They will not keep you standing at that door.

Shall I find comfort, travel-sore and weak?
    Of labour you shall find the sum.
Will there be beds for me and all who seek?
    Yea, beds for all who come.

A Birthday*

My heart is like a singing bird
          Whose nest is in a water'd shoot;
My heart is like an apple-tree
          Whose boughs are bent with thickset fruit;
My heart is like a rainbow shell
          That paddles in a halcyon sea;
My heart is gladder than all these
          Because my love is come to me.

Raise me a dais of silk and down;
          Hang it with vair and purple dyes;
Carve it in doves and pomegranates,
          And peacocks with a hundred eyes;
Work it in gold and silver grapes,
          In leaves and silver fleurs-de-lys;
Because the birthday of my life
          Is come, my love is come to me.

---

* The narrator of "A Birthday" expresses her delight about her love's upcoming birthday. The narrator, who most likely voices Rossetti's own views, compares her heart to various things in nature. She uses the images of a songbird, a fruit-laden apple-tree, and a rainbow to express the depth of her love.

(2) 아서 휴 클러프 Arthur Hugh Clough, 1819–1861

클러프는 이 시기의 종교와 과학 사이의 갈등 속에서 매우 고민한 사람으로 알려졌다. 그는 경건하고도 신앙이 돈독한 어머니의 영향과 토머스 아널드(Thomas Arnold)의 자유주의적인 신교 사상(liberal protestantism)의 영향을 짙게 받았을 뿐만 아니라, 옥스퍼드(Oxford)에서도 뉴먼(Newman)의 권위주의적인 교회 전통 회복 운동과 마주치게 되었다. 그러나 당시에 거세게 불어 닥친 과학 사상과 성서의 역사성에 도전하는 고등 비평(higher criticism)은 그의 신앙을 뒤흔들어 놓고야 말았다. 그는 회의주의에 빠져 진지하게 기독교 신앙을 합리화하려고 노력해 보았지만, 당시 안일주의에 빠져 있던 영국교회나 가톨릭교회의 전통적인 독선적 관행을 받아들일 수 없었다.

그가 학자로 첫 걸음을 내디딜 연구생 자리를 양심에 입각해서 거절한 것도 이런 맥락에서 결정된 일이다. 그는 유럽과 미국으로 떠돌아다녀 보았지만 만족을 얻지 못하였고, 영국 정부의 교육 행정 부서에서 일하다가 건강이 악화되어 세상을 떠났다. 그의 죽음은 매슈 아널드(Matthew Arnold)의 주요한 작품)을 낳게 했다는 점에서 의의를 찾아볼 수 있을 것이다.

1848년에 내놓은 클러프의 첫 작품 「토버너부얼리크의 집」("The Bothie of Tober-na-Vuolich")는 옥스포드 대학생들이 스코트랜드에 여행을 갔다가 그 중 한 사람이 하이랜드(Highland)지방 농부의 딸과 사랑에 빠지는 이야기를 6보격으로 이루어 놓은 시이다. 그의 운문은 흐름이 고르지 못하고 지나치게 평범한 회화로 전락하는 약점을 지니지만 이 작품에서는 그가 스코트랜드의 아름다운 자연을 배경으로 하여 소박하고도 신선한 인물 묘사와 더불어 고전적 목가의 분위기를 잘 살렸기 때문에 그의 시인다운 모습이 가장 잘 나타난다. 자연에 대한 사랑은 그의 정서를 자극하여 그의 문체를 투박함에서 벗어나게 한다. 그의 또 다른 장시 「딥시추스」 ("Dipsychus")는 『파우스트』(*Faust*)를 연상시키는 작품으로서 시인의 세속주의와 이상주의 사이의 분열을 나타낸다.

그는 예리한 지성을 무기로 불합리한 인간의 사고방식에 냉소를 보내고 전통적 신앙에 날카로운 핀잔을 주지만, 자기도 모르는 사이에 회의주의·향략주의적인 흐름으로 전락하는 약점을 보인다. 그뿐만 아니라 그의 갈등과 회의가 더 철저하고 성실하게 파헤쳐지며, 그 고민상이 예술로 승화될 수 있었더라면 좋았을 것이라는 아쉬움을 남긴다. 그의 단시 「싸워봤자 소용없다고 말하지 마라」("Say Not the Struggle Nought Availeth")는 윈스턴 처칠(Winston Churchill)이 제2차 세계 대전 중에 실의에 빠진 영국민을 북돋아 주기 위해서 인용한 후로 그 인기가 올라갔지만 그것은 시적 가치로 말미암은 것이 아니라 위안을 주는 정서와 희망을 주는 요소가 있기 때문이다.

Say not the Struggle nought Availeth*

Say not the struggle nought availeth,
 The labour and the wounds are vain,
The enemy faints not, nor faileth,
 And as things have been they remain.

If hopes were dupes, fears may be liars;
 It may be, in yon smoke concealed,

---

* The poem appeared in 1849, when the poet was 30. The great Irish famine was a recent memory, Reform seemed to have run out of steam in England, monarchism was rising again in France, the revolutionary impulses of Europe in 1848 had petered out, and the slavery issue was heating up in the U.S.A. (where Clough spent parts of his life from childhood on). For liberal-minded folk like Clough there was need of exhortation.

Your comrades chase e'en now the fliers,
       And, but for you, possess the field.

For while the tired waves, vainly breaking
       Seem here no painful inch to gain,
Far back through creeks and inlets making,
       Came, silent, flooding in, the main.

And not by eastern windows only,
       When daylight comes, comes in the light,
In front the sun climbs slow, how slowly,
       But westward, look, the land is bright.

(2014년 중등영어 임용고시 기출문제)

(3) 로버트 브라우닝 Robert Browning, 1812-1889

런던 교외의 캠버웰 출신으로 테니슨과 더불어 빅토리아조를 대표하는 시인이다. 부유한 은행가의 아들로 태어나 가정에서 천재교육을 받아 일찍부터 시재를 나타내었다. 처녀작 시 『폴린』(*Pauline: A Fragment of a Confession*)과 제2작인 극시 『파라셀서스』(*Paracelsus*)는 모두 자서전적 요소를 가진 작품으로, 자기중심적인 회의에 고민하거나 지식만을 탐욕스럽게 추구하는 주인공이, 결국은 무한의 사랑으로 구제받는 모습을 그렸다. 『파라셀서스』는 T. 칼라일과 W. 워즈워스의 주목을 끌었으며, 1837년 코번트 가든에서 상연되었다. 이어 정치적 권력을 쥐느냐, 인류에의 봉사라는 이상을 관철하느냐로 고민하는 청년 시인을 그린, 난해한 이야기 시 『소델로』(*Sordello*)와 소책자 작품 『방울과 석류』(*Bells and Pomegranates No. I: Pippa Passes*)를 출판하였다. 1846년 병약한 여류시인 E. 버레트와 몰래 결혼하였는데, 장인의 반대로 이탈리아로 도주, 그녀가 죽을 때까지 16년간을 주로 피렌체에서 지냈다.

그러는 동안 시집 『남자와 여자』(*Men and Women*) 『등장인물』(*Dramatis Personae*)을 발표하였으며, 또 상대방을 의식하면서 독백하는 형식인 극적 독백의 수법으로 『리포 리피 신부』(*Fra Lippo Lippi*), 『안드레아 델 사르토』 (*Andreadel Sarto*) 등의 명작을 남겼다. 1868-1869년에는 2만 행이 넘는 대작 『반지와 책』(*The Ring and the Book*)을 완성하였다. 이것은 17세기에 로마에 서 일어났던 살인사건을 다룬 내용으로, 한 가지 사건에 대하여 10명의 서 로 다른 성격의 소유자들이 갖는 견해를, 극적 독백의 수법을 자유자재로 구사하여 미묘한 심적 움직임까지 추구하면서 그려낸 작품이다. 작품은 테 니슨의 유연한 용어법과는 대조적으로 난해한 표현이 특징인데, 극적 독백 의 능란한 활용에 의한 복잡한 심리묘사 등은 현대인에게 호소력을 갖는다.

Abt Vogler*

Well, it is earth with me; silence resumes her reign:
    I will be patient and proud, and soberly acquiesce.
Give me the keys. I feel for the common chord again,
    Sliding by semitones till I sink to the minor,—yes,
And I blunt it into a ninth, and I stand on alien ground,
    Surveying awhile the heights I rolled from into the deep;
Which, hark, I have dared and done, for my resting-place is found,
    The C Major of this life: so, now I will try to sleep.

---

* Abt Vogler is written in the voice of an actual historic personage, as are many of Browning's dramatic monologues. Vogler was a composer and musical innovator; in this poem, Browning imagines him aged, growing more infirm, meditating on the purpose and value of his life.

Prospice *

Fear death? —to feel the fog in my throat,
    The mist in my face,
When the snows begin, and the blasts denote
    I am nearing the place,
The power of the night, the press of the storm,
    The post of the foe;
Where he stands, the Arch Fear in a visible form,
    Yet the strong man must go:

My Last Duchess **
Ferrara

That's my last Duchess painted on the wall,
Looking as if she were alive. I call
That piece a wonder, now: Fra Pandolf's hands
Worked busily a day, and there she stands.
Will't please you sit and look at her? I said
"Fra' Pandolf" by design, for never read
Strangers like you that pictured countenance,
The depth and passion of its earnest glance,

---

* Written soon after his wife Elizabeth's passing in 1861, "Prospice" can easily be viewed as one of Browning's most naked declarations. Its basic message is that he (in this case perhaps not a character, but the poet himself) will not falter before death even though its imminence perverts the journey of life, but instead will march forward heroically and face it head-on.

** "My Last Duchess," published in 1842, is arguably Browning's most famous dramatic monologue, with good reason. It engages the reader on a number of levels —historical, psychological, ironic, theatrical, and more. The most engaging element of the poem is probably the speaker himself, the duke.

But to myself they turned (since none puts by
The curtain I have drawn for you, but I)
And seemed as they would ask me, if they durst,
How such a glance came there; so, not the first
Are you to turn and ask thus. Sir, 'twas not
Her husband's presence only, called that spot
Of joy into the Duchess' cheek: perhaps
Fra Pandolf chanced to say "Her mantle laps
Over my lady's wrist too much," or "Paint
Must never hope to reproduce the faint
Half-flush that dies along her throat." Such stuff
Was courtesy, she thought, and cause enough
For calling up that spot of joy. She had
A heart—how shall I say?—too soon made glad,
Too easily impressed; she liked whate'er
She looked on, and her looks went everywhere.
Sir, 'twas all one! My favour at her breast,
The dropping of the daylight in the West,
The bough of cherries some officious fool
Broke in the orchard for her, the white mule
She rode with round the terrace—all and each
Would draw from her alike the approving speech,
Or blush, at least. She thanked men,—good! but thanked
Somehow—I know not how—as if she ranked
My gift of a nine-hundred-years-old name
With anybody's gift. Who'd stoop to blame
This sort of trifling? Even had you skill
In speech—(which I have not)—to make your will
Quite clear to such an one, and say, "Just this
Or that in you disgusts me; here you miss,
Or there exceed the mark"—and if she let

영국시 읽기 227

Herself be lessoned so, nor plainly set

Her wits to yours, forsooth, and made excuse,

—E'en then would be some stooping; and I choose

Never to stoop. Oh sir, she smiled, no doubt,

Whene'er I passed her; but who passed without

Much the same smile? This grew; I gave commands;

Then all smiles stopped together. There she stands

As if alive. Will't please you rise? We'll meet

The company below, then. I repeat,

The Count your master's known munificence

Is ample warrant that no just pretence

Of mine for dowry will be disallowed;

Though his fair daughter's self, as I avowed

At starting, is my object. Nay, we'll go

Together down, sir. Notice Neptune, though,

Taming a sea-horse, thought a rarity,

Which Claus of Innsbruck cast in bronze for me!

(4) 알프레드 로드 테니슨 Alfred Lord Tennyson, 1809–1892

중부 잉글랜드, 랭카셔의 서머스비 출신으로 목사의 아들로 태어나 엄격한 아버지의 교육을 받았다. 1828년 케임브리지 대학의 트리니티 칼리지에 입학하여, 시 「팀북투」("Timbuctoo")로 총장상 메달을 받았다. 이미 형 찰스와 『두 형제 시집』(*Poems by Two Brothers*)을 익명으로 내놓았는데, 실은 장형 프레드릭까지 포함한 3형제 시집이다. 이어 『서정시집』(*Poems, Chiefly Lyrical*)을 발표, L. 헌트에게 인정을 받았고, 1831년 아버지가 죽자 대학을 중퇴하였다. 1832년의 『시집』에는 고전을 제재로 한 「연을 먹는 사람들」("The Lotos-Eaters"), 「미녀들의 꿈」("The Dreams of Fair Women"),

중세에서 제재를 얻은 「샬럿의 아가씨」("The Lady of Shalott"), 그의 예술 관을 보여 주는 「예술의 궁전」("The Palace of Art") 등의 가작이 들어 있다. 이 해 친구 아서 핼럼과 함께 유럽을 여행하였고, 이듬해 핼럼이 죽자 애도의 시를 쓰기 시작하였다. 1842년의 2권본 『시집』에는 「율리시스」 ("Ulysses"), 「록슬리 홀」("Locksley Hall"), 「두 목소리」("Two Voices"), 「고 다이바」("Godiva") 등의 시가 실렸다.

1849년에는 걸작 「인 메모리엄」("In Memoriam")이 출판되었으며, W. 워즈워스의 후임으로 계관시인이 되었다. 이 해에 그는 약혼녀 에밀리 셀 우드와 결혼하였다. 『인 메모리엄』은 17년간을 생각하고 그리던, 죽은 친 구 핼럼에게 바치는 애가로, 어두운 슬픔에서 신에 의한 환희의 빛에 이르 는, 시인의 '넋의 길'을 더듬은 대표작일 뿐만 아니라, 빅토리아 시대의 대 표시이기도 하다. 그 후에도 「모드」("Maud"), 「국왕목가」("Idylls of the King"), 「이녹 아든」("Enoch Arden") 등을 써서 애송되었으며, 여왕으로부 터 영작을 받고, 빅토리아 시대의 국보적 존재가 되었다.

The Lady of Shalott*

  the reaper weary
Listening whispers, ' 'Tis the fairy,
    Lady of Shalott' . . .
Sometimes a troop of damsels glad,
An abbot on an ambling pad . . .

---

* Most critics believe the poem is based on the episode in Arthurian legend of Elaine of Astalot, or the Maid of Astalot, who died of her unrequited love for the famous knight. Tennyson's engagement with Arthurian legend is, of course, most notably seen in his Idylls of the King.

when the moon was overhead

Came two young lovers lately wed;

'I am half sick of shadows,' said

　　　The Lady of Shalott . . .

A bow-shot from her bower-eaves,

He rode between the barley-sheaves . . .

Out flew the web and floated wide;

The mirror crack'd from side to side;

'The curse is come upon me,' cried

　　　The Lady of Shalott.

The Lotos-eaters *

The charmed sunset linger'd low adown

In the red West . . .

And round about the keel with faces pale,

Dark faces pale against that rosy flame,

The mild-eyed melancholy Lotos-eaters came . . .

Death is the end of life; ah, why

Should life all labour be? . . .

But, propt on beds of amaranth and moly,

How sweet (while warm airs lull us, blowing lowly)

With half-dropt eyelid still . . .

Dear is the memory of our wedded lives . . .

---

* "The Lotus Eaters" is a striking poem which begins with a heroic line: "courage! He said
and pointed towards the land". The poem is looking at the human condition and its interest
centers in the conflict between the sense of responsibility and desire to take pleasure.

In Memoriam A. H. H.*

And ghastly thro' the drizzling rain
  On the bald street breaks the blank day . . .
And like a guilty thing I creep
  At earliest morning to the door . . .
To pangs of nature, sins of will,
  Defects of doubt, and taints of blood . . .
I can but trust that good shall fall
  At last—far off—at last, to all,
  And every winter change to spring . . .
An infant crying for the light:
  And with no language but a cry . . .
And finding that of fifty seeds
  She often brings but one to bear . . .
And falling with my weight of cares
  Upon the great world's altar-stairs
That slope thro' darkness up to God . . .
I stretch lame hands of faith, and grope,
And gather dust and chaff, and call
To what I feel is Lord of all,
And faintly trust the larger hope . . .
The living soul was flash'd on mine . . .
At length my trance
  Was cancell'd, stricken thro' with doubt.

---

* "In Memoriam" is often considered Tennyson's greatest poetic achievement. It is a stunning and profoundly moving long poem consisting of a prologue, 131 cantos/stanzas, and an epilogue. It was published in 1850, but Tennyson began writing the individual poems in 1833 after learning that his closest friend, the young Cambridge poet Arthur Henry Hallam, had suddenly died at age 22 of a cerebral hemorrhage. Over the course of seventeen years Tennyson worked on and revised the poems, but he did not initially intend to publish them as one long work.

Crossing the Bar *

Sunset and evening star,
    And one clear call for me!
And may there be no moaning of the bar,
    When I put out to sea,

But such a tide as moving seems asleep,
    Too full for sound and foam,
When that which drew from out the boundless deep
    Turns again home.

Twilight and evening bell,
    And after that the dark!
And may there be no sadness of farewell,
    When I embark;

For tho' from out our bourne of Time and Place
    The flood may bear me far,
I hope to see my Pilot face to face
    When I have crost the bar.

---

* This short but evocative poem is often placed at the end of volumes of Tennyson's poems, as he requested. He wrote it in 1889 when he was 80 years old and recovering from a serious illness at sea, crossing the Solent from Aldworth to Farringford on the Isle of Wight, off the mainland of England. It is said that Tennyson composed it in twenty minutes. Tennyson's illness and old age may have contributed to this very personal and memorable meditation on death.

from The Princess: Tears, Idle Tears *

Tears, idle tears, I know not what they mean,
Tears from the depth of some divine despair
Rise in the heart, and gather to the eyes,
In looking on the happy Autumn-fields,
And thinking of the days that are no more.

Fresh as the first beam glittering on a sail,
That brings our friends up from the underworld,
Sad as the last which reddens over one
That sinks with all we love below the verge;
So sad, so fresh, the days that are no more.

Ah, sad and strange as in dark summer dawns
The earliest pipe of half-awaken'd birds
To dying ears, when unto dying eyes
The casement slowly grows a glimmering square;
So sad, so strange, the days that are no more.

Dear as remember'd kisses after death,
And sweet as those by hopeless fancy feign'd
On lips that are for others; deep as love,
Deep as first love, and wild with all regret;
O Death in Life, the days that are no more!

---

* "Tears, Idle Tears" is one of Tennyson's most famous works, and it has garnered a large
amount of critical analysis. It is a "song" within the larger poem The Princess, published in
1847. In context, it is a song that the poem's Princess commands one of her maids to sing
to pass the time while she and her women take a break from their difficult studies.

(5) 루이스 캐럴 Lewis Carroll, 1832-1898

1832년 1월 27일 영국 체셔 테어스베리에서 성공회 사제의 아들로 출생하였다. 본명은 찰스 루트위지 도즈슨(Charles Lutwidge Dodgson)이다. 럭비학교에서 1851년 옥스퍼드 크라이스트처치 칼리지에 진학하여 수학, 신학, 문학을 공부하였으며, 훗날 모교의 수학 교수를 지냈다. 그는 성직자의 자격을 얻었음에도 내성적인 성격과 말더듬 때문에 평생 설교단에 서지 않았다. 그의 성격은 괴팍했고 다른 사람들과 잘 어울리지 못했다. 엄격한 규칙으로 정한 일상을 고집스럽게 반복했으며 이를 일기에 꼼꼼하게 남겼다. 모든 일상을 기록하여 편지로 주고받았는데 약 9만 9천통의 편지를 보관하였다. 그는 글을 쓰면서 루이스 캐럴이라는 가명을 사용하였다. 그는 크라이스트 칼리지 학장의 딸인 앨리스 리델에게 이야기해 주었던 것을 동화 『이상한 나라의 앨리스』(*Alice's Adventures in Wonderland*)와 그 속편인 『거울 나라의 앨리스』(*Through the Looking-Glass and What Alice Found There*) 등의 유머와 환상이 가득 찬 일련의 작품으로써, 근대 아동문학 확립자의 한 사람이 되었다. 그는 사진에도 상당한 관심을 가지고 있었으며 대학 연구실에서 사진실험을 거치면서 초상사진을 촬영했다. 특히 소녀를 대상으로 많은 사진을 촬영했으며 앨리스 리델이 그의 모델이 되었다. 하지만 앨리스에 대한 지나친 집착으로 얼마 후 그녀의 집안과 의절하게 되었다.

그 밖의 주요작품으로는 『스나크 사냥』(*The Hunting of the Snark*), 『실비와 브루노』(*Sylvie and Bruno*) 등과 시집이 있다. 그의 소설이나 시는 현대의 초현실주의 문학과 부조리문학의 선구자로 간주되며, 난센스 문학의 전형이라고도 할 수 있다. 그는 어린 여자아이들을 좋아하였고 모든 표현은 어린 소녀들을 대상으로 하였다. 평생 독신으로 살았으며 1898년 1월 14일 사망하였다. 그는 빅토리아 왕조의 대표적인 기인의 한 사람으로 일컬어진다.

Haddocks' Eyes *

And now, if e'er by chance I put
My fingers into glue,
Or madly squeeze a right-hand foot
Into a left-hand shoe,
 Or if I drop upon my toe
A very heavy weight,
I weep, for it reminds me so
Of that old man I used to know —
Whose look was mild, whose speech was slow
Whose hair was whiter than the snow,
Whose face was very like a crow,
With eyes, like cinders, all aglow,
Who seemed distracted with his woe,
Who rocked his body to and fro,
And muttered mumblingly and low,
As if his mouth were full of dough,
Who snorted like a buffalo —
That summer evening long ago,
A-sitting on a gate.

---

* "Haddocks' Eyes" is a poem by Lewis Carroll from Through the Looking-Glass. It is sung
by The White Knight in chapter eight to a tune that he claims as his own invention, but
which Alice recognises as "I give thee all, I can no more". By the time Alice heard it, she
was already tired of poetry. It is a parody of "Resolution and Independence" by William
Wordsworth.

(6) 에밀리 브론테 Emily Brontë, 1818–1848

필명은 엘리스 벨(Ellis Bell)로 요크셔 주의 손턴에서 영국 국교회 목사의 딸로 태어났으며, C. 브론테의 동생이고, A. 브론테의 언니이다. 1820년 아버지가 요크셔의 한촌 하워스로 전근하게 되어 에밀리 자매들은 그 황량한 벽지의 목사관에서 자랐다. 1821년 어머니가 죽자 이 자매들은 백모의 손에 양육되다가 1824년 에밀리와 샬럿은 위의 두 언니들과 함께 근처에서 목사의 딸들을 싼 비용으로 맡는 기숙학교에 맡겨졌으나 형편없는 식사로 영양실조와 결핵에 걸려 두 언니들이 이듬해에 사망하자, 놀란 부친은 에밀리와 샬럿을 집에 데려왔다. 이 악덕 기숙학교는 후에 샬럿이 소설『제인 에어』(*Jane Eyre*)에서 분노에 찬 필치로 묘사하고 있다. 1842년에 에밀리는 샬럿과 함께 벨기에의 수도 브뤼셀의 여학교에 유학하여 어학을 공부하고 같은 해에 귀가하였다.

1846년 언니 샬럿, 동생 앤과 셋이서 합저 시집『커러, 엘리스, 액턴벨의 시집』(*Poems by Currer, Ellis*, and Acton Bell, 1846)을 자비 출판했으나 반향이 없었다. 그러나 에밀리는「죄수」("The Prisoner"),「내 영혼은 비겁하지 않노라」("No Coward Soul is Mine") 등의 시편에 의하여 시인으로서 특이한 지위를 차지하고 있다. 1847년에 그녀의 유일한 소설『폭풍의 언덕』(*Wuthering Heights*)이 출판되었으나 이 역시 평이 좋지 못하였으며, 그 이듬해에 폐결핵으로 짧은 생애를 마쳤다. 서정적인 긴박한 심상과 독자적인 깊은 인생 해석으로 가득 차서 순수한 감동을 주는 걸작『폭풍의 언덕』은 오늘날에는 셰익스피어의 『리어왕』(*King Lear*), H. 멜빌의 『백경』(*Moby Dick*)에 필적하는 명작이라고까지 평가되고 있다.

I'm Happiest When Most Away*

I'm happiest when most away
I can bear my soul from its home of clay
On a windy night when the moon is bright
And the eye can wander through worlds of light—
When I am not and none beside—
Nor earth nor sea nor cloudless sky—
But only spirit wandering wide
Through infinite immensity.

(7) 조지 메러디스 George Meredith, 1828-1909

포츠머스 출신으로 부유하고 활달한 양복점 주인이 조부였으나 부친은 평범하고 용렬하였기 때문에 그는 가난이 어떠한 것인지도 알았다. 1842년 독일에 유학하고 18세 때 귀국, 런던에서 법률가의 견습생 노릇을 하다가 문필생활을 결심했다. 1849년 작가 T. L. 피콕의 딸과 결혼하였으며, 아버지와 아들의 대립을 테마로 한 『리처드 페베렐의 시련』(*The Ordeal of Richard Feverel*)과 장편시 『현대의 사랑 및 영국 노변의 시』(*Modern Love, and Poems of the English Roadside*)가 나올 무렵부터 다소 인정을 받기 시작하였다. 그러나 별거 중이던 부인의 사망을 비롯하여 가정적으로는 불행하였다. 그가 작가로서 무르익은 시기는 40세부터 10여 년 간이며 대표작이라

---

* She stresses the importance of being alone in the first line of each stanza; it is clear to us that she is most comfortable when left to recede into her altered consciousness. The entire poem is laying out requisites for the ultimate moment of ecstasy experienced at the end, as the author is finally able to let her self go into the deep relaxation of selflessness. This can be viewed as delving into a creative state, or even a comfortable sleep, where the subject experiences peace and loss of conscious burdens.

고 일컬어지는 소설 『에고이스트』(*The Egoist*), 『크로스웨이즈의 다이아나』 (*Diana of the Crossways*) 등도 이 시기에 썼다.

그는 주지주의 작가라고 불렸으며, 작품 속에서 여성문제를 취급했던 진보파이기도 하였다. 현란하면서도 지극히 난해한 문장이 그의 최대 특색 이라 할 수 있다. 유명해지기 이전의 W. S. 몸도 한때 이런 화려한 문장을 모범으로 삼으려 했었지만, 시대의 변천과 함께 이제는 영국에서도 많이 읽히지는 않는다. 오랫동안 신인의 원고를 선발하는 지위에 있었으며 T. 하디를 일찍 인정했던 일은 유명하다.

Modern Love: I*

By this he knew she wept with waking eyes:
That, at his hand's light quiver by her head,
The strange low sobs that shook their common bed
Were called into her with a sharp surprise,
And strangled mute, like little gaping snakes,
Dreadfully venomous to him. She lay
Stone-still, and the long darkness flowed away
With muffled pulses. Then, as midnight makes
Her giant heart of Memory and Tears
Drink the pale drug of silence, and so beat
Sleep's heavy measure, they from head to feet
Were moveless, looking through their dead black years,

---

* George Meredith's "Modern Love" is his longest poem, and when it was published (a year after his wife died), it was seen as a disturbed work. It is a sonnet sequence consisting of fifty separate sonnets rhyming abba cddc effe ghhg. Meredith's sixteen-line sonnets—a variation on the traditional fourteen-line sonnet—provide an apt structure for presenting interconnected but frequently contradictory feelings and reactions.

By vain regret scrawled over the blank wall.
Like sculptured effigies they might be seen
Upon their marriage-tomb, the sword between;
Each wishing for the sword that severs all.

The Lark Ascending*

He rises and begins to round,
He drops the silver chain of sound,
Of many links without a break,
In chirrup, whistle, slur and shake.
For singing till his heaven fills,
Tis love of earth that he instils.

And ever winging up and up,
Our valley is his golden cup
And he the wine which overflows
to lift us with him as he goes.
Till lost on his aerial rings
In light, and then the fancy sings.

---

* "The Lark Ascending" is a poem of 122 lines by the English poet George Meredith about the song of the skylark. It has been called matchless of its kind, 'a sustained lyric which never for a moment falls short of the effect aimed at, soars up and up with the song it imitates, and unites inspired spontaneity with a demonstration of effortless technical ingenuity... one has only to read the poem a few times to become aware of its perfection.'

(8) 단테 가브리엘 로세티 Dante Gabriel Rossetti, 1828-1882

본명은 가브리엘 샤를 단테 로세티(Gabriel Charles Dante Rossetti)로 런던 출신이며 이탈리아의 망명시인 R. 가브리엘레의 아들로 런던 대학과 왕립 아카데미의 안틱 스쿨에서 수학하고 몇몇 사람의 화가로부터 그림 지도를 받았다. W. H. 헌트를 알게 되어 그와 더불어 '라파엘 전파'를 결성하고 그 중심인물의 한 사람으로 활동하였다. 1850년대에는 신화·성서·문학작품 등을 통하여 얻은 주제로 수채화나 소묘로 서정적 작품을 제작하였다. 그러나 환상적 표현에 대한 흥미와 묘사기술의 부족으로 라파엘 전파 작가들에게 공통된 자연주의적 묘사를 피하였으므로 그 후 그 파에서 떠나 독자적인 화풍을 개척하였다. 후반기의 작품은 수채가 주였으며 감각적 표현으로 기울어졌다. 1860년 연인 엘리자베스 시달과 결혼하였으나 2년 후에 그녀가 자살하자 사실상 은퇴한 것이나 다름없는 생활을 하다가, 만년에는 시작에 몰두하였다.

그의 작풍은 정열·색채감·중세적인 주제와 분위기 등을 특색으로 하고, 신비적이면서도 육감적인 시경을 표출하였다. 대표적인 시작품 『청순한 처녀』(The Blessed Damzel)는 그가 애처의 죽음을 슬퍼한 나머지 그녀의 유해와 함께 매장한 원고를 후에 발굴하여 『시스터 헬렌』(Sister Helen), 『흐름의 비밀』, 『사랑의 야곡』 등의 가편을 함께 수록한 『D. G. 로세티 시집』(The Collected Works of Dante Gabriel Rossetti)을 통하여 발표된 것으로, 요절한 청순한 처녀가 천국의 입구에 기대서서 연인의 승천을 기다리는 내용인데, 신앙이 장식적인 소재로 사용되어 선명한 인상이나 격렬한 감정이 결여된 작품이지만, 빅토리아왕조 영시에 새로운 방향을 제시한 점에서 중요한 의의를 가진다. 1881년에 출판된 『가요와 소네트』(Ballads and Sonnets)는 사랑에서의 영과 육의 관계를 추구한 역작이면서 지나치게 관능적인 연애를 대담하게 노래하여 '육체파'라고 불린 101편의 대표적인 소네트의 연작 『생명의 집』(*The House of Life*)을 비롯하여 다양한 작품이 수록되었다.

Sonnett VI: A Nuptial Sleep*

At length their long kiss severed, with sweet smart:
And as the last slow sudden drops are shed
From sparkling eaves when all the storm has fled,
So singly flagged the pulses of each heart.
Their bosoms sundered, with the opening start
Of married flowers to either side outspread
From the knit stem; yet still their mouths, burnt red,
Fawned on each other where they lay apart.

Sleep sank them lower than the tide of dreams,
And their dreams watched them sink, and slid away.
Slowly their souls swam up again, through gleams
Of watered light and dull drowned waifs of day;
Till from some wonder of new woods and streams
He woke, and wondered more: for there she lay.

---

* "Nuptial Sleep" is a sonnet written by Dante Gabriel Rossetti; it was the final addition to The House of Life: A Sonnet-Sequence in Rossetti's Ballads and Sonnets (1881). (Collins and Rundel 828) The sonnet employs natural and effortless imagery to depict the moment after two lovers consummate their marriage. D. G. Rossetti's explicit topic matter and the eloquent calmness with which he addresses the topic of lovemaking underwent severe criticism by Robert Buchanan in The Fleshly School of Poetry. In "Nuptial Sleep" Rossetti manipulates imagery of 'the everyday' as well as employs metaphors that depict calmness, love, and sensuality.

The Woodspurge *

The wind flapped loose, the wind was still,
Shaken out dead from tree and hill:
I had walked on at the wind's will, —
I sat now, for the wind was still.

Between my knees my forehead was, —
My lips, drawn in, said not Alas!
My hair was over in the grass,
My naked ears heard the day pass.

My eyes, wide open, had the run
Of some ten weeds to fix upon;
Among those few, out of the sun,
The woodspurge flowered, three cups in one.

From perfect grief there need not be
Wisdom or even memory:
One thing then learnt remains to me, —
The woodspurge has a cup of three.

(9) 엘리자베스 배럿 브라우닝 Elizabeth Barrett Browning, 1806-1861

더럼 근교 출신으로 8세 때 그리스어로 호메로스를 읽은 재원이었으나 병약하고 고독하였다. 39세 때 연하의 시인 R. 브라우닝과 결혼하였는데, 그 이전부터 몇 권의 시집을 내었다. 「포르투갈 인으로부터의 소네트」

---

* Every stanza comes to an end at a full-stop, each verse is carefully punctuated, no notable enjambement. The poem seems to be following most of the rules of classical poetry not going out of line, sense of claustrophobia, the author is stuck in his carefully structured poem.

("Sonnets from the Portuguese")는 역시를 가장하여 남편인 R. 브라우닝에 대한 애정을 솔직하게 노래한 작품이다. 장편서사시 「오로라 리」("Aurora Leigh")는 사회문제와 여성문제를, 「캐서귀디의 창」("Casa Guidi Window") 은 이탈리아의 독립에 대한 동정을 노래한 시이다. 결혼 후에는 평생을 피 렌체에서 보냈다. 두 시인의 연애는 V. 울프의 『플러시』(*Flush*)에 의해 널리 알려졌다. 그의 야심작 「오로라 리」는 소설시(novel-poem)라고 할 만한 것 으로서 시의 정신과 형식을 이용하여 당대의 소설적인 내용을 담은 것이 다. 오로라와 사촌 간의 사랑이 이 작품의 근본 줄거리지만 여러 가지 주 제, 즉 시의 성격, 예술의 가치, 여성의 사회적 위치 등에 관한 견해가 멋대 로 짜여 들어가고, 있을 법하지 않은 이야기 줄거리로 말미암아, 또한 빈약 한 구성력 때문에 이것은 소설로서는 실패한 작품이다. 또한 여기 채용된 무운시는 느슨한 데가 너무 많아 때로는 산문과 구별이 잘 되지 않는 경우 도 있다. 그러나 그 대담한 시도는 주목할 만하다. 당시 여성의 정열과 포 부와 사회의식이 이 작품에 뚜렷이 부각되어 있고 낭만주의적 도피주의에 서 벗어나려는 노력이 보인다는 점에서 재음미해야 할 것이다.

XXII. "When our two souls stand up erect and strong..."*

When our two souls stand up erect and strong,
Face to face, silent, drawing nigh and nigher,
Until the lengthening wings break into fire
At either curvèd point, —what bitter wrong

---

* Sonnet 22 is a love poem in the form of a sonnet. A sonnet is a 14-line poem with a specifc rhyme scheme and meter (usually iambic pentameter). This poetry format—which forces the poet to wrap his thoughts in a small, neat package—originated in Sicily, Italy, in the 13th Century with the sonnetto (meaning little song), which could be read or sung to the accompaniment of a lute.

Can the earth do to us, that we should not long
Be here contented? Think! In mounting higher,
The angels would press on us and aspire
To drop some golden orb of perfect song
Into our deep, dear silence. Let us stay
Rather on earth, Belovèd,—where the unfit
Contrarious moods of men recoil away
And isolate pure spirits, and permit
A place to stand and love in for a day,
With darkness and the death-hour rounding it.

How Do I Love Thee?*

How do I love thee? Let me count the ways.
I love thee to the depth and breadth and height
My soul can reach, when feeling out of sight
For the ends of Being and ideal Grace.
I love thee to the level of every day's
Most quiet need, by sun and candlelight.
I love thee freely, as men strive for Right;
I love thee purely, as they turn from Praise.
I love with a passion put to use
In my old griefs, and with my childhood's faith.
I love thee with a love I seemed to lose
With my lost saints,—I love thee with the breath,

---

* All the forty-four poems in Elizabeth Barrett Browning's sonnet sequence *Sonnets from the Portuguese* were written during the period of courtship that preceded her marriage to Robert Browning. As a whole, *Sonnets from the Portuguese* is considered one of the finest poetic sequences in literature. It is Sonnet 43, however, often titled "How do I love thee?" from its memorable first words, which is the best-known of the collection.

Smiles, tears, of all my life!—and, if God choose,
I shall but love thee better after death.

(10) 프란시스 톰슨 Francis Thompson, 1859-1907

영국시인으로 대학에서 가톨릭 신학과 병리학 공부를 했지만 모두 실패하고 1885년 작가가 되고자 런던으로 나왔는데, 빈곤과 결핵으로 고통을 받아서 아편상용자가 되었다. 부랑생활 끝에 가톨릭 잡지의 편집자 메넬부처에게 도움을 받아서 시인으로의 생활을 시작했다. 톰슨의 지적범위는 넓어서 그리스도교적 이념에 적당한 과학정신과 심리분석 그에 세기말적 신비주의가 더해진 것이다. 1888년 『메리 잉글랜드』(*Merry England*)지 편집자 W. 메이넬에게 인정받아 같은 잡지에 시와 산문을 기고하였으며, 1893년에는 처녀작 『시집』(*Poems*)의 걸작 「하늘의 사냥개」("The Hound Of Heaven")는 "나는 신에게서 도망했다. 밤도 낮도 혼의 미로를 방황한다"의 시행으로 시작해서, 신에게 쫓기는 인간의 고뇌를 훌륭하게 묘사하고 있다. 메넬가의 어린이를 노래한 「자매」("Sister Songs"), C. K. D. 파트모아의 영향을 받은 종교적·신비적 테마의 『신시집』등이 있다. 그는 48세 때 가톨릭병원에서 고고한 생애를 끝마쳤다.

The Hound of Heaven*

I FLED Him, down the nights and down the days;
　I fled Him, down the arches of the years;

---

* "The Hound of Heaven" is a poem centering on the pursuit of a sinner by a loving God. Written in a lofty, dignified style that expresses deep feelings, it is classified as an ode. It first appeared in Poems, a collection of Francis Thompson's works published in 1893.

I fled Him, down the labyrinthine ways

  Of my own mind; and in the mist of tears

I hid from Him, and under running laughter.

   Up vistaed hopes I sped;

   And shot, precipitated,

Adown Titanic glooms of chasmèd fears,

  From those strong Feet that followed, followed after.

   But with unhurrying chase,

   And unperturbèd pace,

Deliberate speed, majestic instancy,

   They beat—and a Voice beat

   More instant than the Feet—

'All things betray thee, who betrayest Me.'

(11) 윌리엄 어니스트 헨리 William Ernest Henley, 1849-1903

자신의 잡지를 통해 1890년대 영국 대문호들의 초기 작품을 소개했다. 어려서 결핵을 앓아 나중에 한쪽 발을 절단해야 했다. 다른 한쪽 다리는 그가 에든버러에서 만났던 외과의사 조지프 리스터의 인술과 새롭고 철저한 외과치료법으로 유지될 수 있었다. 에든버러에 있는 병원에서 20개월(1873-75) 동안 입원해 있으면서 병원 생활에 대한 인상적인 자유시를 써서 시인으로서의 명성을 얻었다. 이때의 작품이 『시집』(*A Book of Verses*)에 수록되어 있다. "나는 내 운명의 주인/또한 나는 내 영혼의 선장"이라는 행이 들어있는 가장 인기 있는 시 「인빅투스」("Invictus")도 이 시기에 쓰였다. 로버트 루이스 스티븐슨과의 오랜 우정은 1874년 그가 환자 였을 때 시작된 것으로 헨리는 『보물섬』(*Treasure Island*)에서 불구인 친구를 보살피는 롱 존 실버라는 인물로 그려진다.

건강을 회복한 뒤 편집자로 일하게 되면서 그가 가장 활발하게 활동한 잡지는 1889년 편집장이 된 에든버러의 『스코츠 옵저버』(*Scots Observer*)였다. 이 잡지는 1891년 런던에서 『내셔널 옵저버』(*National Observer*)로 출간되었으며, 정치적인 견해에서는 보수적이었지만, 문학적인 면에서는 진보주의적이어서, 하디·쇼·웰스·배리·키플링 등의 초기 작품들을 게재했다. 편집자와 문학 비평가로서 그는 신예 작가들에게 재능 있는 무명작가들을 발굴·격려하는 데는 호의적이었지만 실적도 없이 이름만 높은 작가들을 맹렬히 비난하는 관대하고도 깐깐한 사람으로 기억되었다. 또한 그는 T. F. 헨더슨과 함께 지금도 상당히 귀중한 로버트 번스의 탄생 100주년 기념 시집을 냈다(1896-97). 그는 이 전집 시집 서문에서 초기의 전기 작가들이 번스를 이상화시키려는 경향에 대응하여 번스의 야성적인 성격을 강조했다. 1888년 이후의 스티븐슨과의 불화와 결혼 후 10년 만에 얻은 딸의 죽음으로 인해 그의 말년은 불행했다. 스티븐슨이 죽은 뒤 헨리는 그에 대하여 신사답지 못한 폭로기사를 썼는데 이 때문에 많은 사람의 비난을 받았다.

Invictus*

Out of the night that covers me,
        Black as the pit from pole to pole,
I thank whatever gods may be

---

* The theme of the poem is the will to survive in the face of a severe test. Henley himself faced such a test. After contracting tuberculosis of the bone in his youth, he suffered a tubercular infection when he was in his early twenties that resulted in amputation of a leg below the knee. When physicians informed him that he must undergo a similar operation on the other leg, he enlisted the services of Dr. Joseph Lister (1827-1912), the developer of antiseptic medicine. He saved the leg. During Henley's twenty-month ordeal between 1873 and 1875 at the Royal Edinburgh Infirmary in Scotland, he wrote "Invictus" and other poems.

For my unconquerable soul.

In the fell clutch of circumstance
 I have not winced nor cried aloud.
Under the bludgeonings of chance
 My head is bloody, but unbowed.

Beyond this place of wrath and tears
 Looms but the Horror of the shade,
And yet the menace of the years
 Finds and shall find me unafraid.

It matters not how strait the gate,
 How charged with punishments the scroll,
I am the master of my fate,
 I am the captain of my soul.

(12) 토머스 하디 Thomas Hardy, 1840–1928

석공의 아들로 잉글랜드 도싯 주 어퍼보컴프턴에서 태어나 1856년 도체스터 건축기사의 제자가 되었고, 1862년 런던의 건축사무소에 들어갔다. 건축공부를 하는 여가에 소설을 쓴 것이 당시 문단의 대가 G. 메레디스에게 인정받았고, 그의 권고로 처녀장편 『최후의 수단』(*Desperate Remedies*)을 간행하였다. 그 후 『녹음 아래에서』(*Under the Greenwood Tree*), 『푸른 눈동자』(*A Pair of Blue Eyes*), 『광란의 무리를 떠나서』(*Far from the Madding Crowd*)로 호평받고, 작가로서의 지위가 확립되었다. 1874년 결혼하고, 손수 지은 도체스터의 저택에 옮겨 살았다.

그의 소설의 대표작으로는 『귀향』(*The Return of the Native*), 『캐스터브

리지의 시장』(*The Mayor of Casterbridge*), 『테스』(*Tess of the d'Urbervilles*), 『미천한 사람 주드』(*Jude the Obscure*) 등이 있지만, 그 밖에도 많은 장·단편 소설을 남겼다. 이들 작품의 거의 모두가 그가 태어났고 또 소설가로 대성한 후에도 계속 살았던 웨식스 지방을 무대로 하였다. 그러나 지명은 모두 가공의 이름인데, 예를 들어 '캐스터브리지'시는 작자가 살고 있던 도체스터 시이다. 이렇듯 한정된 지역을 무대로 삼으면서도 그의 작품이 지방색만을 내세운 문학은 아니고, 인간의 의지와 그것을 비극적으로 짓밟아 뭉개는 운명과의 상극을 주제로 한 비극으로, 그리스 비극·셰익스피어 비극과도 비교할 만하다고 할 수 있다.

더 나아가 19세기 말 영국 사회의 인습, 편협한 종교인의 태도를 용감히 공격하고, 남녀 간의 사랑을 성적인 면에서 대담하게 폭로하였기 때문에 당시의 도덕가들로부터 맹렬한 비난을 받고, 마침내 『미천한 사람 주드』를 끝으로 장편소설 집필을 단념하였다. 그러나 그 후 나폴레옹 시대를 무대로 그의 사상을 몽땅 기울인 장편 대서사시극 『패왕』(*The Dynasts*)을 발표하는 등, 그의 창작활동은 그칠 줄 몰랐다. 1910년 메리크훈장을 받았으며 1912년 상처하고, 2년 후 조수로 있던 여성과 재혼, 그의 만년은 영국 문단의 원로로 자타가 공인하는 존재가 되었다. 사후에 유해는 웨스트민스터 사원의 '시인 코너'에 묻혔는데, 그의 심장만은 고인의 유지에 따라 고향에 있는 부인의 무덤 옆에 묻혔다.

Channel Firing*

That night your great guns, unawares,
Shook all our coffins as we lay,

---

* The poem is registering the fact of war and its cost in human life. Indeed, the piece might

And broke the chancel window-squares,
We thought it was the Judgment-day

And sat upright. While drearisome
Arose the howl of wakened hounds:
The mouse let fall the altar-crumb,
The worms drew back into the mounds,

The glebe cow drooled. Till God called, "No;
It's gunnery practice out at sea
Just as before you went below;
The world is as it used to be:

"All nations striving strong to make
Red war yet redder. Mad as hatters
They do no more for Christés sake
Than you who are helpless in such matters.

"That this is not the judgment-hour
For some of them's a blessed thing,
For if it were they'd have to scour
Hell's floor for so much threatening....

"Ha, ha. It will be warmer when
I blow the trumpet (if indeed
I ever do; for you are men,
And rest eternal sorely need)."

---

be regarded as prescient, for Hardy wrote it in April of 1914, only months before the outbreak of World War I. Yet Hardy is pointing to the costly use of force less to shake a judgmental finger at humankind than to register such use as apparently inescapable. The poem might be said to replace judgments with facts, and Christian theology, which it finds absurd, with history.

So down we lay again. "I wonder,
Will the world ever saner be,"
Said one, "than when He sent us under
In our indifferent century!"

And many a skeleton shook his head.
"Instead of preaching forty year,"
My neighbour Parson Thirdly said,
"I wish I had stuck to pipes and beer."

Again the guns disturbed the hour,
Roaring their readiness to avenge,
As far inland as Stourton Tower,
And Camelot, and starlit Stonehenge.

I Look into my Glass*

I LOOK into my glass,
  And view my wasting skin,
And say, "Would God it came to pass
  My heart had shrunk as thin!"

For then, I, undistrest
  By hearts grown cold to me,
Could lonely wait my endless rest

---

* "I Look Into My Glass" was written when Hardy was only 57 years old and published in 1898. In this poem, Hardy revolves around the impact of time on the human identity. The main theme is the contrast between his aging physical body and his heart which is still young and vibrant. The tone of this poem is thoughtful and there is a rather slow pace which is emphasized by the regular rhyme scheme and numerous punctuations.

With equanimity.

But Time, to make me grieve,
   Part steals, lets part abide;
And shakes this fragile frame at eve
   With throbbings of noontide. (2015년 중등영어 임용고시 기출문제)

The Convergence of the Twain*

(Lines on the loss of the "Titanic")

I

In a solitude of the sea
Deep from human vanity,
And the Pride of Life that planned her, stilly couches she.

II

Steel chambers, late the pyres
Of her salamandrine fires,
Cold currents thrid, and turn to rhythmic tidal lyres.

III

Over the mirrors meant
To glass the opulent
The sea-worm crawls—grotesque, slimed, dumb, indifferent.

---

* "The Convergence of the Twain (Lines on the loss of the "Titanic")" is a poem by Thomas Hardy, published in 1915. The poem describes the sinking of the ocean liner Titanic on 15 April 1912. "Convergence" consists of eleven stanzas (I to XI) of three lines each, following the AAA rhyme pattern.

IV

Jewels in joy designed

To ravish the sensuous mind

Lie lightless, all their sparkles bleared and black and blind.

V

Dim moon-eyed fishes near

Gaze at the gilded gear

And query: "What does this vaingloriousness down here?" ...

VI

Well: while was fashioning

This creature of cleaving wing,

The Immanent Will that stirs and urges everything

VII

Prepared a sinister mate

For her—so gaily great—

A Shape of Ice, for the time far and dissociate.

VIII

And as the smart ship grew

In stature, grace, and hue,

In shadowy silent distance grew the Iceberg too.

IX

Alien they seemed to be;

No mortal eye could see

The intimate welding of their later history,

X

Or sign that they were bent

By paths coincident

On being anon twin halves of one august event,

XI

Till the Spinner of the Years

Said "Now!" And each one hears,

And consummation comes, and jars two hemispheres.

(13) 매슈 아널드 Matthew Arnold, 1822–1888

영국의 근대적 퍼블릭스쿨의 건설자로서 유명한 토머스 아널드의 장남이다. 윈체스터 럭비학교를 거쳐 옥스퍼드 대학에서 공부했으며, 1845년 졸업과 동시에 연구원으로 남았다. 이 가운데에는 뒷날 시인이 된 A. 크라프가 있어, 그들의 교우에서 아널드의 걸작 「학생 집시」("The Scholar Gipsy"), 크라프의 죽음을 애도한 시 「티르시스」("Thyrsis")가 태어났다. 럭비학교의 교직에 있은 지 몇 달 후인 1847년, 추밀원 의장 랜즈다운 경의 비서가 되었고, 1851년 그의 추천으로 장학관에 임명되었으며, 그 해에 결혼하였다.

여러 곳으로 시찰여행을 해야 하는 바쁜 직책으로 시작에 방해가 되었으나, 그는 충실하게 직무를 수행하여 영국 교육제도의 개혁에 힘써 근대적인 국민교육의 건설에 크게 공헌하였다. 1849년에 제1시집 『길 잃은 난봉꾼 및 기타』(The Strayed Reveller and Other Poems)를, 1852년에는 『에트나산 위의 엠페도클레스』(Empedocles on Etna)를 (A)라는 가명으로 출판하였으나 세평을 얻지는 못하였다. 1853년에 이들 구작에 『소랩과 러스텀』(Sohrab and

Rustum) 등의 신작을 더하여 『시집』(New Poems)을 처음으로 '매슈 아널드'라
는 이름으로 내어 호평을 받아 시인으로서의 지위를 확립하였다. 이 후에는
그것을 증보한 『시집』(Poems), 그리스풍의 시극 『메로프』(Merope)를 썼고, 그
후에도 몇 편의 뛰어난 시를 썼으나, 그의 주된 시적 활동은 『시집』으로 끝
났다고 하겠다. 그는 '시는 인생의 비평'이라고 주장한 내성적인 명상 시인
으로 높이 평가받고 있다. 그 시의 기초는 억제된 표현에도 불구하고 낭만
적이며, 잃어가고 있는 젊음을 한탄하고, 회의가 가득 찬 시대를 명상한다.

　　1857년에 옥스퍼드 대학 교수가 되어 10년간 그 직에 있었다. 『호머
번역론』(On Translating Homer) 『켈트 문학 연구』(The Study of Celtic Literature)
는 그의 강의서였다. 문예비평가로서 그를 유명하게 한 것은 『비평시론』
이다. 이것은 그의 사회적인 책임 및 사명감의 소산이고, 이후 『비평론집』
(Essays in Criticism)에 수록하여 현대 비평의 길을 열었다. 이러한 비평의
근저를 그는 '교양에 두어 모든 사상의 중심으로 삼아 영국의 정치·사
회·종교를 비판한 경세의 서 『교양과 무질서』(Culture and Anarchy) 『성 바
울과 프로테스탄트』(St. Paul and Protestantism) 『문학과 도그마』(Literature and
Dogma) 등을 저술하였다.

Growing Old*

What is it to grow old?
Is it to lose the glory of the form,

---

* "Growing Old" as the name says is a poem where Arnold beautifully explains how it feels
when one grows old. In the beginning of the poem, he gives a wonderful question, 'How
does it feel to grow old?' He just puts in simple words asking whether it is just loosing
beauty, or whether it is loosing the luster of the eye or just loosing the looks? Growing old
is far beyond all these is what he says.

The luster of the eye?
Is it for beauty to forego her wreath?
—Yes, but not this alone.

Is it to feel our strength—
Not our bloom only, but our strength—decay?
Is it to feel each limb
Grow stiffer, every function less exact,
Each nerve more loosely strung?

Yes, this, and more; but not
Ah, 'tis not what in youth we dreamed 'twould be!
'Tis not to have our life
Mellowed and softened as with sunset glow,
A golden day's decline.

'Tis not to see the world
As from a height, with rapt prophetic eyes,
And heart profoundly stirred;
And weep, and feel the fullness of the past,
The years that are no more.

It is to spend long days
And not once feel that we were ever young;
It is to add, immured
In the hot prison of the present, month
To month with weary pain.

It is to suffer this,
And feel but half, and feebly, what we feel.

Deep in our hidden heart
Festers the dull remembrance of a change,
But no emotion—none.

It is—last stage of all—
When we are frozen up within, and quite
The phantom of ourselves,
To hear the world applaud the hollow ghost
Which blamed the living man.

Dover Beach*

The sea is calm tonight.
The tide is full, the moon lies fair
Upon the straits; on the French coast the light
Gleams and is gone; the cliffs of England stand,
Glimmering and vast, out in the tranquil bay.
Come to the window, sweet is the night-air!
Only, from the long line of spray
Where the sea meets the moon-blanched land,
Listen! you hear the grating roar
Of pebbles which the waves draw back, and fling,
At their return, up the high strand,
Begin, and cease, and then again begin,
With tremulous cadence slow, and bring

---

* Arguably Matthew Arnold's most famous poem, "Dover Beach" manages to comment on his most recurring themes despite its relatively short length. Its message—like that of many of his other poems—is that the world's mystery has declined in the face of modernity. However, that decline is here painted as particularly uncertain, dark, and volatile.

The eternal note of sadness in.

Sophocles long ago
Heard it on the Ægean, and it brought
Into his mind the turbid ebb and flow
Of human misery; we
Find also in the sound a thought,
Hearing it by this distant northern sea.

The Sea of Faith
Was once, too, at the full, and round earth's shore
Lay like the folds of a bright girdle furled.
But now I only hear
Its melancholy, long, withdrawing roar,
Retreating, to the breath
Of the night-wind, down the vast edges drear
And naked shingles of the world.

Ah, love, let us be true
To one another! for the world, which seems
To lie before us like a land of dreams,
So various, so beautiful, so new,
Hath really neither joy, nor love, nor light,
Nor certitude, nor peace, nor help for pain;
And we are here as on a darkling plain
Swept with confused alarms of struggle and flight,
Where ignorant armies clash by night.

(14) 어니스트 크리스토퍼 다우슨 Ernest Christopher Dowson, 1867-1900

어렸을 때 결핵에 걸린 부모와 함께 쾌적한 휴양지를 찾아 프랑스와 이탈리아를 돌아다니는 등 불안정한 생활을 했다. 1886년 옥스퍼드 대학의 퀸스 칼리지에 들어갔으나, 가세가 기울어 1888년에 중퇴하게 되었고, 양친의 자살, 병에 의한 쇠약, 방종한 생활 등 가장 세기말적인 체험을 했으므로, 그 특징을 충분히 발휘하여 탐미적인 시를 썼다. 특히 숙명적인 여성을 노래한 로맨틱한 시로 알려져 있다. 『시가집』(*Verses*), 시극 『덧없는 사랑의 피에로』(*The Pierrot of the Minute*), 단편집 『딜레마』(*Dilemmas*) 등이 유명하다. 예술을 위한 예술을 신조로 하여 빅토리아 시대의 대중에게 충격을 주려는 의도에서 나온 주제를 다룬 1890년대 영국 시인 그룹 데카당파 (Decadents)에 속하는 매우 재능 있는 시인이다.

1891년 그가 평생 동안 사모한 여인이며 대부분의 시에 영감을 불어넣어 준 아델라이데 폴티노비츠를 만났다. 그녀는 런던의 소호에 있는 자기 부모가 경영하는 '폴란드'라는 식당에서 일하고 있었다. 같은 해 로마 가톨릭으로 개종하여, 가장 유명한 시 「시나라」("Cynara")를 발표했다. 이 시는 "키나라, 나는 내 방식대로 당신에게 충실했습니다"라는 반복어로 널리 알려졌다. 두 사람이 만났을 때 12세에 불과했던 아델라이데는 그의 청혼을 거절했으나 그는 나름대로 6년 동안 애정을 바쳤다. 술과 여자에 빠져 짝사랑의 아픔을 달랬고 시간이 흐를수록 더 광포한 음악과 독한 술을 가까이 하며 그녀를 향한 사랑을 불태웠다.

다우슨은 아서 무어와 함께 쓴 2편의 장편소설 『가면들의 희극』(*A Comedy of Masks*) · 『에이드리언 롬』(*Adrian Rome*)과 단편소설집 『딜레마』 (*Dilemmas*)도 발표했으나, 『시집』(*Verses*) · 『장식물』(*Decorations*) 등의 시를 통해서 명성을 얻었다. 가락과 운율에 꼼꼼하게 집착하여 쓴 서정시는 세련되고 매혹적이다. W. B. 예이츠는 자신의 시 기교가 다우슨의 영향을 받아 많이 발전했음을 시인했다. 루퍼트 브룩의 초기 작품에서도 다우슨의 영향을 찾아볼 수 있다.

Cynara*

Non Sum Qualis Eram Bonae Sub Regno Cynarae

Last night, ah, yesternight, betwixt her lips and mine
There fell thy shadow, Cynara! thy breath was shed
Upon my soul between the kisses and the wine;
And I was desolate and sick of an old passion,
Yea, I was desolate and bowed my head:
I have been faithful to thee, Cynara! in my fashion.

All night upon mine heart I felt her warm heart beat,
Night-long within mine arms in love and sleep she lay;
Surely the kisses of her bought red mouth were sweet;
But I was desolate and sick of an old passion,
When I awoke and found the dawn was gray:
I have been faithful to thee, Cynara! in my fashion.

I have forgot much, Cynara! gone with the wind,
Flung roses, roses riotously with the throng,

---

* Dowson's Cynara represents the lost love who has become a constant obsession. The image the poet briefly draws of her is rather pre-Raphaelite, her "pale, lost lilies" contrasting with the prostitute's "bought red mouth" and the flung roses of dissipation. The diction is archaic: ("yesternight", "betwixt", "yea") but the scenes could not be more fin de siècle, more knowingly decadent. And yet the impression is of pure unfeigned emotion.

Dancing, to put thy pale, lost lilies out of mind;
But I was desolate and sick of an old passion,
Yea, all the time, because the dance was long:
I have been faithful to thee, Cynara! in my fashion.

I cried for madder music and for stronger wine,
But when the feast is finished and the lamps expire,
Then falls thy shadow, Cynara! the night is thine;
And I am desolate and sick of an old passion,
Yea, hungry for the lips of my desire:
I have been faithful to thee, Cynara! in my fashion.

April Love*

We have walked in Love's land a little way,
We have learnt his lesson a little while,
And shall we not part at the end of day,
With a sigh, a smile?

A little while in the shine of the sun,
We were twined together, joined lips forgot
How the shadows fall when day is done,
And when Love is not.

We have made no vows—there will none be broke,
Our love was free as the wind on the hill,

---

* The theme of my poem "April Love" by Ernest Dowson, is love can't last forever and that
sometimes you have to say goodbye. Throughout this poem the speaker talks about his love
towards another person.

There was no word said we need wish unspoke,
We have wrought no ill.

So shall we not part at the end of day,
Who have loved and lingered a little while,
Join lips for the last time, go our way,
With a sigh, a smile.

20세기 영국시 (1890-현재)

1914-18 : World War I
1918 : Gerard Manley Hopkins's poetry published.
1922 : T. S. Eliot's *The Waste Land*; James Joyce's *Ulysses*
1930 : Period of depression and unemployment begins.
1939-45 : World War II
1947 : India and Pakistan become independent nations.
1952 : George VI dies; accession of Elizabeth II.
1991 : Collapse of the Soviet Union.
1994 : Democracy comes to South Africa.

1. 시대적 배경

(1) 1900-45년의 문학

에드워드 시대의 많은 작가들은 새로운 세기에서 그들의 임무란 단호하게 교훈적인 태도를 보이는 것이어야 한다고 생각했다. 『인간과 초인』 (*Man and Superman*)이나 『소령 바버라』(*Major Barbara*)를 비롯한 일련의 재기발랄한 우상 파괴적 희극을 통해 조지 버나드 쇼는 극장을 당대의 주요한 관심사, 즉 정치조직의 문제, 무장과 전쟁의 도덕성, 계급과 직업의 기능,

가족과 결혼의 타당성, 여성해방의 문제 등을 다루는 토론장으로 만들었다. H. G. 웰스, 아널드 베넷, 존 골즈워디, E. M. 포스터 같은 많은 에드워드 시대 소설가들도 영국 사회생활의 결점들을 열심히 탐색했다. 이전 세기에 명성을 누렸던 토머스 하디와 러드야드 키플링 및 힐레어 벨록, G. K. 체스터턴, 에드워드 토머스 등은 미래에 대한 확신이 없었던 까닭에 발라드, 이야기체 시, 풍자, 공상, 지형설명풍의 시, 수필 같은 전통양식을 되살리려고 애썼다. 월터 드 라 메어, 존 메이스필드, 로버트 그레이브스, 에드먼드 블런든 등은 20세기 전반부 영국 문학에서 중요하면서도 종종 무시당한 흐름을 대변한다. 당대의 가장 중요한 글들은 전통적이든, 근대적이든, 희망이나 염려에서 씌어진 것이 아니라 새로운 세기가 문명 전체를 붕괴시키리라는 다소 어두운 느낌에서 비롯된 것이었다. 보어 전쟁에 대한 시에서 하디는 단순하면서도 냉소적으로 제국건설을 위해 인간이 치러야 하는 희생에 대한 질문을 던졌고, 많은 영국 시인들이 이 세기 동안 사용하게 된 어조와 문체를 확립했다. 쇠퇴하는 제국문명의 의미를 가장 충실하고 예리하게 포착한 사람은 미국의 망명작가 헨리 제임스였다. 그는 영국 상류층이 공동체에 대한 도덕적 의무감을 느끼는 것을 높이 평가했다. 그러나 세기말에 이르러 그는 혼란스러운 변화를 주목했다. 대영제국은 구세계의 다른 나라들과 다를 것이 없었으며, 언제나 추악한 탐욕을 숨기지 않았다. 이러한 상황에 대한 제임스의 낙담은 『비둘기의 날개』(*The Wings of the Dove*)·『사자들』(*The Ambassadors*)·『황금의 잔』(*The Golden Bowl*) 같은 후기 작품에서 어두운 환멸의 분위기로 나타났다. 또 다른 망명 작가인 조지프 콘래드는 제임스의 위기감을 공유했으나, 그것을 특정한 문명의 쇠퇴라기보다는 인간성 자체의 타락에 기인한 것으로 보았다. 인간은 의지를 가진 고독하고 낭만적인 존재로서, 자신을 중심에 놓지 않는 세계를 견딜 수 없기 때문에 어떠한 희생을 치르더라도 이 세상에 그의 의미를 강요하려고 한다. 『올메이어의 우행』(*Almayer's Folly*) · 『로드 짐』(*Lord Jim*)에서 그는 이러한 곤경에 공감을 표하는 것처럼 보였다. 그러나 『어둠의 한가운데』(*Heart of Darkness*) · 『노스트로모』(*Nostromo*) · 『비밀요원』(*The Secret Agent*) · 『서구인의 눈으로』(*Under Western Eyes*)에서는 이러한 공감이 눈에 띄게 사라졌다.

1908-14년에 소설가와 시인들은 후기 낭만주의 시대의 문학 관습에 도전하기 시작했다. 인류학 · 심리학 · 철학 · 정치이론 · 정신분석 등의 새 사상에 의해 자극받은 급진적이고 이상적인 정신인 모더니즘이 널리 퍼져 있었다. 이것은 이미지스트라 불리운 영 · 미 시인들의 작품에서 가장 두드러졌는데, 그중 대표적인 작가가 T. E. 흄, F. S. 플린트, 리처드 올딩턴 등의 영국 시인들과 힐다 둘리틀(H. D.), 에이미 로웰 등의 미국시인들이다. 이미지스트들은 언어를 정확한 묘사와 분위기 조성의 수단으로 만들기 위해 시어를 다듬었다. 이러한 목적을 위해 그들은 자유시나 비정형시를 실험했고, 이미지를 주요수단으로 만들었으며, 간결하고 절제된 형식을 사용했다. 제1차 세계대전은 모더니즘 혁명의 초기에 종지부를 찍었고, 영 · 미 모더니스트들은 이상과 혼란스런 현실 사이에 놓인 깊은 심연을 깨닫게 되었다.

2권의 가장 혁신적인 소설 『무지개』(*The Rainbow*) · 『사랑하는 여인들』(*Women in Love*)에서 D. H. 로렌스는 현대문명의 병리현상이 인간정신에 가해진 산업화의 영향 때문이라고 보았다. 그러나 그는 노동계층의 가족생활을 다룬 자전적 소설 『아들과 연인』(*Sons and Lovers*)에서 대단히 효과적으로 이용했던 소설 전통의 관습을 거부하고, 강렬한 인간관계와 열정을 통해 개인이나 집단이 새롭게 태어날 수 있으리라는 희망을 전개하기 위해 신화와 상징에 의존했다. 한편, 런던에 거주한 또 다른 미국 시인이며 극작가 T. S. 엘리엇은 그의 가장 혁신적인 시 『프루프록과 그 밖의 묘사』(*Prufrock and Other Observations*) · 『황무지』(*The Waste Land*)를 통해 현대문명의 질병은 현대인의 정신적 공허와 박탈감에서 비롯되었다고 보았다. 시 전통의 관습을 무시했기 때문에 엘리엇도 로렌스처럼 개인적·집단적 재생의 희망을 전개하기 위해 신화와 상징에 의존했으나, 재생이란 자기부정과 자기부인을 통해 얻어질 수 있다고 주장한 점에서 로렌스와 분명히 구별된다. 로렌스와 엘리엇은 전후시대에 영국에서 영·미 모더니즘을 이끈 지도적 인물이 되었다.

아일랜드의 시인이자 극작가인 윌리엄 버틀러 예이츠와 아일랜드 소설가인 제임스 조이스 역시 중요한 공헌을 했다. 젊었을 때 낭만주의와 라파엘 전파 운동에 영향을 받았던 예이츠는 초기 시와 극에서 자주 애매하고 과장된 언어로 아일랜드의 전설적이고 초자연적인 세계를 환기시켰다. 그의 원숙한 명상시가 지닌 위엄은 대체로 그가 이상화된 아일랜드를 허상이라고 인정했기 때문에 가능했다. 기량이 절정에 달했을 때의 문체는 정열과 정확성을 띠면서 동시에 강력한 상징, 힘찬 리듬, 명료한 어법을 보여준다. 뛰어난 단편모음집 『더블린 사람들』(*Dubliners*)과 자전적인 성격이 강한 소설 『젊은 예술가의 초상』(*A Portrait of the Artist as a Young Man*)에서 조이스는 성과 상상력이 억압된 아일랜드 생활 속에서 개인이 치러야 하는 희생을 묘사하고 있다. 이와는 매우 대조적으로, 『율리시스』(*Ulysses*)는 도시생활이 파노라마처럼 그려진 소설로 성의 묘사가 솔직하고 상상력이 풍부하다.

좀 더 전통적인 작가들, 특히 시인들은 제1차 세계대전의 경험을 사실적이면서 감동적으로 서술했다. 루퍼트 브룩은 전쟁 초기의 이상주의를 그려낸 뒤 전사했다. 시그프리드 서순은 전쟁이 계속되면서 점점 높아가는 분노와 소모감을 포착했다. 윌프리드 오언과 에드먼드 블런던은 참호 속의 전우애뿐만 아니라 전쟁으로 인해 야기된 좀 더 커다란 도덕적 혼돈까지도 표현했다. 전쟁이 끝나가면서 문단을 지배한 분위기는 올더스 헉슬리의 소설에서 볼 수 있듯이 냉소적이면서도 혼란된 것이었다. 그러나 헉슬리의 염세적인 관점은 1930년대에 그의 가장 유명하고 독창적인 소설이며 반유토피아 공상물인 『멋진 신세계』(Brave New World)와 당대 중산층 지식인의 불안을 묘사한 『가자에서 눈이 멀어』(Eyeless in Gaza)에서 가장 완벽하게 표현되었다. 『인도로 가는 길』(A Passage to India)에서 E. M. 포스터는 영국 통치하의 인도에서 다양한 인종적·사회적 집단이 서로 인간적 이해를 추구하다가 겪게 되는 좌절을 다루고 있다. 좀 더 젊고 현대적인 작가들은 블룸즈버리 그룹의 구성원들이었다. 영국 상류층에 속했던 그들 부모세대의 특징인 위선과 사기에 대항하여, 그들은 사생활이나 예술생활에서 시종일관 솔직하려고 노력했다. 이러한 태도는 버지니아 울프의 소설에서 심오하면서도 감동적인 결실을 맺었다. 대단히 섬세하고 서정적인 매력으로 가득 찬 장편·단편 소설에서 그녀는 시간 속에 묶여 있는 자아의 한계를 그려내기 시작했고, 또다른 자아나 어떤 장소 또는 예술작품에 몰두하면 이 한계는 잠시나마 극복될 수 있다고 주장했다. 『댈러웨이 부인』(Mrs. Dalloway)에 큰 영향을 미친 조이스와 더불어 울프는 소설에서 주관성·시간·사건을 처리하는 방식을 변모시켰으며, 전통적인 소설양식은 더이상 적절한 것이 될 수 없다는 느낌을 작가들 사이에 확산시켰다.

1930년대의 많은 글들은 황량하고 염세적인 느낌을 준다. W. H. 오든과 그의 옥스퍼드 대학교 동기인 C. 데이 루이스, 루이스 맥니스, 스티븐 스펜더의 시가 새로운 세대의 진정한 주장으로 곧 인정되었는데, 이는 그들의 시가 절망과 저항감을 조화시켰기 때문이다. 개인적 성향이 어떠했든 간에, 이 시인들은 모두 시에서 어조와 분위기의 급격한 변화, 일상적인 것과 신비한 것의 기이한 병치, 당시 사람들에게 상당히 매력적으로 보였던 진지함과 고상한 정신의 혼합을 보여 주었다. 1914년에 그랬던 것처럼 1939년에도 전쟁이 이 위대한 지성적·창조적 탐닉에 종지부를 찍었다. 이 시기의 걸작은 T. S. 엘리엇의 『4개의 4중주』(*Four Quartets*)로서, 그는 언어·시간·역사에 관한 명상을 통해 폐허의 와중에서 도덕적·종교적 의미를 찾으려 애썼다.

(2) 1945년 이후의 문학

제2차 세계대전이 끝나자 많은 작가들은 전통적인 가치를 갈구했고, 조지 오웰을 비롯한 작가들은 그 당시의 문명을 탐구했다. 오웰의 『동물농장』(*Animal Farm*)은 파시즘에 대한 승리가 어떤 면에서는 전체주의의 확산에 무의식적인 도움을 줄 수도 있다는 쓰디쓴 진실을 다루고 있는 반면, 『1984년』(*Nineteen Eighty-four*)은 개인의 권리를 잠식하는 집단주의가 개인에게 미치는 위험을 경고했으며, 한편 엘리엇은 시를 포기하고 희곡과 비평에 전념했다. 엘리엇의 작품 활동이 뜸한 가운데 절정기에 이른 오든과 그레이브스가 전후 최고의 시인으로 떠올랐다. 부분적으로는 전쟁과 관련된 이유 때문에 초현실주의와 신화가 상당히 중시되고 시에 묵시적·신낭만주의적·수사적 분위기가 발전했다. 이러한 분위기를 표현한 가장 뛰어난 시인으로는 딜런 토머스와 여류시인 에디스 싯웰, 데이비드 개스코인과 조지 바커가 있다. 이블린 워는 전쟁에 대해서 아주 다른 반응을 보였다. 그의 소설 『다시 가본 브라이즈헤드』(*Brideshead Revisited*)는 인간사에서 작용하는 신의 은총을 탐구해보려는 시도였다. 워 세대의 다른 소설가로 전후에 그와 비슷한 명성을 얻은 사람은 앤소니 파웰이다. 파웰의 뛰어난 재능은 12권의 연작소설 『시간의 음악에 맞춰 춤을』(*A Dance to the Music of Time*)에서 뚜렷이 나타난다. 파웰과 워는 당대의 가장 탁월한 문장가였다. 킹즐리 에이미스는 존 웨인, 존 브레인, 앨런 실리토 등 1950년대에 나타난 우상파괴적 소설가 가운데 단연 독보적인 존재이다. 『럭키 짐』(*Lucky Jim*)

은 에이미스 특유의 악의 어린 희극적 관점과 당대의 언어 변화에 대한 남다른 감각에서 나온 작품이다. 에이미스의 중요한 동료로는 아이리스 머독과 앵거스 윌슨이 있는데, 이 두 사람은 에이미스처럼 자유주의적·인본적 전통에 속해 있다. 인물중심의 소설과 현대 소설이론의 긴박한 요구를 서로 조화시키는 것이 극히 중요해졌다. 그렇게 함으로써만 영국 소설이 삶과의 관계를 잃지 않으면서 동시에 예술로서의 활력을 갱신시킬 수 있었다. 당대의 반가운 현상은 신예 작가들과 수많은 원로 소설가들 간의 적극적인 상호 교류였다. 1960년대 이후 우수한 소설가들은 형식의 문제에만 지나치게 관심을 기울이는 경우가 종종 있었으나, 그들은 이러한 관심을 자유주의적 소설에 접목시켜 힘과 다양성을 이끌어내기도 했다. 이러한 예로는 윌리엄 골딩, 앤소니 버제스, 도리스 레싱, 뮤리얼 스파크, V. S. 나이파울을 들 수 있다.

20세기 중반의 가장 주목할 만한 영국 시인 중 한 사람은 필립 라킨이다. 라킨은 마음속에 미묘하고 개인적인 인상들을 채색시키기 위한 단어와 운율을 사용했다. 그는 통제와 조직화에 남다른 재능을 가지고 있으며, 일상성과 단조로움, 고통에서 아름다움을 추출할 수 있었다. 테드 휴스의 작품 역시 중요한데, 그의 작품은 통제된 폭력, 동물적인 본능을 가진 내면성, 인간성의 다듬어지지 않은 측면에 대한 강렬한 탐색 등이 특징이다. 아일랜드 시인 시머스 히니는 1970년대에 등장해, 20세기 후반의 가장 영향력 있는 시인으로 떠올랐다.

전후에 진정으로 급격한 변화가 일어난 곳은 연극 부문이었다. 『성난 얼굴로 돌아보라』(*Look Back in Anger*)에서 존 오즈번은 잘 다듬어진 희곡의 전통을 거부하고, 현대 생활의 강압과 흥분이 관객에게 그대로 전달되도록 만들었다. 그러나 아일랜드 극작가 새뮤얼 베케트가 처음 사용한 혁명적 방법은 이보다 훨씬 더 중요하다. 『고도를 기다리며』(*Waiting for*

Godot)는 장식 없는 무대, 나무 한 그루, 조명만으로 이루어진 극히 간단한 소품과 극도로 절제된 대사만으로도 인간 정신의 내면적이고 잠재적인 활동을 극화함으로써 관객에게 감동과 즐거움을 줄 수 있다는 것을 보여주었다. 베케트는 예술의 유혹적인 환상을 거부하고, 그 대신 가장 단순하고 가장 본질적인 의미의 핵심을 추구했다. 해럴드 핀터는 『생일 파티』(*The Birthday Party*) · 『관리인』(*The Caretaker*) · 『귀향』(*The Homecoming*) 등에서 베케트로부터 모든 것을 해소시킨 극을 쓰는 기법을 배워 그것을 독특한 방식으로 발전시켰다. 좀더 인습적인 극작가들이 인생의 모호하고 불가해한 측면을 설명해야 한다는 의무감을 느끼는 반면, 핀터는 모든 이들이 경험하면서도 제대로 이해하지 못하는 심리적 권력투쟁과 정신적인 위기를 꾸밈없이 제시함으로써 또 다른 유형의 극을 이끌어낼 수 있다는 것을 보여준다. 조 오턴의 소란스럽고 무질서한 희극과 톰 스토파드의 양식적이고 기교가 뛰어난 극들 역시 주목할 만하다.

2. 주요 작가와 작품

(1) T. S. 엘리엇 T. S. Eliot, 1888-1965

미국의 미주리 주 세인트루이스 출신으로 스미스 아카데미를 거쳐 1906년 하버드 대학교에 들어가 철학을 전공하는 한편 프랑스문학을 공부하고 그 상징시에 깊은 관심을 가졌는데, 그 영향은 후에 그의 시작품에 나타나게 된다. 그 밖에도 17세기 영국의 형이상학시와 엘리자베스조 연극을 연구하였다. 하버드 대학교 졸업 후 한때 프랑스의 소르본 대학에 유학, 이어 1914년에 독일에 유학하였으나 제1차 세계대전의 발발로 영국에 피란, 옥스퍼드 대학교에서 연구하였으며, 1915년에 처음으로 지상에 시를 발표하였다. 그 후에도 계속 영국에 머물며 은행원으로 근무하는 한편 시작에 몰두, 1917년에 처녀시집 『프루프록 및 그 밖의 관찰』(*Prufrock and Other Observation*)을 냈고, 이어 1920년에는 처녀평론집 『성스러운 숲』(*The Sacred Wood*)을 내놓아 새로운 문예평론의 입장을 보였다.

그러나 그의 명성을 높여 준 것은 1922년에 그가 편집·창간한 문화평론지 『크라이티어리언』(*Criterion*)에 발표한 『황무지』(*The Waste Land*)이다. 이 작품으로 종래의 미온적인 낭만주의는 자취를 감추게 되었고, 일부 보수적인 시인들의 공격을 받기도 했으나, 20세기 시단의 가장 중요한 작품의 하나로 자리를 굳히게 되었다. 1927년 영국에 귀화하는 동시에 영국 국교로 개종, 1928년에 강행된 평론집 『랜슬롯 앤드루스를 위하여』(*For Lancelot Andrewes*)의 서문에서, '문학적으로는 고전주의자, 정치적으로는 왕정 지지자, 종교적으로는 영국 국교도'임을 선언하였다. 1932년 미국에 돌아가 하버드 대학교 시학 교수 칭호를 받았으며, 그 후에는 주로 런던에 거주하면서, 참신한 문예서적을 많이 간행하는 출판사 'Faber & Faber'의 중역이 되어 영국문단의 중진으로 활동하였고, 1948년에는 노벨문학상을 받았다. 그의 초기의 시는 영국의 형이상학시와 프랑스 상징시에서 받은 영향이 짙으며, 현대문명의 퇴폐상을 그리면서 그 배경으로 신화의 세계를 엿보게 한다.

『황무지』 이후 1930년에 간행된 시집 『재의 수요일』(*Ash Wednesday*)에서는 종교적 색채가 한층 더 짙어졌으며, 그의 시인으로서의 정점은 제2차 세계대전 전부터 쓰기 시작하여 전후에 완성한 『4개의 4중주』(*Four Quartets*)에서 볼 수 있다. 그는 또한 시극에 관심을 가져, 『바위』(*The Rock*), 『성당의 살인』(*Murder in the Catheadral*) 『가족의 재회』(*The Family Reunion*), 『칵테일파티』(*The Cocktail Party*) 등을 발표하였다. 또한 그 동안 간행된 여

러 권의 평론집이 1932년과 1951년에 각각 『평론선집』으로서 정리·간행
되었다. 한편, 그는 문예비평에서 점차 문명비평으로 옮겨가서 『시의 효용
과 비평의 효용』(*The Use of Poetry and the Use of Criticism*), 『이신을 찾아서』
(*After Strange Gods*), 『고금 평론집』(*Essays Ancient and Modern*), 『문화의 정의
에 대한 노트』(*Notes towards the Definition of Culture*) 등을 발표하였다.

Gerontion*

Thou hast nor youth nor age

> *But as it were an after dinner sleep*
> *Dreaming of both.*

Here I am, an old man in a dry month,
Being read to by a boy, waiting for rain.
I was neither at the hot gates
Nor fought in the warm rain
Nor knee deep in the salt marsh, heaving a cutlass,
Bitten by flies, fought.
My house is a decayed house,
And the Jew squats on the window sill, the owner,
Spawned in some estaminet of Antwerp,
Blistered in Brussels, patched and peeled in London.

---

* "Gerontion" is structured in six stanzas. The first introduces the narrator, who describes
himself as an old man who has never really done much with his life. He has had no
passionate involvements, no great battles, and is mindful only of living in a "decayed house,"
by which he refers both to his physical house and to his aging body.

Rhapsody on a Windy Night*

Twelve o'clock.
Along the reaches of the street
Held in a lunar synthesis,
Whispering lunar incantations
Dissolve the floors of memory
And all its clear relations
Its divisions and precisions,
Every street lamp that I pass
Beats like a fatalistic drum,
And through the spaces of the dark
Midnight shakes the memory
As a madman shakes a dead geranium.

Preludes**

I

The winter evening settles down
With smell of steaks in passageways.
Six o'clock.

---

* T. S. Eliot's poem, Rhapsody on a Windy Night, is full of blunt imagery that evokes the individual's increasing isolation in a depleted, worn-out society. "Rhapsody on a Windy Night" is one of the best-loved poems by T S Eliot and one which is sometimes characterised as lyrical and pensive, and more to do with the function of memory than anything else.

** "The Prelude is the greatest long poem in our language after Paradise Lost," says one critic. Its comparison with the great seventeenth-century epic is in some respects a happy one since Milton was (after Coleridge) Wordsworth's greatest idol. "The Prelude" may be classed somewhat loosely as an epic; it does not satisfy all the traditional qualifications of that genre.

The burnt-out ends of smoky days.
And now a gusty shower wraps
The grimy scraps
Of withered leaves about your feet
And newspapers from vacant lots;
The showers beat
On broken blinds and chimney-pots,
And at the corner of the street
A lonely cab-horse steams and stamps.

And then the lighting of the lamps.

II

The morning comes to consciousness
Of faint stale smells of beer
From the sawdust-trampled street
With all its muddy feet that press
To early coffee-stands.
With the other masquerades
That time resumes,
One thinks of all the hands
That are raising dingy shades
In a thousand furnished rooms.

III

You tossed a blanket from the bed,
You lay upon your back, and waited;
You dozed, and watched the night revealing
The thousand sordid images
Of which your soul was constituted;
They flickered against the ceiling.

And when all the world came back

And the light crept up between the shutters

And you heard the sparrows in the gutters,

You had such a vision of the street

As the street hardly understands;

Sitting along the bed's edge, where

You curled the papers from your hair,

Or clasped the yellow soles of feet

In the palms of both soiled hands.

The Love Song of J. Alfred Prufrock*

LET us go then, you and I,

When the evening is spread out against the sky

Like a patient etherized upon a table;

Let us go, through certain half-deserted streets,

The muttering retreats

Of restless nights in one-night cheap hotels

And sawdust restaurants with oyster-shells:

Streets that follow like a tedious argument

Of insidious intent

To lead you to an overwhelming question···.

Oh, do not ask, "What is it?"

Let us go and make our visit.

---

* J. Alfred Prufrock, a presumably middle-aged, intellectual, indecisive man, invites the reader
along with him through the modern city. He describes the street scene and notes a social
gathering of women discussing Renaissance artist Michelangelo. He describes yellow smoke
and fog outside the house of the gathering, and keeps insisting that there will be time to do
many things in the social world.

In the room the women come and go
Talking of Michelangelo.

The yellow fog that rubs its back upon the window-panes,
The yellow smoke that rubs its muzzle on the window-panes
Licked its tongue into the corners of the evening,
Lingered upon the pools that stand in drains,
Let fall upon its back the soot that falls from chimneys,
Slipped by the terrace, made a sudden leap,
And seeing that it was a soft October night,
Curled once about the house, and fell asleep.

And indeed there will be time
For the yellow smoke that slides along the street,
Rubbing its back upon the window panes;
There will be time, there will be time
To prepare a face to meet the faces that you meet;
There will be time to murder and create,
And time for all the works and days of hands
That lift and drop a question on your plate;
Time for you and time for me,
And time yet for a hundred indecisions,
And for a hundred visions and revisions,
Before the taking of a toast and tea.

In the room the women come and go
Talking of Michelangelo.

The Journey Of The Magi*

'A cold coming we had of it,
Just the worst time of the year
For a journey, and such a long journey:
The ways deep and the weather sharp,
The very dead of winter.'
And the camels galled, sorefooted, refractory,
Lying down in the melting snow.
There were times we regretted
The summer palaces on slopes, the terraces,
And the silken girls bringing sherbet.
Then the camel men cursing and grumbling
and running away, and wanting their liquor and women,
And the night-fires going out, and the lack of shelters,
And the cities hostile and the towns unfriendly
And the villages dirty and charging high prices:
A hard time we had of it.
At the end we preferred to travel all night,
Sleeping in snatches,
With the voices singing in our ears, saying
That this was all folly.

Then at dawn we came down to a temperate valley,
Wet, below the snow line, smelling of vegetation;
With a running stream and a water-mill beating the darkness,

---

* The poem is an account of the journey from the point of view of one of the magi. It picks
up Eliot's consistent theme of alienation and a feeling of powerlessness in a world that has
changed. In this regard, with a speaker who laments outliving his world, the poem recalls
Arnold's Dover Beach, as well as a number of Eliot's own works.

And three trees on the low sky,
And an old white horse galloped away in the meadow.
Then we came to a tavern with vine-leaves over the lintel,
Six hands at an open door dicing for pieces of silver,
And feet kiking the empty wine-skins.
But there was no information, and so we continued
And arriving at evening, not a moment too soon
Finding the place; it was (you might say) satisfactory.

All this was a long time ago, I remember,
And I would do it again, but set down
This set down
This: were we led all that way for
Birth or Death? There was a Birth, certainly
We had evidence and no doubt. I had seen birth and death,
But had thought they were different; this Birth was
Hard and bitter agony for us, like Death, our death.
We returned to our places, these Kingdoms,
But no longer at ease here, in the old dispensation,
With an alien people clutching their gods.
I should be glad of another death.

The Four Quartets
Burnt Norton*

I

Time present and time past
Are both perhaps present in time future

---

* Four Quartets are four interlinked meditations with the common theme being man's relationship

And time future contained in time past.
If all time is eternally present
All time is unredeemable.
What might have been is an abstraction
Remaining a perpetual possibility
Only in a world of speculation.
What might have been and what has been
Point to one end, which is always present.
Footfalls echo in the memory
Down the passage which we did not take
Towards the door we never opened
Into the rose-garden. My words echo
Thus, in your mind.

                                    But to what purpose
Disturbing the dust on a bowl of rose-leaves
I do not know.

                                    Other echoes
Inhabit the garden. Shall we follow?
Quick, said the bird, find them, find them,
Round the corner. Through the first gate,
Into our first world, shall we follow
The deception of the thrush? Into our first world.
There they were, dignified, invisible,
Moving without pressure, over the dead leaves,
In the autumn heat, through the vibrant air,
And the bird called, in response to
The unheard music hidden in the shrubbery,

---

with time, the universe, and the divine. In describing his understanding of the divine within
the poems, Eliot blends his Anglo-Catholicism with mystical, philosophical and poetic works
from both Eastern and Western religious and cultural traditions, with references to the
Bhagavad-Gita and the Pre-Socratics as well as St. John of the Cross and Julian of Norwich.

And the unseen eyebeam crossed, for the roses
Had the look of flowers that are looked at.
There they were as our guests, accepted and accepting.
So we moved, and they, in a formal pattern,
Along the empty alley, into the box circle,
To look down into the drained pool.
Dry the pool, dry concrete, brown edged,
And the pool was filled with water out of sunlight,
And the lotos rose, quietly, quietly,
The surface glittered out of heart of light,
And they were behind us, reflected in the pool.
Then a cloud passed, and the pool was empty.
Go, said the bird, for the leaves were full of children,
Hidden excitedly,· containing laughter.
Go, go, go, said the bird: human kind
Cannot bear very much reality.
Time past and time future
What might have been and what has been
Point to one end, which is always present.

(2) 루퍼트 브룩 Rupert Brooke, 1887-1915

럭비 출신으로 럭비 학교 · 케임브리지 대학교를 졸업하였다. 럭비학
교 시절부터 시재를 인정받고, 1911년 처녀시집을 간행하였다. 1913-1914
년 미국 하와이 · 타히티섬 · 오스트레일리아 등지를 여행하며 많은 시를
썼다. 제1차 세계대전에 참전하였다가 그리스에서 병사하였다. 소네트집
『1914년』, 평론집 『존 웹스터와 엘리자베스조 연극』(*John Webster and the
Elizabethan Drama*) 및 H. 제임스의 서문을 붙인 『미국으로부터의 편지』
(*Letters from America*)를 남겼다.

The Soldier*

If I should die, think only this of me;
  That there's some corner of a foreign field
That is for ever England. There shall be
  In that rich earth a richer dust concealed;
A dust whom England bore, shaped, made aware,
  Gave, once, her flowers to love, her ways to roam,
A body of England's breathing English air,
  Washed by the rivers, blest by suns of home.

And think, this heart, all evil shed away,
  A pulse in the eternal mind, no less
    Gives somewhere back the thoughts by England given;
Her sights and sounds; dreams happy as her day;
  And laughter, learnt of friends; and gentleness,
    In hearts at peace, under an English heaven.

(3) 윌프레드 오웬 Wilfred Owen, 1893-1918

웨일스 지방 오즈워스트리 출신으로 어릴 때부터 병약하고 공상적이어서 일찍이 키츠의 영향을 받았다. 1910년 런던대학에 입학하였으나, 중퇴하였다. 1913년에 프랑스로 건너가 보르도에서 가정교사를 하면서 프랑스 사람 특유의 사고방식에 친숙해졌다. 제1차 세계대전이 일어나자 1915년 장교로서 솜 전선에 나갔다. 전장의 인상이나 전쟁에 대한 비판·자책

---

* "The Soldier" is a sonnet in which Brooke glorifies England during the First World War. He speaks in the guise of an English soldier as he is leaving home to go to war. The poem represents the patriotic ideals that characterized pre-war England. It portrays death for one's country as a noble end and England as the noblest country for which to die.

이 어머니와 친구에게 보낸 편지에 남아 있다. 그 해 여름 참호열로 에든 버러 교외의 병원에 입원 중 시인 S. L. 서순(Siegfried (Lorraine) Sassoon) 을 만나 그의 영향을 받았다. 1918년 8월 다시 서부전선으로 나가 전공을 세워 십자훈장을 받았으나, 11월 휴전되기 1주일 전 전사하였다. 내용·기교의 양면에 걸쳐 현대 영국의 시에 많은 영향을 끼쳤다. 특히 종래의 각운을 바꾸어 자유롭게 모운압운을 쓴 것은 특기할 만하다. 작품 중 전장에서 죽인 상대방의 영혼과 지옥에서 만나 서로 이야기한다는 『기묘한 조우』 (*Strange Meeting*)가 가장 특출하다.

Anthem for Doomed Youth*

What passing-bells for these who die as cattle?
    —Only the monstrous anger of the guns.
    Only the stuttering rifles' rapid rattle
Can patter out their hasty orisons.
No mockeries now for them; no prayers nor bells;
    Nor any voice of mourning save the choirs,—
The shrill, demented choirs of wailing shells;
    And bugles calling for them from sad shires.

What candles may be held to speed them all?
    Not in the hands of boys, but in their eyes

---

* This searing poem is one of Owen's most critically acclaimed. It was written in the fall of 1917 and published posthumously in 1920. It may be a response to the anonymous preface from Poems of Today (1916), which proclaims that boys and girls should know about the poetry of their time, which has many different themes that "mingle and interpenetrate throughout, to the music of Pan's flute, and of Love's viol, and the bugle-call of Endeavor, and the passing-bells of death."

Shall shine the holy glimmers of goodbyes.

The pallor of girls' brows shall be their pall;
Their flowers the tenderness of patient minds,
And each slow dusk a drawing-down of blinds.

Dulce Et Decorum Est *

Bent double, like old beggars under sacks,
Knock-kneed, coughing like hags, we cursed through sludge,
Till on the haunting flares we turned out backs,
And towards our distant rest began to trudge.
Men marched asleep. Many had lost their boots,
But limped on, blood-shod. All went lame, all blind;
Drunk with fatigue; deaf even to the hoots
Of gas-shells dropping softly behind.

Gas! GAS! Quick, boys!—An ecstasy of fumbling
Fitting the clumsy helmets just in time,
But someone still was yelling out and stumbling
And flound'ring like a man in fire or lime. —
Dim through the misty panes and thick green light,
As under a green sea, I saw him drowning.

In all my dreams before my helpless sight
He plunges at me, guttering, choking, drowning.

---

* "Dulce et Decorum est" is without a doubt one of, if not the most, memorable and
anthologized poems in Owen's oeuvre. Its vibrant imagery and searing tone make it an
unforgettable excoriation of WWI, and it has found its way into both literature and history
courses as a paragon of textual representation of the horrors of the battlefield.

If in some smothering dreams, you too could pace

Behind the wagon that we flung him in,

And watch the white eyes writhing in his face,

His hanging face, like a devil's sick of sin,

If you could hear, at every jolt, the blood

Come gargling from the froth-corrupted lungs

Bitter as the cud

Of vile, incurable sores on innocent tongues, —

My friend, you would not tell with such high zest

To children ardent for some desperate glory,

The old Lie: Dulce et decorum est

Pro patria mori.

(4) 윌리엄 예이츠 William Butler Yeats, 1865–1939

1865년 더블린 샌디마운트에서 출신으로 화가의 아들로 태어나 더블린 및 런던에서 화가가 되려고 수업하였으나 전향하여 시작에 전념하였다. 최초의 주목할 만한 시집 『오이진의 방랑기』(*The Wandering of Oisin and other Poems*)는 켈트 문학 특유의 유현하고 표묘한 정서를 풍겨, 당시의 세기말 시인들의 호평을 받았으며, 그들과의 교우로 '시인 클럽'의 결성을 보게 되었다. 이 시기의 그는 라파엘 전파의 영향 아래, 낭만적인 주제와 몽환적인 심상을 즐겨 묘사하였다.

1891년 동지들과 더불어 아일랜드 문예협회를 창립, 당시 팽배하던 아일랜드 문예부흥운동에 참가하였으며, 이어 그레고리 부인 등과 협력하여 1899년에 아일랜드 국민극장을 더블린에 창립하였다. 한편 미모의 민족주의자 M. 곤 등을 통해 아일랜드 독립운동에 참가하여 아일랜드 자유국 성립 후에는 원로원 의원이 되었다. 그는 1923년에는 노벨문학상을 수상하였다. 극장 경영, 배우 훈련, 정치 참여 등 그의 시인으로서의 생의 중기는 대체로 실천에 중점을 두었다. 낭만적이고 신화적인 그의 시상은 이 실천으로 하여 정신적 고통을 겪게 되었다. 그러면서도 한편 여전히 심령론 연구를 계속하였고, 1917년에는 무녀와 결혼까지 하였다. 예이츠의 복잡한 후기의 시적 정신이 가장 분명하게 작품에 나타나기 시작한 것은 시집 『탑』(*The Tower*) 등에서 비롯된다 하겠다. 그의 초기 작품에서 보여주던 여성적이고 우미하던 스타일은 딱딱하고 건조한 남성적인 것으로 변화하고, 환상적이던 심상은 금속적이라 할 만큼 구체성을 지닌 심상으로 전화하였다. 그와 동시에 주의의 초점은 그 근저에 깔린 세계관의 심화이다.

그는 시초부터 라파엘 전파, 이어서 상징주의의 영향에서 자연과 대립하여, 자연보다 우월한 것으로서의 예술의 세계를 믿어 왔다. 그의 후기의 고투는 이 자연(자아)의 세계와 자연 부정(예술)의 세계의 상극을 극복하는 고뇌라 해도 무방할 것이다. 이 고뇌를 그는 W. 블레이크의 『예언의 서』를 생각하게 하는, 독자적 신화로써 극복하려고 하였다. 그 기록이 난해한 산문집 『환상』(*A Vision*) 이다. 예이츠의 과제가 현대시의 중추 과제에 이어지는 것은 분명하며, 시인·비평가인 프레이저가 J. 던, J. 밀턴, W. 워즈워스에 그를 비견하는 것도 무리가 아니다.

Sailing to Byzantium*

That is no country for old men. The young
In one another's arms, birds in the trees
—Those dying generations—at their song,
The salmon-falls, the mackerel-crowded seas,

---

* This is Yeats' most famous poem about aging—a theme that preoccupies him throughout

Fish, flesh, or fowl, commend all summer long
Whatever is begotten, born, and dies.
Caught in that sensual music all neglect
Monuments of unageing intellect.

An aged man is but a paltry thing,
A tattered coat upon a stick, unless
Soul clap its hands and sing, and louder sing
For every tatter in its mortal dress,
Nor is there singing school but studying
Monuments of its own magnificence;
And therefore I have sailed the seas and come
To the holy city of Byzantium.

O sages standing in God's holy fire
As in the gold mosaic of a wall,
Come from the holy fire, perne in a gyre,
And be the singing-masters of my soul.
Consume my heart away; sick with desire
And fastened to a dying animal
It knows not what it is; and gather me
Into the artifice of eternity.

Once out of nature I shall never take
My bodily form from any natural thing,
But such a form as Grecian goldsmiths make

The Tower. The poem traces the speaker's movement from youth to age, and the corresponding geographical move from Ireland, a country just being born as Yeats wrote, to Byzantium. Yeats felt that he no longer belonged in Ireland, as the young or the young in brutality, were caught up in what he calls "sensual music." This is the allure of murder in the name of republicanism, which disgusted Yeats.

Of hammered gold and gold enamelling
To keep a drowsy Emperor awake;
Or set upon a golden bough to sing
To lords and ladies of Byzantium
Of what is past, or passing, or to come.

(2000년 중등영어 임용고시 기출문제)

Byzantium*

Miracle, bird or golden handiwork,
More miracle than bird or handiwork,
Planted on the star-lit golden bough,
Can like the cocks of Hades crow,
Or, by the moon embittered, scorn aloud
In glory of changeless metal
Common bird or petal
And all complexities of mire or blood.

Under Ben Bulben**

Swear by what the sages spoke
Round the Mareotic Lake

---

* This poem Byzantium by William Butler Yeats is written after four years of his writing the poem entitled "Sailing to Byzantium". The poem "Byzantium" is parallel to "Sailing to Byzantium". Both poems are the poems about escape from a world of flux to the kingdom of permanence.

** "Under Ben Bulben" is a long poem of ninety-four lines divided into six movements celebrating William Butler Yeats's vision of an artistically integrated spiritual reality. He exhorts readers and artists to share this vision for the fulfillment of the human race through art.

That the Witch of Atlas knew,
Spoke and set the cocks a-crow.

Swear by those horsemen, by those women
Complexion and form prove superhuman,
That pale, long-visaged company
That air in immortality
Completeness of their passions won;
Now they ride the wintry dawn
Where Ben Bulben sets the scene.

Here's the gist of what they mean.

Leda and the Swan*

A sudden blow: the great wings beating still
Above the staggering girl, her thighs caressed
By the dark webs, her nape caught in his bill,
He holds her helpless breast upon his breast.

How can those terrified vague fingers push
The feathered glory from her loosening thighs?
And how can body, laid in that white rush,
But feel the strange heart beating where it lies?

A shudder in the loins engenders there

---

* The myth of Leda and the Swan is a familiar one from Classical mythology. Zeus fell in love
with a mortal, Leda the Trojan queen, and raped her while taking on the form of a swan
to protect his identity. She became pregnant with Helen of Troy. That Helen was part
goddess helps to explain how her beauty brought about the destruction of two civilizations.

The broken wall, the burning roof and tower
And Agamemnon dead.

                                    Being so caught up,
So mastered by the brute blood of the air,
Did she put on his knowledge with his power
Before the indifferent beak could let her drop?

Down By the Salley Gardens*

Down by the salley gardens
    my love and I did meet;
She passed the salley gardens
    with little snow-white feet.
She bid me take love easy,
    as the leaves grow on the tree;
But I, being young and foolish,
    with her would not agree.

In a field by the river
    my love and I did stand,
And on my leaning shoulder
    she laid her snow-white hand.
She bid me take life easy,
    as the grass grows on the weirs;
But I was young and foolish,
    and now am full of tears.

---

* "Down by the Salley Gardens" is kind of a poet's way of playing with famous songs and
changing them to his own liking. The story goes that Yeats heard this old Irish folk song
one day, and was so tickled by it that he took it upon himself to give it his own spin.

Cloths of Heaven *

Had I the heavens' embroidered cloths,
Enwrought with golden and silver light,
The blue and the dim and the dark cloths
Of night and light and the half-light,
I would spread the cloths under your feet:
But I, being poor, have only my dreams;
I have spread my dreams under your feet;
Tread softly because you tread on my dreams.

Easter 1916 **

I have met them at close of day
Coming with vivid faces
From counter or desk among grey
Eighteenth-century houses.
I have passed with a nod of the head
Or polite meaningless words,
Or have lingered awhile and said

---

* This short, love, lyric poem "He Wishes for the Cloths of Heaven" composed by the well
known Irish poet W. B. Yeats has expressed his personal feeling for his beloved. The poet
himself is identified as the main character in the poem. Here he says that if he had some
fine cloths of gold and silver embellished with fine colors, he would spread them on the
ground where his beloved would walk. But because of his poverty, he could not afford
such heavenly comfort to her.

** Easter 1916 by William Butler Yeats is a poem about an Irish immature revolutionary plan
which became unsuccessful to overthrow the British reign in Ireland. About fifteen hundred
people participated in this revolution to seize the government office building of Dublin on
Easter morning, but three hundred of them were killed on the spot, and more than two
hundred people were taken as prisoner and tortured.

Polite meaningless words,
And thought before I had done
Of a mocking tale or a gibe
To please a companion
Around the fire at the club,
Being certain that they and I
But lived where motley is worn:
All changed, changed utterly:
A terrible beauty is born.

The Second Coming*

Turning and turning in the widening gyre
The falcon cannot hear the falconer;
Things fall apart; the centre cannot hold;
Mere anarchy is loosed upon the world,
The blood-dimmed tide is loosed, and everywhere
The ceremony of innocence is drowned;
The best lack all conviction, while the worst
Are full of passionate intensity.

Surely some revelation is at hand;
Surely the Second Coming is at hand.
The Second Coming! Hardly are those words out
When a vast image out of Spiritus Mundi

---

* In The Second Coming poet's mind was filled with gloom in consequence of the side-spread murder and bloodshed in Ireland in the course of the Easter rebellion of 1916. The Irish civil war that followed the great war of 1914-1919 and various other events in Europe added to that gloom.

Troubles my sight: a waste of desert sand;
A shape with lion body and the head of a man,
A gaze blank and pitiless as the sun,
Is moving its slow thighs, while all about it
Wind shadows of the indignant desert birds.

The darkness drops again but now I know
That twenty centuries of stony sleep
Were vexed to nightmare by a rocking cradle,
And what rough beast, its hour come round at last,
Slouches towards Bethlehem to be born?

After Long Silence*

Speech after long silence; it is right,
All other lovers being estranged or dead,
Unfriendly lamplight hid under its shade,
The curtains drawn upon unfriendly night,
That we descant and yet again descant
Upon the supreme theme of Art and Song:
Bodily decrepitude is wisdom; young
We loved each other and were ignorant.

---

* Yeats complains that the wisdom of old age is insufficient compensation for the loss of
loveliness and physical love. And in other places he curses the mental and physical
insufficiencies that come with age.

When You Are Old*

When you are old and grey and full of sleep,
And nodding by the fire, take down this book,
And slowly read, and dream of the soft look
Your eyes had once, and of their shadows deep;

How many loved your moments of glad grace,
And loved your beauty with love false or true,
But one man loved the pilgrim soul in you,
And loved the sorrows of your changing face;

And bending down beside the glowing bars,
Murmur, a little sadly, how Love fled
And paced upon the mountains overhead
And hid his face amid a crowd of stars.

Among School Children**

I

I walk through the long schoolroom questioning;
A kind old nun in a white hood replies;

---

* "When You Are Old" was written for Maud Gonne. It is based on Ronsard's "Quand Vous Serez Bien Vieille," Sonnets Pour Helene (1578), which maintains the Maud Gonne/Helen of Troy parallel that Yeats so often draws. The idea of love in age is an ancient one, meant to express the fact that love inheres not merely in youth, but in something deeper and more lasting.

** The central themes of "Among School Children" are best exemplified in the central action: A sixty-year-old official is visiting with elementary school children. The age-old poetic themes of innocence versus experience, naïveté versus wisdom, and youth versus age permeate every stanza of the poem.

The children learn to cipher and to sing,
To study reading-books and histories,
To cut and sew, be neat in everything
In the best modern way—the children's eyes
In momentary wonder stare upon
A sixty-year-old smiling public man.

II

I dream of a Ledaean body, bent
Above a sinking fire, a tale that she
Told of a harsh reproof, or trivial event
That changed some childish ·day to tragedy—
Told, and it seemed that our two natures blent
Into a sphere from youthful sympathy,
Or else, to alter Plato's parable,
Into the yolk and white of the one shell.

(5) 데이비드 허버트 로렌스 David Herbert Lawrence, 1885-1930

D. H. 로렌스는 영국 노팅엄셔 주의 탄광촌 이스트우드 출생하여 조부시절부터 광부였던 아버지와, 조선기사 딸로 교사를 지낸 중류계급 출신인 어머니와의 계급 차에서 오는 계속적인 불화가, 어린 시절의 그의 성격 형성에 많은 영향을 끼쳤다. 이러한 사정들이 뒷날 그의 문학에 흐르는 주제의 한 원형을 이루었다. 노팅엄 대학 사범부를 졸업한 후 1909년부터 3년간 런던 교외 크로이든의 초등학교에서 교편을 잡았다. 1910년 12월에 어머니를 여의고 1912년 봄에는 노팅엄 대학 시절의 은사 E. 위클리의 부인이며 6세나 연상인 프리다와 사랑에 빠져 둘이서 독일 · 이탈리아 등을 전전하였는데, 『아들과 연인』(*Sons and Lovers*, 1913)은 이때에 쓴 것이다.

1914년에 영국으로 돌아와 프리다와 정식으로 결혼하였고, 제1차 세계 대전 때는 아내가 적국인이라는 이유와 그 밖의 이유로 박해를 받아 전쟁과 사람들의 광기를 저주하면서 영국 각지를 유랑하였다. 1915년에는 『무지개』(*The Rainbow*)를 발표하였는데 성 묘사가 문제되어 곧 발매금지를 당하였다. 『무지개』에서 취급된 남녀관계의 윤리문제는, 다음해에 완성하여 1920년에 예약 한정판으로 낸 『사랑하는 여인들』(*Women in Love*)에서 더철저히 파헤쳤다. 대전이 종결된 뒤 1919년 11월 이후 세계 각처를 방랑하였는데, 『아론의 지팡이』(*Aaron's Rod*), 『캥거루』(*Kangaroo*), 『날개 있는 뱀』(*The Plumed Serpent*) 등의 장편에는 예언자적인 독특한 세계관이 담겨 있으며, 만년에 피렌체에서 완성한 『채털리 부인의 사랑』(*Lady Chatterley's Lover*)은 『무지개』나 『사랑하는 여인들』에서 충분히 나타내지 못하였던 그의 성철학을 펼친 작품이며 외설시비로 오랜 재판을 겪은 후 미국에서는 1959년에, 영국에서는 1960년에야 비로소 완본 출판이 허용되었다.

Snake*

A snake came to my water trough
On a hot, hot day, and I in pajamas for the heat,
To drink there.

In the deep, strange-scented shade of the great dark carob tree
I came down the steps with my pitcher
And must wait, must stand and wait, for there he was at the trough
before me.

---

* "Snake" can be understood on two levels, as narrative and as symbol. On the simpler level, a Lawrence-like speaker encounters a snake at "his" water trough. Rapt by nearly hypnotic fascination, he allows the snake to drink, without taking action.

He reached down from a fissure in the earth-wall in the gloom
And trailed his yellow-brown slackness soft-bellied down, over the edge of the stone trough
And rested his throat upon the stone bottom,
And where the water had dripped from the tap, in a small clearness,
He sipped with his straight mouth,
Softly drank through his straight gums, into his slack long body,
Silently.

Someone was before me at my water trough,
And I, like a second-comer, waiting.

He lifted his head from his drinking, as cattle do,
And looked at me vaguely, as drinking cattle do,
And flickered his two-forked tongue from his lips, and mused a moment,
And stooped and drank a little more,
Being earth-brown, earth-golden from the burning bowels of the earth
On the day of Sicilian July, with Etna smoking.

The voice of my education said to me
He must be killed,
For in Sicily the black, black snakes are innocent, the gold are venomous.

And voices in me said, If you were a man
You would take a stick and break him now, and finish him off.

But must I confess how I liked him,
How glad I was he had come like a guest in quiet, to drink at my water trough

And depart peaceful, pacified, and thankless
Into the burning bowels of this earth?

Was it cowardice, that I dared not kill him?
Was it perversity, that I longed to talk to him?
Was it humility, to feel so honored?
I felt so honored.

And yet those voices:
If you were not afraid, you would kill him!

And truly I was afraid, I was most afraid,
But even so, honored still more
That he should seek my hospitality
From out the dark door of the secret earth.

He drank enough
And lifted his head, dreamily, as one who has drunken,
And flickered his tongue like a forked night on the air, so black
Seeming to lick his lips,
And looked around like a god, unseeing, into the air,
And slowly turned his head,
And slowly, very slowly, as if thrice adream
Proceeded to draw his slow length curving round
And climb the broken bank of my wall-face.

And as he put his head into that dreadful hole,
And as he slowly drew up, snake-easing his shoulders, and entered
further,
A sort of horror, a sort of protest against his withdrawing into that

horrid black hole,
Deliberately going into the blackness, and slowly drawing himself after,
Overcame me now his back was turned.

I looked round, I put down my pitcher,
I picked up a clumsy log
And threw it at the water trough with a clatter.

I think it did not hit him;
But suddenly that part of him that was left behind convulsed in
undignified haste,
Writhed like lightning, and was gone
Into the black hole, the earth-lipped fissure in the wall-front
At which, in the intense still noon, I stared with fascination.

And immediately I regretted it.
I thought how paltry, how vulgar, what a mean act!
I despised myself and the voices of my accursed human education.

And I thought of the albatross,
And I wished he would come back, my snake.

For he seemed to me again like a king,
Like a king in exile, uncrowned in the underworld,
Now due to be crowned again.

And so, I missed my chance with one of the lords
Of life.
And I have something to expiate:
A pettiness. (2013년 중등영어 임용고시 기출문제)

(6) 위스턴 오든 Wystan Hugh Auden, 1907-1973

영국 요크셔 출신으로 옥스퍼드 대학교 졸업하고 1930년대에 과격한 발언과 실험적 시법의 개척으로 알려진 이른바 '1930년대 시인'의 중심인물로서 영국시단에서 크게 활약하였다. 특히 C. D. 루이스, S. 스펜더, L. 맥니스 등은 작품의 내용이나 시풍마저 오든의 영향을 크게 받았고, 개인적인 친분도 있어 일괄하여 '오든 그룹'이란 명칭으로 부르고 있다. 영국시절의 대표작에는 『시집』(*Poems*), 『연설자들』(*The Orators*), 『보라 여행자여』(*Look, Stranger!*), 이 밖에도 C. 이셔우드와 합작으로 쓴 시극이나 맥니스와의 합작인 자서전적 아이슬란드 기행시, 에스파냐내란을 주제로 한 유명한 시편 등이 있다. 사상적이라기보다는 감성적인 측면에서 좌경적이기는 하였으나, 동시에 프로이트에 대한 관심도 컸다. 따라서 한편으로는 핍박받는 빈민의 비참함과 비정의 사회에 대한 양심의 가책이 도사리고 있으면서, 다른 한편으로는 예술가로서의 개인적인 염원이 있어 이 양자의 상극 또는 조정이 시의 주제였다.

기법 면에서도 고대 영시풍의 단음절 낱말을 많이 써서 조롱이 섞인 경시와 모멸을 덧붙인 독특한 스타일을 만들어 냈다. 제2차 세계대전 중에 미국의 국적을 취득한 후로는 영국 성공회에 귀의하여 작품도 현저하게 종교적 색채를 더해 갔다. 주요 작품에는 『새해의 편지』(*New Year Letter*) 『한동안』(*For the Time*) 『불안의 시대』(*The Age of Anxiety*) 『아킬레스의 방패』(*The Shield of Achilles*) 『클리오의 찬가』(*Homage to Clio*) 등 다수가 있다.

Funeral Blues*

Stop all the clocks, cut off the telephone,
Prevent the dog from barking with a juicy bone,
Silence the pianos and with muffled drum
Bring out the coffin, let the mourners come.

Let aeroplanes circle moaning overhead
Scribbling on the sky the message 'He is Dead'.
Put crepe bows round the white necks of the public doves,
Let the traffic policemen wear black cotton gloves.

He was my North, my South, my East and West,
My working week and my Sunday rest,
My noon, my midnight, my talk, my song;
I thought that love would last forever: I was wrong.

The stars are not wanted now; put out every one,
Pack up the moon and dismantle the sun,
Pour away the ocean and sweep up the wood;
For nothing now can ever come to any good.

Lullaby**

Lay your sleeping head, my love,
Human on my faithless arm;

---

* The poem in the format readers usually see it today is a dirge, or a lament for the dead. Its tone is much more somber than early iterations, and the themes more universal, although it speaks of an individual. It has four stanzas of four lines each with lines in varying numbers of syllables but containing about four beats each.

Time and fevers burn away
Individual beauty from
Thoughtful children, and the grave
Proves the child ephemeral:
But in my arms till break of day
Let the living creature lie,
Mortal, guilty, but to me
The entirely beautiful.

Soul and body have no bounds:
To lovers as they lie upon
Her tolerant enchanted slope
In their ordinary swoon,
Grave the vision Venus sends
Of supernatural sympathy,
Universal love and hope;
While an abstract insight wakes
Among the glaciers and the rocks
The hermit's carnal ecstasy.

Certainty, fidelity
On the stroke of midnight pass
Like vibrations of a bell,
And fashionable madmen raise
Their pedantic boring cry:
Every farthing of the cost,
All the dreaded cards foretell,

** The poem begins with the speaker addressing his lover, perhaps in a post-coital situation. He looks down at the lover sleeping on his own "faithless" arm, giving the reader a bit of pause regarding what kind of lullaby or love poem this is.

Shall be paid, but from this night
Not a whisper, not a thought,
Not a kiss nor look be lost.

Beauty, midnight, vision dies:
Let the winds of dawn that blow
Softly round your dreaming head
Such a day of welcome show
Eye and knocking heart may bless,
Find the mortal world enough;
Noons of dryness find you fed
By the involuntary powers,
Nights of insult let you pass
Watched by every human love.

(7) 스티비 스미스 Stevie Smith, 1902-1971

본명은 플로렌스 마가렛 스미스(Florence Margaret Smith)로 그는 익살스럽고 정감 있으나 값싼 감상은 배제된 작품을 통해 독창적이고 영감에 찬 개성을 표현했다. 거의 평생 동안 런던 북부 교외 팔머스그린에 있는 집에서 숙모와 단둘이 살았다. 그곳에서 학교를 다닌 뒤부터 1950년대 초까지는 런던에 있는 잡지사의 비서로 일했다. 그 후 집에서 작품 활동을 하면서, 자신을 키워준 숙모가 1968년 96세로 죽을 때까지 돌보았다. 스미스의 시 가운데는 팔머스그린과 그곳 주민들을 주제로 한 것도 몇 편 있다.

1960년대에는 그녀의 시낭송이 유명해져서 라디오 방송과 음반 취입도 하게 되었다. 때로는 자신이 직접 시에 곡을 붙이기도 했다. 의식의 흐름 기법을 사용한 『싸구려 종이 소설』(*Novel on Yellow Paper*), 『변방에서』(*Over the*

Frontier), 『휴일』(*The Holiday*) 등 3편의 소설을 썼으며, 단편소설·문학평론·수필 등도 썼으나 시에서 가장 높은 평가를 받았다. 『스티비 스미스 시집』(*The Collected Poems of Stevie Smith*)에는 서버풍의 소묘가 삽화로 들어가 있는데, 초기 시집 『우리 모두에게 좋은 시절이 있었네』(*A Good Time Was Had By All*), 『고요히 가라앉다』(*Not Waving but Drowning*)가 포함되어 있으며, 시 『고요히 가라앉다』는 여러 시선집에 실려 있다. 그녀의 시행은 대개 짧고 서술적이며, 운율이 불규칙하고 모음조화와 변칙적인 각운을 따른다는 점에서 주목할 만하다. 간결한 문체는 윌리엄 블레이크를 연상시키며, 존 베처먼과도 비교되기도 한다. 그녀는 진지한 주제를 아주 명료하게 진술하여 유치하다는 비난을 자주 들었으며, 죽음의 주제를 반복해서 다루었다.

『재선집』(*Me Again: Uncollected Writings of Stevie Smith, Illustrated by Herself*)은 산문, 편지, 이전에 미발간된 시들을 묶은 유고집이다. 케이 딕이 쓴 『아이비와 스티비』(*Ivy and Stevie: Conversations and Reflections*)는 데임 아이비 콤프턴 버넷과의 대화 녹음을 토대로 한 것이다. 『스티비』(*Stevie*)는 휴 화이트모어의 희곡으로 1977년 출판되었다. 화이트모어가 제작·감독을 맡은 영화 『스티비』는 1978년 런던에서 처음 상영되었고 1981년에는 뉴욕에서 상영되었다.

Our Bog Is Dood*

Our Bog is dood, our Bog is dood,
They lisped in accents mild,
But when I asked them to explain

---

* Stevie Smith's original poem, "Our Bog is Dood," seems like a Dr. Seuss copycat: made up words, repetitive rhyming, and an illogical, nonsensical storyline. One can't help but wonder, though, if Smith intended for "Bog" to have a much deeper meaning than some of Seuss's more famous works—think *Green Eggs and Ham* and *The Cat in the Hat*.

They grew a little wild.
How do you know your Bog is dood
My darling little child?

We know because we wish it so
This is enough, they cried,
And straight within each infant eye
Stood up the flame of pride,
And if you do not think it so
You shall be crucified.

Then tell me, darling little ones,
What's dood, suppose Bog is?
Just what we think, the answer came,
Just what we think it is.
They bowed their heads. Our Bog is ours
And we are wholly his.

But when they raised them up again
They had forgotten me
Each one upon each other glared
In pride and misery
For what was dood, and what their Bog
They never could agree.

Oh sweet it was to leave them then,
And sweeter not to see,
And sweetest of all to walk alone
Beside the encroaching sea,
The sea that soon should drown them all,
That never yet drowned me.

Not Waving but Drowning*

Nobody heard him, the dead man,
But still he lay moaning:
I was much further out than you thought
And not waving but drowning.

Poor chap, he always loved larking
And now he's dead
It must have been too cold for him his heart gave way,
They said.

Oh, no no no, it was too cold always
(Still the dead one lay moaning)
I was much too far out all my life
And not waving but drowning.

(8) 필립 아서 라킨 Philip Arthur Larkin, 1922-1985

영국 워릭셔 주 코번트리 출신으로 옥스퍼드 대학교를 졸업하였다.
1950년대 초에 일어난 신시운동 무브먼트(The Movement)파의 대표적인
시인으로서 과작이지만, 제2차 세계대전 후의 영국 시에 끼친 영향이 크다.
반 모더니즘의 자세로 일관하여 개인적 체험과 평범한 일상생활에서 소재
를 얻어서 간결한 말과 전통적인 시형을 사용하여 노래하였다. 『교회를 방
문하다』(*Church Going*)는 어느 현대시집에나 수록되어 있을 정도로 대표작

---

* "Not Waving but Drowning" comes straight out of the longest, darkest night of the British
  poet Stevie Smith's soul. That's really saying something, too, because Smith is well known
  for a career's worth of gloomy and morbid lines.

이다. 시집에 『북의 배』(*The North Ship*), 『성령강림절의 결혼식』(*The Whitsun Weddings*) 『높은 창』(*High Windows*) 등이 있다. 1960년대 이후는 T. 하디에 심취하여 하디를 현대시의 아버지라고 하는 명시선집 『옥스포드 판 20세기 영국시』(*The Oxford Book of Twentieth Century English Verse*)를 편집하였다. 소설에는 『질』(*Jill*), 『겨울 처녀』(*A Girl in Winter*) 등이 있다.

The Large Cool Store*

The large cool store selling cheap clothes
Set out in simple sizes plainly
(Knitwear, Summer Casuals, Hose,
In Browns and greys, maroons and navy)
Conjures the weekday world of those

Who leave at dawn low terraced houses
Timed for factory, yard and site.
But past the heaps of shirts and trousers
Spread the stands of Modes For Night:
Machine-embroidered, thin as blouses,

Lemon, sapphire, moss-green, rose
Bri-Nylon Baby-Dolls and Shorties
Flounce in clusters. To suppose
They share that world, to think their sort is
Matched by something in it, shows

---

* This poem is a description of a Marks and Spencers shop in Larkin's time. Since then, they have moved further upmarket, but in the 1950s, M&S was a shop much like the Primark of today—selling cheap, though slightly dated, fashionable clothes.

How separate and unearthly love is,
Or women are, or what they do,
Or in our young unreal wishes
Seem to be: synthetic, new
And natureless in ecstasies.

The Whitsun Weddings*

That Whitsun, I was late getting away:
    Not till about
One-twenty on the sunlit Saturday
Did my three-quarters-empty train pull out,
All windows down, all cushions hot, all sense
Of being in a hurry gone. We ran
Behind the backs of houses, crossed a street
Of blinding windscreens, smelt the fish-dock; thence
The river's level drifting breadth began,
Where sky and Lincolnshire and water meet.

All afternoon, through the tall heat that slept
    For miles inland,
A slow and stopping curve southwards we kept.
Wide farms went by, short-shadowed cattle, and
Canals with floatings of industrial froth;
A hothouse flashed uniquely: hedges dipped
And rose: and now and then a smell of grass

---

* "The Whitsun Weddings" is a deceptively leisurely sounding poem in eight ten-line stanzas. The title refers to the British tradition of marrying on the weekend of Whitsunday or Pentecost (the seventh Sunday after Easter) to take advantage of the early summer "bank holiday" or long weekend.

Displaced the reek of buttoned carriage-cloth
Until the next town, new and nondescript,
Approached with acres of dismantled cars.

(9) 테드 휴스 Ted Hughes, 1930-1998

휴스의 시는 감상이 전적으로 배제되어 있으며, 거칠고 부조화스러운 시행 속에서 동물들의 교활함과 야만스러움을 강조한 것이 특징이다. 그의 인간관도 지성보다는 야성을 강조하고 있는데, 그의 깊은 통찰력이 뛰어난 지성의 소산임을 생각할 때 이것은 아이러니가 아닐 수 없다. 그는 요크셔 웨스트라이딩 지방의 방언을 시의 색채에 조화시켰다. 케임브리지 펨브룩 칼리지를 다니면서 민담·문화인류학에 관심을 가졌으며, 이러한 관심사를 자신의 시에 반영했다. 1956년 미국의 시인 실비아 플래스와 결혼했고, 1957년 두 사람은 미국을 여행했으며, 그해 첫 시집 『빗속의 독수리』(*The Hawk in the Rain*)를 발간했다. 뒤이어 톰 건과 함께 『시선집』(*Selected Poems*)을 발표했다. 톰 건은 영시를 위해 새로운 방향을 모색하는 시인으로서 종종 휴스와 공동 작업을 했다. 1963년 부인 플래스가 자살한 이후 거의 3년 동안 시작에서 손을 뗀 그는 사진작가·삽화가 등과 공동으로 『북극성 아래서』(*Under the North Star*)를 펴냈다. 그는 아동도서도 많이 썼는데 그의 어린 시절을 회상한 『엘밋의 유고』(*Remains of Elmet*)가 있다. 1965년 이래 런던에서 발행하는 『번역에 있어서의 현대 시』(*Modern Poetry in Translation*)지의 공동 편집자로 재직하고 있으며, 1984년 영국 계관시인이 되었다.

Sam*

It was all of a piece to you
    That was your horse, the white calm stallion, Sam,
    Decided he'd had enough
    And started home at a gallop. I can live
    Your incredulity, your certainty
    That this was it. You lost your stirrups. He galloped
    Straight down the white line of the Barton Road.
    You lost your reins, you lost your seat —
    It was grab his neck and adore him
    Or free-fall. You slewed under his neck,
    An upside-down jockey with nothing
    Between you and the cataract of macadam,
    That horribly hard, swift river,
    But the propeller terrors of his front legs
    And the claangour of the iron shoes, so far beneath you.

Luck was already there. Did you have a helmet?
    How did you cling on? Baby monkey
    Using your arms and legs for clinging steel.
    What saved you? Maybe your poems
    Saved themselves, slung under that plunging neck,
    Hammocked in your body over the switchback road.

You saw only blur. And a cyclist's shock-mask,
    Fallen, dragging his bicycle over him, protective.

---

* In her first year at Cambridge, Plath had hired an old horse called Sam who was expected
  to be placid, but bolted with the inexperienced rider on his back. While it was a frightening
  and dangerous experience, Plath recalled it as a time when she felt immensely alive.

I can feel your bounced and dangling anguish,
Hugging what was left of your steerage.
How did you hang on? You couldn't have done it.
Something in you not you did it for itself.
You clung on, probably near unconscious.
Till he walked into his stable. That gallop
Was practice, but not enough, and quite useless.

When I jumped a fence you strangled me
One giddy moment, then fell off,
Flung yourself off and under my feet to trip me
And tripped me and lay dead. Over in a flash.

Hawk Roosting*

I sit in the top of the wood, my eyes closed.
Inaction, no falsifying dream
Between my hooked head and hooked feet:
Or in sleep rehearse perfect kills and eat.

The convenience of the high trees!
The air's buoyancy and the sun's ray
Are of advantage to me;
And the earth's face upward for my inspection.

My feet are locked upon the rough bark.

---

* Ted Hughes' poem 'Hawk Roosting' on its literal level of meaning is an expression of a bird
of prey, the hawk, which is sitting on a tree and meditating about its power of destruction,
its ability to suppress change, and its conceited arrogance and superiority.

It took the whole of Creation
To produce my foot, my each feather:
Now I hold Creation in my foot

Or fly up, and revolve it all slowly —
I kill where I please because it is all mine.
There is no sophistry in my body:
My manners are tearing off heads —

The allotment of death.
For the one path of my flight is direct
Through the bones of the living.
No arguments assert my right:

The sun is behind me.
Nothing has changed since I began.
My eye has permitted no change.
I am going to keep things like this.

(10) 앨프리드 하우스먼 A. E. Housman, 1859-1936

하우스먼은 영국 옥스퍼드대를 졸업하고 23세에 특허국의 관리가 된 이후 야간에 대영박물관에서 11년간 독학 후, 제1급의 고전학자로 인정받아 런던대와 케임브리지대에서 라틴문학을 가르쳤다. 그가 남긴 간결하고도 고전미 넘치는 150여 편의 서정시는 시공을 넘어 세계인들의 사랑을 받고 있다. 하우스먼의 소박한 시는 그 자체로 스토리텔링이다. 아무런 비평이나 해설을 곁들이지 않아도 애인이 살포시 던져주는 사과 한 알처럼 독자들의 손에 실감 있게 잡힌다.

Loveliest of Trees*

Loveliest of trees, the cherry now
Is hung with bloom along the bough,
And stands about the woodland ride
Wearing white for Eastertide.

Now, of my threescore years and ten,
Twenty will not come again,
And take from seventy springs a score,
It only leaves me fifty more.

And since to look at things in bloom
Fifty springs are little room,
About the woodlands I will go
To see the cherry hung with snow. (1999년 중등영어 임용고시 기출문제)

A Shropshire Lad.

XIII. When I was one-and-twenty**

When I was one-and-twenty
    I heard a wise man say,

---

* A. E. Housman's "Loveliest of Trees, the Cherry Now" consists of three four-line, essentially iambic stanzas, or quatrains, in which the poet, through his observation of the beauty of the natural world, is reminded of the brevity of his own life and resolves, henceforth, to experience life with intensity.

** It comes from a collection of 63 poems called A Shropshire Lad. But, if you think that Housman was a country boy frolicking in the fields of Shropshire, you couldn't be further off the mark. Houseman wrote them while he was in London. It turns out that he hadn't even been to Shropshire.

'Give crowns and pounds and guineas
  But not your heart away;
Give pearls away and rubies
  But keep your fancy free.'
But I was one-and-twenty,
  No use to talk to me.

When I was one-and-twenty
  I heard him say again,
'The heart out of the bosom
  Was never given in vain;
'Tis paid with sighs a plenty
  And sold for endless rue.'
And I am two-and-twenty,
  And oh, 'tis true, 'tis true.

LIV. With rue my heart is laden*

With rue my heart is laden
  For golden friends I had,
For many a rose-lipt maiden
  And many a lightfoot lad.

By brooks too broad for leaping
  The lightfoot boys are laid;
The rose-lipt girls are sleeping
  In fields where roses fade.

---

* The poet is recalling the boys and girls—the lads and lasses—he knew earlier in life, and is
saddened. He tells us that his heart is laden—loaded, weighted down—with rue, that is, with
sorrow and regret.

(11) 셰이머스 히니 Seamus Heaney, 1939-2013

북아일랜드 예이츠 이후 아일랜드 시인으로는 가장 뛰어나다는 평가를 받는다. 1961년 북아일랜드의 수도 벨파스트의 퀸스 대학교를 졸업했다. 이후, 조셉스 교육대학교와 퀸스 대학교에서 강의했고, 1966년 첫 시집 『어느 자연주의자의 죽음』(*Death of a Naturalist*)을 발표하면서 등단했다. 1972년 북아일랜드의 분규를 목격하고 남아일랜드로 이주했으며, 1982-1994년 하버드 대학교와 옥스퍼드 대학교 교환교수를 지냈다. 아일랜드인이면서 영국식 교육을 받아야 했던 유년의 체험이 어두운 상상력의 근저를 이루면서, 초기에는 조국의 비극적 역사를 직시한 작품을 많이 발표했으며, 이후 시의 서정성을 노래하면서 문학성을 인정받았다. 아일랜드 문학아카데미상 (1971), 『선데이타임스』 봉블랑 상(1988) 등을 받았으며, 1995년 노벨문학상을 수상했다. 그의 시는 사물 자체의 음악성을 발견하여 이를 깊이 있게 표현하고 있다. 주요시집으로 『어느 자연주의자의 죽음』, 『겨울나기』(*Wintering Out*), 『들일』(*Field Work*), 『스테이션 아일랜드』(*Station Island*) 등이 있다.

The Forge*

All I know is a door into the dark.
Outside, old axles and iron hoops rusting;
Inside, the hammered anvil's short-pitched ring,
The unpredictable fantail of sparks
Or hiss when a new shoe toughens in water.

---

* From a strictly formal point of view, "The Forge" is a sonnet. As is typical of Seamus Heaney's work, however, and reflective of this poem's unobtrusive depths, it is more interesting for the ways in which it departs from conventional sonnet forms than for its attachment to them.

The anvil must be somewhere in the centre,
Horned as a unicorn, at one end and square,
Set there immoveable: an altar
Where he expends himself in shape and music.
Sometimes, leather-aproned, hairs in his nose,
He leans out on the jamb, recalls a clatter
Of hoofs where traffic is flashing in rows;
Then grunts and goes in, with a slam and flick
To beat real iron out, to work the bellows.

Blackberry-Picking*

Late August, given heavy rain and sun
For a full week, the blackberries would ripen.
At first, just one, a glossy purple clot
Among others, red, green, hard as a knot.
You ate that first one and its flesh was sweet
Like thickened wine: summer's blood was in it
Leaving stains upon the tongue and lust for
Picking. Then red ones inked up and that hunger
Sent us out with milk cans, pea tins, jam-pots
Where briars scratched and wet grass bleached our boots.
Round hayfields, cornfields and potato-drills
We trekked and picked until the cans were full
Until the tinkling bottom had been covered

---

* The poem deals with the glory and harshness of nature (there are some links with Perch and Death of a Naturalist). The metaphorical image 'summer's blood was in it' is a reminder of the darker side as well, although nature seems a living thing, the eating of the berry causes a bleeding, 'leaving stains upon the tongue and lust for picking'.

With green ones, and on top big dark blobs burned
Like a plate of eyes. Our hands were peppered
With thorn pricks, our palms sticky as Bluebeard's.
We hoarded the fresh berries in the byre.
But when the bath was filled we found a fur,
A rat-grey fungus, glutting on our cache.
The juice was stinking too. Once off the bush
The fruit fermented, the sweet flesh would turn sour.
I always felt like crying. It wasn't fair
That all the lovely canfuls smelt of rot.
Each year I hoped they'd keep, knew they would not.

(12) 존 메이스필드 John Masefield, 1878-1967

헤리퍼드셔의 변호사 아들로 출생하여 어려서 아버지를 여의고 13세
에 선원이 되어 각지를 전전하였다. 1895년 선원을 그만두고 뉴욕으로 건
너가 노동자로 일하면서 인생의 밑바닥 생활을 체험하였고, 이때부터 문학
에 대한 관심도 깊어졌다. 1897년 귀국, 언론계에 발을 들여 놓고 런던에
정주하였다. 1902년 시집 『해수의 노래』(Salt-Water Ballads)로 인정을 받기
시작, 1919년에는 대표작인 서사시 「여우 레이나르드」("Reynard the Fox")
를 발표하였다. 1930년에는 계관시인이 되었다.

그의 시의 짜임새는 매끈하지 못하지만 알기 쉬운 운문으로 해양과
이국의 정서, 사회적 관심이 넘치는 그의 시는 한동안 많은 대중 독자들을
매료하였다. 그는 시 이외에도 극·소설·평론·수필 등 다양한 글을 썼다.
사회의 허위를 벗기어 인간애를 나타낸 『낸의 비극』(The Tragedy of Nan),
사극 『폼페이 대제의 비극』(The Tragedy of Pompey the Great) 등의 작품이 있
다.

The West Wind*

It's a warm wind, the west wind, full of birds' cries;
  I never hear the west wind but tears are in my eyes.
  For it comes from the west lands, the old brown hills,
  And April's in the west wind, and daffodils.

It's a fine land, the west land, for hearts as tired as mine,
  Apple orchards blossom there, and the air's like wine.
  There is cool green grass there, where men may lie at rest,
  And the thrushes are in song there, fluting from the nest.

"Will you not come home, brother? You have been long away.
  It's April, and blossom time, and white is the spray;
  And bright is the sun, brother, and warm is the rain,
  Will you not come in, brother, home to us again?

Larks are singing in the west, brother, above the green wheat,
  So will ye not come home, brother, and rest your tired feet?
  I've a balm for bruised hearts, brother, sleep for aching eyes,"
  Says the warm wind, the west wind, full of birds' cries.

It's the white road westwards is the road I must tread
  To the green grass, the cool grass, and rest for heart and head,
  To the violets and the brown brooks and the thrushes' song,
  In the fine land, the west land, the land where I belong.

---

* the poet starts by describing,with very poetic imagery of birds, how the west wind is different from other winds 'it's a warm wind, full of birds' cries.' There is a touch of melancholy, perhaps home-sickness as he describes how it brings tears too, and memories from an old land.

Sea Fever *

I must go down to the seas again, to the lonely sea and the sky,
And all I ask is a tall ship and a star to steer her by;
And the wheel's kick and the wind's song and the white sail's shaking,
And a grey mist on the sea's face, and a grey dawn breaking.

I must go down to the seas again, for the call of the running tide
Is a wild call and a clear call that may not be denied;
And all I ask is a windy day with the white clouds flying,
And the flung spray and the blown spume, and the sea-gulls crying.

I must go down to the seas again, to the vagrant gypsy life,
To the gull's way and the whale's way where the wind's like a whetted knife;
And all I ask is a merry yarn from a laughing fellow-rover,
And quiet sleep and a sweet dream when the long trick's over.

(13) 제라드 홉킨스 Gerard Manley Hopkins, 1844-1889

홉킨스는 에식스 스트랫퍼드에서 출생하여 옥스퍼드 대학교에서 공부하였다. 가톨릭으로 개종하여 뉴먼 추기경의 제자가 되었고, 1884년에는 더블린대학교 그리스어 교수에 취임하였다. 생전에는 시를 한 편도 발표하지 않았으나 그의 친구 브리지스가 홉킨스의 시 수 편을 시화집에 발표하였고, 또 1918년에는 주가 붙은 『홉킨스 시집』을 간행하여 주목받았다.

그의 시는 아주 독창적인 것으로 '도약률'(sprung rhythm)이라는 운율

---

* ohn Masefield's poem "Sea-Fever" expresses a sailor's powerful longing to return to the sea. The poem's rhythm creates a sense of the sailor's experiences at sea. The imagery and sensory details create a mood of freedom and adventure. Personification, simile, and metaphor enhance the emotional tone and romanticize life at sea.

법을 이용하였고, 또 두운을 많이 써서 이미지와 암유의 복잡한 구성을 시도, 의미의 강력한 집중을 나타내었다. 작품의 내용은 다양했지만 주로 자연과 종교에 관한 것이 많았다. 특히 1875년 겨울 독일에서 추방된 수녀 5명이 템스 강 하구에서 난파하여 익사한 사건을 읊은 「도이칠란트호의 난파」("The Wreck of the Deutschland")는 유명하다.

Binsey Poplars

felled 1879 *

My aspens dear, whose airy cages quelled,
   Quelled or quenched in leaves the leaping sun,
  All felled, felled, are all felled;
    Of a fresh and following folded rank
         Not spared, not one
        That dandled a sandalled
     Shadow that swam or sank
On meadow & river & wind-wandering weed-winding bank.

  O if we but knew what we do
     When we delve or hew—
   Hack and rack the growing green!
     Since country is so tender
    To touch, her being só slender,
    That, like this sleek and seeing ball

---

* The poet mourns the cutting of his "aspens dear," trees whose delicate beauty resided not only in their appearance, but in the way they created "airy cages" to tame the sunlight. These lovely trees, Hopkins laments, have all been "felled." He compares them to an army of soldiers obliterated. He remembers mournfully the way they their "sandalled" shadows played along the winding bank where river and meadow met.

But a prick will make no eye at all,

Where we, even where we mean

To mend her we end her,

When we hew or delve:

After-comers cannot guess the beauty been.

Ten or twelve, only ten or twelve

Strokes of havoc unselve

The sweet especial scene,

Rural scene, a rural scene,

Sweet especial rural scene.

The Windhover*

To Christ our Lord

I caught this morning morning's minion, king-

dom of daylight's dauphin, dapple-dawn-drawn Falcon, in his riding

Of the rolling level underneath him steady air, and striding

High there, how he rung upon the rein of a wimpling wing

In his ecstasy! then off, off forth on swing,

As a skate's heel sweeps smooth on a bow-bend: the hurl and gliding

Rebuffed the big wind. My heart in hiding

Stirred for a bird,—the achieve of, the mastery of the thing!

Brute beauty and valour and act, oh, air, pride, plume, here

Buckle! AND the fire that breaks from thee then, a billion

Times told lovelier, more dangerous, O my chevalier!

---

* "The windhover" is a bird with the rare ability to hover in the air, essentially flying in place
while it scans the ground in search of prey. The poet describes how he saw (or "caught")
one of these birds in the midst of its hovering.

No wonder of it: shéer plód makes plough down sillion
Shine, and blue-bleak embers, ah my dear,
Fall, gall themselves, and gash gold-vermilion.

(14) 윌리엄 헨리 데이빗 William Henry Davies, 1871-1940

헨리 데이빗은 웨일즈 시인이자 작가인 윌리엄 헨리 데이빗은 웨일즈의 뉴포트에서 출생하였다. 그는 영국과 미국에서 그의 삶의 중요한 시기를 대부분을 부랑자나 떠돌이 일꾼으로 보냈지만, 그의 시대의 가장 인기 있는 시인 중 한명이 되었다. 그의 작품의 주요한 주제는 인간의 상태가 자연 그대로 반영되는 방식인 삶의 고통과 방랑하는 모험심과 그가 만났던 다양한 캐릭터들에 관한 것이다. 그의 작품의 많은 부분이 그 장르의 다른 이들에 의해 쓰인 스타일과 주제에 어울리지 않을지라도 그는 보통 조지안 시인(Georgian Poets) 중 한 명으로 생각된다. 그의 첫 시집 『영혼의 파괴자와 다른 시들』(*The Soul's Destroyer and Other Poems*)은 그가 34세 일 때 발간되었다.

Leisure*

What is this life if, full of care,
We have no time to stand and stare.

No time to stand beneath the boughs
And stare as long as sheep or cows.

---

* In "Leisure", W. H. Davies explores the importance of leisure of everyday life. The speaker begins by asking a rhetorical question, "What is life?" This begins a continuous, slow, and harmonious rhythm Davies emphasizes the fact that you need to disregard the things that aren't truly important and to pace yourself.

No time to see, when woods we pass,
Where squirrels hide their nuts in grass.

No time to see, in broad daylight,
Streams full of stars, like skies at night.

No time to turn at Beauty's glance,
And watch her feet, how they can dance.

No time to wait till her mouth can
Enrich that smile her eyes began.

A poor life this is if, full of care,
We have no time to stand and stare.

(2006년 중등영어 임용고시 기출문제)

(15) 프란시스 콘퍼드 Frances Cornford, 1886-1960

찰스 다윈의 손녀딸이며 영국의 시인인 콘퍼드는 슬프면서도 익살스
런 시 「열차 밖의 어떤 뚱뚱한 숙녀에게」("To a Fat Lady Seen From the
Train")로 가장 잘 알려져 있다. 그녀는 『시집』(*Collected Poems*)을 1954년에
펴냈고, 1959년 시 부문 퀸스 상을 받았다.

Childhood*

I used to think that grown-up people chose
To have stiff backs and wrinkles round their nose,

---

* The poem childhood shows the reality of how children look at adults. Children are portrayed

And veins like small fat snakes on either hand,
On purpose to be grand.
Till through the banister I watched one day
My great-aunt Etty's friend who was going away,
And how her onyx beads had come unstrung.
I saw her grope to find them as they rolled;
And then I knew that she was helplessly old,
As I was helplessly young. (2011년 중등영어 임용고시 기출문제)

To a Fat Lady Seen From the Train*

O why do you walk through the fields in gloves,
Missing so much and so much?
O fat white woman whom nobody loves,
Why do you walk through the fields in gloves,
When the grass is soft as the breast of doves
And shivering sweet to the touch?
O why do you walk through the fields in gloves,
Missing so much and so much?

(16) 앤 바바라 리들러 Anne Barbara Ridler, 1912-2001

영국 출신의 시인인 리들러는 다운 하우스 학교에서 교육을 받았고,
이후에 그녀의 여교장 올리브 윌리스(Olive Willis)의 전기를 출판하였다.

---

with their lack of experience on the real world and how little they know about the world
they have yet to experience but then they realize how little they know about the world and
have an epiphany that becoming an adult is part of life as well as becoming old.

* That triolet form is damnably insistent once it's got a grip in your head. Either way this
poem seems to me such an oddity; a curious mixture of romanticism and mean-spiritedness.

플로렌스와 로마에서 6개월을 보낸 후, 그녀는 런던에 있는 킹스 칼리지에서 저널리즘 학위를 받았다. 1938년 그녀는 후에 번힐(Bunhill) 출판사의 매니저가 된 옥스퍼드 대학의 출판부 비비안 리들러와 결혼하여 두 딸과 두 아들을 낳았다.

C. S. 루이스(Lewis)의 동료인 그녀는 잉클링스(Inklings) 그룹에 열광하였으며, T. S. 엘리엇과 가까이 지내며 그녀는 엘리엇 전집을 위하여 엘리엇의 시에 나타난 이미지를 암시하는 짧지만, 강한 이미지의 시 "I Who am Here Dissembled"를 썼다. 1940년대 짧은 시기 동안에 리들러는 또한 『카인』(*Cain*, 1943)과 『그늘진 공장: 예수 탄생극』(*Shadow Factory: A Nativity Play*, 1945)으로 성공적인 시극 작가로서 활동을 하였다.

At Parting

Since we through war awhile must part
Sweetheart, and learn to lose
Daily use
Of all that satisfied our heart:
Lay up those secrets and those powers
Wherewith you pleased and cherished me these two years:

Now we must draw, as plants would,
On tubers stored in a better season,
Our honey and heaven;
Only our love can store such food.
Is this to make a god of absence?
A new-born monster to steal our sustenance?

We cannot quite cast out lack and pain.

Let him remain-what he may devour

We can well spare:

He never can tap this, the true vein.

I have no words to tell you what you were,

But when you are sad, think, Heaven could give no more.

Before Sleep

Now that you lie

In London afar,

And may sleep longer

Though lonelier,

For I shall not wake you

With a nightmare,

Heaven plant such peace in us

As if no parting stretched between us.

The world revolves

And is evil;

God's image is

Wormeaten by the devil;

May the good angel

Have no rival

By our beds, and we lie curled

At the sound unmoving centre of the world.

In our good nights

When we were together,

We made, in that stillness

Where we loved each other,
A new being, of both
Yet above either:
So, when I cannot share your sleep,
Into this being, half yours, I creep.

(17) 주디스 비버리지 Judith Beveridge, 1956-

주디스 비버리지는 현대 호주 시인이자 편집자 그리고 학자이다. 그
는 영국 런던에서 출생하여 1960년에 그녀의 부모와 함께 호주에 도착하
였다. 시드니 기술대학(University of Technology, Sydney)에서 학사학위를
받고 그는 환경개선 연구원으로서 도서관에서 일했다. 현재 그녀는 뉴캐슬
(Newcastle) 대학교와 시드니(Sydney) 대학교에서 창작법을 강의하고 있으
며, 『민진』(*Meanjin*)의 편집자로서 일하고 있다.

Orb Spider

I saw her, pegging out her web
thin as a pressed flower in the bleaching light.
From the bushes a few small insects
clicked like opening seed-pods. I knew some
would be trussed up by her and gone next morning.
She was so beautiful spinning her web
above the marigolds the sun had made
more apricot, more amber; any bee
lost from its solar flight could be gathered
back to the anther, and threaded onto the flower
like a jewel.

She hung in the shadows
as the sun burnt low on the horizon
mirrored by the round garden bed. Small petals
moved as one flame, as one perfectly-lit hoop.
I watched her work, produce her known world,
a pattern, her way to traverse
a little portion of the sky;
a simple cosmography, a web drawn
by the smallest nib. And out of my own world
mapped from smallness, the source
of sorrow pricked, I could see
immovable stars.
Each night
I saw the same dance in the sky,
the pattern like a match-box puzzle,
tiny balls stuck in a grid until shaken
so much, all the orbits were in place.
Above the bright marigolds
of that quick year, the hour-long day,
she taught me to love the smallest transit,
that the coldest star has planetesimal beauty.
I watched her above the low flowers
tracing her world, making it one perfect drawing.

(2013년 중등영어 임용고시 기출문제)

To The Islands

I will use the sound of wind and the splash
  of the cormorant diving and the music
any boatman will hear in the running threads
  as they sing about leaving for the Islands.

I will use a sinker's zinc arpeggio as it
   rolls across a wooden jetty and the sound
of crabs in the shifting gravel and the scrape
   of awls across the hulls of yachts.

I will use the wash-board chorus of the sea
   and the boats and the skiffler's skirl
of tide-steered surf taken out by the wind
   through the cliffs. Look—I don't know

much about how to reach the Islands, only
   what I've heard from the boatman's song
and from a man who walked the headland
   to find a place in the rocks free of salt

and osprey. But perhaps I can use
   the bladder-wrack and barnacle, the gull
wafting above the mussels and the bird
   diving back to sea. Perhaps I can use

the song sponge divers sing to time each dive
   and then use their gasps as they lift
their bags onto the skiffs. Perhaps
   the seapool whispers of the sun-downers

or the terns above the harbour are what
   the divers sing to as they hold their
breath and swim the silent minutes through
   with prayer. I will use the gull's height

and the limpet's splash and the wasps' nest
  hanging like a paper lamp under the pier
and the little boat sailing out. Even the
  fishermen lugging shoals over the stones,

even the sailors shift-walking the decks,
  even the end-blown note of a shell leveled
towards the horizon. I will use the eagle's
  flight moored in the eyes of children

and the voices of men, the ones, they say,
  who've made it, though perhaps the purlin
creaking on its rafter, the gull squawking
  from the jetty, the wind calling

along the moorings and the notes the divers
  hear in the quiet waters of their breathing
as they seek release through depths
  are all I'll, know about finding the Islands.

Meanwhile, I'll use the sound of sunlight
  filling the sponges and a diver's saturated
breathing in the lungs of an oarsman
  rowing weightless cargo over the reefs.

III

미국시 읽기

제1장

19세기 미국시

1. 시대적 배경

1830년에서 40년 사이에 미국 사회의 변경은 빠르게 서쪽으로 이동하고 있었다. 윌리엄 쿠퍼(William Cooper)의 뒤를 이은 작가들은 서부의 변경을 미국의 삶에 관한 문학의 소재로 보기 시작했다. 그러나 동부 연안의 여러 도시에는 대서양 공동체로서의 국가의 오랜 이상이 아직 살아 있었다. 그것은 매사추세츠와 버지니아의 문화가 국가적 문화의 모델이 되어야 한다는 정서에서 비롯된 것이었다. 이 시기에 보스턴을 비롯하여 인접 소도시들은 지적 흥분과 활기로 가득하였다. 하버드 교수인 에드워드 채닝(Edward Channing)이 1818년에 세운 『북미평론』(*North American Review*)은 자신들의 사상을 확산시키는데 바빴다. 1826년 이래 순회 강사들이 보스턴과 뉴잉글랜드의 시골 지역에 문화와 과학에 관한 지식을 전파하였다. 보스턴의 젊은 지식인들은 "새로운 정신 영역"을 논하였고, 과거의 낡은 애국주의에 식상해 하였다. 미국의 힘과 부는 더 이상 그들의 관심을 끌지 못하였다. 그들은 내면의 삶을 탐구하고 싶어 했다. 그들은 그리스, 독일, 인도의 철학자들을 섭렵하였다. 많은 이들이 자신의 삶과 느낌을 일기로 남겼다. 이들 가운데는 채식주의자나 나체주의자도 있었다.

이 시기에 미국 사회 전반에는 미국적이라 할 특징들이 두드러지게 나타났다. 흔히 미국의 르네상스(American Renaissance)라 불리던 이 시기의 중요한 특성은 서부 팽창 과정에서 생긴 개인주의이다. 이것은 한 개인과 다른 개인이 달라지려는 의지로써, 경제적 자립과 무한한 기회를 잡아보려는 팽창기의 미국인들에게 적합한 것이었다. 이것은 경제적 의미에서 유동성, 강인성, 탄력성을 강조하는 것이다. 1831-32년 사이에 미국을 방문한 프랑스의 알렉시 드 토크빌(Alexis De Tocqueville)은 『미국 민주주의』(*Democracy in America*)라는 책에서 미국 사회의 유동성이 미국의 실용주의적 특성과 낙관주의적 진보의 개념을 바탕으로 한 민주주의 제도의 수립에 기여했음을 지적한다. 이것은 모든 개인이 자신을 초월하여 신과 하나가 될 수 있다는 초월주의의 기틀을 마련하였다. 초월주의자들(Transcendentalists)은 철학의 체계보다는 느낌과 신앙의 운동을 추구하였고, 선조의 보수적인 청교도주의(Puritanism)나, 보다 새롭고 자유로운 유일신주의 신앙(Unitarianism)도 거부하였다. 그들은 두 종교 모두 "부정적이고, 차가우며, 생명이 없는 것"으로 보았다. 그들 또한 그리스도를 지혜를 가르치는 자로서 존경했지만, 셰익스피어나 위대한 철학자들의 작품도 마찬가지로 중요한 것으로 생각하였다. 그들은 이성보다는 감정과 직관을 통해서 진리를 발견하려고 하였다. 초기 초월주의자인 오레스테스 브라운슨(Orestes Brownson)에 따르면 이 운동은 "인간에게서 직관적으로 진리를 아는 능력 ...감각을 초월하는 지식의 질서를 발견하는 것"이었다. 헨리 데이비드 소로(Henry David Thoreau)는 "지혜는 탐구하는 것이 아니라 보는 것"이라고 하였다. 초월주의자들은 인간과 자연의 모든 곳에서 신을 발견하였다. 여러 가지 면에서 자연 자체가 그들의 "성서"였다. 새와 구름과 나무, 그리고 눈이 그 들에게는 특별한 의미를 지니고 있었다. 이 같은 자연의 이미지가 일종의 언어를 창조하였고, 이러한 언어를 통하여 그들은 인간 영혼에 이미 심어진 사상을 발견하였다.

시와 관련해서 19세기에 접어들면서 미국 시는 영국의 영향력에서 점차 벗어나고 있었다. 19세기 초반의 미국 시는 여전히 영국의 18세기 낭만시의 영향을 받고 있었지만 그 내용면에서는 미국적인 소재를 사용함으로써 미국적인 독창성을 가미해 가고 있었다. 19세기 초의 미국시는 비록 형식과 기교면에선 영국의 낭만시를 모방하고 있었지만 그 내용면에선 영국의 낭만시에서는 찾아볼 수 없는 미국적인 지명과 식물의 이름 등을 시어로 활용함으로써 미국적인 풍경과 미국적인 감성을 담은 독특한 시들을 탄생시켰다. 남북전쟁 이후에는 급격하게 진행된 산업화의 영향으로 인간과 사회, 인간과 자연에 대한 고민을 시로 표현하는 작품들이 등장하기 시작했다. 또한 자연을 통한 자기 성찰의 내용을 표현하는 시들이 등장하면서 미국의 자연이 미국시의 중요한 소재이자 주제가 되었다. 새롭게 탄생한 국가의 건설과 발전에 대한 열망이나 민주주의에 대한 찬미 등을 노래한 시들이 등장하기 시작한 것도 19세기 미국시의 한 특징으로 볼 수 있다.

2. 주요 작가와 작품

(1) 필립 프레노 Philip Freneau, 1752-1832

필립 프레노는 1752년 와인 상인이었던 피에르 프레노(Pierre Freneau)의 장남으로 태어났다. 뉴저지 주에서 성장했고, 프린스턴 대학에 입학하여 목사가 되기 위해 공부했다. 프린스턴 대학을 졸업하고 잠시 교직에 있었지만 곧 그만 두었다. 독립전쟁이 발발하자 그는 영국을 신랄하게 비판하는 글을 써서 발표하기도 했다. 그러나 그는 독립혁명에 직접 참전하지는 않았고 미국을 떠나 서인도제도에서 머물며 글을 쓰기도 했다. 프레노는 다시 미국으로 돌아와 민병대에 가입해 활동하기도 했고, 영국군에게 붙잡혀 감옥선에 6주정도 수감되어 고초를 겪기도 했다. 이후 그는 그가 감옥선에서 겪었던 경험을 「영국 감옥선」("The British Prison Ship")이라는 강력한 반영국적인 어조의 시를 통해 발표했다. 이러한 이유로 필립 프레노는 "미국 혁명의 시인"(The Poet of the American Revolution)으로 불리기도 했다. 필립 프레노의 시는 영국의 낭만시의 전통을 이어받기도 했지만 시적언어와 소재 면에서 영국의 낭만시에서는 찾아 볼 수 없는 지극히 미국적인 언어와 소재를 사용하여 미국적인 자연과 미국적인 정서를 담은 시를 썼다.

The Indian Burying Ground *

In spite of all the learned have said,
    I still my old opinion keep;
The posture, that we give the dead,
    Points out the soul's eternal sleep.

Not so the ancients of these lands —
    The Indian, when from life released,
Again is seated with his friends,
    And shares again the joyous feast.

---

* "The Indian Burying Ground" is a short lyric poem of forty lines celebrating the spirits of Native Americans haunting their sequestered graves in the North American wilderness. It is an early American example of the Romantic movement in Western literature.

His imaged birds, and painted bowl,
    And venison, for a journey dressed,
Bespeak the nature of the soul,
    Activity, that knows no rest.

His bow, for action ready bent,
    And arrows, with a head of stone,
Can only mean that life is spent,
    And not the old ideas gone.

Thou, stranger, that shalt come this way,
    No fraud upon the dead commit—
Observe the swelling turf, and say
    They do not lie, but here they sit.

Here still a lofty rock remains,
    On which the curious eye may trace
(Now wasted, half, by wearing rains)
    The fancies of a ruder race.

Here still an aged elm aspires,
    Beneath whose far-projecting shade
(And which the shepherd still admires)
    The children of the forest played!

There oft a restless Indian queen
    (Pale Shebah, with her braided hair)
And many a barbarous form is seen
    To chide the man that lingers there.

By midnight moons, o'er moistening dews;
    In habit for the chase arrayed,
The hunter still the deer pursues,
    The hunter and the deer, a shade!

And long shall timorous fancy see
    The painted chief, and pointed spear,
And Reason's self shall bow the knee
    To shadows and delusions here.

(2) 윌리엄 칼런 브라이언트 William Cullen Bryant, 1794-1878

윌리엄 칼런 브라이언트는 1794년 매사추세츠 주의 커밍턴 (Cummington)에서 출생했다. 그의 아버지 피터 브라이언트(Peter Bryant) 는 의사였으며 이후 매사추세츠 주의 입법의원이 되었다. 그는 법률을 공 부하였으며, 이후 변호사로 활동하기도 했지만 결국 시를 쓰는 일에 더욱 매료되었다. 그는 알렉산더 포프(Alexander Pope)와 같은 시인들의 작품에 영향을 받았다. 그는 시를 통해 삶과 죽음에 대한 철학적인 고민과 자신의 정치적인 신념을 표명하기도 했다. 그의 대표작 『죽음에 대한 고찰』 (*Thanatopsis*)은 자연의 일부로서의 인간에 대해 그의 깊은 명상을 전하고 있다. 그를 유명하게 했던 『금지령』(*The Embargo*)은 토머스 제퍼슨 대통령 을 신랄하게 공격하는 내용을 담고 있었기 때문에 시가 출판되자마자 뜨 거운 반향을 불러 일으켰다.

Thanatopsis*

To him who in the love of Nature holds
Communion with her visible forms, she speaks
A various language; for his gayer hours
She has a voice of gladness, and a smile
And eloquence of beauty, and she glides
Into his darker musings, with a mild
And healing sympathy, that steals away
Their sharpness, ere he is aware. When thoughts
Of the last bitter hour come like a blight
Over thy spirit, and sad images
Of the stern agony, and shroud, and pall,
And breathless darkness, and the narrow house,
Make thee to shudder, and grow sick at heart; —
Go forth, under the open sky, and list
To Nature's teachings, while from all around —
Earth and her waters, and the depths of air —
Comes a still voice —

Yet a few days, and thee

The all-beholding sun shall see no more
In all his course; nor yet in the cold ground,
Where thy pale form was laid, with many tears,
Nor in the embrace of ocean, shall exist
Thy image. Earth, that nourished thee, shall claim
Thy growth, to be resolved to earth again,

---

* "Thanatopsis" is written as an encouragement for mankind. The title is composed of two words: thanatos, which means 'death', and opsis, which means 'view', so thanatopsis actually means a 'view of death'.

And, lost each human trace, surrendering up
Thine individual being, shalt thou go
To mix for ever with the elements,
To be a brother to the insensible rock
And to the sluggish clod, which the rude swain
Turns with his share, and treads upon. The oak
Shall send his roots abroad, and pierce thy mould.

　　　Yet not to thine eternal resting-place
Shalt thou retire alone, nor couldst thou wish
Couch more magnificent. Thou shalt lie down
With patriarchs of the infant world—with kings,
The powerful of the earth—the wise, the good,
Fair forms, and hoary seers of ages past,
All in one mighty sepulchre.　The hills
Rock-ribbed and ancient as the sun,—the vales
Stretching in pensive quietness between;
The venerable woods—rivers that move
In majesty, and the complaining brooks
That make the meadows green; and, poured round all,
Old Ocean's gray and melancholy waste,—
Are but the solemn decorations all
Of the great tomb of man. The golden sun,
The planets, all the infinite host of heaven,
Are shining on the sad abodes of death,
Through the still lapse of ages. All that tread
The globe are but a handful to the tribes
That slumber in its bosom.—Take the wings
Of morning, pierce the Barcan wilderness,
Or lose thyself in the continuous woods
Where rolls the Oregon, and hears no sound,

Save his own dashings—yet the dead are there:
And millions in those solitudes, since first
The flight of years began, have laid them down
In their last sleep—the dead reign there alone.
So shalt thou rest, and what if thou withdraw
In silence from the living, and no friend
Take note of thy departure? All that breathe
Will share thy destiny. The gay will laugh
When thou art gone, the solemn brood of care
Plod on, and each one as before will chase
His favorite phantom; yet all these shall leave
Their mirth and their employments, and shall come
And make their bed with thee. As the long train
Of ages glide away, the sons of men,
The youth in life's green spring, and he who goes
In the full strength of years, matron and maid,
The speechless babe, and the gray-headed man—
Shall one by one be gathered to thy side,
By those, who in their turn shall follow them.

    So live, that when thy summons comes to join
The innumerable caravan, which moves
To that mysterious realm, where each shall take
His chamber in the silent halls of death,
Thou go not, like the quarry-slave at night,
Scourged to his dungeon, but, sustained and soothed
By an unfaltering trust, approach thy grave,
Like one who wraps the drapery of his couch
About him, and lies down to pleasant dreams.

(3) 랄프 왈도 에머슨Ralph Waldo Emerson, 1803-1882

　　미국의 철학자이자 시인인 에머슨은 1803년 매사추세츠 주의 보스턴에서 태어났다. 아버지가 유니테리언 교회(Unitarian church)의 목사였기 때문에 어려서부터 종교적으로 아버지의 영향을 많이 받았다. 어려서 목사였던 아버지가 돌아가셨기 때문에 가난한 어린 시절을 보냈으나 어머니의 열정적인 교육열로 인해 그를 포함한 형제들 모두가 하버드 대학을 졸업했다. 에머슨은 하버드를 졸업 후 목사직을 잠시 수행하기도 했지만 아내의 죽음과 종교적 교리에 대한 본질적인 회의로 인해 목사직을 그만두고 10개월간의 유럽여행을 떠났다. 그는 그곳에서 워즈워드와 콜리지를 비롯한 낭만주의 대가들을 만나 낭만주의 정신에 대한 교감을 나누었다. 귀국 후 에머슨은 영국으로부터 진정한 정신적 문화적 독립의 필요성을 역설하면서 미국적인 가치와 철학의 필요성을 주장했다. 1836년 발표한 『자연』(*Nature*)은 과거의 방식을 맹목적으로 추종하는 것으로부터 벗어나 새로운 환경에 맞는 새로운 방식과 사상의 중요성을 강조하고 있다. 에머슨은 『자연』에서 미국의 진정한 사상적 독립에 대한 필요성을 언급하고 있는 것이다. 『자연』의 첫 머리는 과거의 방식에 무비판적으로 순응하는 시대의 잘못을 지적하는 것으로 시작하고 있다. 『자연』을 발표한 후 에머슨은 초절주의 클럽(Transcendental Club)을 결성했다. 초절주의(Transcendentalism)는 에머슨이 『자연』을 발표한 1836년부터 1860년대까지 일어났던 미국의 종교, 문학, 철학 전반에 걸쳐서 일어났던 일종의 정신운동으로 이해할 수 있다. 종교적인 관점에서 볼 때 초절주의는 유니태리아니즘(Unitarianism)이 철학적으로 발전한 것으로 볼 수 있다. 유니태리아니즘은 윌리엄 엘러리 채닝(William Ellery Channing)에 의해 체계화되었으며, 청교도들의 엄격한 캘빈주의(Calvinism)에 반발하여 개인의 자유의지를 중시하면서 개인이 신과 하나가 될 수 있다고 믿었다. 초절주의는 유니테리어니즘과 낭만주의 문학정신이 결합하여 개인의 자유의지를 바탕으로 직관을 통해 보편적인 진리와 모든 자연과 생명에 깃든 "대영혼"(Over-Soul)을 느낄 수 있다고 믿었다.

Days*

Daughters of Time, the hypocritic Days,
Muffled and dumb like barefoot dervishes,
And marching single in an endless file,
Bring diadems and fagots in their hands.
To each they offer gifts after his will,
Bread, kingdoms, stars, and sky that holds them all.
I, in my pleached garden, watched the pomp,
Forgot my morning wishes, hastily
Took a few herbs and apples, and the Day
Turned and departed silent. I, too late,
Under her solemn fillet saw the scorn.

Each and All**

Little thinks, in the field, yon red-cloaked clown,
Of thee from the hill-top looking down;
The heifer that lows in the upland farm,

---

* "Days" is a poem written by Ralph Waldo Emerson. This poem is about the narrator watching the days pass him by. He feels as if he is missing out on his own life while watching others. He is, perhaps, also lazy. Emerson personifies "Days" by giving it actions that people would have, such as giving people something and calling it a "her".

** "Each and All" echoes the idea—which Emerson voices in many places—that things by

Far-heard, lows not thine ear to charm;
The sexton, tolling his bell at noon,
Deems not that great Napoleon
Stops his horse, and lists with delight,
Whilst his files sweep round yon Alpine height;
Nor knowest thou what argument
Thy life to thy neighbor's creed has lent.
All are needed by each one;
Nothing is fair or good alone.
I thought the sparrow's note from heaven,
Singing at dawn on the alder bough;
I brought him home, in his nest, at even;
He sings the song, but it pleases not now,
For I did not bring home the river and sky; —
He sang to my ear, — they sang to my eye.
The delicate shells lay on the shore;
The bubbles of the latest wave
Fresh pearls to their enamel gave;
And the bellowing of the savage sea
Greeted their safe escape to me.
I wiped away the weeds and foam,
I fetched my sea-born treasures home;
But the poor, unsightly, noisome things
Had left their beauty on the shore,
With the sun, and the sand, and the wild uproar.
The lover watched his graceful maid,
As 'mid the virgin train she stayed,

---

themselves are unaffecting and even ugly but that when placed in context, usually their natural context, they become beautiful. Even putrefaction, Emerson writes, is beautiful when seen as the source of new life.

Nor knew her beauty's best attire

Was woven still by the snow-white choir.

At last she came to his hermitage,

Like the bird from the woodlands to the cage; —

The gay enchantment was undone,

A gentle wife, but fairy none.

Then I said, "I covet truth;

Beauty is unripe childhood's cheat;

I leave it behind with the games of youth:" —

As I spoke, beneath my feet

The ground-pine curled its pretty wreath,

Running over the club-moss burrs;

I inhaled the violet's breath;

Around me stood the oaks and firs;

Pine-cones and acorns lay on the ground;

Over me soared the eternal sky,

Full of light and of deity;

Again I saw, again I heard,

The rolling river, the morning bird; —

Beauty through my senses stole;

I yielded myself to the perfect whole.

Brahma*

IF the red slayer think he slays,

   Or if the slain think he is slain,

---

* "Brahma" is an excellent reflection and representation of Ralph Waldo Emerson's work as a whole. Though he is more widely known as a writer of essays, several of his poems may be seen as keys to his use of style and theme in all of his work, and this is one of those poems.

They know not well the subtle ways
    I keep, and pass, and turn again.

Far or forgot to me is near;
    Shadow and sunlight are the same;
The vanish'd gods to me appear;
    And one to me are shame and fame.

They reckon ill who leave me out;
    When me they fly, I am the wings;
I am the doubter and the doubt,
    And I the hymn the Brahmin sings.

The strong gods pine for my abode,
    And pine in vain the sacred Seven;
But thou, meek lover of the good!
    Find me, and turn thy back on heaven.

(4) 에밀리 디킨슨 Emily Dickinson, 1830-1886

에밀리 디킨슨은 19세기와 20세기의 문학적 감수성을 연결하는 역할을 하고 있다. 과격한 개인주의자였던 그녀는 매사추세츠 주의 작은 칼뱅주의 마을 애머스트에서 태어나 평생을 보냈다. 그녀는 결혼하지 않았던데다 외부적으로는 별 사건이 일어나지 않았지만 내면적으로는 격렬한, 예사롭지 않은 삶을 살았다. 그녀는 자연을 사랑했으며 뉴잉글랜드 시골의 새, 동물, 식물, 계절의 변화 등에서 깊은 영감을 얻었다. 디킨슨은 감수성이 너무 풍부했던 나머지 말년을 은둔자로 보냈다. 그녀는 아마도 시를 쓰기 위해 은둔자가 되었는지도 모른다. 그녀는 시를 쓰는 것 이외에도 변호

사이자 애머스트의 유명 인사이며 후에 연방의원이 된 아버지를 위해 집 안일을 하면서 하루하루를 보냈다.

디킨슨은 독서를 많이 하지는 않았지만 성경, 윌리엄 셰익스피어의 작품, 고전 신화 관련 작품들을 꿰뚫고 있었다. 디킨슨은 당시 가장 은둔하는 문학인이었기에 이러한 책들만이 그녀의 진정한 스승이었다. 수줍음 많았고, 작품을 거의 발표하지도 않았으며, 또 세상에 알려지지도 않았던 이 시골 여성이 19세기 최고의 미국 시들을 창조해냈다는 사실은, 그녀의 시가 재발견된 1950년대 이래 독자들을 매혹시키고 있다. 디킨슨의 간결하면서 이미지즘적인 스타일은 휘트먼에 비해 더욱 현대적이며 혁신적이다. 그녀는 한 단어로 표현할 수 있을 때 결코 두 단어를 사용하는 일이 없었고, 거의 속담처럼 응축된 스타일로 추상적인 사고와 구체적인 사물을 결합했다. 그녀의 수작들은 군더더기가 하나도 없다. 다수의 시들은 현 시대의 감수성을 조롱하고 있고, 어떤 시들은 심지어 이교도적이기까지 하다. 그녀는 때로 놀라울 정도로 실존적인 깨달음을 보여주고 있다. 그녀는 포처럼 마음의 어둡고 감추어진 부분을 탐구하면서 죽음과 무덤을 극화하기도 했다. 하지만 그녀는 꽃과 벌 같은 단순한 사물들도 찬미했다. 그녀의 시는 대단한 지적 능력을 보여주고 있으며 시간에 갇힌 인간 의식의 한계에 대한 고통스런 역설을 일깨우고 있다. 그녀는 뛰어난 유머 감각을 지니고 있었으며 그녀가 다루는 주제의 범위와 묘사 방법은 놀라울 정도로 다양했다. 그녀의 시의 제목은 일반적으로 토머스 H. 존슨이 1955년 표준판에서 할당한 번호로 알려져 있다. 그녀의 시는 불규칙한 대문자와 대시(dash, ―)로 북적댄다.

1855년 목사인 찰스 워즈워즈를 만나 칼뱅주의적 정통주의의 영향을 받게 되었다. 그녀의 시는 자연과 사랑 외에도 퓨리터니즘(청교도주의)을 배경으로 한 죽음과 영원 등의 주제를 많이 다루었다. 같은 시대의 영국의 여류시인 C. C. 로제티와 유사한 점도 있으나, 디킨슨의 시가 훨씬 더 경질적인 요소를 지니고 있어, 19세기 낭만파의 시풍보다도 17세기의 형이상학파 시인(metaphysical poet)의 시풍에 가까웠다.

운율에서나 문법에서나 파격적인 데가 있었기 때문에 19세기에서는 인정을 받지 못했으나, 20세기에 들어와서 이미지즘이나 형이상학적인 시의 유행과 더불어 높이 평가받게 되었다. 1955년 하버드 대학에서 『전시집』(*The Poems of Emily Dickinson*)이 발간되었고, 1958년에 『전서간집』이 간행되었다.

I'm nobody! Who are you?*

I'm nobody! Who are you?
Are you nobody, too?
Then there's a pair of us—don't tell!
They'd banish—you know!

How dreary to be somebody!
How public like a frog
To tell one's name the livelong day
To an admiring bog!

---

* This poem opens with a literally impossible declaration—that the speaker is "Nobody." This nobody-ness, however, quickly comes to mean that she is outside of the public sphere; perhaps, here Dickinson is touching on her own failure to become a published poet, and thus the fact that to most of society, she is "Nobody."

How happy is the little Stone*

How happy is the little Stone
That rambles in the Road alone,
And doesn't care about Careers
And Exigencies never fears —
Whose Coat of elemental Brown
A passing Universe put on,
And independent as the Sun
Associates or glows alone,
Fulfilling absolute Decree
In casual simplicity —

The Soul selects her own Society**

The Soul selects her own Society —
Then — shuts the Door —
To her divine Majority —
Present no more —

Unmoved — she notes the Chariots — pausing —
At her low Gate —

---

* This poem by Emily Dickinson suggests that it is much easier and more enjoyable being a
small, inconsequential object overlooked by everybody else than it is to be human and to
have all the responsibility and obligation that comes with that identity.

** "The Soul Selects Her Own Society" is believed to have been written in 1862, a year during
which Dickinson supposedly produced more than 300 poems. Significantly, the poem can be
read as a description of the artist's experience: the Soul, perhaps a poet, freely chooses to
close herself off from the world in order to pursue the solitary, interior life of creativity and
self-discovery.

Unmoved—an Emperor be kneeling
Upon her Mat—

I've known her—from an ample nation—
Choose One—
Then—close the Valves of her attention—
Like Stone—

Because I could not stop for Death*

Because I could not stop for Death—
He kindly stopped for me—
The Carriage held but just Ourselves—
And Immortality.

We slowly drove—He knew no haste
And I had put away
My labor and my leisure too,
For His Civility—

We passed the School, where Children strove
At Recess—in the Ring—
We passed the Fields of Gazing Grain—
We passed the Setting Sun—

---

* In this poem, Dickinson's speaker is communicating from beyond the grave, describing her journey with Death, personified, from life to afterlife. In the opening stanza, the speaker is too busy for Death ("Because I could not stop for Death—"), so Death—"kindly"—takes the time to do what she cannot, and stops for her.

Or rather—He passed us—
The Dews drew quivering and chill—
For only Gossamer, my Gown—
My Tippet—only Tulle—

We paused before a House that seemed
A Swelling of the Ground—
The Roof was scarcely visible—
The Cornice—in the Ground—

Since then—'tis Centuries—and yet
Feels shorter than the Day
I first surmised the Horses' Heads
Were toward Eternity—

There's a certain Slant of light *

There's a certain Slant of light,
Winter Afternoons—
That oppresses, like the Heft
Of Cathedral Tunes—

Heavenly Hurt, it gives us—
We can find no scar,
But internal difference—
Where the Meanings, are—

---

* This poem focuses only on the effect of a certain kind of light that the speaker notices on
winter afternoons. It quickly becomes clear that this is not going to be a poem extolling
nature or winter light's virtues, for this light "oppresses."

None may teach it—Any—
'Tis the seal Despair—
An imperial affliction
Sent us of the Air—

When it comes, the Landscape listens—
Shadows—hold their breath—
When it goes, 'tis like the Distance
On the look of Death—

These are the days when birds come back*

These are the days when birds come back,
A very few, a bird or two,
To take a backward look.

These are the days when skies put on
The old, old sophistries of June,—
A blue and gold mistake.

Oh, fraud that cannot cheat the bee,
Almost thy plausibility
Induces my belief,

Till ranks of seeds their witness bear,

---

* This trochaic poem, with Dickinson's irregular punctuation, has an irregular rhyme scheme
with the 1st and 2nd lines sometimes rhyming with near rhyme, but not always. It's theme
is a twist on the sacred religious theme of Communion. It compares the return of birds to
a fraud that threatens to "cheat the bees." It invites children to partake of the ritual of
returning waves of nature's patterns.

And softly through the altered air
Hurries a timid leaf!

Oh, sacrament of summer days,
Oh, last communion in the haze,
Permit a child to join,

Thy sacred emblems to partake,
Thy consecrated bread to break,
Taste thine immortal wine!

I like to see it lap the Miles＊

I like to see it lap the Miles—
And lick the Valleys up—
And stop to feed itself at Tanks—
And then—prodigious step

Around a Pile of Mountains—
And supercilious peer
In Shanties—by the sides of Roads—
And then a Quarry pare

To fit it's sides
And crawl between

＊ This poem, although the subject is never named explicitly, only referred to as "it," is about
a train. The speaker enjoys watching this train traveling through the country, imagining it as
a kind of giant horse figure, going fast and far and licking up the country side. She imagines
it feeding itself at tanks—ostensibly, either filling with new passengers at train stations, or
being refueled.

Complaining all the while
In horrid—hooting stanza—
Then chase itself down Hill—

And neigh like Boanerges—
Then—prompter than a Star
Stop—docile and omnipotent
At it's own stable door—

There's been a Death, in the Opposite House*

There's been a Death, in the Opposite House,
As lately as Today—
I know it, by the numb look
Such Houses have—alway—

The Neighbors rustle in and out—
The Doctor—drives away—
A Window opens like a Pod—
Abrupt—mechanically—

Somebody flings a Mattress out—
The Children hurry by—
They wonder if it died—on that—

---

* This poem is describes what goes on in a house in which someone has recently died. The tone is matter of fact, much like a reporter would notice details. Without mentioning death, she describes all the things that go on after a death: she mentions the "numbness" of the house, but that is the appearance of those who come and go rather than that of the building; neighbors "rustle" in and out, perhaps offering support; the doctor has done all he can, so he leaves.

I used to—when a Boy—

The Minister—goes stiffly in—
As if the House were His—
And He owned all the Mourners—now—
And little Boys—besides—

And then the Milliner—and the Man
Of the Appalling Trade—
To take the measure of the House—

There'll be that Dark Parade—

Of Tassels—and of Coaches—soon—
It's easy as a Sign—
The Intuition of the News—
In just a Country Town—

I heard a Fly buzz*

I heard a Fly buzz—when I died—
The Stillness in the Room
Was like the Stillness in the Air—
Between the Heaves of Storm—

The Eyes around—had wrung them dry—
And Breaths were gathering firm

---

* This poem is another where the speaker is writing from beyond the grave, and like "Because I could not stop for Death," it is describing the scene of the speaker's death, although in a very different way.

For that last Onset—when the King
Be witnessed—in the Room—

I willed my Keepsakes—Signed away
What portions of me be
Assignable—and then it was
There interposed a Fly—

With Blue—uncertain stumbling Buzz—
Between the light—and me—
And then the Windows failed—and then
I could not see to see—

This Is My Letter To The World*

This is my letter to the world,
That never wrote to me,—
The simple news that Nature told,
With tender majesty.
Her message is committed
To hands I cannot see;
For love of her, sweet countrymen,
Judge tenderly of me!

---

* "This Is My Letter to the World" is a work of metafiction; that is, it is literature that is consciously self-referential and highlights rather than conceals the work as a created piece of art. In the first line, the speaker makes clear exactly what this text is: a letter.

Time and Eternity*

There's been a death in the opposite house
    As lately as to-day.
I know it by the numb look
    Such houses have alway.
The neighbors rustle in and out,
    The doctor drives away.
A window opens like a pod,
    Abrupt, mechanically;
Somebody flings a mattress out,—
    The children hurry by;
They wonder if It died on that,—
    I used to when a boy.
The minister goes stiffly in
    As if the house were his,
And he owned all the mourners now,
    And little boys besides;
And then the milliner, and the man
    Of the appalling trade,
To take the measure of the house.
    There'll be that dark parade
Of tassels and of coaches soon;
    It's easy as a sign,—
The intuition of the news
    In just a country town.

---

* "Time and Eternity" is the culminating work of Ananda Kentish Coomaraswamy's career, a career increasingly dedicated to an advocacy of the perennial philosophy. The essence of the perennial philosophy is vitalist and mystic rather than empirical or rationalistic in the modernist sense.

I Died for Beauty, but was Scarce *

I died for beauty, but was scarce
Adjusted in the tomb,
When one who died for truth was lain
In an adjoining room.

He questioned softly why I failed?
"For beauty," I replied.
"And I for truth,—the two are one;
We brethren are," he said.

And so, as kinsmen met a night,
We talked between the rooms,
Until the moss had reached our lips,
And covered up our names.

I taste a liquor never brewed**

I taste a liquor never brewed—
From Tankards scooped in Pearl—
Not all the Frankfort Berries
Yield such an Alcohol!

---

* The speaker says that she died for Beauty, but she was hardly adjusted to her tomb before
a man who died for Truth was laid in a tomb next to her. When the two softly told each
other why they died, the man declared that Truth and Beauty are the same, so that he and
the speaker were "Brethren." The speaker says that they met at night, "as Kinsmen," and
talked between their tombs until the moss reached their lips and covered up the names on
their tombstones.

** Emily Dickinson did not give titles to most of her poems, so they are generally referred to

Inebriate of air —am I —
And Debauchee of Dew —
Reeling —thro' endless summer days —
From inns of molten Blue —

When "Landlords" turn the drunken Bee
Out of the Foxglove's door —
When Butterflies —renounce their "drams" —
I shall but drink the more!

Till Seraphs swing their snowy Hats —
And Saints —to windows run —
To see the little Tippler
Leaning against the —Sun!

(5) 에드거 앨런 포 Edgar Allan Poe, 1809–1849

앨런 포는 1809년 1월 19일 미국 보스턴에서 유랑극단 배우 출신의
부모 아래 태어났다. 2세 때는 아버지가 집을 나가고 어머니까지 폐결핵으
로 여읜 뒤, 담배상이던 숙부 존 앨런(John Allan)에게 3세 때 입양되며 '에
드거 앨런 포'(Edgar Allan Poe)라는 이름을 얻게 되었다. 1826년 버지니아
대학교에 입학했으나 숙부와의 불화로 재정적 지원이 줄어들자, 학비 마련
을 위해 도박에 뛰어들었고 빚더미에 올라 이듬해 학교를 중퇴하였다. 같
은 해인 1827년 시집 『티무르와 그 밖의 시』(*Tamerlane and Other Poems*)를

---

by their first lines. The editor of the 1955 edition of her poems, Thomas H. Johnson,
attempted to number them according to the order of their composition; "I taste a liquor
never brewed —" is listed as number 214. Dickinson sometimes left alternate versions of her
poems, and the version discussed here is what Johnson believed to be her final one.

발표하며 시단에 데뷔했으나, 생활고로 육군에 자원입대하게 되었다.

1831년부터는 미국 볼티모어에서 미망인인 숙모 마리아 클렘(Maria Clemm)의 집에서 기거하였고, 1833년 10월 『볼티모어 토요일 방문자』(*The Baltimore Saturday Visiter*)지의 단편소설 50달러 현상 공모에 단편 『병 속의 수기』(*Found in a Bottle*)가 당선되면서 주목을 받았다. 그 결과 1835년 문예지 『남부문학통신』(*Southern Literary Messenger*)의 편집자로 근무하기 시작했으나, 신랄한 비평문을 여과 없이 수록해 반발을 불러일으킨 탓에 1837년 퇴사하였다. 1835년에는 당시 13세였던 사촌 여동생 버지니아 클렘(Virginia Clemm)과 26세의 나이로 결혼한 뒤, 리치먼드와 필라델피아에서 편집자 생활을 근근이 유지해 왔다. 그 후 1838년 단편 『리지아』(*Ligeia*)에 이어, 최초의 장편소설 『아서 고든 핌의 이야기』(*The Narrative of Arthur Gordon Pym of Nantucket*)를 발간하며 창작 활동에 돌입했다. 1839년에는 단편 『윌리엄 윌슨』(*William Wilson*)과 『어셔 가의 몰락』(*The Fall of the House of Usher*)을 발표했고, 이듬해인 1840년 첫 단편집으로 『그로테스크하고 아라베스크한 이야기』(*Tales of the Grotesque and Arabesque*)를 2권으로 묶어 출간하였다.

또한 1845년 『이브닝 미러』(*The Evening Mirror*)지에 발표했던 시편 『갈가마귀』(*The Raven*)가 집중 조명을 받으며 유럽 문단에까지 이름을 알리게 되었다. 그러나 1842년부터 지병으로 투병생활을 하던 아내 버지니아 클렘의 병세가 결핵으로 악화되면서 1847년 1월 끝내 사망하기에 이르렀다. 사별의 충격으로 우울증에 시달리던 그는 아편을 복용하거나 자살을 시도하기까지 했다. 버지니아 클렘의 무덤을 배회하는 등 피폐한 생활을 이어가던 끝에 사별한 아내를 추모하는 내용의 마지막 시 『애너벨 리』(*Annabel Lee*)를 1849년 발표하였다. 이밖에도 『헬렌에게』(*To Helen*) 등의 시편을 통해 아름다움과 암울한 상념 등에 천착하여 음악적 리듬감을 효과적으로 표현한 순수시를 선보이며 미국의 대표적인 낭만주의 시인으로도 손꼽힌다.

The Raven*

Once upon a midnight dreary, while I pondered, weak and weary,
Over many a quaint and curious volume of forgotten lore—
    While I nodded, nearly napping, suddenly there came a tapping,
As of some one gently rapping, rapping at my chamber door.
"'Tis some visitor," I muttered, "tapping at my chamber door—
        Only this and nothing more."

    Ah, distinctly I remember it was in the bleak December;
And each separate dying ember wrought its ghost upon the floor.
    Eagerly I wished the morrow;—vainly I had sought to borrow
    From my books surcease of sorrow—sorrow for the lost Lenore—
For the rare and radiant maiden whom the angels name Lenore—
        Nameless here for evermore.

To Helen**

Helen, thy beauty is to me
    Like those Nicéan barks of yore,
That gently, o'er a perfumed sea,
    The weary, way-worn wanderer bore
    To his own native shore.

---

* "The Raven" is the most famous of Poe's poems, notable for its melodic and dramatic qualities. The meter of the poem is mostly trochaic octameter, with eight stressed-unstressed two-syllable feet per lines.

** The narrator praises Helen for her beauty, which he compares to a ship bringing a "weary, wayworn wanderer" to his home. Her classic beauty has reminded him of ancient times, and he watches her stand like a statue while holding a stone lamp.

On desperate seas long wont to roam,
　Thy hyacinth hair, thy classic face,
Thy Naiad airs have brought me home
　To the glory that was Greece,
　And the grandeur that was Rome.

Lo! in yon brilliant window-niche
　How statue-like I see thee stand,
The agate lamp within thy hand!
　Ah, Psyche, from the regions which
　Are Holy-Land!

Annabel Lee*

It was many and many a year ago,
In a kingdom by the sea,
That a maiden there lived whom you may know
By the name of ANNABEL LEE;
And this maiden she lived with no other thought
Than to love and be loved by me.

I was a child and she was a child,
In this kingdom by the sea;
But we loved with a love that was more than love-
I and my Annabel Lee;

---

* Long ago, "in a kingdom by the sea," lived Annabel Lee, who loved the narrator. Both she and the narrator were children but knew love more powerful than that of the angels, who envied them. A wind chilled and killed Annabel, but their love was too strong to be defeated by angels or demons. The narrator is reminded of Annabel Lee by everything, including the moon and the stars, and at night, he lies by her tomb by the sea.

With a love that the winged seraphs of heaven
  Coveted her and me.

And this was the reason that, long ago,
  In this kingdom by the sea,
  A wind blew out of a cloud, chilling
  My beautiful Annabel Lee;
So that her highborn kinsman came
  And bore her away from me,
  To shut her up in a sepulchre
  In this kingdom by the sea.

The angels, not half so happy in heaven,
  Went envying her and me-
Yes! —that was the reason (as all men know,
  In this kingdom by the sea)
That the wind came out of the cloud by night,
  Chilling and killing my Annabel Lee.

But our love it was stronger by far than the love
  Of those who were older than we-
Of many far wiser than we-
And neither the angels in heaven above,
  Nor the demons down under the sea,
Can ever dissever my soul from the soul
  Of the beautiful Annabel Lee.

For the moon never beams without bringing me dreams
  Of the beautiful Annabel Lee;
And the stars never rise but I feel the bright eyes
  Of the beautiful Annabel Lee;

And so, all the night-tide, I lie down by the side
  Of my darling- my darling- my life and my bride,
  In the sepulchre there by the sea,
  In her tomb by the sounding sea.

(6) 헨리 롱펠로우 Henry Wadsworth Longfellow, 1807-1882

롱펠로우는 메인 주의 포틀랜드 출신으로 보든 대학교 졸업 후 약 3년 동안 유럽에 유학하고, 귀국 후 모교의 근대어학 교수가 되었다. 1835년 하버드 대학교 교수가 되기 전에 또 다시 유럽으로 갔으며, 이때 첫 번째 부인을 잃었다. 스위스에서 프랑세즈 애플턴을 발견하고 그녀를 산문 이야기 『하이페리온』(*Hyperion, a Romance*)의 여주인공으로 묘사하였다가 그녀의 반감을 사기도 했으나 1843년 드디어 그녀와 결혼하였다. 그러나 이 두 번째 부인도 1861년 불행한 사고로 불타 죽었다. 18년간 하버드 대학 교수직에 있었으며, 그 동안 케임브리지에 살면서 많은 시작을 발표하였다. 그 중에서도 식민지 전쟁을 배경으로 한 비련의 이야기 『에반젤린』(*Evangeline*), 핀란드의 『칼레발라』의 영향을 받고서 쓴 인디언의 신화적 영웅 이야기 시「하이어워사의 노래」("The Song of Hiawatha"), 청교도 군인의 연애 이야기 「마일즈 스탠디시의 구혼」("The Courtship of Miles Standish and Other Poems") 등의 장시가 유명하다.

그의 시는 독창성과 직감의 깊이는 없으나, 유럽의 시적 전통, 특히 유럽 대륙 여러 나라의 민요를 솜씨있게 번안·번역함으로써 미국 대중에게 전달한 공적은 크다. 오늘날 최대 걸작으로 높이 평가되는 작품은 단테의 『신곡』 번역에 붙인 소네트 『신곡』으로, 그의 다른 시에서는 볼 수 없는 사상의 깊이가 보인다.

Snow-flakes*

Out of the bosom of the Air,
    Out of the cloud-folds of her garments shaken,
Over the woodlands brown and bare,
    Over the harvest-fields forsaken,
        Silent, and soft, and slow
        Descends the snow.

Even as our cloudy fancies take
    Suddenly shape in some divine expression,
Even as the troubled heart doth make
    In the white countenance confession,
        The troubled sky reveals
        The grief it feels.

This is the poem of the air,
    Slowly in silent syllables recorded;
This is the secret of despair,
    Long in its cloudy bosom hoarded,
        Now whispered and revealed
        To wood and field.

---

* "Snowflakes" conveys the experience of loss and bereavement, both of which Longfellow experienced. His first wife, who died in childbirth, informed the poem Hyperion. He suffered facial burns when he tried to rescue his second wife who died in a fire following this he grew a beard to conceal his scars.

Serenade from "The Spanish Student"*

STARS of the summer night!
   Far in yon azure deeps,
Hide, hide your golden light!
   She sleeps!
My lady sleeps!
   Sleeps!

Moon of the summer night!
   Far down yon western steeps,
Sink, sink in silver light!
   She sleeps!
My lady sleeps!
   Sleeps!

Wind of the summer night!
   Where yonder woodbine creeps,
Fold, fold thy pinions light!
   She sleeps!
My lady sleeps!
   Sleeps!

Dreams of the summer night!
   Tell her, her lover keeps
Watch! while in slumbers light
   She sleeps!

---

* "Serenade" takes place while Preciosa is asleep in her chamber before Victorian enters the scene by the balcony. The two are in love. "Serenade" is written as four stanzas with seven lines each. The final three lines in each stanza are the same. Each stanza contains the rhyme scheme ABABBB. The first and third lines all end with the same word in each stanza.

My lady sleeps!

    Sleeps!

The Sound of the Sea*

The sea awoke at midnight from its sleep,
  And round the pebbly beaches far and wide
  I heard the first wave of the rising tide
Rush onward with uninterrupted sweep;
A voice out of the silence of the deep,
A sound mysteriously multiplied
As of a cataract from the mountain「s side,
Or roar of winds upon a wooded steep.
So comes to us at times, from the unknown
And inaccessible solitudes of being,
The rushing of the sea-tides of the soul;
And inspirations, that we deem our own,
Are some divine foreshadowing and foreseeing
Of things beyond our reason or control.

A Psalm of Life**

What The Heart Of The Young Man Said To The Psalmist.
Tell me not, in mournful numbers,

---

* "The Sound of the Sea" is a sonnet by Henry Wadsworth Longfellow, describing the sounds of the sea and relating it to human inspiration. Through only auditory images of the sea and other powerful natural forces, Longfellow effectively alludes to the nature of human inspiration. Through detailed and sensory imagery, Longfellow communicates the subtle details of the human soul and how inspiration functions.

Life is but an empty dream!
For the soul is dead that slumbers,
And things are not what they seem.

Life is real! Life is earnest!
And the grave is not its goal;
Dust thou art, to dust returnest,
Was not spoken of the soul.

Not enjoyment, and not sorrow,
Is our destined end or way;
But to act, that each to-morrow
Find us farther than to-day.

Art is long, and Time is fleeting,
And our hearts, though stout and brave,
Still, like muffled drums, are beating
Funeral marches to the grave.

In the world's broad field of battle,
In the bivouac of Life,
Be not like dumb, driven cattle!
Be a hero in the strife!

Trust no Future, howe'er pleasant!
Let the dead Past bury its dead!

** "A Psalm of Life" was once very widely read and just as widely admired. Today, however,
the poem is often mocked for its allegedly incoherent imagery and its supposedly empty
rhetoric. In the poem, the speaker responds to Biblical (specifically, Old Testament) teachings
that all human life is vain and that human beings, made of dust, eventually return to dust.

Act,—act in the living Present!
    Heart within, and God o'erhead!

Lives of great men all remind us
    We can make our lives sublime,
And, departing, leave behind us
    Footprints on the sands of time;

Footprints, that perhaps another,
    Sailing o'er life's solemn main,
A forlorn and shipwrecked brother,
    Seeing, shall take heart again.

Let us, then, be up and doing,
    With a heart for any fate;
Still achieving, still pursuing,
    Learn to labor and to wait.

(7) 월트 휘트먼 Walt Whitman, 1819–1892

휘트먼은 뉴욕 주 롱아일랜드 출신으로 아버지는 목수였는데, T. 페인(1737-1809)의 인권사상 등에 심취하였고, 어머니는 네덜란드 이민 출신으로 자유롭고 민주적인 기풍을 지녔다. 4세 때 브루클린으로 이주, 가정 사정으로 초등학교를 중퇴하여 인쇄소 직공으로 있으면서 독학으로 교양을 쌓았다. 1835년 고향에 돌아가 초등학교 교사, 신문 편집 등에 종사하였다. 그 후 뉴욕으로 옮겨 저널리스트로 활동하기 시작하여, 1846년에는 브루클린의 미국 민주당계 일간지 『이글』(*Eagle*)의 편집자가 되었다. 그러나 1848년 '프리 소일(free soil) 운동'을 지지하는 그의 논설이 민주당 보수파의 분노를 사게 되어 사임, 전부터의 염원이던 프리 소일파의 주간신문 『자유민』(*Freeman*)을 창간하여 그 주필로 활약하였다. 그러나, 또다시 민주당 보수파의 공격을 받고 겨우 1년 만에 사임하였다. 1850년대에 들어서자, 그는 합승마차의 마부석 옆에 앉거나 나룻배에 타거나 하여 민중의 생태를 관찰하고, 또는 아버지의 목수 일을 도우며 많은 시간을 독서와 사색으로 보냈다. 이 내부 침잠의 시기를 거쳐서 그의 시인으로의 전신이 이루어졌다. 1855년 시집 『풀잎』(*Leaves of Grass*)을 자비로 출판하였는데, 이것은 종래의 전통적 시형을 크게 벗어나 미국의 적나라한 모습을 고스란히 받아들여 찬미한 것이었다. 그러나 제3판(1860)에 이르자, 새로 수록된 『카라마스』 등의 시군을 통해서 사랑과 연대라고 하는 일정한 주장이 표면화하기 시작하여, 이른바 '예언자 시인'으로의 변모를 드러냈다. 논문 『민주주의의 미래상』(*Democratic Vistas*)에서도 미국사회의 물질주의적인 경향을 비판하고, '인격주의'의 필요성을 주장하였다.

1862년 겨울, 남북전쟁에 종군 중이던 동생 조지가 부상당한 것이 계기가 되어, 1863년 이후는 관청에 근무하면서 워싱턴의 병원에서 부상병을 간호하기도 하였다. 어떻든 남북전쟁을 극복하고 통일을 지킬 수 있었다는 것은 그에게는 커다란 기쁨이었으며, 자신의 고통과 죽음을 견디는 젊은 병사들의 모습을 직접 목격한 경험은 그의 마음속에 미국의 미래에 대한 희망을 불러일으켰다. 1865년, 남북전쟁을 소재로 하는 72페이지의 작은 시집 『북소리』(Drum-Taps)를 출판하고, 이듬해 링컨 대통령에 대한 추도시 「앞뜰에 라일락이 피었을 때」("When Lilacs Last in the Dooryard Bloom'd")를 포함한 24페이지의 『속편』을 출판해서 곧 『풀잎』에 재록하였다.

1873년에 중풍의 발작이 있었으나 요양에 전념, 1879년에는 서부 여행, 1880년에는 캐나다 여행도 할 수 있을 만큼 회복되었다. 1882년에는 산문집 『자선일기 기타』를 출판, 문명도 높아졌다. 1884년에는 『풀잎』의

인세로 세운 뉴저지주 캠던의 미클가 자택에는 내외의 방문자가 빈번히 드나들었다. 그러나 체력도 약해졌지만 그 자신은 점차 염세주의로 기울었으며, 1888년 재차 중풍이 발작한 후, 1892년 폐렴으로 세상을 떠났다.

I Sit and Look Out*

I sit and look out upon all the sorrows of the world, and upon all oppression and shame;

I hear secret convulsive sobs from young men, at anguish with themselves, remorseful after deeds done;

I see, in low life, the mother misused by her children, dying, neglected, gaunt, desperate;

I see the wife misused by her husband—I see the treacherous seducer of young women;

I mark the ranklings of jealousy and unrequited love, attempted to be hid—I see these sights on the earth;

I see the workings of battle, pestilence, tyranny—I see martyrs and prisoners;

I observe a famine at sea—I observe the sailors casting lots who shall be kill'd, to preserve the lives of the rest;

I observe the slights and degradations cast by arrogant persons upon laborers, the poor, and upon negroes, and the like;

All these—All the meanness and agony without end, I sitting, look out upon,

See, hear, and am silent.

---

* "I sit and look out" is a poem about modern society. The narrator is looking out of the window at life—and all that he sees is Sorrow, Suffering, Corruption and Degradation of society. The advent of capitalism and industrialization has had a tremendous impact on the moral values of the people who choose to be detailed observers, as echoed in the title.

O Captain! My Captain!*

1

O CAPTAIN! my Captain! our fearful trip is done;
The ship has weather'd every rack, the prize we sought is won;
The port is near, the bells I hear, the people all exulting,
While follow eyes the steady keel, the vessel grim and daring:
　　But O heart! heart! heart!
　　　O the bleeding drops of red,
　　　　Where on the deck my Captain lies,
　　　　　Fallen cold and dead.

2

O Captain! my Captain! rise up and hear the bells;
Rise up—for you the flag is flung—for you the bugle trills;
For you bouquets and ribbon'd wreaths—for you the shores a-crowding;
For you they call, the swaying mass, their eager faces turning;
　　Here Captain! dear father!
　　　This arm beneath your head;
　　　　It is some dream that on the deck,
　　　　　You've fallen cold and dead.

3

My Captain does not answer, his lips are pale and still;
My father does not feel my arm, he has no pulse nor will;
The ship is anchor'd safe and sound, its voyage closed and done;
From fearful trip, the victor ship, comes in with object won;

---

* The poem is an elegy to the speaker's recently deceased Captain, at once celebrating the safe
and successful return of their ship and mourning the loss of its great leader.

Exult, O shores, and ring, O bells!
    But I, with mournful tread,
        Walk the deck my Captain lies,
            Fallen cold and dead

Song of Myself (1892 version)*

1

I celebrate myself, and sing myself,
And what I assume you shall assume,
For every atom belonging to me as good belongs to you.

I loafe and invite my soul,
I lean and loafe at my ease observing a spear of summer grass.

My tongue, every atom of my blood, form'd from this soil, this air,
Born here of parents born here from parents the same, and their
parents the same,
I, now thirty-seven years old in perfect health begin,
Hoping to cease not till death.

Creeds and schools in abeyance,
Retiring back a while sufficed at what they are, but never forgotten,
I harbor for good or bad, I permit to speak at every hazard,
Nature without check with original energy.

---

* "Song of Myself," the longest poem in Leaves of Grass, is a joyous celebration of the human
  self in its most expanded, spontaneous, self-sufficient, and all-embracing state as it observes
  and interacts with everything in creation and ranges freely over time and space.

6

A child said What is the grass? fetching it to me with full hands;
How could I answer the child? I do not know what it is any more than he.

I guess it must be the flag of my disposition, out of hopeful green stuff woven.

Or I guess it is the handkerchief of the Lord,
A scented gift and remembrancer designedly dropt,
Bearing the owner's name someway in the corners, that we may see and remark, and say Whose?

Or I guess the grass is itself a child, the produced babe of the vegetation.

Or I guess it is a uniform hieroglyphic,
And it means, Sprouting alike in broad zones and narrow zones,
Growing among black folks as among white,
Kanuck, Tuckahoe, Congressman, Cuff, I give them the same, I receive them the same.

And now it seems to me the beautiful uncut hair of graves.

Tenderly will I use you curling grass,
It may be you transpire from the breasts of young men,
It may be if I had known them I would have loved them,
It may be you are from old people, or from offspring taken soon out of their mothers' laps,
And here you are the mothers' laps.

This grass is very dark to be from the white heads of old mothers,
Darker than the colorless beards of old men,
Dark to come from under the faint red roofs of mouths.

O I perceive after all so many uttering tongues,
And I perceive they do not come from the roofs of mouths for
nothing.

I wish I could translate the hints about the dead young men and
women,
And the hints about old men and mothers, and the offspring taken
soon out of their laps.

What do you think has become of the young and old men?
And what do you think has become of the women and children?

They are alive and well somewhere,
The smallest sprout shows there is really no death,
And if ever there was it led forward life, and does not wait at the end
to arrest it,
And ceas'd the moment life appear'd.

All goes onward and outward, nothing collapses,
And to die is different from what any one supposed, and luckier.

36
Stretch'd and still lies the midnight,
Two great hulls motionless on the breast of the darkness,
Our vessel riddled and slowly sinking, preparations to pass to the one
we have conquer'd,

The captain on the quarter-deck coldly giving his orders through a countenance white as a sheet,

Near by the corpse of the child that serv'd in the cabin,

The dead face of an old salt with long white hair and carefully curl'd whiskers,

The flames spite of all that can be done flickering aloft and below,

The husky voices of the two or three officers yet fit for duty,

Formless stacks of bodies and bodies by themselves, dabs of flesh upon the masts and spars,

Cut of cordage, dangle of rigging, slight shock of the soothe of waves,

Black and impassive guns, litter of powder-parcels, strong scent,

A few large stars overhead, silent and mournful shining,

Delicate sniffs of sea-breeze, smells of sedgy grass and fields by the shore, death-messages given in charge to survivors,

The hiss of the surgeon's knife, the gnawing teeth of his saw,

Wheeze, cluck, swash of falling blood, short wild scream, and long, dull, tapering groan,

These so, these irretrievable.

48

I have said that the soul is not more than the body,

And I have said that the body is not more than the soul,

And nothing, not God, is greater to one than one's self is,

And whoever walks a furlong without sympathy walks to his own funeral drest in his shroud,

And I or you pocketless of a dime may purchase the pick of the earth,

And to glance with an eye or show a bean in its pod confounds the learning of all times,

And there is no trade or employment but the young man following it may become a hero,

And there is no object so soft but it makes a hub for the wheel'd universe,
And I say to any man or woman, Let your soul stand cool and composed before a million universes.

And I say to mankind, Be not curious about God,
For I who am curious about each am not curious about God,
(No array of terms can say how much I am at peace about God and about death.)

I hear and behold God in every object, yet understand God not in the least,
Nor do I understand who there can be more wonderful than myself.

Why should I wish to see God better than this day?
I see something of God each hour of the twenty-four, and each moment then,
In the faces of men and women I see God, and in my own face in the glass,
I find letters from God dropt in the street, and every one is sign'd by God's name,
And I leave them where they are, for I know that wheresoe'er I go,
Others will punctually come for ever and ever.

제2장

20세기 미국시

1. 시대적 배경

1909년에 런던에서 자신의 첫 시집 『사람들』(*Personae*)을 발표한 에즈라 파운드(Ezra Pound)는 런던에 머물고 있던 일단의 젊은 영미시인들에게 나아갈 방향을 1911년에 젊은 영국 사상가인 흄(T. E. Hulme)과 함께 제시했다. 그들은 곧 사상파 시인으로 알려지게 되었다. 그들은 새로운 시 운동을 시작했고 그들의 성명을 발표했다. 여기에는 힐다 두리틀(Hilda Doolittle), 윌리엄 칼로스 윌리엄스(William Carlos Williams), 에이미 로월(Amy Lowell) 등의 미국시인들이 참여했고, 이들의 시는 사상파 시집에 모아져서 발표되었다. 그들의 시는 자유시 및 다른 실험적인 형식의 발달을 가져왔다. 그들은 1912년에 시카고에서 창간된 『시: 운문잡지』(*Poetry: A Magazine of Verse*)의 성공에도 기여했다. 이 시기에 로빈슨(Robinson)은 자신의 시적 재능을 최대로 발휘하여 『하늘을 등진 사나이』(*The Man Against the Sky*), 『멀린』(*Merlin*) 등을 발표했다. 프로스트(Robert Frost)는 1913년에 첫 시집을 내었고 1923년에 네 번째 시집을 발표했다. 중서부 출신의 발라드 시인인 바첼 린지(Vachel Lindsay)는 1913년부터 1917년 사이에 세 권의 시집을 발표하여 시단에서의 명성을 확고히 했다. 중서부지방의 삶을 시적으로 비평하는 일은 1915년에 나온 매스터스(Edgar Lee Masters)의 『스푼 강 명시 선집』 (*Spoon River Anthology*)으로 시작되었는데 더 인상적인 작품은 샌드버그(Carl Sandburg)의 시였다. 샌드버그는 1916년에서 1920년 사이에 자유시 형식으로 중서부 보통사람들의 삶을 탐구하는 세 권의 시집을 발표하였다. 밀레 (Edna St. Vincent Millay)는 1917년에 첫 시집을 발표했고 엘리엇(T. S. Eliot)은 1920년에 두 번째 시집을 발표하여 그의 성숙한 특성을 여실히 보여주었다.

금세기의 미국시는 제 2차 세계대전이 발발할 때까지 점점 더 상징주의적으로 되어갔고, 이전의 문학작품에 대한 인유나 신화적 의미의 암시에 더욱 의존하게 되었으며 지적인 깊이나 뛰어난 재기를 향하여 나아가는 경향이 있었다. 사상파 시인들과 파운드는 프랑스 상징주의자들, 고전 작품, 12,13세기의 프랑스 서정시인들, 이태리의 문예부흥과 고대의 중국과 일본의 시형식에서 영감을 발견했다. 엘리엇의 박학다식은 또한 철학적 영감, 종교사상, 동양의 신비주의 및 인류학 지식을 강조했다. 엘리엇 등은 엘리자베스 시대의 시인과 극작가뿐만 아니라 자코방(Jacobean) 시대의 영국 형이상학파 시인들을 재발견했다.

강렬하고 격렬한 형이상학적 이미지는 시의 지적인 긴장과 상징적 범주를 고양시켰다. 그럼으로써 시는 보다 어려워졌고, 사상의 정서적 의미를 표현하는 보다 나은 도구가 되었다. 매클리시(MacLeish), 스티븐스(Stevens), 윌리엄스(Williams), 마리안 무어(Marianne Moore), 커밍스(Cummings), 크레인(Crane) 및 랜섬(Ransom)과 테이트(Tate)와 같은 내슈빌(Nashville)의 "도망자" 그룹(Fugitives)의 시에 특징적인 것은 형이상학적 경향이다.

1920년대는 1929년에 재정적 붕괴로 이어지는 대공황으로 끝났다. 히틀러(Hitler)와 무솔리니(Mussolini)의 등장과 더불어 공황 시기는 경제적 빈곤, 이념적 불안, 미국적 가치의 전반적 재평가를 초래했다. 많은 작가들이 전통적인 미국의 이상주의에 대한 충실의 깊이를 발견했다. 매클리시는 『새로 발견된 나라』(New Found Land)와 『정복자』(Conquistador)를 발표하고 그 후 10년 동안 민주주의의 선전물을 쓰는 데 주력했다. 집산주의자들에게 공감을 보이며 시를 쓰기 시작했던 샌드버그는 민중을 사랑하고 있음을 보여주는 『국민, 예스』(The People, Yes)를 1936년에 발표하고 링컨의 전기를 방대하게 연구했다.

두 차례에 걸친 세계대전 사이에 성장한 일단의 시인들이 시의 활력을 되찾게 하였다. 이 시인들은 금세기 중반의 영미시인들에게 공통된 질문이었던 잃어버린 자아에 대한 불안이나 개인적 실체를 탐구했다. 뮤리엘 루카이저(Muriel Rukeyser)는 『만가』(Elegies)에서 감동적인 긍정을 표현했고, 원시생활과 종교에서 일찍이 영감을 발견했다. 존 홈즈(John Holmes)는 자신의 시는 "자신을 발견하려는 노력"이라고 말하며, 모든 사람들을 위한 시를 썼다.

뢰스케(Theodore Roethke)와 로월(Robert Lowell)은 비범한 힘으로 표준 시인의 반열에 올랐다. 두 사람 모두 과거에 배경을 두고 있다. 뢰스케에게는 이용할 수 있는 과거가 성서적 유산이었다. 그는 동물, 식물뿐만 아니라 심지어는 무생물에서도 생명력을 관찰함으로써 인간이 되는 것의 일반적 의미를 발견했다. 로월에게는 이용할 수 있는 과거가 복합적인 가정과 사회와 문화적 전통이었다.

리처드 윌버(Richard Wilbur)와 리처드 에버하트(Richard Eberhart)는 공통점이 많다. 그들 둘 다 주목할 만한 자연시를 썼다. 그들 모두 타고난 재치와 꼼꼼하고 경제적인 스타일을 숙달함으로써 사회적 환경을 이해했다. 그들은 미묘하고 활기찬 이미저리에 의해 고양된 깊은 의미가 있는 장시를 썼다.

20년대에 출생한 다른 시인들은 눈부신 성공과 참을 수 없는 좌절을 모두 경험하고 경우에 따라서는 자살하거나 요절함으로써 끝나기도 했다. 『꿈 노래』(*The Dream Songs*)에 실린 한 연작시에서 존 베리맨(John Berryman)은 조숙했던 델모어 슈와르츠(Delmore Schwartz)와 랜달 자렐(Randall Jarrell)처럼 개인의 역할을 강조했다.

윌리엄 스타포드(William Stafford)처럼 나이든 시인도 있었지만 대부분 1920년대에 출생한 시인들이 진정 제 2차 세계대전의 경험을 물려받았다. 그들은 자동화, 규격화, 대중문화 등에 의해 비인간화되지는 않았다. 비록 몇몇은 인간의 비인간성이나 민주주의가 그 잠재력을 실현시키지 못함으로써 소외되기는 하였으나 대부분은 자아탐구에 대하여 걱정하지 않았다. 그들은 이 상태가 전반적으로 인류를 위하여 존재한다는 사실을 인식했고, 그들의 작품은 어느 시대든 진정한 문학이 그렇듯이 현재 인간이 처해있는 난관을 시인이 인식하고 있다는 인상을 지니고 있다.

현실을 파악하고 그로부터 무언가를 창조하려한 이 세대를 대표하는 시인들은 아직 규정되지 않던 심리적 현실, 특히 개인들 서로의 관계의 실상을 직시한다. 제임스 디키(James Dickey), 로버트 블라이(Robert Bly), 실비아 플라스(Sylvia Plath) 같은 몇몇 시인들은 지극히 일반적인 것 이외에는 공통점이 없다. 그러나 대부분은 물질주의를 거부하고 앨런 긴즈버그(Allen Ginsberg)와 개리 슈나이더(Gary Snyder)가 말한 바 있는 미래의 삶의 질에 대하여 두려움을 갖고 있다. 대부분의 시인들이 불공평을 깊이 느끼고 있지만 사회적인 문제를 직접 다룬 훌륭한 시를 쓴 시인은 거의 없다. 최근 시인들의 업적 중 가장 인상적이고 영속적인 것은 새로운 언어, 정확하고 때로는 아름다운 미국의 속어, 비유적 등가물에 있어서의 상응하는 직접성, 통제되지만 유연한 리듬에 정통하다는 점이다. 그들은 모두 우리의 일상 언어를 유명하게 했다. 이러한 영감은 휘트먼(Whitman), 엘리엇(Eliot), 스티븐스(Stevens), 윌리엄스(Williams), 뢰스케(Roethke) 및 로월(Lowell)이나 삶으로부터 온 것이다.

20세기 미국 시는 두 가지 흐름으로 나누어진다. 그 하나는 전통적인 방법과 주제를 고수한 로버트 프로스트와 로빈슨의 현대적시의 흐름이다. 다른 하나는 월러스나 윌리엄스의 모더니스트 시의 흐름이다.

(1) 시적 전통

모더니스트 시의 흐름과 다르게 전통적 시의 전통을 고수한 대표적인 시인이 바로 로빈슨과 프로스트이다. 여기서는 프로스트를 중심에 두고 살펴본다. 프로스트는 애국적 보수주의와 전통적인 인본주의적 가치들을 대변한다고 할 수 있다. 그런데 그의 시는 동시대의 시와는 다른 성격을 지닌다. 먼저 프로스트는 파운드나 엘리엇의 모더니즘과는 다른 미국의 시적 전통을 나타낸다. 첫째, 엘리엇이나 파운드가 붕괴된 문화를 반영하고 유럽의 기대는 반면 프로스트는 미국의 토착민적 시골 정신을 예찬하며 마크 트웨인과 연관되는 지방색이 두드러진 유머를 계속한다. 둘째, 파운드와 엘리엇이 방대한 고전적 지식에 의존하는 반면 프로스트는 가벼운 지식을 활용한다. 셋째, 엘리엇의 목소리는 권위의 근거를 추구하며 시끄러운 반면 프로스트의 목소리는 더 일관되고 자기주장이 강하다. 넷째, 엘리엇의 시는 자유시를 주로 구가하지만 프로스트는 새로운 전통적인 시적양식을 선호하였다. 그는 전통적인 형식적 한계 내에서 시를 쓰고자 하였다. 전통적 시 형식을 사용함에 있어서 프로스트는 엘리엇과 파운드와 다르다. 뿐만 아니라 그의 대부분의 시는 의미의 측면에서 엘리엇과 달리 포프처럼 교훈적이다. 그는 무언가를 말하려는 시인이고 그의 매력적인 은유와 기술적인 기교와 일상적인 언어사용이 그의 시를 뛰어나게 만든다.

(2) 모더니스트 시

20세기 미국의 주류 시는 모더니스트 시의 흐름에 속한다. 여기서는 윌리엄 카를로스 윌리엄스와 윌러스 스티븐스 두 명의 모더니스트 시인에 초점을 맞추어 볼 것이다. 먼저 윌리엄스는 엘리엇과 파운드가 과거로 돌아가고 유럽 문화에서 의미를 찾으려는 경향에 반대하여 동시대 미국의 잊혀진 삶에 목소리를 부여하려는 새로운 토속적인 시를 옹호하였다. 그는 현실과의 직접적인 대면을 기록하기 위해 전통적인 시적 구조와 결별하고 자연스러운 미국 일상어로 이루어진 자유시를 실험하였다. 형식은 주제에 의해 지배되어야한다고 보았다. 그는 사물을 가능한 한 정확하고 경제적으로 제시하는데 관심을 가지고 있었다. 그의 시는 이미지의 사진 같은 명료성을 주장한다. 그는 이처럼 지나친 객관주의를 내세워 사물자체에 집착하였으며 상징주의나 의미를 거부하는 그의 태도는 일관성이나 기피, 생동감이 결여된 모더니스트 시를 초래하였다. 스티븐스도 윌리엄스처럼 모든 기존의 신화와 믿음을 거부하였다. 그는 개인이 자신의 세계를 만들 필요성을 강조한다. 스티븐스가 자아를 세계의 중심으로 창조자로 내세우는 것은 미국 전통의 핵심이다. 그에게 현실은 의식이다. 그가 말하는 현실도 결국은 시적 현실을 의미한다. 결국 그의 시는 시 속의 시를 탐구하거나 시 자체에 탐닉하는 경향을 보인다.

2. 주요 작가와 작품

(1) 로버트 프로스트 Robert Frost, 1874-1963

프로스트는 샌프란시스코 출신으로 남부 옹호파인 아버지가 남군의 R. 리 장군의 이름을 그대로 아들의 이름으로 한 것이라고 전한다. 10세 때 아버지가 변사하여 뉴잉글랜드로 이주, 오랫동안 버몬트의 농장에서 청경우독의 생활을 계속하였다. 그 경험을 살려 후에 이 지방의 소박한 농민과 자연을 노래함으로써 현대 미국 시인 중에서 가장 순수한 고전적 시인으로 꼽힌다.

이후 교사·신문기자로 전전하다가 1912년 영국으로 건너갔는데, 그 것이 시인으로서의 새로운 출발이 되었다. E. 토머스, R. 브룩 등의 영국시인과 친교를 맺을 기회를 얻었으며, 그들의 추천으로 처녀시집『소년의 의지』(*A Boy's Will*)가 런던에서 출판되었고, 이어『보스턴의 북쪽』(*North of Boston*)이 출간됨으로써 시인으로서의 지위를 확립하였다. 이 두 시집에는 대표작「풀베기」("Birches"),「돌담의 수리」("Mending Wall") 등이 수록되었다. 1915년에 귀국하여 미국에서도 신진시인으로 환영받았다. 이듬해 제3시집『산의 골짜기』(*Mountain Interval*), 그 후『뉴햄프셔』(*New Hampshire*),『서쪽으로 흐르는 개울』(*West-Running Brook*),『표지의 나무』(*A Witness Tree*) 등이 발표되었다.

신과 대결하는 인간의 고뇌를 그린 시극『이성의 가면』(*A Masque of Reason*)과 성서의 인물을 현대에 등장시킨『자비의 가면』(*A Masque of Mercy*)을 거쳐 1962년에『개척지에서』(*In the Clearing*)를 출판하였는데, 이것이 최후의 시집이 되었다. 또 J. F. 케네디 대통령 취임식에 자작시를 낭송하는 등 미국의 계관시인적 존재였으며, 퓰리처상을 4회 수상하였다.

Out, Out—*

The buzz saw snarled and rattled in the yard
And made dust and dropped stove-length sticks of wood,
Sweet-scented stuff when the breeze drew across it.
And from there those that lifted eyes could count
Five mountain ranges one behind the other
Under the sunset far into Vermont.
And the saw snarled and rattled, snarled and rattled,
As it ran light, or had to bear a load.
And nothing happened: day was all but done.
Call it a day, I wish they might have said
To please the boy by giving him the half hour
That a boy counts so much when saved from work.
His sister stood beside him in her apron
To tell them 'Supper.' At the word, the saw,
As if to prove saws knew what supper meant,
Leaped out at the boy's hand, or seemed to leap—
He must have given the hand. However it was,
Neither refused the meeting. But the hand!
The boy's first outcry was a rueful laugh,
As he swung toward them holding up the hand
Half in appeal, but half as if to keep
The life from spilling. Then the boy saw all—
Since he was old enough to know, big boy
Doing a man's work, though a child at heart—
He saw all spoiled. 'Don't let him cut my hand off—
The doctor, when he comes. Don't let him, sister!'

---

* Frost uses the method of personification to great effect in this poem. The buzz saw, though
technically an inanimate object, is described as a cognizant being, aggressively snarling and
rattling as it does its work.

So. But the hand was gone already.
The doctor put him in the dark of ether.
He lay and puffed his lips out with his breath.
And then—the watcher at his pulse took fright.
No one believed. They listened at his heart.
Little—less—nothing!—and that ended it.
No more to build on there. And they, since they
Were not the one dead, turned to their affairs.

Meeting and Passing*

AS I went down the hill along the wall
There was a gate I had leaned at for the view
And had just turned from when I first saw you
As you came up the hill. We met. But all
We did that day was mingle great and small
Footprints in summer dust as if we drew
The figure of our being less than two
But more than one as yet. Your parasol
Pointed the decimal off with one deep thrust.
And all the time we talked you seemed to see
Something down there to smile at in the dust.
(Oh, it was without prejudice to me!)
Afterward I went past what you had passed
Before we met and you what I had passed.

(2012년 중등영어 임용고시 기출문제)

---

* "Meeting and Passing" is a little bit hard to understand the true meaning of. What did Frost "pass" in the dust before he met the woman? Anyway, the poem is about how he met a woman and they spent a lot of time together having fun, however, she looked down and smiled and saw something in the dust that Frost put there. This poem is written as one stanza. It is rhymed as ABBAABBCDEDEFF. It is a Shakespearean Sonnet.

Stopping by Woods on a Snowy Evening*

Whose woods these are I think I know.
His house is in the village though;
He will not see me stopping here
To watch his woods fill up with snow.

My little horse must think it queer
To stop without a farmhouse near
Between the woods and frozen lake
The darkest evening of the year.

He gives his harness bells a shake
To ask if there is some mistake.
The only other sound's the sweep
Of easy wind and downy flake.

The woods are lovely, dark and deep,
But I have promises to keep,
And miles to go before I sleep,
And miles to go before I sleep. (2008년 교육과정 평가원 기출문제)

---

* On the surface, this poem is simplicity itself. The speaker is stopping by some woods on a
snowy evening. He or she takes in the lovely scene in near-silence, is tempted to stay longer,
but acknowledges the pull of obligations and the considerable distance yet to be traveled
before he or she can rest for the night.

The Road Not Taken*

Two Roads diverged in a yellow wood,
And sorry I could not travel both
And be one traveler, long I stood
And looked down one as far as I could
To where it bent in the undergrowth;

Then took the other, as just as fair,
And having perhaps the better claim,
Because it was grassy and wanted wear;
Though as for that the passing there
Had worn them really about the same,

And both that morning equally lay
In leaves no step had trodden black.
Oh, I kept the first for another day!
Yet knowing how way leads on to way,
I doubted if I should ever come back.

I shall be telling this with a sigh
Somewhere ages and ages hence:
Two roads diverged in a wood, and I-
I took the one less traveled by,
And that has made all the difference.

---

* The narrator comes upon a fork in the road while walking through a yellow wood. He
  considers both paths and concludes that each one is equally well-traveled and appealing.
  After choosing one of the roads, the narrator tells himself that he will come back to this
  fork one day in order to try the other road.

(2) 칼 샌드버그 Carl Sandburg, 1878–1967

샌드버그는 스웨덴계 이민의 아들로 일리노이 주 출신으로 집이 가난하여 어려서부터 갖가지 노동에 종사하다가 아메리카-에스파냐 전쟁에 종군하였다. 제대 후에는 고향에 있는 롬버드 대학에서 고학으로 공부하였으며, 그 뒤 신문기자가 되어 정치운동에도 관여하는 한편, 시작에도 손을 대었다. 1914년에 잡지 『포에트리』(*Poetry*)에 「시카고」("Chicago")라는 작품을 발표하여 일약 시인으로서의 명성을 얻었다. 그의 시는 시카고라는 근대도시를 대담 솔직하게 취급, 부두 노동자나 트럭 운전사들이 쓰는 속어나 비어까지도 시에 도입, 전통적인 시어에 집착하는 사람들에게 충격을 주었다.

1916년에 「시카고」를 포함하여 중서부 지방의 자연을 노래한 작품을 모아 『시카고 시집』(*Chicago Poems*)을 출판, 뒤이어 『옥수수 껍질을 벗기는 사람』(*Cornhuskers*), 『연기와 강철』(*Smoke and Steel*), 『전 시집』(*Complete Poems*) 등을 간행하였다. 그는 또 링컨 연구자로도 유명하여 대작 『링컨, 대초원 시대』(*Abraham Lincoln: the Prairie Years*) 『링컨, 남북전쟁 시대』(*Abraham Lincoln: the War Years*)를 썼고, 이 밖에 각지의 민요와 전설을 모은 『아메리카 민요집』(*The American Songbag*), 자서전 『언제나 젊은 이방인들』(*Always the Young Strangers*) 등을 남겼다.

Fog*

The fog comes
on little cat feet.

---

* The image is the fog itself and Sandburg uses the metaphor of the stealth, quickness, unpredictability and silence of a cat to describe the fog. I would say this technique is a derivative technique of zoomorphism. Zoomorphism is when you describe something (usually humans) in animal terms or with characteristics of an animal; "hungry as a wolf."

It sits looking
over harbor and city
on silent haunches
and then moves on.

Chicago *

Hog Butcher for the World,
　　Tool Maker, Stacker of Wheat,
　　Player with Railroads and the Nation's Freight Handler;
　　Stormy, husky, brawling,
　　City of the Big Shoulders:

They tell me you are wicked and I believe them, for I have seen your
painted women under the gas lamps luring the farm boys.
And they tell me you are crooked and I answer: Yes, it is true I have
seen the gunman kill and go free to kill again.
And they tell me you are brutal and my reply is: On the faces of
women and children I have seen the marks of wanton hunger.
And having answered so I turn once more to those who sneer at this
my city, and I give them back the sneer and say to them:
Come and show me another city with lifted head singing so proud to
be alive and coarse and strong and cunning.
Flinging magnetic curses amid the toil of piling job on job, here is a
tall bold slugger set vivid against the little soft cities;
Fierce as a dog with tongue lapping for action, cunning as a savage

---

* "Chicago" started Sandburg's literary rise, and many critics consider it one of his best poems.
Certainly it is one of the most anthologized. "Chicago" contains most of the characteristics
that made Sandburg famous: It breaks with conventional poetic versification, deals with the
"unpoetic," and expresses his lifelong faith in the American people's resilience.

pitted against the wilderness,

  Bareheaded,

  Shoveling,

  Wrecking,

  Planning,

  Building, breaking, rebuilding,

Under the smoke, dust all over his mouth, laughing with white teeth,

Under the terrible burden of destiny laughing as a young man laughs,

Laughing even as an ignorant fighter laughs who has never lost a battle,

Bragging and laughing that under his wrist is the pulse, and under his
ribs the heart of the people,

                    Laughing!

Laughing the stormy, husky, brawling laughter of Youth, half-naked,
sweating, proud to be Hog Butcher, Tool Maker, Stacker of Wheat,
Player with Railroads and Freight Handler to the Nation.

Happiness *

I asked the professors who teach the meaning of life to tell
      me what is happiness.
And I went to famous executives who boss the work of
      thousands of men.
They all shook their heads and gave me a smile as though
      I was trying to fool with them
And then one Sunday afternoon I wandered out along
      the Desplaines river

---

* This poem relates to ours because it is all about finding the meaning of happiness. Besides
the titles both being about happiness, the context inside of the poems are very similar. In
this poem Carl Sandburg talks about how he went to all of these highly educated people and
asked them all the same question, "What is happiness?".

And I saw a crowd of Hungarians under the trees with
    their women and children and a keg of beer and an
    accordion.

(3) 에즈라 파운드 Ezra Pound, 1885-1972

아이다호 주 출신으로 펜실베이니아 대학교에서 공부한 후 1909년 영국으로 건너가, 언제나 이미지즘과 그 밖의 신문학 운동의 중심이 되어 T. S. 엘리엇과 J. 조이스를 세상에 소개하였다. 상징파와 같은 애매한 표현을 싫어하여, 언어를 조각과 같이 구상적으로 구사할 것을 주장하였다. 시집에는 『가면』(*Personae*), 『휴 셀윈 모벌리』(*Hugh Selwyn Mauberley*), 『캔토스』(*The Cantos*) 등이 있다. 특히 『캔토스』는 엘리엇의 「황무지」("The Waste Land")와 마찬가지로, 과거와 현재를 자유롭게 동시에 구사한 신화적 방법으로 장편시를 시도한 것이다. 그 연작의 하나인 「피산 캔토스」("Pisan Cantos")에 의해서 보링겐 상을 받았다.

In a Station of the Metro*

The apparition of these faces in the crowd;
Petals on a wet, black bough.

---

* In this quick poem, Pound describes watching faces appear in a metro station. It is unclear whether he is writing from the vantage point of a passenger on the train itself or on the platform. The setting is Paris, France, and as he describes these faces as a "crowd," meaning the station is quite busy. He compares these faces to "petals on a wet, black bough," suggesting that on the dark subway platform, the people look like flower petals stuck on a tree branch after a rainy night.

The Lake Isle*

O God, O Venus, O Mercury, patron of thieves,
Give me in due time, I beseech you, a little tobacco-shop,
With the little bright boxes
piled up neatly upon the shelves
And the loose fragment cavendish
and the shag,
And the bright Virginia
loose under the bright glass cases,
And a pair of scales
not too greasy,
And the votailles dropping in for a word or two in passing,
For a flip word, and to tidy their hair a bit.

O God, O Venus, O Mercury, patron of thieves,
Lend me a little tobacco-shop,
or install me in any profession
Save this damn'd profession of writing,
where one needs one's brains all the time.

---

* There comes a point in everybody's life when a thought of a getaway from the lives we live crosses our mind. For some it's just an image that pops up and quickly disappears with its unrealistic theme and others can't get it out of their mind, dwelling about it their whole life. Although, most people do think of an escape, they don't particularly know what they want. In his poem "The Lake Isle", Ezra Pound puts down on paper the simple things he longs for in life, revealing us the picture of the milieu he wants to escape to.

(4) 윌리엄 윌리엄스 William Carlos Williams, 1883–1963

윌리엄스는 뉴저지 주의 러더퍼드 출신으로 영국인 아버지와 푸에르토리코계의 어머니 사이에서 태어났다. 펜실베이니아 대학교 의학부 졸업, 유럽에 유학한 후에 출생지에서 개업하였으며, 평생을 시작에 몰두하였다. E. 파운드 등과의 교유에서 이미지즘의 영향을 받아 초기의 시집 『신 포도』 (Sour Grape)와 『봄과 모든 것』(Spring and All)으로 신선한 즉물적 시풍을 확립하였다. 과장된 상징주의를 배제하고 평명한 관찰을 기본으로 한 '객관주의'의 시를 표방하였고, 시집 『브뢰헬의 그림, 기타 시들』(Pictures from Brueghel and Other Poems)로 1963년 퓰리처상을 받았다. 또한 5부작 『패터슨』 (Paterson)은 특히 유명하여 비근한 제재로 일상의 언어를 구사하여 장대한 서사시를 엮어냈다. 미국시단을 대표하는 시인의 한 사람이었다.

This Is Just To Say*

I have eaten
the plums
that were in
the icebox

and which
you were probably
saving
for breakfast

---

* The rhythm of everyday speech, the absence of punctuation, the title, the message of "I have eaten/ the plums," and the brevity of "This Is Just to Say" combine to suggest that the poem poses as a hastily scribbled note. The pose may convey the theme of Williams's poem. If so, the parallel between this particular poem and a note is a crucial issue.

Forgive me
they were delicious
so sweet
and so cold

The Red Wheelbarrow*

so much depends
upon

a red wheel
barrow

glazed with rain
water

beside the white
chickens.

Spring And All**

By the road to the contagious hospital
under the surge of the blue

* What "depends upon" a red wheelbarrow, white chickens, and rain? The reader is aware of
the usefulness—in the case of rain, the necessity—of these things in the external world. The
things referred to in the poem are also particular instances of types and classes of things—
the wheelbarrow being a machine, for example, on which life also depends.

** "Spring and All" is a poem of only twenty-seven lines, yet it echoes some of the imagery
as well as the concepts of T. S. Eliot's The Waste Land (1922) and is filled with Williams's

mottled clouds driven from the
northeast—a cold wind. Beyond, the
waste of broad, muddy fields
brown with dried weeds, standing and fallen

patches of standing water
the scattering of tall trees

All along the road the reddish
purplish, forked, upstanding, twiggy
stuff of bushes and small trees
with dead, brown leaves under them
leafless vines—

Lifeless in appearance, sluggish
dazed spring approaches—

They enter the new world naked,
cold, uncertain of all
save that they enter. All about them
the cold, familiar wind—

Now the grass, tomorrow
the stiff curl of wildcarrot leaf

One by one objects are defined—
It quickens: clarity, outline of leaf

---

desire to break with poetic tradition. The poem reveals this in the second and third words
of the title. Spring is one of the most traditional themes of poetry; "and All" deflates it.

But now the stark dignity of
entrance—Still, the profound change
has come upon them: rooted they
grip down and begin to awaken

(5) 로버트 로웰 Robert Lowell, 1917–1977

보스턴 출신으로 J. 로웰의 자손으로 1940년 캐니언 대학 졸업하였다.
대학 재학 중에 시인·평론가인 J. 랜섬에게 배웠고, 제2차 세계대전 때는
징병거부로 투옥된 일도 있다. 그의 시는 어둡고 엄격한 윤리적 진지성과
강하고 풍부한 리듬이 뛰어나다. 시집으로 『하느님과 닮지 않은 땅』(*Land
of Unlikeness*), 『위어리 경의 성』(*Lord Weary's Castle*), 『전기 습작』(*Life Studies*)
이외에 번역·번안시를 모은 『모방』(*Imitations*)이 있다.

Memories of West Street and Lepke*

Only teaching on Tuesdays, book-worming
in pajamas fresh from the washer each morning,
I hog a whole house on Boston's
"hardly passionate Marlborough Street,"
where even the man
scavenging filth in the back alley trash cans,

---

* The poetic nature of this poem lies in the way in which its stanzas are presented in a
possible chronological order. The stanzas have seemingly little connection with each other,
however they could be a timeline of memories throughout a person's life just as the title
suggests. Clearly the poem could be recounted as a summary of one's life, but what is most
exceptional about this poem is that it seems to recount a list of bad or darker things in life.
the poem is also written in a romantic meter, however the topics are very dark; involving jail
drugs and death by electric chair.

has two children, a beach wagon, a helpmate,
and is a "young Republican."
I have a nine months' daughter,
young enough to be my granddaughter.
Like the sun she rises in her flame-flamingo infants' wear.

These are the tranquillized Fifties,
and I am forty. Ought I to regret my seedtime?
I was a fire-breathing Catholic C. O.,
and made my manic statement,
telling off the state and president, and then
sat waiting sentence in the bull pen
beside a Negro boy with curlicues
of marijuana in his hair.

Given a year,
I walked on the roof of the West Street Jail, a short
enclosure like my school soccer court,
and saw the Hudson River once a day
through sooty clothesline entanglements
and bleaching khaki tenements.
Strolling, I yammered metaphysics with Abramowitz,
a jaundice-yellow ("it's really tan")
and fly-weight pacifist,
so vegetarian,
he wore rope shoes and preferred fallen fruit.
He tried to convert Bioff and Brown,
the Hollywood pimps, to his diet.
Hairy, muscular, suburban,
wearing chocolate double-breasted suits,
they blew their tops and beat him black and blue.

I was so out of things, I'd never heard
of the Jehovah's Witnesses.
"Are you a C. O.?" I asked a fellow jailbird.
"No," he answered, "I'm a J. W."
He taught me the "hospital tuck,"
and pointed out the T-shirted back
of Murder Incorporated's Czar Lepke,
there piling towels on a rack,
or dawdling off to his little segregated cell full
of things forbidden the common man:
a portable radio, a dresser, two toy American
flags tied together with a ribbon of Easter palm.
Flabby, bald, lobotomized,
he drifted in a sheepish calm,
where no agonizing reappraisal
jarred his concentration on the electric chair —
hanging like an oasis in his air
of lost connections....

Skunk Hour*

For Elizabeth Bishop

Nautilus Island's hermit
heiress still lives through winter in her Spartan cottage;
her sheep still graze above the sea.
Her son's a bishop. Her farmer
is first selectman in our village,
she's in her dotage.

---

* "Skunk Hour" is the last poem in Life Studies, and as such it was meant to sum up the
themes and tone of the collection and suggest some sort of resolution.

Thirsting for
the hierarchic privacy
of Queen Victoria's century,
she buys up all
the eyesores facing her shore,
and lets them fall.

The season's ill —
we've lost our summer millionaire,
who seemed to leap from an L. L. Bean
catalogue.   His nine-knot yawl
was auctioned off to lobstermen.
A red fox stain covers Blue Hill.

And now our fairy
decorator brightens his shop for fall,
his fishnet's filled with orange cork,
orange, his cobbler's bench and awl,
there is no money in his work,
he'd rather marry.

One dark night,
my Tudor Ford climbed the hill's skull,
I watched for love-cars.   Lights turned down,
they lay together, hull to hull,
where the graveyard shelves on the town. . . .
My mind's not right.

A car radio bleats,
'Love, O careless Love . . . .' I hear
my ill-spirit sob in each blood cell,

as if my hand were at its throat . . . .
I myself am hell,
nobody's here —

only skunks, that search
in the moonlight for a bite to eat.
They march on their soles up Main Street:
white stripes, moonstruck eyes' red fire
under the chalk-dry and spar spire
of the Trinitarian Church.

I stand on top
of our back steps and breathe the rich air —
a mother skunk with her column of kittens swills the garbage pail
She jabs her wedge-head in a cup
of sour cream, drops her ostrich tail,
and will not scare.

(6) 에드윈 로빈슨 Edwin Arlington Robinson, 1869–1935

메인 주의 벽촌인 틸벨리 타운에서 자라, 하버드 대학교 중퇴 후 뉴욕에서 시집 『밤의 아이들』(*The Children of the Night*)을 냈으나 인정을 받지 못하였다. 한동안 세관에 근무한 뒤, 1916년 『하늘을 등지고 선 사나이』(*The Man Against the Sky*)로 이름이 알려졌고, 아서왕 전설에서 소재를 딴 3부작 『멀린』(*Merlin*), 『랜슬롯』(*Lancelot*), 『트리스트럼』(*Tristram*)으로 퓰리처상을 받았다. 그 후에 『시집』(*Collected Poems*)과 『두 번 죽은 사나이』(*The Man Who Died Twice*)로 역시 퓰리처 상을 받았다. 실의와 소외의 와중에서 인간의 영위를 노래한 그의 작품은 높이 평가된다.

Richard Cory*

Whenever Richard Cory went down town,
We people on the pavement looked at him:
He was a gentleman from sole to crown,
Clean favored, and imperially slim.

And he was always quietly arrayed,
And he was always human when he talked;
But still he fluttered pulses when he said,
"Good-morning," and he glittered when he walked.

And he was rich—yes, richer than a king—
And admirably schooled in every grace:
In fine, we thought that he was everything
To make us wish that we were in his place.

So on we worked, and waited for the light,
And went without the meat, and cursed the bread;
And Richard Cory, one calm summer night,
Went home and put a bullet through his head.

---

* "Richard Cory," which first appeared in The Children of the Night and remains one of
Robinson's most popular poems, recalls the economic depression of 1893. At that time,
people could not afford meat and had a diet mainly of bread, often day-old bread selling for
less than freshly baked goods. This hard-times experience made the townspeople even more
aware of Richard's difference from them, so much so that they treated him as royalty.

Haunted House *

Here was a place where none would ever come
For shelter, save as we did from the rain.
We saw no ghost, yet once outside again
Each wondered why the other should be so dumb;
And ruin, and to our vision it was plain
Where thrift, outshivering fear, had let remain
Some chairs that were like skeletons of home.

There were no trackless footsteps on the floor
Above us, and there were no sounds elsewhere.
But there was more than sound; and there was more
Than just an axe that once was in the air
Between us and the chimney, long before
Our time. So townsmen said who found her there.

(7) 윌리스 스티븐스 Wallace Stevens, 1879-1963

펜실베이니아 주 리딩 출신으로 하버드 대학교 뉴욕 법과대학에서 공부하고 변호사가 되었다. 그 후 보험회사로 옮겨 1934년 부사장까지 되었다. 직장 생활을 하는 틈틈이 이미지스트의 기관지 『포에트리』에 기고하였다. 40세가 넘어 처녀시집 『하모니엄』(*Harmonium*)을 발표하였는데, 프랑스의 상징주의 영향을 많이 받은 작품으로 평가된다.

그의 시는 풍부한 이미지와 난해한 은유가 특색이며, 시집 『질서의 관

---

* That larger something is hinted at in "The Haunted House," in which a married couple suddenly sense the scary possibility that they might not really know each other. Robinson's work suggests that loneliness, a sense of separation from one another, and also from ultimate meanings, is an inescapable human condition.

넘』(*Ideas of Order*), 『푸른 기타를 든 사나이』(*The Man with the Blue Guitar*) 이후로 형이상학적인 경향을 짙게 풍겼다. 『시집』(*Collected Poems*)으로 퓰리처상을 수상하였고, 또한 『필요한 천사』(*The Necessary Angel*) 같은 뛰어난 시평론도 남겼다.

The Snow Man*

One must have a mind of winter
To regard the frost and the boughs
Of the pine-trees crusted with snow;

And have been cold a long time
To behold the junipers shagged with ice,
The spruces rough in the distant glitter

Of the January sun; and not to think
Of any misery in the sound of the wind,
In the sound of a few leaves,

Which is the sound of the land
Full of the same wind
That is blowing in the same bare place

For the listener, who listens in the snow,

---

* "The Snow Man" is a short fifteen-line poem divided into five tercets. The title conjures up an image of a human artifact. The resemblance between a real human figure and a snowman, however, is hardly exact, for a high degree of conventional stylization goes into the making of a snowman—differently sized balls for head, torso, and limbs, coals for eyes, carrot for nose, and so on.

And, nothing himself, beholds
Nothing that is not there and the nothing that is.

The Emperor of Ice-Cream*

Call the roller of big cigars,
The muscular one, and bid him whip
In kitchen cups concupiscent curds.

Let the wenches dawdle in such dress
As they are used to wear, and let the boys
Bring flowers in last month's newspapers.

Let be be finale of seem.

The only emperor is the emperor of ice-cream.

Take from the dresser of deal.

Lacking the three glass knobs, that sheet
On which she embroidered fantails once
And spread it so as to cover her face.

If her horny feet protrude, they come

---

* The Emperor of Ice-Cream is the most popular poem of Wallace Stevens. Stevens "plots"
this story into two equal stanzas: one for the kitchen where the ice cream is being made, and
another for the bedroom where the corpse awaits decent covering. He "plots" it further by
structuring the poem as a series of commands from an unknown master of ceremonies,
directing-in a diction f extreme oddness-the neighbors in their funeral duties.

To show how cold she is, and dumb.

Let the lamp affix its beam.

The only emperor is the emperor of ice-cream.

(8) 실비아 플라스 Sylvia Plath, 1932-1963

신화라는 말이 꼭 들어맞는 미국의 대표적 여성 시인 실비아 플라스
(Sylvia Plath)는 1932년 매사추세츠에서 보스턴대학의 생물학 교수이자 땅
벌 연구의 세계적 권위자였던 오토 플라스와 아우렐리아의 딸로 태어났다.
독일계였던 아버지는 실비아가 여덟 살 때 당뇨병으로 유명을 달리하는데,
이 사건을 실비아의 삶과 작품 세계에 지울 수 없는 상흔이 된다. 1950년
장학생으로 스미스여대에 입학한 실비아는 이미 400편이 넘는 시를 썼으
며 자신에게 깊은 감명을 준 많은 서적의 목록을 소유하고 있었다. 1952년
『마드모아젤』지 공모전에 단편 「민튼 씨네 집에서 보낸 일요일」이 입상하
면서 작품이 게재되었고 1953년부터 『마드모아젤』의 객원편집기자로 활동
했다. 그리고 이 시기에 수면제를 먹고 자살을 시도하게 된다. 이때의 경험
은 1963년에 발표한 자전적 소설 『벨자』(*The Bell Jar*)에 묘사되고 있다.

충격요법과 심리요법을 병행한 치료 기간을 거친 후 실비아는 학업을
계속하는 한편 문학적으로도 성공을 거둔다. 1955년 스미스 대학을 졸업한
실비아는 풀브라이트 스칼라십으로 케임브리지에서 공부하게 된다. 1956
년에 영국의 시인 테드 휴스와 결혼하고 1957년-58년까지 모교인 스미스
대학에서 영문학 강사로 재직한다. 1960년 4월에는 딸 프리다가 태어난다.
같은 해 10월에는 실비아의 첫 번째 시집인 『거상』(*The Colossus*)이 영국에

서 출판된다. 이 시집에 실린 시들은 대단히 정교하고 치밀하게 쓰였으며 실비아의 고독한 인생의 미로를 명백하게 계시하고 있다.

영국 데본의 작은 마을에서 살던 실비아와 테드는 아들 니콜라스가 태어난 해인 1962년 10월부터 별거에 들어간다. 이때의 고통은 오히려 실비아의 시 세계에 생명을 불어넣은 듯 그녀는 그 무렵 한 달에 서른 편의 시를 써내는 열정을 보여주다가 마침내 1963년 2월 11일 가스오븐에 머리를 처박고 자살함으로써 서른 살의 천재 여성 시인 실비아는 참혹한 비극으로 자신의 삶을 마감한다.

Ariel*

Stasis in darkness.
Then the substanceless blue
Pour of tor and distances.

God's lioness,
How one we grow,
Pivot of heels and knees!—The furrow

Splits and passes, sister to
The brown arc
Of the neck I cannot catch,

Nigger-eye
Berries cast dark
Hooks—

---

* "Ariel" depicts a woman riding her horse in the countryside, at the very break of dawn. It details the ecstasy and personal transformation that occurs through the experience.

Black sweet blood mouthfuls,
Shadows.
Something else

Hauls me through air—
Thighs, hair;
Flakes from my heels.

White
Godiva, I unpeel—
Dead hands, dead stringencies.

And now I
Foam to wheat, a glitter of seas.
The child's cry

Melts in the wall.
And I
Am the arrow,

The dew that flies
Suicidal, at one with the drive
Into the red

Eye, the cauldron of morning.

Lady Lazarus*

I have done it again.
One year in every ten
I manage it —

A sort of walking miracle, my skin
Bright as a Nazi lampshade,
My right foot

A paperweight,
My face a featureless, fine
Jew linen.

Peel off the napkin
O my enemy.
Do I terrify? —

The nose, the eye pits, the full set of teeth?
The sour breath
Will vanish in a day.

Soon, soon the flesh
The grave cave ate will be
At home on me

---

* "Lady Lazarus" is a poem commonly understood to be about suicide. It is narrated by a woman, and mostly addressed to an unspecified person. The narrator begins by saying she has "done it again." Every ten years, she manages to commit this unnamed act. She considers herself a walking miracle with bright skin, her right foot a "paperweight," and her face as fine and featureless as a "Jew linen".

And I a smiling woman.
I am only thirty.
And like the cat I have nine times to die.

This is Number Three.
What a trash
To annihilate each decade.

What a million filaments.
The peanut-crunching crowd
Shoves in to see

Them unwrap me hand and foot—
The big strip tease.
Gentlemen, ladies

These are my hands
My knees.
I may be skin and bone,

Nevertheless, I am the same, identical woman.
The first time it happened I was ten.
It was an accident.

The second time I meant
To last it out and not come back at all.
I rocked shut

As a seashell.
They had to call and call
And pick the worms off me like sticky pearls.

Dying
Is an art, like everything else.
I do it exceptionally well.

I do it so it feels like hell.
I do it so it feels real.
I guess you could say I've a call.

It's easy enough to do it in a cell.
It's easy enough to do it and stay put.
It's the theatrical

Comeback in broad day
To the same place, the same face, the same brute
Amused shout:

'A miracle!'
That knocks me out.
There is a charge

For the eyeing of my scars, there is a charge
For the hearing of my heart—
It really goes.

And there is a charge, a very large charge
For a word or a touch
Or a bit of blood

Or a piece of my hair or my clothes.
So, so, Herr Doktor.
So, Herr Enemy.

I am your opus,
I am your valuable,
The pure gold baby

That melts to a shriek.
I turn and burn.
Do not think I underestimate your great concern.

Ash, ash —
You poke and stir.
Flesh, bone, there is nothing there —

A cake of soap,
A wedding ring,
A gold filling.

Herr God, Herr Lucifer
Beware
Beware.

Out of the ash
I rise with my red hair
And I eat men like air.

Daddy*

You do not do, you do not do
Any more, black shoe

---

* "Daddy," comprised of sixteen five-line stanzas, is a brutal and venomous poem commonly understood to be about Plath's deceased father, Otto Plath.

In which I have lived like a foot
For thirty years, poor and white,
Barely daring to breathe or Achoo.

Daddy, I have had to kill you.
You died before I had time—
Marble-heavy, a bag full of God,
Ghastly statue with one gray toe
Big as a Frisco seal

And a head in the freakish Atlantic
Where it pours bean green over blue
In the waters off beautiful Nauset.
I used to pray to recover you.
Ach, du.

(9) 힐다 둘리틀 Hilda Doolittle, 1886-1961

필명은 H.D. E.I.을 사용했으며, 파운드와 사귀어 이미지즘 운동에 가담한 바 있다. 1913년 영국의 시인이자 소설가인 R. 앨딩턴과 결혼한 후유럽에 거주하였다. 1937년 이혼했으나 이미지즘에 가장 충실한 시인으로간주된다. 『바다 유원지』(Sea Garden) 이후 많은 시집이 있고, 전쟁을 다룬『벽은 넘어지지 않는다』(The Walls Do Not Fall)로 시작되는 3부작은 역작으로 평가받고 있다.

Heat *

O wind, rend open the heat,
cut apart the heat,
rend it to tatters.

Fruit cannot drop
through this thick air—
fruit cannot fall into heat
that presses up and blunts
the points of pears
and rounds the grapes.

Cut the heat—
plough through it,
turning it on either side
of your path.

Pear Tree**

Silver dust
lifted from the earth,
higher than my arms reach,

---

* This poem is about oppression, hope, and the struggle to overcome obstacles. In this poem, the heat symbolizes oppression and the wind is representative of hope and resilience. The middle stanza of the poem, regarding the growth of good fruit, is a metaphor, describing that if a person lets oppression and harassment get to them; and they start believing what people are saying, they cannot accomplish great things because they think that they are not good enough.

** The poem is mostly an expression of her fascination with a beautiful pear tree. In this poem, the pear tree is described as a beautiful with silver dust which just out of her reach

you have mounted.
O silver,
higher than my arms reach
you front us with great mass;

no flower ever opened
so staunch a white leaf,
no flower ever parted silver
from such rare silver;

O white pear,
your flower-tufts,
thick on the branch,
bring summer and ripe fruits
in their purple hearts.

Oread*

Whirl up, sea —
whirl your pointed pines,
splash your great pines
on our rocks,
hurl your green over us,
cover us with your pools of fir.

---

to her. If you just plainly see the words without the meanings behind them you would only
see a huge tree that is glazed in silver buds.

* "Oread" well represents H. D.'s early lyrical verse and the Imagist movement of poetry
early in the twentieth century. Terse and compact, the poem crisply conveys the natural
forces at work, or called upon to work, by the series of active verbs and imperatives —
"whirl," "splash," "hurl," and "cover." The hard-hitting lines stress a sense of urgency for
nature to fulfill this request.

(10) 마지 피어시 Marge Piercy, 1936-

1936년 미국 디트로이트에서 태어나 가난한 노동자 가정에서 자랐다. 가족 중 최초로 대학 교육을 받은 그녀는 미시건 대학교에 장학생으로 입학하여 영문학을 전공했다. 촉망받는 대학생 작가에게 수여하는 홉우드 상을 여러 번 받았고 훗날 노스웨스턴 대학교에서 박사 학위를 받았다.

대학 졸업 후 비서, 계산원, 강사 등 여성 임시직 노동자의 생활을 전전하며 생계를 이어 간 그녀는 계급과 여성 문제에 대해 좀 더 진지하게 고민하며, 사회운동에 적극 참여하기 시작했다. 1960년대 초 '민주사회를 위한 학생 연합' 뉴욕 지부장을 맡아 베트남전 반대 운동에 참여했고, 한편으로 소설 『빠른 몰락』(*Going Down Fast*), 『독수리를 춤춰 잠들게 하라』(*Dance The Eagle To Sleep*)를 발표하며 작품 활동을 시작했다.

1971년에 케이프코드로 이주한 이후 본격적으로 여성운동에 관심을 기울였고, 오랫동안 동료로 지낸 아이라 우드와 1982년에 결혼했다. 희곡 『마지막 백인 계급』(*The Last White Class*)을 공동 집필했던 두 사람은 소설 『폭풍의 물결』(*Storm Tide*) 역시 함께 작업했다. 『뉴욕 타임즈』 베스트셀러였던 『입대』(*Gone To Soldiers*)를 비롯하여 『한줄기로 땋은 삶』(*Braided Lives*), 『여자의 갈망』(*The Longings of Women*) 등 여러 작품이 대중의 사랑을 받았고, 회상록 『고양이와의 동침』(*Sleeping with Cats*) 역시 호평을 받았다. 『그, 그녀, 그것』(*He, She And It*)으로 최고의 과학소설에 수여하는 아서 C. 클락 상을 받기도 했다. 피어시는 글을 쓰지 않을 때는 양심의 가책을 느끼는 정치적 작가로 자신을 정의한다. 지금까지 소설 열일곱 권과 시집 열일곱 권을 발표한 그녀는 여전히 열렬한 사회운동가이자 작가로서 왕성히 활동하고 있다.

A Work Of Artifice*

The bonsai tree
in the attractive pot
could have grown eighty feet tall
on the side of a mountain
till split by lightning.
But a gardener
carefully pruned it.
It is nine inches high.
Every day as he
whittles back the branches
the gardener croons,
It is your nature
to be small and cozy,
domestic and weak;
how lucky, little tree,
to have a pot to grow in.
With living creatures
one must begin very early
to dwarf their growth:
the bound feet,
the crippled brain,
the hair in curlers,
the hands you
love to touch. (2007년 중등영어 임용고시 기출문제)

---

* "A Work of Artifice," by the American poet Marge Piercy, is a small poem about a large
subject. The poem describes how a bonsai tree, which in nature has the potential to grow
to an enormous height, is instead carefully pruned so that it becomes something miniature—a
mere, tiny glimpse of its potential self.

(11) 에드워드 에스틀린 커밍스 Edward Estlin Cummings, 1894-1962

일반적으로 E. E. 커밍스로 알려진 에드워드 에스틀린 커밍스는 유머, 세련미, 사랑과 에로티시즘에 대한 찬미, 구두점에 대한 실험과 시각적 형식 등의 특징을 지닌 매력적이고 새로운 시를 창작했다. 화가이기도 했던 그는, 시가 우선적으로 언어 예술이 아니라 시각적인 예술로 변했음을 인지한 첫 번째 미국 시인이었다. 그는 자간과 들여쓰기를 남다르게 구사했으며, 대문자를 거의 사용하지 않았다.

윌리엄스와 마찬가지로 커밍스는 구어체, 날카로운 이미지, 대중문화에서 비롯된 단어들을 사용했다. 또한 윌리엄스와 마찬가지로 시를 자유롭게 배열하였다. 그의 시 「이제 막」("in Just")은 독자들에게 중간에 빠진 생각들을 채우도록 하고 있다.

in Just — *

in Just —
spring   when the world is mud —
luscious the little
lame balloonman

whistles   far   and wee

---

* In only twenty-four lines, E. E. Cummings captures both the feeling and the meaning of spring. Only in spring, or "just" in spring, is the world a kind of wonderful mud bath for children. Spring rains make puddles in which children love to play. Spring is a carnival season — a time to celebrate nature — which accounts for the appearance of the "balloonman," who adds a festive air to the season.

and eddieandbill come
running from marbles and
piracies and it's
spring

when the world is puddle-wonderful

the queer
old balloonman whistles
far   and   wee
and bettyandisbel come dancing

from hop-scotch and jump-rope and

it's
spring
and

            the
                    goat-footed

balloonMan   whistles
far
and
wee

I carry your heart with me(i carry it in)*

i carry your heart with me(i carry it in
my heart)i am never without it(anywhere
i go you go,my dear; and whatever is done
by only me is your doing, my darling)
i fear
no fate(for you are my fate, my sweet)i want
no world(for beautiful you are my world, my true)
and it's you are whatever a moon has always meant
and whatever a sun will always sing is you

here is the deepest secret nobody knows
(here is the root of the root and the bud of the bud
and the sky of the sky of a tree called life; which grows
higher than soul can hope or mind can hide)
and this is the wonder that's keeping the stars apart

i carry your heart(i carry it in my heart)

(12) 샤론 올즈 Sharon Olds, 1942-

샤론 올즈는 1942년에 샌프란시스코에서 태어났다. 독실한 기독교 가
정에서 자라고 스탠포드 대학을 졸업한 후 컬럼비아 대학에서 영어학 분

---

* The poem opens with the speaker declaring, "i carry your heart with me(i carry it in my
heart)." He goes on to stress the sense of unity he (we're just assuming it's a he) feels with
the one he loves. Everything he does and feels is connected to her (again, just our gender
assumption here). His fate and his world is her alone. The meaning of nature is also shared
with the speaker's love. Finally, the "tree of life" or the "secret nobody knows" has its roots
in the wonder of love and its limitless possibilities.

야에서 박사학위를 받았다. 그 즈음 그녀는 그 무엇을 바쳐서도 시인이 되기로 결심한다. 지금까지 8권의 시집을 냈고 그녀의 시는 크게 주목을 받고 있다. 그녀는 선정적 언어를 사용한다. 섹스에 관한 시라면 단연코 샤론 올즈를 따라올 자가 없을 것이다. 그녀는 1980년의 첫 시집 첫 시에서부터 아버지를 "좆"(cock)으로 어머니를 "씹"(cunt)으로 부르는 데서 기분이 더 나아졌다고 선언하였고, 1992년의 네 번째 시집 『아버지』(*The Father*)에 실린 시 「찌꺼기 소나타」("Waste Sonata")에서 "나는 더러운 말을 사랑해요"라고 말하고 있다. 그녀의 시에 전혀 거리낌 없이 등장하는 성 기관 및 성 행위와 관련된 비속어들은 독자에게 충격을 줄만하다. 시인이 불러일으키고자 하는 감정을 증폭하는 데 기여하는 것으로 보인다.

Rite of Passage *

As the guests arrive at my son's party
they gather in the living room —
short men, men in first grade
with smooth jaws and chins.
Hands in pockets, they stand around
jostling, jockeying for place, small fights
breaking out and calming. One says to another
How old are you? Six. I'm seven. So?
They eye each other, seeing themselves
tiny in the other's pupils. They clear their throats

---

* The poem "Rites of Passage" depicts the birthday party of her first grade son. As the poem goes on, one can see the metaphoric imagery laid in to resemble the coming of age for a man. Men will have "hands in pockets" as "they stand around jostling, jockeying for a place" in the world.

a lot, a room of small bankers,
they fold their arms and frown. I could beat you
up, a seven says to a six,
the dark cake, round and heavy as a
turret, behind them on the table. My son,
freckles like specks of nutmeg on his cheeks,
chest narrow as the balsa keel of a
model boat, long hands
cool and thin as the day they guided him
out of me, speaks up as a host
for the sake of the group.
We could easily kill a two-year-old,
he says in his clear voice. The other
men agree, they clear their throats
like Generals, they relax and get down to
playing war, celebrating my son's life.

Waste Sonata*

I think at some point I looked at my father
 and thought He's full of shit. How did I
 know fathers talked to their children,
 kissed them? I knew, I saw him and judged him.
 Whatever he poured into my mother
 she hated, her face rippled like a thin
 wing, sometimes, when she happened to be near him,

---

* A powerful lament over a father's wasted life, and the "purgatory" of living in a household
 dominated by alcoholism and marital discord. Strong and graphic language weaves a complex
 web of conflicting emotions: hatred and self-hatred, scorn and pity, condemnation and
 forgiveness

and the liquor he knocked into his body
felled him, slew the living tree,
loops of its grain started to cube,
petrify, coprofy, he was a
shit, but I felt he hated being a shit,
he had never imagined it could happen, this drunken
sleep was a spell laid on him—
by my mother! Well, I left to them
the passion of who did what to whom, it was a
baby in their bed they were rolling over on,
but I could not live with hating him.
I did not see that I had to. I stood
in that living room and saw him drowse
like the prince, in slobbrous beauty, I began
to think he was a kind of chalice,
a grail, his love the goal of a quest,
yes! He was the god of love
and I was a shit. I looked down at my forearm—
whatever was inside there
was not good, it was white stink,
bad manna. I looked in the mirror
and as I looked at my face the blemishes
arose, like pigs up out of the ground
to the witch's call. It was strange to me
that my body smelled sweet, it was proof I was
demonic, but at least I breathed out,
from the sour dazed scum within,
my father's truth. Well it's fun talking about this,
I love the terms of foulness. I have learned
to get pleasure from speaking of pain.

But to die, like this. To grow old and die

a child, lying to herself.

My father was not a shit. He was a man

failing at life. He had little shits

travelling through him while he lay there unconscious —

sometimes I don't let myself say

I loved him, anymore, but I feel

I almost love those shits that move through him,

shapely, those waste foetuses,

my mother, my sister, my brother, and me

in that purgatory.

(13) 존 랜섬 John Crowe Ransom, 1888-1974

테네시 주 풀래스키 출신으로 1903년 내슈빌 시의 밴더빌트 대학교에 입학한 후 다시 1910년에 영국으로 건너가 옥스퍼드 대학교에서 공부하였다. 귀국하여 모교의 영문학 교수가 되고 잡지 『퓨지티브』(*The Fugitive*)를 창간하였다. 이후 이 잡지를 중심으로 모인 문인들을 퓨지티브 그룹이라고 불렀으며, 남부 문학운동의 지도자가 되었다. 이 무렵 그는 남부의 토지재분운동을 시작하였고 농본주의를 역설하였다. 잡지는 3년 만에 휴간되었으나 1939년 『케니언 리뷰』(*The Kenyon Review*)를 창간하여 편집자가 되고, 또 케니언 대학교의 교수로도 활약하였다. 이후 1958년 70세로 은퇴할 때까지 교수와 잡지편집자로서 문단에 크게 기여하였고, 뉴크리티시즘의 중심인물로서 1930년대부터 평생 동안 문학의 분석적 비평의 확립을 위하여 크게 공헌하였다.

저서에는 『세계의 육체』(*The World's Body*) 『신비평』(*the New Critics*)이 있다. 시인으로서는 주지적인 작풍으로 엄격히 통제당하는 이미지, 긴밀한 구성 등이 특히 눈에 띈다. 시집으로 『신에 관한 시』(*Poems about God*) 『한기와 열병』(*Chills and Fever*) 『시선집』(*Selected Poems*) 등이 있다.

Piazza Piece*

I am a gentleman in a dustcoat trying
To make you hear. Your ears are soft and small
And listen to an old man not at all,
They want the young men's whispering and sighing.
But see the roses on your trellis dying
And hear the spectral singing of the moon;
For I must have my lovely lady soon,
I am a gentleman in a dustcoat trying.

I am a lady young in beauty waiting
Until my truelove comes, and then we kiss.
But what grey man among the vines is this
Whose words are dry and faint as in a dream?
Back from my trellis, Sir, before I scream!
I am a lady young in beauty waiting.

(2010년 중등영어 임용고시 기출문제)

---

* Written as a Petrarchan sonnet (fourteen lines of iambic pentameter rhyming abbaacca deeffd), "Piazza Piece" illustrates Ransom's skill with traditional forms. The octave (first eight lines) and sestet (remaining six lines) are an attempted dialogue between age (an elderly man) and youth (a young lady). Their differing attitudes make "Piazza Piece" essentially a debate poem (two characters argue the merits of diametrically opposite philosophical positions)

Bells for John Whiteside's Daughter *

There was such speed in her little body,
And such lightness in her footfall,
It is no wonder her brown study
Astonishes us all.

Her wars were bruited in our high window.
We looked among orchard trees and beyond
Where she took arms against her shadow,
Or harried unto the pond

The lazy geese, like a snow cloud
Dripping their snow on the green grass,
Tricking and stopping, sleepy and proud,
Who cried in goose, Alas,

For the tireless heart within the little
Lady with rod that made them rise
From their noon apple-dreams and scuttle
Goose-fashion under the skies!

But now go the bells, and we are ready,
In one house we are sternly stopped
To say we are vexed at her brown study,
Lying so primly propped.

---

* "Bells for John Whiteside's Daughter" shows Ransom's pattern of addressing ultimate
  metaphysical issues and using the conventional quatrain form to impose order that distances
  speaker and reader from the emotions involved. The occasion for the bells is the funeral of
  John Whiteside's daughter.

(14) 랜스턴 휴스 Langston Hughes, 1902–1967

미주리 주 조플란 출신으로 컬럼비아 대학교를 중퇴하고, 1925년 『기회』(*Opportunity*)지 현상모집 시 부문에 1등으로 입선하였다. 처녀시집 『슬픈 블루스』(*The Weary Blues*), 제2시집 『유대인의 나들이옷』(*Fine Clothes to the Jew*)을 발표하여 블루스나 민요를 능숙하게 구사하는 시풍으로 1920년대 흑인 문예부흥의 기수가 되었다. 제2차 세계대전 후에는 흑인신문 『시카고 디펜더』의 칼럼을 담당하며 일련의 『심플 소설』을 발표하였다. 시집 『편도 차표』(*One-Way Ticket*), 『엄마에게 물어 봐』(*Ask Your Mama*), 소설 『웃음이 없지는 않다』(*Not Without Laughter*), 단편집 『심플, 가슴 속을 털어놓다』(*Simple Speaks His Mind*), 자서전 『대양』(*The Big Sea*) 등이 있다.

Dream*

Hold fast to dreams
For if dreams die
Life is a broken-winged bird
That cannot fly.
Hold fast to dreams
For when dreams go
Life is a barren field
Frozen with snow.

---

* The speaker advises the reader to hold onto dreams, because if dreams die, life will be like a bird with damaged wings that cannot fly. When dreams go away, life is "barren field" covered with frozen snow.

Life is Fine*

I went down to the river,
I set down on the bank.
I tried to think but couldn't,
So I jumped in and sank.

I came up once and hollered!
I came up twice and cried!
If that water hadn't a-been so cold
I might've sunk and died.

But it was Cold in that water! It was cold!

I took the elevator
Sixteen floors above the ground.
I thought about my baby
And thought I would jump down.

I stood there and I hollered!
I stood there and I cried!
If it hadn't a-been so high
I might've jumped and died.

But it was High up there! It was high!

---

* The spirited and jaunty "Life is Fine" is not one of Hughes's more well-known works, but has many similarities to his other poems. It tells the story of a man with a jubilant spirit and the ability to remain optimistic in the face of personal despair. It is energetic and musical, and the structure resembles that of a blues song.

So since I'm still here livin',
I guess I will live on.
I could've died for love—
But for livin' I was born

Though you may hear me holler,
And you may see me cry—
I'll be dogged, sweet baby,
If you gonna see me die.

Life is fine! Fine as wine! Life is fine!

(15) 앨런 긴즈버그 Allen Ginsberg, 1926-1998

미국으로 이민 온 러시아인이 어머니인 유대계 시인으로, 콜롬비아 대학을 졸업한 후, 샌프란시스코에서 방랑하면서 G. 슈나이더나 L. 파린게티들과 교류하고, 황폐한 세대를 대담하게 묘사한 산문적 시집 『울부짖다』 (*Howl and Other Poems*)에서 일약 비트 제너레이션의 교조가 되었다. 이어서 정신병원에서 죽은 모친 나오미를 위해서 감동적인 진혼가 『카디시』 (*Kaddish and Other Poems*)를 썼다. 환상적인 체험을 구해서 마약을 하고, 1961년에는 인도에 가서 수행하는데 돌아오는 길에 일본에 들러서 슈나이더와 선을 공부하고, 교토~도쿄간의 급행열차 안에서 새로운 자기각성을 경험하였다. 귀국 후 만트라를 주장해서 데모의 선두에 서고, 사회적인 의식이 농후한 작품을 발표하고 있다. 베트남 전쟁기에 쓰인 시집 『아메리카 몰락』(*The Fall of America: Poems of These States*)은 그의 화이트맨적인 예언자 시인의 풍모를 잘 전하고 있다.

Howl

For Carl Solomon*

I saw the best minds of my generation destroyed by madness,
    starving hysterical naked,
dragging themselves through the negro streets at dawn looking
    for an angry fix,
angelheaded hipsters burning for the ancient heavenly
    connection to the starry dynamo in the machinery of night,
who poverty and tatters and hollow-eyed and high sat up smoking
    in the supernatural darkness of cold-water flats floating
    across the tops of cities contemplating jazz,
who bared their brains to Heaven under the El and saw
    Mohammedan angels staggering on tenement roofs
    illuminated,
who passed through universities with radiant cool eyes
    hallucinating Arkansas and Blake-light tragedy among the
    scholars of war,
who were expelled from the academies for crazy & publishing
    obscene odes on the windows of the skull,
who cowered in unshaven rooms in underwear, burning their
    money in wastebaskets and listening to the Terror through
    the wall,
who got busted in their pubic beards returning through Laredo
    with a belt of marijuana for New York,

  . . .

---

* Part III of "Howl" is the poem's most direct address to Carl Solomon, the person to whom the poem is dedicated. Ginsberg met Solomon during a brief stay in the Columbia Presbyterian Psychological Institute in 1949. In the poem, Ginsberg names the mental institution Rockland, and the refrain of the third part of the poem is Ginsberg crying to Solomon that: "I'm with you in Rockland!"

A Supermarket in California*

What thoughts I have of you tonight, Walt Whitman, for I walked down the sidestreets under the trees with a headache self-conscious looking at the full moon.

In my hungry fatigue, and shopping for images, I went into the neon fruit supermarket, dreaming of your enumerations!

What peaches and what penumbras! Whole families shopping at night! Aisles full of husbands! Wives in the avocados, babies in the tomatoes!—and you, García Lorca, what were you doing down by the watermelons?

I saw you, Walt Whitman, childless, lonely old grubber, poking among the meats in the refrigerator and eyeing the grocery boys.

I heard you asking questions of each: Who killed the pork chops? What price bananas? Are you my Angel?

I wandered in and out of the brilliant stacks of cans following you, and followed in my imagination by the store detective.

We strode down the open corridors together in our solitary fancy tasting artichokes, possessing every frozen delicacy, and never passing the cashier.

Where are we going, Walt Whitman? The doors close in a hour. Which way does your beard point tonight?

(I touch your book and dream of our odyssey in the supermarket and feel absurd.)

Will we walk all night through solitary streets? The trees add shade

---

* "A Supermarket in California" begins with Ginsberg recounting a particular vision he had one night while living in Berkeley, California. He opens by setting the scene: he is walking down a street, under trees and a full moon, having "thoughts" of Walt Whitman.

to shade, lights out in the houses, we'll both be lonely.

Will we stroll dreaming of the lost America of love past blue
automobiles in driveways, home to our silent cottage?

Ah, dear father, graybeard, lonely old courage-teacher, what America
did you have when Charon quit poling his ferry and you got out on
a smoking bank and stood watching the boat disappear on the black
waters of Lethe?

(16) 메리엔 무어 Marianne Moore, 1887-1972

미주리 주의 세인트루이스 출신으로 1909년 브린 모어 칼리지를 졸업
하고 칼라일 상과대학에서 공부하였다. 뉴욕공립도서관의 사서직에 있다가,
1925년 문예잡지 『다이얼』(*The Dial*)의 편집에 참여하였다. 이미지즘의 영
향에서 출발하여, 그 후에 '사물주의'(Objectivism)를 표방하는 독특한 시풍
을 수립하였다. 그의 시는 명확한 이미지를 나타내고, 섬세하면서도 냉정하
여 잘 억제되어 있고, 기지와 역설이 풍부하였다. 그 중에서도 『시선집』
(*Selected Poems*)과 『시 모음집』(*Collected Poems*)이 유명하다. 이 밖에도 『시집』
(*Poems*) 『관찰』(*Observations*)과 라 퐁텐의 『우화시』의 운문 번역 『라 퐁텐의
우화집』(*The Fable of La Fontaine*), 평론집 『편애』(*Predilections*) 등이 있다.

Poetry*

I, too, dislike it: there are things that are important beyond
　　all this fiddle.
　　Reading it, however, with a perfect contempt for it, one

---

* The poem is best known for the shocking first line, in which Moore states that she dislikes

          discovers in

    it after all, a place for the genuine.

        Hands that can grasp, eyes

          that can dilate, hair that can rise

            if it must, these things are important not because a

high-sounding interpretation can be put upon them but because

        they are

    useful. When they become so derivative as to become

        unintelligible,

the same thing may be said for all of us, that we

        do not admire what

      we cannot understand: the bat

          holding on upside down or in quest of something to

eat, elephants pushing, a wild horse taking a roll, a tireless

        wolf under

    a tree, the immovable critic twitching his skin like a horse

        that feels a flea, the base-

ball fan, the statistician —

      nor is it valid

         to discriminate against "business documents and

school-books"; all these phenomena are important. One must make

    a distinction

    however: when dragged into prominence by half poets, the

      result is not poetry,

---

poetry. The remaining two lines of the 1967 version present some problems because she does not exemplify the word "genuine" after stating that there is "a place for the genuine" in poetry. In the original version, however, Moore illustrates precisely what poetry she repudiates and what poetry she admires.

nor till the poets among us can be

   "literalists of

    the imagination" —above

      insolence and triviality and can present

for inspection, "imaginary gardens with real toads in them,"

   shall we have

  it. In the meantime, if you demand on the one hand,

  the raw material of poetry in

   all its rawness and

   that which is on the other hand

    genuine, you are interested in poetry.

The Fish*

wade

through black jade.

   Of the crow-blue mussel-shells, one keeps

   adjusting the ash-heaps;

    opening and shutting itself like

an

injured fan.

   The barnacles which encrust the side

   of the wave, cannot hide

    there for the submerged shafts of the

---

* "The Fish" marked a turning point in Moore's development. Even though she would later write poems that were as good, critics note that she never excelled in achieving a more perfect integration of images and ideas. She creates precise images of natural things in terms that also denote human characteristics. These build upon one another to express an eternal truth—that all life forces contain death.

sun,

split like spun

        glass, move themselves with spotlight swiftness

        into the crevices —

                in and out, illuminating

the

turquoise sea

        of bodies. The water drives a wedge

        of iron through the iron edge

                of the cliff; whereupon the stars,

pink

rice-grains, ink-

        bespattered jelly fish, crabs like green

        lilies, and submarine

                toadstools, slide each on the other.

All

external

        marks of abuse are present on this

        defiant edifice —

                all the physical features of

ac-

cident —lack

        of cornice, dynamite grooves, burns, and

        hatchet strokes, these things stand

                out on it; the chasm-side is

dead.

Repeated

        evidence has proved that it can live

        on what can not revive

               its youth. The sea grows old in it.

(17) 시어도어 로스케 Theodore Roethke, 1908-1963

미시건 주 출신으로 미시건 대학교와 하버드 대학교를 졸업하고 라파
예트 대학교, 펜실베이니아 주립대학교 등을 거쳐 워싱턴 대학교 교수를
지냈다. 그의 작품에는 지적 분위기를 풍기는 정형시와, 쉬르리얼리즘(초현
실주의)의 경향을 띤 자유시가 있다. 어린 시절과 노년기를 노래한 자유시
에는 뛰어난 작품이 많다. 주요시집 『오픈 하우스』(*Open House*) 『잃어버린
아들과 그 밖의 시』(*The Lost Son and Other Poems*) 『각성』(*The Waking*) 『바람
의 말』(*Words for the Wind*) 등이 있다.

Cuttings *

Sticks-in-a-drowse droop over sugary loam,
Their intricate stem-fur dries;
But still the delicate slips keep coaxing up water;
The small cells bulge;

---

* This poem, one of the most frequently reprinted of the "greenhouse" series, shows Roethke's
close attention to the plant world and his identification with it. His sense of unity with the
rest of life transcends the ordinary and becomes a spiritual experience, while at the same
time remaining grounded in everyday reality. The highly emotional poem is also written using
a style and themes that could only be Roethke's.

One nub of growth
Nudges a sand-crumb loose,
Pokes through a musty sheath
Its pale tendrilous horn.

My Papa's Waltz*

The whiskey on your breath
Could make a small boy dizzy;
But I hung on like death:
Such waltzing was not easy.

We romped until the pans
Slid from the kitchen shelf;
My mother's countenance
Could not unfrown itself.

The hand that held my wrist
Was battered on one knuckle;
At every step you missed
My right ear scraped a buckle.

You beat time on my head
With a palm caked hard by dirt,
Then waltzed me off to bed
Still clinging to your shirt.

---

* In "My Papa's Waltz," Theodore Roethke imaginatively re-creates a childhood encounter with his father but also begins to attempt to understand the meaning of the relationship between them. The poem may be read as a warm memory of happy play, but when one is familiar with the rest of Roethke's work, a darker view of the event emerges.

The Waking*

I wake to sleep, and take my waking slow.
I feel my fate in what I cannot fear.
I learn by going where I have to go.

We think by feeling. What is there to know?
I hear my being dance from ear to ear.
I wake to sleep, and take my waking slow.

Of those so close beside me, which are you?
God bless the Ground!   I shall walk softly there,
And learn by going where I have to go.

Light takes the Tree; but who can tell us how?
The lowly worm climbs up a winding stair;
I wake to sleep, and take my waking slow.

Great Nature has another thing to do
To you and me; so take the lively air,
And, lovely, learn by going where to go.

This shaking keeps me steady. I should know.
What falls away is always. And is near.
I wake to sleep, and take my waking slow.
I learn by going where I have to go.

---

* The title suggests the central idea of the poem: a discovery of the fundamental paradox of
  human life. The "waking" to which the poet refers involves the broad assertion that life
  leads to death. More precisely, the poet has grasped the insight that living (waking), which
  involves coming to new awarenesses, ultimately leads only to dying (sleep).

Open House*

My secrets cry aloud.
I have no need for tongue.
My heart keeps open house,
My doors are widely swung.
An epic of the eyes
My love, with no disguise.

My truths are all foreknown,
This anguish self-revealed.
I'm naked to the bone,
With nakedness my shield.
Myself is what I wear:
I keep the spirit spare.

The anger will endure,
The deed will speak the truth
In language strict and pure.
·I stop the lying mouth:
Rage warps my clearest cry
To witless agony.

---

* "Open House" is the title poem of Theodore Roethke's first volume of poetry. Friend and fellow poet Stanley Kunitz proposed the book title before Roethke actually had written the poem. Then, upon completing the poem, Roethke placed it at the front of the manuscript, suggesting that both the poem and its theme were to serve as an introductory promise for the poet's first work as well as for his entire career.

(18) 리처드 윌버 Richard Wilbur, 1921-

윌버는 뉴욕에서 태어나 앰허스트 대학을 졸업하고 하버드 대학에서 석사학위를 받고 그 이후, 하버드 대학 과 그 밖의 여러 대학에서 강의를 하였다. 『아름다운 변화들과 다른 시들』(*The Beautiful Changes, and Other Poems*), 『예식과 다른 시들』(*Ceremony, and Other Poems*)이라는 두 권의 시집을 낸 뒤 외국 작가들의 작품을 번역하였다. 1957년에 『이 세상의 것들』(*Things of This World*)로 퓰리처상과 전미 도서상을 받았으며, 『신작 및 시모음집』(*New and Collected Poems*)으로 두 번째 퓰리처 상을 받았다. 1987년 윌버는 로버트 펜 워런(Robert Penn Warren)의 뒤를 이어 미국의 2대 계관시인이 되었다.

그의 시를 주제적으로 특징짓는 것은 상반되는 것들 간의 균형이다. 그것은 존재하는 것 자체의 빛나는 의의를 표현하려고 하면서도 세계 속의 구체적인 사물들을 자세히 식별한다. 그는 세계를 추상적인 것과 구체적인 것, 풍성함과 곤궁함이 어우러져내는 통합된 실재를 그린다.

A Summer Morning*

Her young employers, having got in late
From seeing friends in town
And scraped the right front fender on the gate,
Will not, the cook expects, be coming down.

---

* In "A Summer Morning," he tells how the cook and the gardener, because their rich young employers got in late, enjoy the beautiful big gardens and house on a sunny morning, "Possessing what the owners can but own," bringing a moral insight to a small incident that would gladden Saint Francis.

She makes a quiet breakfast for herself,
The coffee-pot is bright,
The jelly where it should be on the shelf.
She breaks an egg into the morning light,

Then, with the bread-knife lifted, stands and hears,
The sweet efficient sounds
Of thrush and catbird, and the snip of shears
Where, in the terraced backward of the grounds,

A gardener works before the heat of the day.
He straightens for a view
Of the big house ascending stony-gray
Out of his beds mosaic with the dew.

His young employers having got in late,
He and the cook alone
Receive the morning on their old estate,
Possessing what the owners can but own.

The Pardon*

My dog lay dead five days without a grave
In the thick of summer, hid in a clump of pine
And a jungle of grass and honey-suckle vine.
I who had loved him while he kept alive

---

* Death and life are intertwined in such a way that one cannot come without the other.
Richard Wilbur uses graphic description to clearly express this in his work "The Pardon,"
through a series of events that ultimately bring a man to learn to mourn, after causing him
a lifetime without love.

Went only close enough to where he was
To sniff the heavy honeysuckle-smell
Twined with another odor heavier still
And hear the flies' intolerable buzz.

Well, I was ten and very much afraid.
In my kind world the dead were out of range
And I could not forgive the sad or strange
In beast or man. My father took the spade

And buried him. Last night I saw the grass
Slowly divide (it was the same scene
But now it glowed a fierce and mortal green)
And saw the dog emerging. I confess

I felt afraid again, but still he came
In the carnal sun, clothed in a hymn of flies,
And death was breeding in his lively eyes.
I started in to cry and call his name,

Asking forgiveness of his tongueless head.
..I dreamt the past was never past redeeming:
But whether this was false or honest dreaming
I beg death's pardon now. And mourn the dead.

Two Voices in a Meadow*

A Milkweed

Anonymous as cherubs
Under the crib of God,
White seeds are floating
Out of my burst pod.
What power had I
Before I learned to yield?
Shatter me, great wind:
I shall possess the field

A Stone

As casual as cow-dung
Under the rib of God,
I lie where chance would have me,
Up to the ears in sod.
Why should I move? To move
Befits a light desire.
The sill of heaven would founder,
Did such as I aspire.

---

* As meta-poetry: The poem is about the poem and the power of poetry. The great wind is
also the spirit of poetic inspiration, by which Wilbur bursts open the milkweed so that the
seeds posses the field of my mind—if I yield. From here on out, every time I see milkweed,
it'll burst out anew.

(19) 제니 코진 Jeni Couzyn, 1942-

남아공 출신의 캐나다 시인인 그녀는 나탈(Natal) 대학교에서 교육을 받고 1966년 영국으로 이주하였다. 이후 그녀는 프리랜서 작가로 자신을 알렸고, 1975년 캐나다 시민이 되었고 1976년에 브리티시 콜롬비아 주 빅토리아 대학에 전속작가로 임명받았다. 1970년에 그녀의 첫 시집 『비행』(*Flying*)과 이후 『태어날 시간』(*A Time to be Born*, 1981), 『익사하는 삶: 시선집』(*Life by Drowning: Selected Poems*, 1985), 그리고 『바로 그것이다』(*That's It*, 1993) 등을 출판하였다. 코진의 시는 여성의 사회적, 정치적이고 창의적인 결과에 반복적으로 관심을 갖는다. 탁월한 말솜씨로 예술에 대한 그녀의 인식과 광범위한 사회적인 접근에 대한 그녀의 시에 대한 욕망은 그녀의 글에 분명하게 반영되었다. 그녀의 풍성하게 이루어진 시들의 대부분은 아프리카에서의 어린 시절을 주로 다루고 있다.

My Father's Hands

My father's hands
are beautiful, they can
fix this moth's wing and make
machines
they can mend the fuse when the world
goes dark
can make light swim and walls jump
in around me again.
I can see my mother's face again.

You must take good care of them with

your finest creams
never let the nails break or
skin go dry, only those wise fingers
know how to fix the thing
that makes my doll cry and they make
small animals out of clay.

Never let blades or anything sharp
and hurtful near them
don't let bees or nettles
sting them don't let fire or burning oil
try them.

My father's hands are beautiful, take
good care of them. (2003년 중등영어 임용고시 기출문제)

(20) 데이비드 채프먼 베리 David Chapman Berry, 1942-

데이비드 채프먼 베리는 1942년에 빅스버그(Vicksburg)에서 태어났지만, 그린빌(Greenville)에서 성장하였다. 그는 델타 스테이트 대학(Delta State College)을 졸업한 후, 의대 입학이 거절된 뒤에 제너럴 모터스에서 1년간 일을 하였다. 이후 그가 그의 첫 번째 시집 『사이공 묘지』(*Saigon Cemetery*, 1972)를 썼던 베트남에서 의료봉사자로 일했다. 고향으로 돌아온 후, 그는 테네시 대학교에 대학원 과정에 등록하여 그곳에서 1973년 박사학위를 받았다. 그는 지금 서든 미시시피 대학교에 영문학 교수로 근무하고 있다.

On Reading Poems to a Senior Class at South High*

Before
I opened my mouth
I noticed them sitting there
as orderly as frozen fish
in a package.

Slowly water began to fill the room
though I did not notice it
till it reached
my ears

and then I heard the sounds
of fish in an aquarium
and I knew that though I had
tried to drown them

with my words
that they had only opened up
like gills for them
and let me in.

Together we swam around the room
like thirty tails whacking words
till the bell rang

---

* "On Reading Poems to a Senior Class at South High", the author, David Chapman Berry, has relied on metaphors and similes to carry out his view of a typical literature class and a teacher's view of teaching. The setting of the poem is in a senior literature class, at South High School.

puncturing
a hole in the door

where we all leaked out

They went to another class
I suppose and I to home

where Queen Elizabeth
my cat met me
and licked my fins
till they were hands again. (2003년 중등영어 임용고시 기출문제)

(21) 캐시 송 Cathy Song, 1955-

캐시 송은 한국계 미국인 아버지와 중국계 미국인 어머니를 가진 하와이 출신의 미국의 여류시인이다. 그녀는 서정적인 시집 『사진 신부』(Picture Bride, 1983)에서 자신의 가족을 통해 역사를 극화하고 있다. 많은 아시아 계 미국인 시인들은 문화적 다양성을 탐색하고 있다. 캐시 송이 시 「식물성 공기」("The Vegetable Air", 1988)에서 묘사한 소가 어슬렁거리는 광장, 중국 식당, 비딱하게 걸린 코카콜라 현수막 등이 있는 초라한 마을은 뿌리 없는 다문화적인 동시대의 삶을 상징하고 있는데, 이런 삶은 예술을 통해, 특히 이 시의 경우에는 카세트에 담긴 오페라를 통해 참을 만한 것이 된다.

Picture Bride*

She was a year younger
than I,
twenty-three when she left Korea.
Did she simply close
the door of her father's house
and walk away. And
was it a long way
through the tailor shops of Pusan
to the wharf where the boat
waited to take her to an island
whose name she had
only recently learned,
on whose shore
a man waited,
turning her photograph
to the light when the lanterns
in the camp outside
Waialua Sugar Mill were lit
and the inside of his room
grew luminous
from the wings of moths
migrating out of the cane stalks?
What things did my grandmother
take with her? and when

---

* The picture bride of Song's poem is the grandmother of the poem's speaker. The grandmother is the object of meditation for her granddaughter, a persona who closely resembles the author in age, gender, and ethnic background (Song's father and mother are of Korean and Chinese ancestry, respectively).

she arrived to look
into the face of the stranger
who was her husband,
thirteen years older than she,
did she politely untie
the silk bow of her jacket,
her tent-shaped dress
filling with the dry wind
that blew from the surrounding fields
where the men were burning the cane?

(2007년 중등영어 임용고시 기출문제)

(22) 메이 스웬슨 May Swenson, 1913-1989

메이 스웬슨은 미국의 시인이자 극작가이다. 그녀는 저명한 비평가 헤롤드 블룸(Harold Bloom)에 의해 자주 묘사되는 20세기 가장 중요하고 독창적인 시인중 하나로 평가받고 있다. 그녀는 마가렛(Margaret)과 댄 아더 스웬슨(Dan Arthur Swenson)의 첫째 아이로 스웨덴어가 주로 사용되고 영어가 제2의 언어로 쓰이는 몰몬(Mormon) 가정의 10자녀 중 장녀로 성장하였다. 레즈비언으로서 그녀는 종교적인 이유로 다소 그녀의 가족들은 그녀를 피했다. 『성상 연구』(*Iconographs*, 1970)와 같은 그녀의 많은 시 작품들은 아이들을 위한 것이었다. 그녀는 또한 노벨 수상자인 토마스 트란스트뢰메르(Tomas Tranströmer)와 같은 동 시대의 스웨덴 시인의 작품들을 번역하였다.

Question*

Body my house
my horse my hound
what will I do
when you are fallen

Where will I sleep
How will I ride
What will I hunt

Where can I go
without my mount
all eager and quick
How will I know
in thicket ahead
is danger or treasure
when Body my good
bright dog is dead

How will it be
to lie in the sky
without roof or door
and wind for an eye

With cloud for shift
how will I hide? (2008년 중등영어 임용고시 기출문제)

---

* This poem clearly is a question of what will happen when the should leaves the body. The
  body is its house, its hound, and horse. It is the souls residence, senses and mobility,
  without it will the soul ever be the same? How shall he function without his body? This
  poem deals with the question of what will happen when the soul and the body part.

The Woods At Night*

The binocular owl,
fastened to a limb
like a lantern
all night long,

sees where all
the other birds sleep:
towhee under leaves,
titmouse deep

in a twighouse,
sapsucker gripped
to a knothole lip,
redwing in the reeds,

swallow in the willow,
flicker in the oak —
but cannot see poor
whippoorwill

under the hill
in deadbrush nest,
who's awake, too —
with stricken eye

---

* This poem is a marvel of rhythm and sound effect. Alliteration, assonance, internal and end
rhyme are all here, and create a wonderful musicality. For example, stanza 1: The binocular
owl, ('binocular owl' and 'long') fastened to a limb like a lantern (limb, like lantern, long,
leaves, lip) all night long, and the repetition (which itself 'repeats, repeats, repeats' in last
stanza) of the 'oo' 'ee' and 'w' sounds throughout the entire poem.

flayed by the moon
her brindled breast
repeats, repeats, repeats its plea
for cruelty.

(23) 빌리 콜린스 Billy Collins, 1941-

뉴욕 태생의 미국시인으로 2001년부터 2003년까지 계관시인 직을 맡았으며 현재는 뉴욕시립대학교(CUNY) 레먼 칼리지 영문학 교수로 재직 중이다. 9/11사태 희생자들을 추모하여 「이름들」("The Names")이라는 자작시를 계관시인의 자격으로 국회에서 낭송했다. 콜린스는 다양한 여러 인쇄 매체에 자신의 시를 발표해 오고 있으며, 자신의 시집을 낭송한 녹음 CD를 발표하기도 했다. 시인 스티븐 던은 콜린스에 대해 이렇게 말했다. "언제나 빌리 콜린스의 시는 우리가 현재 어디 있는지를 알게 해주는 것 같다. 그렇다고 그가 가는 방향을 늘 알 수 있는 것은 아니다. 그가 도착하는 곳에 나도 도착하고 싶다. 열등한 시인은 그럴지 몰라도, 콜린스는 우리에게 아무것도 숨기지 않는다. 그는 자신이 발견한 것을 우리가 명료하게 엿듣도록 허락한다."

The History Teacher*

Trying to protect his students' innocence
   he told them the Ice Age was really just
   the Chilly Age, a period of a million years
   when everyone had to wear sweaters.

---

* The speaker in the story is not described or told about in any way and it is therefore very

And the Stone Age became the Gravel Age,
named after the long driveways of the time.

The Spanish Inquisition was nothing more
than an outbreak of questions such as
"How far is it from here to Madrid?"
"What do you call the matador's hat?"

The War of the Roses took place in a garden,
and the Enola Gay dropped one tiny atom on Japan.

The children would leave his classroom
for the playground to torment the weak
and the smart,
mussing up their hair and breaking their glasses,

while he gathered up his notes and walked home
past flower beds and white picket fences,
wondering if they would believe that soldiers
in the Boer War told long, rambling stories
designed to make the enemy nod off.

(2011년 중등영어 임용고시 기출문제)

---

difficult to attach a name or character to him. However we can exclude some instances. It is not the teacher himself neither one of the children in the class due to him telling about them in third person. The speaker also knows what the teacher is thinking.

Weighing the Dog*

It is awkward for me and bewildering for him
as I hold him in my arms in the small bathroom,
balancing our weight on the shaky blue scale,

but this is the way to weigh a dog and easier
than training him to sit obediently on one spot
with his tongue out, waiting for the cookie.

With pencil and paper I subtract my weight
from our total to find out the remainder that is his,
and I start to wonder if there is an analogy here.

It could not have to do with my leaving you
though I never figured out what you amounted to
until I subtracted myself from our combination.

You held me in your arms more than I held you
through all those awkward and bewildering months
and now we are both lost in strange and distant neighborhoods.

---

* In Billy Collins's Weighing the Dog, he conveyed a much deeper concept than simply
weighing a dog. It talked about a broken relationship. The dog symbolized his lover.

Introduction to Poetry*

I ask them to take a poem
and hold it up to the light
like a color slide

or press an ear against its hive.

I say drop a mouse into a poem
and watch him probe his way out,

or walk inside the poem's room
and feel the walls for a light switch.

I want them to waterski
across the surface of a poem
waving at the author's name on the shore.

But all they want to do
is tie the poem to a chair with rope
and torture a confession out of it.

They begin beating it with a hose
to find out what it really means.

---

* In "Introduction to Poetry", the writer, Billy Collins sends a message that readers should be patient and open minded when reading poems in order to see the meaning, yet not over-analyze. The dramatic situation is Billy Collins is speaking (I think) to all readers about the way one should read poetry. The poem teaches the reader how to read and dive into a poem, using many literary devices and tone to do so. Collins's use of literary devices really helped the poem take the shape it took in my mind.

(24) 린다 파스탄 Linda Pastan, 1932-

파스탄은 유대계 미국 시인으로 뉴욕에서 출생하였다. 그녀는 가족생활이나 가정, 어머니의 상태, 여성의 결혼, 노화, 죽음뿐만 아니라 삶과 관계의 파괴와 같은 주제를 다루는 짧은 시를 쓰는 것으로 유명하다. 그녀는 최소 12권의 시집과 수많은 에세이집을 출판하였다. 그녀의 시집 두 권은 내셔널북어워드(National Book Award)와 로스앤젤레스 타임즈북 상(Los Angeles Times Book Prize)에 후보로 지명되었다.

To A Daughter Leaving Home*

When I taught you
at eight to ride
a bicycle, loping along
beside you
as you wobbled away
on two round wheels,
my own mouth rounding
in surprise when you pulled
ahead down the curved
path of the park,
I kept waiting
for the thud
of your crash as I

---

* "To A Daughter Leaving Home" is a very poignant, bittersweet piece of poetry. In the poem, the parent is teaching his or her daughter how to ride a bike. The entire poem, even though it's discussing watching the daughter ride away on her bike, is an extended metaphor about life.

sprinted to catch up,
while you grew
smaller, more breakable
with distance,
pumping, pumping
for your life, screaming
with laughter,
the hair flapping
behind you like a
handkerchief waving
goodbye.

Love Poem*

I want to write you
a love poem as headlong
as our creek
after thaw
when we stand
on its dangerous
banks and watch it carry
with it every twig
every dry leaf and branch
in its path

---

* In essence "love poem" describes the idea a woman has for writing her lover a poem which would embody the rushing current of the headlong love that they have. The love described within the actual poem embodies a love which is all encompassing and sometimes overwhelming but that the two lovers are in it together. The theme is quite simply the power of love in a relationship and this is communicated in a diction that is very conversational yet lyrical.

every scruple

when we see it

so swollen

with runoff

that even as we watch

we must grab

each other

and step back

we must grab each

other or

get our shoes

soaked we must

grab each other

(25) 레이첼 해더스 Rachel Hadas, 1948-

레이첼 해더스는 미국시인, 교사, 수필가이자 번역가이다. 그녀의 가장 최근의 수필집 『클래식: 수필들』(*Classics: Essays*, 2007)이고 그녀의 가장 최근의 시집은 『식욕의 고통』(*The Ache of Appetite*, 2010)이다. 그녀는 구겐하임 재단 기금(Guggenheim Fellowship), 인그램 메릴 재단 수상(Ingram Merrill Foundation Grants), 폴저 셰익스피어 라이브러리로부터 O. B. 하디슨 상 수상(the O. B. Hardison Award from the Folger Shakespeare Library)과 미국 아카데미로부터 문학상(Award in Literature from the American Academy)과 예술과 문학 위원회(Institute of Arts and Letters)로부터 다양한 수상을 하였다.

The Red Hat *

It started before Christmas. Now our son
officially walks to school alone.
Semi-alone, it's accurate to say:
I or his father track him on the way.
He walks up on the east side of West End,
we walk on the west side. Glances can extend
(and do) across the street; not eye contact.
Already ties are feelings and not fact.
Straus Park is where these parallel paths part;
he goes alone from there. The watcher's heart
stretches, elastic in its love and fear,
toward him as we see him disappear,
striding briskly. Where two weeks ago,
holding a hand, he'd dawdle, dreamy, slow,
he now is hustled forward by the pull
of something far more powerful than school.

The mornings we turn back to are no more
than forty minutes longer than before,
but they feel vastly different-flimsy, strange,
wavering in the eddies of this change,
empty, unanchored, perilously light
since the red hat vanished from our sight.

(2012년 중등영어 임용고시 기출문제)

---

* "The Red Hat" is a poem about the emotions a parent goes through in letting their child
go and gain more independence. The author expresses these emotions using such tools as
symbolism. The narrator of the story is describing the event in which their son started
walking to school on his own.

(26) 주디스 비버리지 Judith Beveridge, 1956-

주디스 비버리지는 현대 호주 시인이자 편집자 그리고 학자이다. 그는 영국 런던에서 출생하여 1960년에 그녀의 부모와 함께 호주에 도착하였다. 시드니 기술대학(University of Technology, Sydney)에서 학사학위를 받고 그는 환경개선 연구원으로서 도서관에서 일했다. 현재 그녀는 뉴캐슬(Newcastle) 대학교와 시드니(Sydney) 대학교에서 창작법을 강의하고 있으며, 『민진』(*Meanjin*)의 편집자로서 일하고 있다.

Orb Spider*

I saw her, pegging out her web
thin as a pressed flower in the bleaching light.
From the bushes a few small insects
clicked like opening seed-pods. I knew some
would be trussed up by her and gone next morning.
She was so beautiful spinning her web
above the marigolds the sun had made
more apricot, more amber; any bee
lost from its solar flight could be gathered
back to the anther, and threaded onto the flower
like a jewel.
  She hung in the shadows
as the sun burnt low on the horizon
mirrored by the round garden bed. Small petals

---

* This poem is about the poet observing nature and comparing it to humans. The poet watches the orb spider spin its web and the orb spider teaches the human world lessons through out the poem. In the "Orb Spider" Judith Beveridge conveys that nature is perfect and humans have a lot to learn from the nature.

moved as one flame, as one perfectly-lit hoop.
I watched her work, produce her known world,
a pattern, her way to traverse
a little portion of the sky;
a simple cosmography, a web drawn
by the smallest nib. And out of my own world
mapped from smallness, the source
of sorrow pricked, I could see
immovable stars.
  Each night
I saw the same dance in the sky,
the pattern like a match-box puzzle,
tiny balls stuck in a grid until shaken
so much, all the orbits were in place.
Above the bright marigolds
of that quick year, the hour-long day,
she taught me to love the smallest transit,
that the coldest star has planetesimal beauty.
I watched her above the low flowers
tracing her world, making it one perfect drawing.

(2013년 중등영어 임용고시 기출문제)

(27) 마거릿 애트우드 Margaret Atwood, 1939-

마거릿 애트우드는 1939년 11월 캐나다 오타와에서 태어나 온타리오
와 퀘벡에서 자랐다. 그녀의 가족은 곤충학자인 아버지를 따라 매년 봄이면
북쪽 황야로 갔다가 가을에는 도시로 돌아오곤 했다. 어울릴 친구가 별로
없었던 애트우드에게는 독서가 유일한 놀이였다. 다양한 책을 다독했으며,
6세부터 글을 쓰기 시작하여 16세에 전문 작가가 되기로 결심했다. 토론토

대학과 하버드 대학에서 영문학을 공부하며 대학 문예 잡지에 많은 시와 단편 소설을 발표했다. 스물한 살에 출간한 첫 시집 『서클 게임』(The Circle Game)으로 캐나다 총리 상을 수상했다. 이후 장편소설 『떠오름』(Surfacing)으로 작가로서 본격 적으로 이름을 알리기 시작했다. 수많은 소설과 시를 발표하며 20세기 캐나다를 대표하는 여성작가로 추앙받고 있으며, 평론과 TV 드라마, 동화 등 다방면에 걸쳐 활발한 창작 활동을 하고 있다.

애트우드는 캐나다 최초의 페미니즘 작가라는 평가를 받고 있는데, 그 외에도 캐나다와 캐나다인의 정체성, 미국을 비롯한 유럽 국가들과의 외교 관계, 환경 문제, 인권 문제, 현대 예술 등 다양한 주제를 폭넓게 다루고 있다. 2000년에 『눈먼 암살자』(The Blind Assassin)로 부커 상을 수상하며 일반 대중과 평단의 찬사를 고루 받았다. 『신탁 여인』(Lady Oracle), 『시녀 이야기』(The Handmaid's Tale), 『고양이 눈』(Cat's Eye) 등 뛰어난 작품들을 꾸준히 발표하고 있다. 브리티시컬럼비아 대학, 토론토 요크 대학에서 영문학 교수를 역임하였고, 현재 국제사면위원회, 캐나다 작가협회, 민권운동 연합회 등에서 활동 중이다.

Siren Song*

This is the one song everyone
would like to learn: the song
that is irresistible:

---

* "Siren Song," by the Canadian author Margaret Atwood, is spoken by one of the sirens of classical mythology. Sirens were often imagined as figures who were partly women and partly birds. They sat along sea coasts and sang songs so appealing that the mariners who heard this singing might easily be lured to their deaths, often by shipwreck.

the song that forces men
to leap overboard in squadrons
even though they see the beached skulls

the song nobody knows
because anyone who has heard it
is dead, and the others can't remember.

Shall I tell you the secret
and if I do, will you get me
out of this bird suit?

I don't enjoy it here
squatting on this island
looking picturesque and mythical

with these two feathery maniacs,
I don't enjoy singing
this trio, fatal and valuable.

I will tell the secret to you,
to you, only to you.
Come closer. This song

is a cry for help: Help me!
Only you, only you can,
you are unique

at last. Alas
it is a boring song
but it works every time.

| 인용문헌 |

김재환 역. 『노튼 영문학 개관 I』: 중세-왕정복고시대와 18세기. 서울: 까치
　　　글방, 2003.
　――――.『노튼 영문학 개관 II』: 낭만주의 시대-20세기. 서울: 까치글방,
　　　2005.
Spurr, Barry. *Studying Poetry*. 2nd. New York: Macmillan, 2006.
Thomas R. Arp and Greg Johnson. *Perrine's Sound and Sense: An Introduction*
　　　to Poetry. 11th. Boston: Wadsworth, 2005.
<http://www.bartleby.com/>
<http://www.gradesaver.com/>
<http://www.poemhunter.com/>
<http://www.poets.org/>
<http://www.poetryfoundation.org/>

| 지은이 **황치복**

가톨릭대학교 철학(신학)과를 졸업하고 서강대학교 대학원에서 종교학 석사를 수료했고, 건국대학교 대학원에서 영어영문학 석·박사학위를 취득했으며, 현재 전주대학교 사범대학 영어교육과 교수로 재직 중이다. 미국소설학회와 한국문학과종교학회 편집위원을 역임했으며, 현재 한국존스타인벡학회 총무, 한국영어교육연구학회 부회장, 대한영어영문학회 학술이사 등 다양한 학회에서 활동 중이다. 저서로는『존 스타인벡 소설과 영화』, 『존 스타인벡의 문학과 삶』, 『미국소설과 서술기법』(공저) 등이 있으며 영미소설 및 시에 관한 다수의 논문을 발표했다.

영미시의 감상과 이해

초판 1쇄 발행일 2015년 9월 21일

지은이 황치복
발행인 이성모
발행처 도서출판 동인
주 소 서울시 종로구 혜화로3길 5 118호
등 록 제1-1599호
TEL   (02) 765-7145 / FAX (02) 765-7165
E-mail dongin60@chol.com
I S B N 978-89-5506-676-0
정 가 20,000원

※ 잘못 만들어진 책은 바꿔 드립니다.